My

BROWN-EYED
*E*ARL

My

BROWN-EYED
*E*ARL

ANNA BENNETT

St. Martin's Paperbacks

This is a work of fiction. All of the characters, organizations, and events portrayed in this novel are either products of the author's imagination or are used fictitiously.

MY BROWN-EYED EARL

Copyright © 2016 by Anna Bennett.
Excerpt from *I Dared the Duke* Copyright © 2017 by Anna Bennett.

All rights reserved.

For information address St. Martin's Press, 175 Fifth Avenue, New York, NY 10010.

ISBN: 978-1-250-10090-0

Our books may be purchased in bulk for promotional, educational, or business use. Please contact your local bookseller or the Macmillan Corporate and Premium Sales Department at 1-800-221-7945, ext. 5442, or by e-mail at MacmillanSpecialMarkets@macmillan.com.

Printed in the United States of America

St. Martin's Paperbacks edition / October 2016

St. Martin's Paperbacks are published by St. Martin's Press, 175 Fifth Avenue, New York, NY 10010.

10 9 8 7 6 5 4 3 2 1

For Mike
Because when the zombie apocalypse hits,
I know you'll protect us
and secure the necessities,
like Netflix and donuts.
And for a thousand other reasons.

Chapter ONE

London, May 1817

Miss Margaret Lacey—Meg, to her family and friends—had the odd but unshakable feeling that the next half hour could alter the course of her life. Forever.

Which was just as well, because heaven knew that she and her sisters couldn't remain on their current paths—not if they wished to keep a roof over their heads and food in their bellies.

"Trust me, Meg. You're perfect for this position." Her friend Charlotte linked an arm through Meg's and bustled her down the street toward a row of elegant Mayfair townhouses.

"*Perfect* is a bit of a stretch." Meg had hoped to find work as a companion to an aging dowager, fetching fans and lemonade. Elderly people, she understood. Persons under the age of twelve were another matter entirely. "Shouldn't a governess have a way with children?"

"You've two younger sisters," Charlotte said.

"They're only a few years younger, and the only useful thing I've taught them is how to ignore insults from puffed-up debutantes."

"Nonsense. You're kind, intelligent, and patient. I've no doubt you can manage a pair of six-year old girls." Charlotte stopped and faced Meg. "Show me your best governess expression."

Meg glanced sideways at her friend and gave her an encouraging sort of smile.

"That will never do."

"Why not?"

Charlotte sighed. "*The look* is your primary weapon."

"Weapon? You said they were six."

"Suppose the twins complain about doing their sums. A good governess does not deign to argue with her charges. She simply gives them *the look*. Now, let's see it."

"Very well." Meg did her best to imitate the withering, mildly disdainful expression that had seemed etched onto her own governess's face.

Charlotte grimaced and bit her bottom lip.

Oh dear. "They're not going to do their sums, are they?"

"Heavens no. They'll think you've eaten a bad kipper." Charlotte took her arm, pulling her along once more. "Never mind—we shall work on that. But I can assure you that you *are* qualified. Honestly, Meg," she added with a warm smile, "any child would be lucky to have you as a governess."

Meg swallowed. She liked children, truly she did, in spite of their tendency to be terrifyingly unpredictable. "Let us hope I can convince my potential employers."

And convince them she must. Dear Uncle Alistair would never admit it, but Meg and her sisters had been a tremendous burden on him and his dwindling fortune. He'd generously taken them in after the unexpected and tragic deaths of her parents eight years ago. But now she was twenty-three, old enough to venture out on her own— and to try to save Uncle Alistair from debtor's prison.

"Employer, actually," Charlotte corrected. "He is a bachelor, and apparently at a loss for what to do with the twins."

Meg arched an eyebrow. "A bachelor with twins?"

"I don't know the details of his situation, but I'm certain you'll learn more during the interview." Charlotte pulled a scrap of paper from the pocket of her cloak and compared the address on it to the one above a stately town house entrance boasting polished stone steps and a gleaming black door. "This is it. You don't want to be late."

"No, of course not." Meg smoothed her hands down the skirt of her lilac dress, which was three years old and the nicest she owned. "Wait. You haven't told me his name."

"He's an earl." Charlotte consulted her paper. "Lord Castleton."

Oh no. The edges of Meg's vision turned fuzzy, and she stumbled on the pavement.

Charlotte steadied her. "You look as though you've seen a ghost. What's wrong?"

Everything. Lord Castleton was the man her parents had chosen for her to marry.

She'd been a sullen, spot-faced fifteen-year-old when they'd summoned her to the drawing room to meet him. Mama and Papa assumed she'd be thrilled with the arrangement. After all, he was a handsome, strapping young man who would one day be an earl—more than the plain daughter of a vicar could hope for. And it wasn't as though they'd be wed right away. He and Meg could get to know each other over the next few years—easily accomplished, as his family owned the estate next to their humble cottage.

Meg hadn't objected to the match in theory—she wasn't daft. But she *had* objected to the way he'd looked at her, with the thinly veiled dread and horror of a young man receiving a life sentence in Newgate.

Her pride simply wouldn't tolerate it.

So she had tossed her head, crossed her arms, leveled her gaze at him, and said, "I would sooner shave my head and enter the convent than marry you."

Burning at the memory, Meg pressed her gloved palms to her cheeks and turned to her friend. She'd never revealed that particular chapter of her past to Charlotte. It was tied up with too many painful memories. And did not cast her in a favorable light. "I can't do it."

"But you must! He's expecting you."

"Are you certain? That is, is he aware that I'm the candidate?"

Charlotte shrugged. "I'm sure Lord Torrington informed him. Why are you suddenly so anxious? Do you know the earl?"

Meg swallowed. "I used to—before he inherited the earldom." She'd been careful to avoid him once she and her sisters came to London, which was easy, for they did not move in the same circles. He was the ton's golden boy, while she lived in the shadows. "I fear I made an awful impression."

"You are being far too dramatic," Charlotte said. "He probably doesn't even remember the encounter."

Meg knew the words were meant to comfort and reassure, but the idea that he might have forgotten their meeting—the one that haunted her daily—pained her even more. "I suppose you are correct." He had no doubt moved on. Still, it was horribly awkward to be in the position of needing his approval now.

Charlotte narrowed her pretty gray eyes. "Why do I feel like there is more to this story?"

"I promise to tell you the whole of it. Later." Meg drew a long breath and willed her heartbeat to slow to a civilized pace. "Suffice it to say that if I was nervous before, I'm doubly so now. The earl is not likely to overlook my lack of experience." Not when paired with her past indecorous behavior.

"It's natural to feel some trepidation before an interview," Charlotte said kindly. "Is there more to it than that? Have you changed your mind about wanting the position?"

Meg hesitated only a moment. "No. Of course I still need it. It was just a shock, learning that my prospective employer is the earl." She could not afford—quite literally— to let her pride overrule her good sense. "If he's willing to consider entrusting his children to me, the least I can do is meet with him."

"Please, forget everything I said before. Just be your usual, charming self."

Meg squeezed Charlotte's hands. "Thank you for arranging the interview. I shall endeavor not to embarrass you or Lord Torrington." She winked at her friend. "But no promises."

"Go on. You'll be late." Charlotte gave her a little push toward the grand town house. "Tea this Sunday afternoon?"

"Of course."

"With any luck, you'll be a governess by then."

Meg's belly twisted in knots, but she managed a cheerful smile as she ascended the stone steps on wobbly legs. "Yes, luck. And there's some comfort in knowing the interview can't *possibly* go as badly as the ghastly scene I've conjured in my mind."

"The young lady applying for the governess position is waiting for you in the drawing room, my lord."

William Ryder, the Earl of Castleton, peeled his face off the surface of his mahogany desk and growled. "Damn it, Gibson. I asked not to be disturbed."

Unperturbed, the butler set a tray on the corner of the desk. "Yes, I am quite aware, my lord. But you made that request three hours ago. I hoped that your, ah, condition would be much improved by now, and—"

"For the love of God, call it what it is."

The butler's forehead creased. "Begging your pardon?"

"It's not a *condition*. It's the devil of a hangover."

"So it would seem. In any event, I assumed that you would wish to keep the scheduled appointment. However, if you would like me to send her away—"

"No." Will rubbed eyelids that felt like they'd been singed from the inside out. "I need to deal with the problem."

As if on cue, one half of the problem slid down the hall outside his study, squealing in an octave that set Will's teeth on edge.

"My turn!" called her sister, a matching blond-haired sprite. A second later she, too, glided over the polished floorboards on stockinged feet, colliding with the first twin and sending the pair of them sprawling onto the floor.

"You should have waited," cried the first.

"You should have moved out of the way," retorted the second.

Will pressed his fingertips to a throbbing temple. "Gibson!"

"Allow me, my lord." Turning to the girls, he said, "Diana. Valerie. Young ladies do not skate across the floor in their stockings."

"They should," said one. "It's quite fun."

The butler cleared his throat, and two spots of color appeared on his cheeks. "I suggest that the two of you return to the nursery," he said sharply. "At once."

With another chorus of head-splitting squeals, the twins scrambled to their feet and tore down the hallway.

"I don't believe I've ever seen you so flustered, Gibson." Will smiled. "I daresay I'm feeling a little better."

"All too happy to serve as a source of amusement," the butler said dryly. He plucked a cup from the serving tray on Will's desk, filled it with steaming, pungent coffee, and set it in front of him.

"I suppose I shouldn't add anything to this," Will said, taking a few scalding sips.

"It would rather defeat the purpose."

"Fine. Let's get this interview over with. Bring the governess here."

Gibson's gaze flicked around the room as though he were mentally cataloging all the reasons why a respectable young miss should not enter the decidedly male realm: the snifter of brandy and half-filled glass on the sideboard, the painting of a nude Aphrodite above the mantle, the discarded cravat draped over the arm of his chair. "If you're certain, my lord."

"I am." This was killing poor Gibson.

"Shall I ring for Phelps?"

Will leaned back in his chair and spread his arms. "Why would I need my valet?"

"Forgive me for mentioning it, my lord, but you look somewhat disheveled. I thought perhaps Phelps could tidy you up."

"Blast it, Gibson. I don't require tidying. I'm looking for a governess, not a mistress." But then, maybe his butler was trying to tell him something. "Wait. Is she . . . ?"

"Is she *what*, my lord?"

Will wanted to say *comely* or *beautiful*. "Young?"

"She is. And not at all your usual sort of companion."

"Then why all the fuss, damn it? Show her in here."

The butler's nostrils flared in his otherwise stony face. "As you wish, my lord." He turned stiffly and headed toward the drawing room at a glacial pace.

Hell. Will leaned forward on his elbows and pinched

the bridge of his nose. Somehow, in the space of a week, his highly ordered, luxurious life had fallen apart.

First, Marina, the beautiful widow he'd been seeing, hinted that she wanted more than the mutually pleasurable arrangement they'd agreed to, forcing Will to break things off with her.

Next, his recently deceased cousin's mistress showed up on Will's doorstep with the twin girls, threatening to leave them at an orphanage unless he took them in.

And then last night, he attended a dinner party in honor of his mother's birthday. In front of a dozen guests, she announced her sole wish: that her son marry before she turned fifty—in exactly one year. After choking on his wine, Will promised to give the matter some thought.

Then he had gone directly to his club and drunk himself into oblivion.

Jesus. He stood, ran his hands through his hair, and checked his reflection in a mirror between a pair of bookcases. Gibson was right—he looked like hell.

Bad enough to scare off a potential governess.

He swiped the cravat off his chair, slung it around his neck, hastily tied it in some semblance of a knot, and buttoned his jacket. There was nothing to be done about the stubble on his chin or the faint imprint the desk blotter had left on his cheek, so he threw back the rest of his coffee and congratulated himself. Within the hour he'd have a governess to manage the twins, and at least *one* aspect of his life would be set to rights.

Gibson was already shuffling down the corridor. "My lord," he intoned from the doorway, "may I present Miss Lacey."

Will blinked. Lacey . . . it was a common name. Surely the potential governess couldn't be—

She glided into the study and cast a wary look his way.

"Good afternoon, Lord Castleton. It's a pleasure to see you again."

Dear God. It *was* her. The vicar's daughter who thought she was too damned good for him. Standing in his study, cloaked in a drab dress that might have been lilac once but now more closely resembled gray. No ribbons adorned her brown hair. No ringlets framed her face. In fact, the only decoration she wore was the light smattering of freckles across her nose.

The butler raised his bushy brows. "I was not aware that you were already acquainted."

"Thank you, Gibson. That will be all."

The butler left reluctantly, closing the door behind him.

Miss Lacey pressed her lips together as though she longed to say something and silence herself at the same time. From what he recalled of her tongue, it was best kept under lock and key.

"What on earth are you doing here?" Will demanded.

"Applying for the governess position. I assumed you knew."

"No," he said curtly.

"I see." She glanced over her shoulder at the door. "Perhaps it would be better if I—"

"Be seated, Miss Lacey." He inclined his head toward the armchair in front of his desk.

She hesitated, and for a moment he thought she'd refuse. But then she walked toward the chair, looked at the seat, and froze. Just as stubborn as he remembered, unbiddable as ever.

He bristled. "Perhaps you'd prefer to remain standing for the entire interview?"

"No. It's only . . ."

"You object to meeting in my study?"

She narrowed eyes that were not quite green, but not

quite brown either. "No, but I hoped to avoid sitting on this." In one, fluid motion she leaned over the chair, picked up a pink, lace-edged scrap of satin between her thumb and index finger, and dangled it in front of his face.

Chapter TWO

Lord Castleton snatched the frilly handkerchief from Meg's hand. He started to stuff it in his pocket, apparently thought better of it, and shoved it into a desk drawer. "Let me assure you, Miss Lacey. Nothing untoward has occurred here in my study."

Perhaps not. But something untoward had definitely occurred *somewhere*.

Meg sat in the chair in front of his desk, glad she no longer had to rely on her shaking legs for support. "I'm certain that's none of my concern."

"I'm glad we agree."

She *was* curious, though. If her parents had had their way, the man who was now sitting across from her and cursing under his breath would have been her husband. Difficult as it was to fathom, she would have been his countess, probably blessed with a couple of children at this point.

The sight of him now, sporting rumpled clothes, a scowling face, and a foul mood, made her think she had dodged a rather nasty bullet.

The earl steepled his fingers under his chin, dark with stubble. "Now then, why don't you begin by telling me why you've been reduced to applying for a governess position?"

Dear Lord, this was humiliating—not needing to work, but having to explain herself. To him. She didn't want to reveal just how desperate she was. Or confess that suitors weren't exactly lining up outside her front door.

"My two sisters and I live with my uncle, Lord Wiltmore." Meg studied the earl's face, waiting for the moment he realized she was one of the infamous Wilting Wallflowers.

The ton had cruelly dubbed Meg, Beth, and Julie thus after their first season had proved highly unsuccessful. The cause of their disgrace was a reputation-shattering combination of unfashionable gowns and their uncle's eccentric behavior. Revealing her connection to Uncle Alistair inevitably prompted one of two responses: derision or pity. The former was far easier to accept than the latter.

The earl stared intently, his expression betraying nothing. "Go on."

"My uncle has been very good to us, but I cannot impose on his generosity forever."

"Why not?"

Because Uncle Alistair is down to four loyal servants who've not been paid in six months. Because caring for my sisters and me has drained whatever meager savings he once had. Because Beth and Julie deserve to own at least one pretty pair of slippers.

Gripping the arms of the chair, she said, "I prefer to make my own way."

"Interesting. I had expected you to spout some drivel about adoring children or having a passion for teaching."

She probably should have. "I do not consider such sentiments *drivel*, my lord."

"But they aren't *your* sentiments, are they, Miss Lacey?"

Meg swallowed. She'd anticipated questions about her lack of experience and references, but the earl's inquiries were even more difficult to answer. For they were personal. "Of course I like children," she assured him. "Perhaps you could tell me a bit more about your daughters."

He laughed—a deep, soulful sound that stirred something in her belly. "For one, they're not my daughters. What else would you like to know?"

What else, indeed? "Their names?"

"Diana and . . ." He dragged a hand through thick, dark hair. ". . . Violet. Er, I think that's right."

Meg searched her mind for another question, hoping to remain on the offensive. "And you are their guardian?"

He shook his head as if he'd protest, then stood abruptly and turned his back to her. "I suppose I am. For now."

Meg's heart went out to the girls. She knew all too well what it felt like to be passed off to a distant relative. At fifteen, she herself had felt like an odd and worthless family heirloom—the sort that no one wants but that no one can quite manage to give away to strangers, either. Uncle Alistair's offer to take them in had been a godsend.

"Where are the girls' parents?"

He turned, fixing an icy gaze on her. "Forgive me. I was under the impression that *I* would ask the questions at this interview."

Drat. She raised her chin. "Ask away."

"You've never been a governess before?"

"No."

"And what makes you think that you're qualified?"

If he thought to intimidate her with rudeness, his plan backfired. His sharp tone only served to raise her ire, erasing the nervousness she'd felt earlier. "I tutored my younger sister in French." A bit of a stretch perhaps, but she *had* helped Beth conjugate a few verbs and taught her some more colorful phrases.

He raised a dark brow, incredulous. "Your reference is your younger sister?"

"Of course not. I believe we've already established that this would be my first governess position, but everyone must begin somewhere, my lord. Furthermore, my friend Charlotte—er, Miss Winters—is an experienced governess and has promised to share the lessons that she's created for her own young charge."

"This Miss Winters sounds like a gem. The perfect candidate. Perhaps *she* should be the one to apply for the position."

"She's already in the employ of your friend, Lord—" She stopped herself, for he didn't deserve a civil response.

Frustration propelled her from her chair, but it was pride that made her lean across the ridiculously large desk and narrow her eyes at the earl. "Never mind. This meeting was a waste of time. I hereby withdraw my application."

There was no denying it—he'd behaved like an ass. Clearly, Miss Lacey brought out the worst in him.

But she was correct on one count. The interview *was* a waste of time. She had thought marrying him was beneath her. How on earth would she manage to *work* for him? Merely requesting an update on the girls' progress could well cause her to bite his head off.

And yet . . .

Will admired her fiery personality. Even the drab gown she wore couldn't detract from the passionate sparks, couldn't stamp them out.

"I apologize for my foul mood," he said. "It has less to

do with you and more to do with the lingering, unfortunate effects of over-imbibing last evening. Still, inexcusable."

She sniffed as if to say his admission was hardly a surprise. "I accept your apology. Nevertheless, I shall take my leave."

The slightly husky tone of her voice warmed his blood. If his own governess had sounded like that, he would have followed her around like a puppy. He cast Miss Lacey a rueful smile and bowed politely. "I agree that would be for the best."

She inclined her head, gracefully crossed the Aubusson rug, and, with the dignity befitting a queen, opened the study door.

Only to be bowled over by the twins, who seemed to have been launched into the room by a catapult.

Good God. He rounded the desk and stared in horror at the tangle of arms and legs writhing on the floor of his study. At the bottom of the pile, Miss Lacey struggled to no avail. One twin had landed across her waist, pinning her to the floor. The other lay crosswise over her knees.

"Girls!" he bellowed. "What the dev—" He stopped himself—just barely. "Remove yourselves from Miss Lacey at once."

"We just wanted to know who you were talking to. We didn't mean to—" said one.

Will looped an arm around her torso, extricated her from the heap, and did the same with her sister.

Miss Lacey sat up, dazed. Will crouched beside her. "Are you all right?"

"Yes. That is, I think so." She reached for her bonnet, which looked like an elephant and not a slight lass had sat upon it.

Will scooped up the hat, tried valiantly to restore it to

some semblance of its former shape, and handed it to her. Several chestnut locks had escaped the thick knot at her nape, and while this no doubt served as a source of distress for Miss Lacey, he thought the effect charming.

Odd, that.

It might have been her mussed hair or her pink cheeks or her slightly parted lips, but she looked almost . . . attractive.

Definitely not the same gangly, scowling girl who'd rejected him eight years earlier.

"Shouldn't you help her up, Lord Castleton?" piped one of the twins behind him.

"It's what a gentleman would do," remarked the other.

"Silence!" He turned to glare at them, mostly because they were correct. His hangover returned in full force.

"I can manage." Miss Lacey sprang nimbly to her feet, smoothed the stray curls behind her ears, and brushed out her skirts.

Will faced the girls, arms crossed over his chest. "It is especially bad form to eavesdrop and knock a person to the floor before introductions have been made."

One of the girls thrust her hand at Miss Lacey. "I'm Diana. Pleased to meet you."

"The pleasure is mine. I'm Miss Lacey." She shook the girl's hand and turned to her twin, who clutched a doll tightly to her chest. "Lord Castleton has told me a bit about you both. You must be Violet."

"No." Tears welled in blue eyes too big for her face, and her lower lip trembled. "My name isn't Violet." She cast an accusatory glance at Will, who suddenly felt about three inches tall.

"Her name is Valerie," Diana said helpfully. "A far better name than Violet."

"Agreed," Miss Lacey said quickly. "It's no contest."

Her gaze flicked from Valerie to Will and back. "Please forgive my mistake. Lord Castleton said your name was *Valerie*—I'm certain—and then I went and botched it."

Valerie brightened instantly, beaming at Will like he was some sort of hero. He stared at Miss Lacey in wonder. With a small fib she'd elevated him from scoundrel to prince. What type of sorceress was she?

"It was lovely meeting you both," she said to the twins, "but I really must go."

The truth hit him like a thunderbolt. He couldn't let her walk out of his study. There were a dozen reasons why she was the wrong candidate, but the radiant smile Valerie wore trumped them all. "Wait."

"What is it, my lord?"

"I'd like you to reconsider."

The look she gave him was polite but regretful. "I think we both know I'm not right for this position."

After the series of unfortunate events that comprised the interview, he hadn't expected her to readily accept. But he was encouraged by the fact that thus far she'd made no threats of head shaving or convents.

"I think you *are* right for the position," he said smoothly. He was used to getting what he wanted. Now that he knew what—or, rather, whom—he wanted, it was a mere matter of negotiating the terms.

And he fully intended to win.

Meg had no intention of changing her mind. She was going to have to ask Charlotte to help her find another position. And yet, she couldn't resist the opportunity to hear Lord Castleton grovel.

"What are you saying, my lord?"

His mouth curled into a slow, dangerous smile. "I'm offering you the job."

She wondered if he'd forgotten about the twins, who

stood behind him, absorbing every word of the conversation. "And what brought about this sudden change of heart?"

He shrugged impossibly broad shoulders. "Perhaps my hangover has finally worn off."

"I see." But his casual air and charming banter did not fool her. A horn had just sounded, signaling the start of the hunt—and she, a prospective governess, was the fox he pursued. "I'm afraid I cannot accept."

"How can you say no? We haven't even discussed the terms."

"The particular terms are irrelevant. I won't be swayed by an extra afternoon off."

He chuckled, sending a shiver down her spine. "I was under the impression that you needed the income."

Heaven help her, she did. But surely, another opening would come along, wouldn't it? "I will find something else."

"Let's discuss your salary."

"There's nothing to discuss." She tried not to think about the new spectacles that Uncle Alistair desperately needed or the pretty rose-colored shawl that Julie longed for. Meg couldn't be bought—not by the earl.

"Whatever your friend, Miss Winters, makes . . . I'll double it."

She gasped. "Why?"

"Because I wish to reach an agreement. Right now." He sauntered closer, his hard arm brushing against hers as he bent toward her ear. "Every woman has her price."

She bristled at his words and the obvious innuendo. "Not I, my lord. Of all people, I should have thought you'd learned that by now."

He rubbed his chin and smiled, seemingly unperturbed. "You are a formidable negotiator, Miss Lacey. Very well, then. I shall triple Miss Winter's salary and also put you up in the blue guest chamber—it has the best view of the garden." He paced a moment, as if he'd let that sink in, then smiled smugly. "Now do we have a deal?"

"We do not." Later she might kick herself for refusing his offer, but at the moment pride firmly held the reins. "Money is not the only consideration in a decision such as this."

"So true." He ambled toward the twins, stood behind them, and patted their unruly blond curls. "Girls, how would you like to have Miss Lacey as your special new friend?"

"Friend? I hardly think a governess is the same thing as—"

"Oh, yes!" The twins bounced on their toes as if their glee were too much to contain.

"They've never had a governess before," the earl said in a stage whisper. "I thought we should ease into it."

No. There would be no *easing in* of anything. How dare he use those poor little girls as pawns?

Meg knelt before them and looked earnestly into their hopeful blue eyes. "I've no doubt Lord Castleton will find someone better suited to the position." Probably by this time tomorrow.

"Better suited? What does that mean?" asked Diana, her little nose crinkling. "You don't want to be friends with us?"

Valerie wrung her tiny hands. "We're sorry we knocked you down earlier."

"I'm not cross about that," Meg assured her. "Of course I'd like to be your friend, but circumstances don't allow—" She sighed. "It's complicated."

"That's what Mama said when she brought us here . . . before she left us." Diana scowled at the memory. Valerie whimpered.

Meg shot the earl a withering glance before returning her attention to the girls.

"Everything will be fine," Meg said. "You'll see."

"Mama said that, too." Valerie sniffled. "But *nothing's* been fine. I miss her."

Diana draped an arm around her sister's shoulders and raised her pointy chin. "Don't fret, Val. I'll take care of you till Mama comes back."

Meg flicked her gaze to Lord Castleton, who gave a somber shake of his head.

So, their mother wasn't coming back for them.

The poor, brave dears. She swallowed the knot in her throat. The girls' wan faces reflected all the grief and fear she'd felt eight years ago after losing her parents, her home, and the only life she'd ever known. What she would have given then for someone who understood that she needed to be a child for a while longer. For someone to assure her that she'd be safe and protected—maybe even loved.

No, she couldn't walk away from these two. "What if I agreed to stay, just for a little while?"

"Would you?" Diana asked, one part hopeful and one part suspicious.

Meg nodded and was almost bowled over again when Valerie threw her arms around her neck. Diana hung back, watchful and cautious, but Meg detected a reluctant smile.

"Will you come see the nursery? I could show you where Molly sleeps," Valerie asked.

"Molly's her doll," Diana provided helpfully.

"Miss Lacey and I have a few matters to discuss," the earl interjected. "But you'll have plenty of time with her in the days ahead. Run along now."

"I shall see you soon," Meg assured them, and they bounded out of the room, leaving her quite alone with Lord Castleton.

"It seems we have a deal after all," he gloated.

Her palm itched to slap the self-satisfied smile off

his face. "For the *girls'* sake, I've agreed to a temporary assignment."

"Excellent. I shall honor the terms I set forth earlier."

"That's very . . . generous."

"And I expect you to begin working tomorrow morning."

"But—"

He raised his brows. "Unless you'd prefer to start this evening?"

Meg smiled sweetly. "No."

"I thought not."

She had much to do. Beth and Julie didn't even know about the interview, and now she had to let them know she was moving into the earl's residence—at least for a while.

As she exited the study, Lord Castleton strolled behind her, triumphing no doubt.

"What made you change your mind about me?" she asked over her shoulder.

"They need you," he said simply. "Even an idiot like me could see that."

She laughed in spite of herself. "Well, they need *someone.*"

"Not me. I promise to stay out of your way."

Of course he would. The great Lord Castleton couldn't be bothered with a pair of heartbroken little girls or their plain, unfashionable governess. He was now free to resume his drunken bachelor activities, leaving the rest of them to their own devices.

And that was clearly for the best.

Chapter THREE

"Did you have a nice time with Charlotte?" Beth looked up from her sewing, blew an errant chestnut curl away from her face, and smiled.

Meg hung her hat and shawl on a peg in the front hallway, then joined Beth on the settee in the cozy parlor. Smaller and easier to heat than the drawing room, it was where the sisters spent most of their time. As Meg looked around at the stacks of books and piles of unfinished sketches and stories, she felt a pang—a hint of the homesickness that was sure to come. "We only had a brief visit, but she is well."

"Brief? You were gone most of the afternoon." Beth squinted at her needle as she gracefully guided it through the hem of a gown pooled in her lap. "Did you stop somewhere else?"

"Yes." Meg tried to keep the nervousness from her voice. "I have news. Where's Julie?"

"She went to check on Uncle Alistair. You know how he is—he gets so absorbed in his research that he forgets to eat. What is this news? It sounds very mysterious."

"I'll tell you both when Julie returns." Meg picked up the sleeve of the navy dress draped across Beth's legs. "I thought you'd already let the hem out of this."

"I did, but I think I can stretch another inch out of it. Shouldn't Julie have stopped growing by now?"

"Did I hear my name?" Julie breezed into the parlor and placed her hands on her slender hips. "Meg, you're back!"

"She is, and she has something to tell us." Beth scooted over and patted the settee cushion beside her.

Ignoring the invitation, Julie clasped her hands under her chin. "How exciting. Don't tell me—let me guess. We've received a ball invitation?"

"No, darling. Nothing as exciting as that, I'm afraid," Meg said. The youngest of the trio, Julie was the only one who still became dreamy-eyed at the mention of a ball. "Come sit, and I'll explain everything."

Julie kicked off her slippers and tucked her long legs on the settee beneath her. Beth plopped her sewing onto the table in front of them. "I don't like the sound of this. What's going on?"

Meg let out a long, slow breath. "It's wonderful news, actually."

Beth narrowed her pretty blue eyes. "Then why do you seem so anxious?"

"Well, this afternoon after I met with Charlotte . . . I went on an interview."

"An interview?" cried Julie. "For what?"

"A governess position caring for young girls—twins." Meg paused. "I was offered the job . . . and I start tomorrow. I'll need to pack my things tonight."

Julie pressed trembling fingers to her throat. "But . . . but why would you seek a governess position?"

"I think you know," said Meg, lowering her voice to a whisper. "Uncle Alistair can barely afford the few servants he has left. I had to do *something* to help, and this job pays well. I'll be able to cover some of the household expenditures. Maybe even set aside enough to buy new gowns for both of you." She desperately wanted her sisters to make decent matches—even if it was too late for her.

Julie shook her head. "Oh, Meg. I don't want a new gown if it means you have to move out. We're the Lacey girls, remember? We stay together, no matter what."

It had been their mantra after the death of their parents. When well-meaning relatives planned to farm each sister out to a different second cousin, the girls had pleaded to stay together—and Uncle Alistair had valiantly come to their rescue.

"I'm not abandoning you," Meg said. "I'll still be in London, just a few blocks away. But you must realize things are different now that we're grown."

"She's right," Beth said to her younger sister. "I've examined each line of the budget. I've scrimped and saved everywhere I possibly can, and the truth is . . . we can't go on as we are. Besides, we knew we couldn't stay together *forever*. One day soon, you could have an offer of marriage."

"An offer of marriage?" Julie rolled her eyes. "From whom? I can't even recall the last time an eligible gentleman asked me to dance. Unless we're counting Lord Winston."

Beth shuddered at the mention of the portly baron old enough to be their grandfather. "I don't think we should consider him eligible for anything."

"Agreed," said Meg. "Our prospects are admittedly few. Which only proves my point—we must seize control of our futures. *Before* one of us is reduced to accepting a marriage proposal from a toothless widower."

"This all just seems so sudden," Julie fretted. "Can't you wait till next week?"

"I'm afraid not. The twins are in desperate need of

guidance." She smiled at the thought of their freckled faces and turned-up noses. "You'd adore them. They remind me of the two of you when you were younger—full of energy and a small dose of mischief. Sadly, I have the distinct impression that their parents are unable or unwilling to care for them."

"How awful," cried Beth. "At least we spent much of our childhood with Mama and Papa before . . ."

Guilt sliced through Meg, as it always did at the mention of her parents' death. *She* was the one who had set events in motion that horrifying day, and nothing her sisters said could ever convince her otherwise. "The twins are only six years old, and I'm not at all sure how I will manage them, but I need to try . . . for their sakes."

Beth sighed. "I think that's lovely."

Julie gave a nod. "It sounds as though those little girls need you even more than I do. Which is saying a lot."

"Did Charlotte arrange the interview?" Beth asked.

"Yes, tell us how this all came about," Julie urged. "And who will be your employer? Is it someone we know?"

Oh dear. Meg had dreaded this part of the conversation, but there was no avoiding it, so she attempted a bright smile. "You'll never guess."

"I don't know anyone with twin girls," Beth mused.

"He's a bachelor," Meg said. "The girls aren't his daughters, but they currently live with him."

Julie's eyes went round. "A bachelor! Is he handsome?"

Meg squirmed. Handsome? If one liked the tall, dark, and dashing type. Still, good looks couldn't make up for his rakish ways and extreme arrogance. "I wouldn't venture to say. But I'm sure you've already formed your own opinion, for you are both acquainted with the earl—Lord Castleton."

Beth and Julie blinked, then froze. Silence descended upon the parlor. At the same time, a cloud drifted in front of the sun, and the glow that had drenched the room in warmth faded to a chilly shadow.

Beth swallowed. "We are not *that* desperate yet, are we, Meg?"

"Won't it be terribly awkward?" Julie chimed in.

"Perhaps. However, I agreed to take the position on a temporary basis for the girls' sake. And for ours. I confess it's not an ideal situation, but he has promised to keep his distance, and I shall do the same."

"While you're living in the same house?" Julie asked, skeptical.

"It's a large house." Meg thanked heaven for that. "Now, who wants to help me pack?"

"Pack?" Uncle Alistair ambled into the parlor, spectacles propped on his balding head. "By Jove! Never say that my ever-industrious niece is embellishing on an expedition of some sort, leaving us for foreign and exigent lands."

Meg found her uncle's habit of occasionally choosing the wrong word endearing—but unfortunately most of the ton did not. She went to him and gave his ink-stained fingers a squeeze. "I wouldn't dream of it. But I must leave for a while, as I just told Beth and Julie. I've accepted a governess position."

His jovial expression evaporated, leaving him looking every bit of his seventy years. "But . . . but why, my dear? This is your home—it's where you belong."

"Of course it is. But I've always wished to work with children," she fibbed. "And now that a wonderful opportunity has come along, I hope you'll be happy for me. I shall still be here in London, and I promise to visit often."

He swiped at the stray white hairs above his ears, fine strands that seemed perpetually in motion. "Far be it from me to deny you the chance to pursue your life's ambivalence. But this place won't be the same without your sunny dispossession. I will miss you."

Meg hugged him, savoring the soft, yet solid feel of his shoulders. "I'll miss you too, Uncle. And I shall never forget how good you've been to me—to all of us."

"To your new governess." Alec, Lord Torrington, raised his glass in a salute and took a large gulp.

"To one problem solved," Will added, before taking a swig of his own drink. Miss Lacey had started that morning. Why, then, did his life seem more complicated than ever?

He'd come to his club to escape the suddenly domestic feel of his house. Somehow, in the span of a week, he'd acquired two rambunctious girls, made a nursery out of a perfectly good bedchamber, and saddled himself with a reluctant governess.

Alec chuckled. "I'm surprised you didn't farm the little urchins out to a couple in the country—somewhere they wouldn't be underfoot."

"I considered it, believe me." But his cousin, Thomas, had adored his daughters, and Will had once promised that he'd provide for the girls if the unthinkable happened. And then it had—his hale and hearty cousin, the closest thing Will had to a brother, had fallen off his horse and broken his neck. Will couldn't send his girls away.

Shaking off his grief, he snorted. "At least now they'll be too busy learning their sums to terrorize my house. I understand that Miss Winters arranged for the interview. Please let her know I'm in her debt."

At the mention of Miss Winters, Alec took on the look of a lovesick fool. "Charlotte was happy to do it. Miss Lacey's her friend."

Will stared into his brandy, debating how much to tell

Alec. If the women were friends, then Miss Lacey had surely shared the sordid tale. And Miss Winters would delight in passing it along. In short, Alec would soon know that Will's new governess had rejected him outright.

Damn.

He might as well tell Alec before he heard it from someone else.

"Miss Lacey and I actually have a history," Will began.

"The devil you say!" Alec leaned forward in his leather chair. "Did you . . . and she . . ."

"No, blast you." Although the idea intrigued Will far more than it should. "Her family's cottage wasn't far from my estate—my father's at the time—in Oxfordshire. She's a few years younger than I, but we were acquainted as children."

Alec grinned. "This grows more interesting by the minute."

Will shot him a withering look. "My father informed me at age twenty that I was to marry the vicar's daughter, Miss Lacey."

Alec spewed his brandy. "What?"

"Believe me, I was as shocked as you are now," Will said. "We had no close bond to their family and little to gain from the match. But my father would brook no argument."

"So you agreed?"

"Ostensibly. I thought I'd delay the marriage for a few years and in the meantime give her plenty of reasons to cry off."

Alec shook his head with equal parts disgust and admiration. "You're a heartless bastard, do you know that?"

"Me?" Will snorted. "When Miss Lacey learned of the arrangement, she declared she'd rather shave her head and enter a convent than marry me."

Alec threw his head back and laughed—until tears trickled from his damned eyes.

"It was a long time ago." Will looked around the club, hoping Alec's outburst hadn't attracted too much attention.

Alec swiped the back of his hand across his cheek. "Why on earth would a girl with no prospects reject a future earl? And an almost handsome one at that?"

Because she was too bloody proud for her own good. "I came upon her swimming in the lake one day."

"You did *not*."

Will shrugged. "It was all quite innocent, I assure you. I was fishing, looking for a place to cast my line—"

"Is that what we're calling it these days?"

Leveling a glare, Will made an admittedly weak attempt at a defense. "I'd fished there dozens of times without seeing anyone. And when I stumbled upon her discarded dress and saw her bare arms and legs splashing in the water . . . well, I did what any red-blooded boy would have done."

"Good God. No wonder she rejected you."

Will raked a hand through his hair. "Don't be an ass. I gaped. For a few seconds. She saw me and screamed. I ran. The end."

Alec erupted into another hearty round of laughter.

"Damn it. I shouldn't have told you."

"No, no, no. I'm glad you did. It's just ironic."

"How so?"

"You really don't know, do you?"

"What in hell's name are you talking about?"

"Your new governess is one of Lord Wiltmore's Wall-flowers." Alec leaned back and lit a cigar.

Suddenly wary, Will loosened his cravat. "Wait. You know her?"

"We're not acquainted, but I know of her. She and her two sisters were taken in by their uncle some years ago. He's a good-humored fellow"—Alec traced a circle in the air beside his head—"and stark raving mad."

Ah yes, she'd mentioned her uncle—but had made him sound more valiant knight than bumbling bedlamite. "What else do you know about her?"

Alec shrugged. "Not much. She blends into the background at most affairs, probably because she dresses more modestly than a maid. But if anyone should dare to insult her addle-brained uncle, she launches into a passionate defense. At the peril of her own reputation."

So, she was loyal—to a fault. Will snorted. "Let's hope she hasn't inherited her uncle's eccentricities."

Thoughtful, Alec blew out a thin ribbon of smoke. "I doubt it. Not if Charlotte recommended her. But she *does* sound like the sort of woman who knows her mind."

"Yes," Will mused. "That's exactly what I'm afraid of."

Will returned from his club a few hours later to a house that was blissfully still and quiet. In the foyer, a note on the silver salver beside the front door caught his eye—a letter, addressed to him, in Marina's handwriting.

He hadn't seen his beautiful mistress—*ex*-mistress, he mentally corrected himself—in four days. He held the heavy paper under his nose, inhaling her expensive French perfume. Perhaps she missed him and was willing to return to their previous arrangement—the one where she demanded nothing from him but pleasure. Maybe the note held an invitation.

He slid a finger beneath the red wax seal, unfolded the paper, and squinted at the multitude of loops and flourishes.

Dearest Will,
    Our silly quarrel has gone on to long. Return to my bed, darling, and persuade me to forgive you. There is no reason for us to be a part.

                                                          M.

Her words trailed across the paper like a lover's kisses, conjuring countless evenings they'd enjoyed one another. But, Jesus, her spelling was atrocious. Why hadn't he noticed before?

He glanced at the grandfather clock standing sentry in the hall. Just after midnight. Not too late for a visit to Marina's flat. But he was not interested in begging forgiveness. Or any other favors.

With a shrug, he tossed the note back on the salver and began to walk upstairs—until the soft glow of a lamp in the library beckoned.

He followed it but drew up short in the doorway. Miss Lacey sat at the desk near the fireplace, where an orange log sizzled on the grate. Only she was more slumped than sitting, her forehead buried in an open book.

And if he was not mistaken, she snored.

Bemused, he walked closer. An inkwell, some scribbled notes, and an array of books cluttered the desk before her, as though she'd been working most of the evening. He'd known she'd be a diligent employee. Partly because she was devoted to the girls, but also because she was hell-bent on proving herself to him. She had a chip on her shoulder the size of Windsor Castle.

But in sleep, she appeared smaller—less contrary. Her shawl bunched around her waist, and her simple dress revealed the long, lean lines of her back. Fine curls clung to her nape, tempting him to taste the smooth skin there.

He'd never imagined Miss Lacey could look so soft, so vulnerable, so—

Crackle.

The log in the fireplace popped and crumbled, waking her.

Her head snapped up and she gasped, placing her palms flat on the desk.

"Good evening, Miss Lacey," Will drawled. "Or should I say good morning?"

"My lord," she said breathlessly. "What are you doing here?"

"I live here."

She clutched a hand to her chest and looked around the room, at the desk and at him—clearly needing a moment to regain her composure. "I was preparing some lessons for the girls. I must have drifted off."

Arching a brow he said, "Let's hope that the girls find your lessons more stimulating."

She scowled, which he deserved, but he couldn't resist sparring with her.

With her usual, brisk efficiency, she straightened the desk, creating a neat stack of books and notes. "It is actually fortunate that I found you here—"

"I found *you*," he corrected. "But please, proceed."

She rolled her eyes. "I've a request to make—on the girls' behalf. Diana and Valerie require some new dresses."

"That seems reasonable." Miss Lacey could buy the hellions entire wardrobes as long as she kept them out of his hair.

"If we expect them to behave like young ladies, we should ensure they *look* like young ladies."

"You've convinced me, Miss Lacey. Done."

"Thank you." The tight lines around her mouth revealed how much those words had cost her. "Don't worry. The girls don't need anything fancy or outrageously expensive. I won't take them to a modiste."

"Would you consider taking yourself?"

She blinked, clearly offended. "I beg your pardon."

"To the modiste. I don't mean to insult, but your own gowns leave something to be desired." They were atrocities.

Eyes sparking with fury, she rounded the desk and stood toe-to-toe with him. "What I wear," she ground out, "is none of your concern."

"I think it is," he countered. "Appearances matter. You said as much yourself in regard to the twins."

"That's different!"

"Furthermore," he continued blandly, "your appearance reflects on me. I can't have my new governess mistaken for a scullery maid."

"Scullery maid? How dare you—"

"Rest assured, I shall cover the cost. Heaven forbid it should come out of the exorbitant salary I'm paying you." It would be worth it to see her wearing something . . . silk. In a mossy green to match her eyes. Preferably low-cut.

"I am not some mistress that you can dress like a doll," she sputtered. Had she been reading his thoughts? "And while you may be my employer, you have *no* say over what I choose to wear."

He eyed her unfortunate excuse for a dress. It flattered her figure about as much as a monk's robe. "You're not honestly telling me you *choose* to wear a gown the unappetizing shade of a mushroom?"

She crossed her arms, challenging him. "Actually, I am."

They stared at one another for several moments. Will couldn't say exactly what was happening between them, but he hadn't felt so alive, so invigorated in . . . forever.

"Very well then," he conceded, for even the best generals knew when to retreat. "You can purchase a mud-colored bonnet to match."

"No thank you." She batted thick lashes and flashed a mockery of a smile. "I already own one." She snatched her papers off the desk, clutched them to her chest, and stormed past him. "You know, on second thought," she called over her shoulder. "I probably *should* take the girls to a modiste. And to the milliner's. And to the book shop as well."

Holy hell. He waved an arm at the book-covered walls surrounding them. "What about all these?"

"I assume you will spare no expense when it comes to the girls' education?"

"No, but—"

"I thought not," she said smugly.

"In fact, I think it's important that I join you for a shopping trip of this magnitude." What in God's name was he saying?

She snorted, incredulous. "Surely you have more important things to do."

About a dozen. "No."

With a huff, she marched back to him and raised her chin. She stood so close that he could see the subtle rise and fall of her chest, the constellation of freckles across the bridge of her nose, the flecks of gold in her eyes. The corner of her pretty mouth curled into a smile.

As if she knew the mesmerizing effect she had on him.

"Since you are at our disposal—" she began.

He frowned. "I didn't say that."

"We will make a day-long outing of it. After we make our *many* purchases"—she tapped a slender finger on her chin—"we shall take the girls to Hyde Park for fresh air and a chance to play."

"Play? Shouldn't they return to the nursery to memorize poems or something?"

"And after the park, we shall stop at Gunter's for ice cream."

He opened his mouth to object, but then he imagined Miss Lacey, closing her eyes in ecstasy as she savored a creamy spoonful of ice cream. Six hours of carrying parcels might be worth that one moment.

"What's your favorite flavor?" he asked, the huskiness

of his voice betraying his wickedness. "Peach? Orange? Or something more exotic . . . like jasmine?"

She shot him the blistering look mastered by governesses the world 'round. "You," she said evenly, "will never—ever—know."

Chapter FOUR

"Oh, look at this one!" Valerie pointed to a sapphire silk evening gown in the fashion magazine she and her sister leafed through. "So pretty."

"You'd only spill jam on it," Diana said.

"I suppose you're right." Valerie sighed.

Meg thanked the shopkeeper, who was wrapping several items for them, and placed a hand on Valerie's shoulder. "It *is* a very fancy dress."

"That's what I told her!" Diana shook her head like a dowager duchess frustrated by the frivolities of the young.

Meg let her fingers trail over the magazine page, tracing the delicate beading at the bottom of the gown. "However, I think every girl deserves to have at least one fancy dress in her armoire. Why don't we ask the dressmaker if she could fashion something in a similar shade of blue—to match your pretty eyes?"

Valerie's chest swelled and her eyes shone as she nodded, as though she was too overcome to speak.

"Shall I add a blue gown to your order?" The shopkeeper

winked at Meg. "Something suitable for a princess's tea party?"

"Please." Meg squashed the guilt niggling at her belly. The earl could afford it. "And shall we find something equally fancy for you, Miss Diana?" Meg flipped the pages of the magazine, hoping to entice her.

"No, thank you. I like the gowns we picked out. And the hats and gloves and stockings. But I *love* my new boots." She extended her foot and swiveled her ankle, admiring a tiny forest green half-boot. I can't wait to see how fast I can run."

"Let's try to keep the mud off of them for a day or two at least," Meg teased.

"What about you, Miss Lacey?" Valerie fingered a swatch of deep rose silk on the counter as she gazed up at Meg. "Do you have a fancy dress in your armoire?"

"Me?" Meg chuckled as she glanced down at her faded lilac gown. "I'm afraid not."

"Shouldn't you have at least one?"

Behind the counter, the shopkeeper coughed into her hand, as if to second Valerie's suggestion.

Meg tore her eyes away from the stylish designs gracing the pages of the magazine. She'd love nothing more than to own a gorgeous gown that was made especially for her, in a shimmery fabric that would sparkle in the candlelight as she twirled around a ballroom. How lovely would it feel to have silk skimming over her skin and swirling about her legs while she moved in time to the music?

But it was a secret desire—one Meg barely admitted to herself.

"Governesses have no need of ball gowns," she said matter-of-factly.

"Neither do six year olds," Diana pointed out. She

grabbed the silk swatch from her sister and thrust it beneath Meg's chin, as the dressmaker had done for the girls earlier. "This color looks pretty with your hair. See?"

Meg hazarded a glance in the looking glass on the counter. The fabric *was* a delectable shade of pink. "Nonsense."

"It's not," Diana pouted. "You said every girl should have one fancy dress."

"I must agree," Lord Castleton interjected, startling them all. He strode into the shop and joined them at the counter.

Meg had almost—but not quite—forgotten he waited for them outside. He'd escorted them on all their errands that morning but had opted to remain in the coach while the girls ordered their dresses. He must have grown very weary of waiting if he'd deemed it necessary to enter this eminently feminine realm.

Ironically, surrounded by snippets of lace, silks, and frippery, he looked larger, more masculine, than ever.

Meg closed the fashion magazine and slid it aside. "I apologize for the delay, my lord. Our purchases are being wrapped, and we shall be ready momentarily."

"Do not think to change the subject, Miss Lacey," he said smoothly. "Your charge here . . ."

"Diana," she provided.

Inclining his head, he continued, "Diana makes an excellent point. You *should* have one nice gown."

"That is none of your concern," Meg said evenly. She mustn't lose her temper in front of the twins. "Besides, this shopping trip is for *the girls*."

"True. But it seems as though *the girls* wish for you to have a new dress." He pointed at the square of rose silk that Diana held. "What's that?"

"A fabric sample." Diana raised it to Meg's shoulder. "Wouldn't this look pretty on Miss Lacey?"

Valerie sighed dreamily. "Divine."

Meg plucked the silk from Diana's fingers and returned it to the counter. "Look, our packages are ready. Let's ask the footman to load them onto the coach, shall we?" Grabbing one hand of each twin, she started toward the dress shop's door.

Only to be blocked by the earl. Or, more precisely, his torso. His very broad, very hard, and very immovable torso.

"What is your rush, Miss Lacey? This outing was meant to be productive, but fun as well—was it not?"

"Yes, of course." Meg could feel the twins gazing up at her, anxious to see how she'd fare in a minor power struggle with Lord Castleton. "However, if you'll recall, we have a rather full schedule."

His mouth curled in amusement. "Are you always so regimented . . . so rigid?"

Meg bristled. Perhaps she was a bit . . . inflexible. But so much of life was outside of one's control. She saw no harm in maintaining order where possible. "Some of us," she ground out, "do not have the luxury of indulging every whim, nor the freedom to blow wherever the wind takes us."

"Like a dandelion seed?" Valerie interjected.

Meg squeezed her little hand. "Exactly."

"I'm not suggesting you abandon your duties, steal away on a ship, and sail to the West Indies, for God's sake. I'm merely encouraging you to take the same advice you gave the girls. Order one fancy gown to keep in your armoire."

"Why?" A pretty dress wouldn't stop the ton from ridiculing her and her sisters. It wouldn't transform her from a wallflower to a diamond of the first water. *Why* did he care?

"Because even though you think it's frivolous and extravagant, you might need it one day." He leaned toward her slightly. "You might *want* it."

Lord help her, she did. But even more than she wanted a pretty gown for herself, she wanted one for each of her sisters. Maybe she should let the earl buy her a gown so that she could give it to them. It would be too short for Julie, but Beth could wear it, and perhaps add some lace to the bottom to make it work for Julie too.

Her heart may have been tempted, but pride was in control. "While I appreciate your concern for my hypothetical needs and wants," she said stiffly, "I can assure you that an elegant gown would serve me no purpose beyond collecting dust and attracting moths."

The earl seemed to consider this as he crossed his arms, his wide shoulders and muscular biceps testing the seams of his dark green, tailored jacket. His eyes, brown as melted chocolate, searched her face with an intensity that unsettled her. He didn't understand why she defied him, couldn't accept it. And something in his gaze told her that he would not be content until he knew all her secrets—the fears and desires she held so closely that not even her sisters were aware of them.

A shiver ran the length of her spine, but she would not yield, nor would she apologize.

An odd combination of puzzlement and hurt flashed across his face so quickly she might have imagined it. He pressed his lips together, then nodded—a silent admission of defeat.

Why, then, did she not feel victorious?

"I have no wish to contribute to the proliferation of dust and moths in your armoire," he said with a wry smile. Turning his attention to the girls, he added, "Having survived the ordeal of dress shopping, I think we have earned a visit to the park. What do you say?"

"Yes!" they exclaimed in unison.

"I'll let the footman know the packages are ready," Meg offered.

"No need." Lord Castleton shot a charming grin at the shopkeeper as he scooped up their purchases and marched toward the shop door. The shopkeeper gripped the edge of the counter as though she feared she'd swoon, while another of the shop's patrons fanned herself—vigorously.

Meg wanted to roll her eyes. So the earl carried a few packages. That hardly qualified him for knighthood.

"Are you coming, Miss Lacey?" he called over his shoulder. "If you've reconsidered and have decided to order a gown, we'll be happy to wait."

"No," she said through gritted teeth. "I'm quite done with shopping."

Meg would have liked to cling to her contrary mood for the remainder of the afternoon, but the glorious spring day made it nigh impossible. As she, Lord Castleton, and the girls strolled along the pebbled footpath in the dappled shade, a warm breeze eased some of the tightness from her shoulders. The earl steered their little group to a bench at the edge of the Serpentine and waved an arm at the surrounding lawn. "Ladies, how do you fancy this spot?"

"Perfect!" Valerie said.

Diana tossed a ball from hand to hand. "*Now* may we play?"

"Of course," Meg said with a smile. "Shall we have a game of catch?"

"Yes!" the girls cried in unison.

"Not I." The earl lowered himself onto the bench, stretched out his long legs, and crossed them at the ankles.

"My question was directed toward the *girls*, my lord."

"Was it?" he said, his mouth curling into a dangerous smile. "I don't know whether to be relieved or insulted."

"Either way, we shall leave you to your own devices." Meg led the twins away from the path where London's elite strolled. Why should she care if the earl was embarrassed to be seen with her? If he were so shallow that he would shun a person for being a bit unfashionable, then she would not waste a single thought on him.

"Stay away from the water, girls. I'll not have you falling in. Come, here's a nice open space." Meg and the twins quickly formed a triangle and tossed the ball to one another. Each time the ball flew over their heads, Diana and Valerie squealed in delight and chased it with glee. Their laughter washed over Meg, soothing some of her hurt. *They* didn't seem to mind that she dressed like a kitchen maid.

If only she hadn't goaded the earl in the library last night, they wouldn't have had to endure his company today. But he'd provoked her, and she'd responded in kind, and he'd ultimately called her bluff, blast it all.

"Miss Lacey." Valerie pointed across the lawn. "I think the woman over there is waving to you."

Meg turned and raised a hand to her brow, shielding her eyes from the sun. Several yards away, Charlotte waved happily as a young girl skipped beside her.

"Who are they?" Diana asked.

"My friend Miss Winters and her charge, Abigail."

"I think she's our age," Valerie said.

"I believe she is." Meg cast a glance at the bench behind her where the earl had been joined by a pretty blond-haired woman in a stunning pink gown. The woman slowly twirled a yellow parasol trimmed in delicate lace while she giggled at something Lord Castleton had said. Her maid stood to the side of them, a discreet distance away. No, the earl would not mind if she introduced the twins to Charlotte and Abigail.

He was too busy making his next conquest to notice. In fact, Meg doubted he'd notice if she and the girls toppled head-first into the Serpentine.

"Meg!" Charlotte cried as she approached. "What a

lovely surprise." Pink-cheeked and breathless, she pulled Meg into a quick, fierce hug. "How are you faring—well, I hope?"

She cast a meaningful glance over her shoulder toward the earl. "Quite."

Charlotte followed her gaze and nodded. "Well, then," she said to the girls, smiling, "we must all become acquainted, for I've a feeling we'll be spending many afternoons together."

After introductions, Meg handed the ball to Abigail. "Here, you may take my place in the game. You'll keep up with these two far better than I."

While the girls played, Meg and Charlotte walked to the shade of a stately oak nearby. "It's so wonderful to see you," Charlotte said. "You look very well, indeed. Are you happy?"

The question caught Meg off guard. She couldn't very well tell her friend the truth—not after she'd been so kind as to arrange the interview. "I miss Beth and Julie, of course. But the twins are delightful."

Charlotte raised a brow. "And the earl?"

"So far, we've managed to tolerate each other."

"What?" Charlotte's forehead knitted. "He hasn't done anything . . . untoward, I hope?"

"No," Meg reassured her. "It's not that." She frowned as the girls drifted across the lawn, farther away from her. "I'm going to bring them back here." She started toward them, but Charlotte placed a hand on her arm.

"They're fine. Let them enjoy a bit of freedom."

Meg relaxed. Unlike her, Charlotte knew what she was doing. And the girls *were* in plain sight. "Tell me this gets easier."

"It does. Building trust takes time."

Meg nodded but was unsure whether her friend referred to the children or the earl.

"You said that there was some history between you and Lord Castleton," Charlotte said. "When did you two meet?"

"Ages ago. We used to be neighbors." Meg glanced back at the earl. He and his beautiful companion had begun strolling down the path by the lake. She might as well tell Charlotte the whole sordid tale. "I was barely fifteen when—"

"Diana!" Valerie shouted. "Stop!" Several yards away, she stared helplessly as her twin sprinted across the park lawn, head down, her new boots churning up the grass.

Meg ran to Valerie's side. "Where's she going?"

"She told us to count how long it takes her to run to the other side of the road and back."

Meg's heart plummeted. "That's Rotten Row." She lifted the front of her gown and took off, running after Diana. The little girl seemed oblivious to the phaeton careening down the path, pulled by horses galloping like their tails were aflame.

"Diana!" she cried, shouldering her way past a man puffing on a pipe.

But the girl kept moving, closer to the road and the out-of-control phaeton.

Her slippers slapping the ground as she ran, Meg gasped for air, and called out again, louder. "Diana!"

The little girl stumbled to a stop in the middle of the road. She spun around to face Meg, her blond curls blowing in the breeze. Smiling, she raised her hand to wave.

Then froze.

She stared wide-eyed at the huge horses barreling down the dirt path toward her.

Never in her life had Meg felt so powerless. Not when her parents announced she'd marry a man she barely knew. Not when she'd been forced to leave the only home she'd ever known. Not ever.

She *had* to reach Diana in time.

Meg sprinted. She launched herself at Diana, knocking her off her feet. The girl tumbled into the grass, out of danger.

But Meg's chest slammed onto the dirt, knocking the breath from her lungs. With the horses almost upon her, she struggled to her feet, but her slipper caught on the hem of her dress, and she landed on her knee with a bone-jarring thud.

The ground vibrated with the pounding of hooves. Dear God. She was about to be trampled.

Chapter FIVE

Her throat thick with dust, Meg couldn't breathe, much less scream.

She braced herself for the inevitable pain. She wasn't ready to die, and yet—

Whoosh. A blur of dark green dove in front of the horses' hooves. *Bam.* A large body landed on top of her, forcing the air from her lungs. Strong hands grasped her shoulders and pulled her away from the hooves, the dust, and the danger.

She rolled over the ground like a log, the man on top of her one moment, she on top of him the next. And when they finally jolted to a stop beside a row of prickly hedges, both of them clinging to each other and breathing hard, she was on top.

Meg pressed her hands against the solid wall of his chest, and raised her head to look at her rescuer.

Lord Castleton. Naturally.

He wore a lopsided grin that, in spite of her brush with death, made her very aware that he was a man and she was a woman—lying atop him.

"Are you quite well, Miss Lacey?" A polite inquiry on the face of it, but his arched brow and suggestive tone made it wholly improper.

"I believe so," she rasped. "But Diana—"

"Is fine." He pushed himself to sitting, holding her firmly on his lap. Concern darkened his brown eyes. "You, however, seem like you could use a glass of brandy."

Brandy? "Not at all. That is, I am concerned for Diana." She swallowed and closed her eyes briefly, to erase the image of what might have been.

She squashed the strong and sudden urge to cry. What was she doing, pretending to be a governess? Thanks to her incompetence, a little girl had almost died. "I must check on her."

Meg clambered off the earl, perhaps not as elegantly as she might have, because he swallowed an oath when her knee came in contact with a certain—male—part of his anatomy.

Blast it all. Cringing, she scrambled to her feet and knelt beside Diana. "Let me see you." Meg placed her palms on the girl's cheeks, studied every inch of her face, and found nary a scratch. "Does anything hurt? Can you move your arms and legs?"

"Of course," Diana said, out of breath but smiling. "Did you see how fast I ran in my new boots?"

Relief coursed through Meg, but she had to make Diana understand that she couldn't dash off, unchaperoned. And she certainly couldn't run in the vicinity of Rotten Row. "You were very fast, indeed. But I don't think you realize the danger you were in or what could have happened." Diana's little face crumpled, but Meg pressed on. "Those horses were huge, and you almost—"

"Beat me in a footrace," Lord Castleton interrupted smoothly.

Meg glanced over her shoulder at the earl, who

approached with a slight limp, as though he hadn't quite recovered from the injury her wayward knee had inflicted. "I beg your pardon?"

"Diana almost outran me."

The girl grinned. "Actually, I *did* outrun you."

The earl chuckled. "So you did. At least I managed to best Miss Lacey."

Meg frowned. "This isn't a laughing matter, my lord." It was bad enough that she'd let it happen. Diana had been in peril—and it was all her fault. "I don't think you should make light of it."

Lord Castleton gave Diana a conspiratorial wink and jabbed a thumb at Meg. "Sore loser."

Meg blinked and opened her mouth to scold the earl or Diana or . . . *someone*. But Diana giggled.

And even if discipline *was* called for, well, the timing seemed all wrong. Something a proper governess surely would have known.

"Meg! Are you all right?" Charlotte hurried across the lawn, Abigail and Valerie in tow. "You took such a tumble!"

"I fear I tackled her," the earl said without a hint of remorse.

Meg ignored him. "I'm fine. Diana is too."

"Thank goodness." Valerie released Charlotte's hand and threw her arms around her sister.

"You're squeezing too hard," Diana complained to her twin. Looking up at Meg, she asked, "May we go to Gunter's now?"

Meg stood, surprised to find that her knees wobbled a bit. The earl grabbed her elbow, steadying her, while Charlotte fussed over her wrinkled gown and the leaf stuck in her hair.

"Gunter's?" Meg repeated. The girls had been looking forward to it, but she was still worried about Diana.

Perhaps they should return to the house and summon a doctor.

She looked to Lord Castleton, but neither his heavy-lidded gaze nor his uncurving mouth gave any indication of his preference. "I don't know." She turned to Charlotte, hoping that her friend would provide some guidance. What was a governess to do after one of her charges was nearly trampled?

Charlotte gave her an encouraging nod. "It might be just the thing to cheer everyone . . . if you're sure you're feeling well enough."

"I am." The twins began to bounce happily. "It appears the girls are as well. Will you and Abigail join us?"

"I'm afraid we can't. We came to the park for a brief outing but must return home and resume our penmanship lesson."

The earl nodded approvingly. "It is encouraging to hear that not *all* impressionable girls while away the entire day shopping for gowns, playing ball in the park, and eating ice cream. Your commitment to educating your young charge is to be commended, Miss Winters."

Charlotte cast Lord Castleton a wary glance. "I know that Miss Lacey is equally committed. It's all a matter of balance, my lord."

"If you say so." Inclining his head in her direction, he said, "Good day, Miss Winters. I'm going to bid farewell to a friend, then I'll meet the rest of you at the coach."

He walked away, his strides a bit shorter and slower than usual. Good Lord, perhaps Meg had injured him worse than she thought.

She held the twins' hands and began walking back across the park. "Please, no more running for today, girls."

Charlotte shot her a sympathetic smile. "You know, it's not your fault, Meg."

Well, of course it was. If she couldn't keep them safe,

she wasn't fit to be a governess. "To quote the earl, 'If you say so.'"

"Honestly. It could have happened to me or anyone. *I'm* the one who told you to let them have some freedom, remember?"

"I knew that Diana had new boots and that she wanted to test them out. But I only worried about the Serpentine . . . it never occurred to me that she'd run—"

"Children are unpredictable. These things happen."

Meg stopped and faced her friend. "Today's outing could have ended in tragedy, Charlotte. And it happened in my first week as a governess. In front of my employer."

Charlotte winced. "That part was unfortunate. But you mustn't lose confidence."

"No danger of that," Meg replied. "To lose something, you must first possess it."

Her friend laughed. "Everything's going to work out. You'll see."

Near a bench beside the water, the earl spoke to the lovely young lady he'd abandoned—temporarily, at least—in order to rescue Diana. And Meg. The blond woman didn't seem to mind his disheveled cravat, grass-stained trousers, or dusty jacket. In fact, she gazed at him with adoration. As though he were some sort of hero.

And he was. Even Meg couldn't deny it. He'd literally swept her off her feet and protected her with his body. His very large, hard, strong body.

"Meg?" Charlotte waved a hand in front of Meg's face. "Hmm?"

"I was asking if you still wanted to meet on Sunday."

"Oh, yes. Of course."

Charlotte's brow knit. "You seem a little dazed from that fall. After Gunter's, you should take to your bed and rest until dinner."

Meg rolled her eyes. "Yes, ma'am."

"Here comes the earl now. I'll see you soon."

Charlotte and Abigail waved good-bye to the girls, and Lord Castleton helped the twins into the coach. When he offered his hand to Meg, she pretended not to see it and deposited herself on the seat between the girls. She'd had quite enough physical contact with the earl for one day. Nay, for an entire fortnight.

The twins squirmed on either side of Meg as they debated the merits of potential ice cream flavors. "Someone should invent suet pudding ice cream," Valerie announced. "I would eat that."

"As would I," Diana said with a shrug. "But it's rather boring. I should like to taste something more exciting, like cricket leg ice cream."

"You would not," Valerie retorted.

"How do you know?"

Their friendly bickering reminded Meg of her own sisters, and she smiled; but a glance across the coach revealed the earl was not similarly amused. With his crossed arms, clenched jaw, and brooding stare, he was the picture of intimidation. A chill raced down her spine.

Meg couldn't fault him for being angry with her. She was angry with herself. And she owed the earl an apology.

As the coach started rolling down the street, Meg cleared her throat. "My lord," she began.

He blinked and dragged his gaze away from the storefronts that glided past his window. "What is it, Miss Lacey?" He spoke with the exasperation of someone interrupted in the middle of a particularly vexing math problem.

Undaunted, she lifted her chin. "Regarding the incident in the park earlier. I feel that I must apo—"

"No," he snapped.

"But I—"

"We will not have this conversation now." He let the final word hang in the air for a moment, and his implication was clear: whatever he intended to say could not be said in front of the girls. "See me in my study before dinner this evening. Seven o'clock, sharp."

Meg's throat constricted, so she simply nodded.

He must mean to sack her.

One grave mistake had effectively dashed her plans to save Uncle Alistair from debtor's prison, see her sisters marry well, and gain a modicum of independence. How could she have been so careless? Her heart sank, and not just because of the money. Even now, Valerie's small hand was nestled in her own, and Diana's head leaned against her shoulder. Meg had disappointed them, too.

She sighed. She had lasted barely two days in her governess position. Approximately one day longer than she'd expected.

Chapter SIX

Will poured himself a generous drink and sank into one of the pair of armchairs that flanked the fireplace in his study. As the first swallow of brandy blazed a path down his throat, he started to cross his legs—and immediately thought better of it.

Jesus. His stones still hadn't recovered entirely. It felt like they'd been hit by a battering ram rather than his governess's knee.

Maybe it served him right, because before Miss Lacey had nearly unmanned him, he had been undeniably aroused. Hard as a pine tree.

Even now, his cock swelled at the memory of her soft breasts pressed against his chest. Her lithe legs had straddled him, her thighs squeezing his hips with just the right amount of pressure. And when she'd lifted her head to look at him, a silky chestnut curl had fallen across his cheek, tempting him to spear his fingers through her hair and obliterate what was left of the tidy knot at her nape.

If there was one thing he could absolutely not resist, it was balancing a beautiful woman on top of him—even one as contrary as Miss Lacey. The combination of her full breasts bouncing above, her bottom pressing deliciously against his cock, and the unexpected interest in her sparkling eyes had instantly triggered his desire.

Cursing, he adjusted himself, threw back the rest of his brandy, and glanced at the clock on the mantle.

Two minutes to seven. Miss Lacey would not be late. She was rigid—a slave to rules—which was probably a useful and admirable trait in a governess. Unfortunately, it was a terrible trait in a lover. Not that he had any intention of bedding her. It was just a damned shame that someone as beautiful and passionate as she should be so . . . regimented.

But Will had realized a couple of other things in the park, as well. First, he was responsible for the twins. He'd known it before, on an intellectual level. But today, as the phaeton had careened down Rotten Row and Diana stood there defenseless, he'd *felt* it. In his gut. And it was terrifying. When he'd promised his cousin that he'd take care of the girls, he'd had no idea what he was signing up for, but he couldn't go back on his word. He wouldn't.

The second thing Will had learned was that Miss Lacey was all too willing to sacrifice her own well-being for the sake of her charges. She'd put herself in the path of charging horses in order to rescue Diana, and if Will hadn't swept her out of the way . . .

Christ. Heart pounding in his chest, he stood and refilled his glass.

Which led to his third and final revelation of the day. He had to protect Miss Lacey, too. For the sake of his own sanity. He couldn't worry about her and the girls every time they wanted to go for a walk in the park, for God's sake.

At the sound of footsteps, he checked the clock again. Predictably punctual, to the second.

"Good evening, my lord." Miss Lacey stood at the threshold of his study, wringing her hands. The drab, navy gown she wore lent her face a pale, almost ghostly pallor. She had removed the bits of grass from her hair and the smudges of dirt from her cheeks, effectively erasing all traces of their intimate, if accidental, encounter. Pity, that.

Will waved a hand at the chair beside him. "Come in, please. Sit."

She perched on the edge of the seat, folded her hands in her lap, and pursed her lips, adopting a pose that could have been called either *Demure Governess* or *Determined Spinster*. "Earlier in the coach," she began, "you did not allow me to speak."

"Why do I have the feeling you're about to rectify that now?"

"I would be remiss if I did not thank you for coming to my aid in the park."

Will nodded. Perhaps it wasn't the most graceful thank-you, but she was a proud creature, and, if he were honest, he respected that about her. In an effort to meet her halfway, he said, "I regret that I had to tackle you. I would have avoided doing so if it were possible."

"I understand. It was the lesser of two evils. I am in your debt."

Will started to disagree and say she owed him nothing, but checked himself and mentally tucked her admission in his pocket. It might prove useful in future dealings with his governess. "The important thing is that no one was hurt."

"Yes, about that." She wrung her hands some more. "I feel that I must apologize for"—her cheeks instantly flushed bright pink—"the extremely unfortunate and entirely accidental contact that my knee happened to make with your . . ."

Will raised both brows and feigned ignorance. "With my *what*, Miss Lacey?"

The flush on her cheeks deepened and spread like a strawberry-colored ink stain, crawling down her pretty neck and disappearing behind the ridiculously high collar of her gown. "You know very well what I'm referring to."

"You give me far too much credit. I'm not a reader of minds." It was not well done of him, but damned if he could resist the chance to tease her.

She blew out a long breath and shot him a wary look. "Very well. I shall attempt to clarify as best I can. You were on the ground, and I was on—" She shook her head and started over. "We were *both* on the ground—"

Will frowned for effect. "That's not precisely the way I remember it, but do go on."

"I was attempting to stand," she continued through gritted teeth, "when my knee made incidental and regrettably injurious contact with . . ."

He leaned forward. "Yes?"

She crossed her arms, frustration rolling off of her in waves. "You know." For the briefest of moments her gaze darted to the front of his trousers before returning to his face. Good God. It was incredibly improper and arousing as hell.

He leaned an elbow on the mantle behind him and crossed his legs at the ankles, hoping to create room in his trousers for his growing erection. "I confess that I *do* know, Miss Lacey. The question is, do *you*?"

"I know enough, my lord," she tossed back at him. "And frankly, I'm not impressed."

If he'd been sipping brandy, he would have choked on it. "You're not?"

"No," she sniffed. "It seems exceedingly . . . fragile."

"*Fragile*?"

She shrugged. "Consider the damage I inflicted with my knee. I wasn't even trying."

"Truly? Because I'm beginning to have my doubts about that."

She gasped. "You are thwarting my attempts to apologize for hurting you. Why do you enjoy humiliating me so?"

He opened his mouth to reply, then sank into the chair opposite her. Jesus, he was an ass. "It was poorly done of me. If it's any consolation, it wasn't my intention to embarrass you, so much as . . . to challenge you."

She pressed her fingertips to her temple and squinted as though she felt a headache coming on. "To challenge me? I don't understand."

"I enjoy sparring with you." After he'd goaded her so mercilessly, she deserved to know the truth of it. "You're a worthy opponent, Miss Lacey."

Her spine stiffened. "If you want a sparring partner, Lord Castleton, I suggest you find one at Jackson's Saloon. I am only a governess—and not a very good one at that," she added, more to herself than to him. "Which brings me to the real reason I wished to speak to you and what I wanted to say earlier, in the coach."

Ah, yes. If Will wasn't mistaken, she'd been on the verge of tendering her resignation. But if he let her leave, then he'd have to hire someone else, and where the devil was he going to find another governess willing to throw herself in front of charging thoroughbreds for the sake of a pair of little hellions? He'd be damned if he'd waste countless hours interviewing scores of bookish spinsters.

Time to nip her thoughts of resigning in the bud.

He crossed his arms and said, "If you'll recall, Miss Lacey, I am the one who summoned *you* here."

"Yes, but I—"

"Can speak your mind after I've spoken mine," he finished for her. "Fair enough?"

Meg bit her tongue and nodded. The earl paced thoughtfully in front of the fireplace, rubbing the light stubble on his chin as he no doubt debated the best way to inform her that he was sacking her. It didn't really matter whether he fired her or she quit, but she did wonder if there was a limit to how much humiliation a person could endure in one day. Surely, she was nearing the threshold by now.

"There will be no more incidents like the one that occurred today," he said smoothly, as if it were just that easy to command it so.

"It was inexcusable," Meg agreed. "I should never have let the girls wander off. My carelessness could have resulted in—"

"Miss Lacey," the earl drawled, "a brief pause is not an invitation to speak."

Meg bristled. "No? I rather thought that was how conversations worked, my lord."

A smug smile spread across his face, and she realized she had fallen into the trap of sparring with him once more.

"Please, continue," she said.

Lord Castleton inclined his dark head. "In order to avoid a repeat performance, you and the twins shall not depart the house unless accompanied by a footman. Harry will keep a close eye on you during each and every outing. You will not leave this house without him."

After a period of silence, during which Meg's blood heated to a rolling boil, the earl waved his palm magnanimously. "Your turn. I'm sure you have plenty to say."

Oh, she did, and most of it wasn't fit for polite conversation. She took another moment, exhaled, and said, "Allow me to make sure I understand. You want a footman to follow the twins and me every time we go for a stroll in the garden? We are essentially prisoners, allowed to leave the premises only when closely guarded?"

"You are being rather dramatic, Miss Lacey. This town house is a far cry from Newgate, and I am taking this measure to ensure the girls' well-being."

Meg's blood bubbled a little more. "You think me incapable of keeping them safe."

"The twins attract calamities like dogs' fur attracts burrs. I doubt any one person can keep them out of trouble, but Harry will lend his assistance by looking out for them. He will protect you, as well, if necessary."

The glare she shot at him should have turned him to stone. "I *don't* require protection."

"You did today." There was no mocking or triumph in his voice, but rather a gravity that stunned her into silence. "I can't be with you all the time, but I can see that someone else is." His brown eyes darkened as he looked at her, willing her to understand. His whole body tensed as he waited for her response.

It was, perhaps, the most vulnerable and honest she'd ever seen him. Beneath the usual masks of *Overbearing Earl* and *Dissolute Rake*, there was a man who might genuinely care for her. Not in a romantic way, but enough to be concerned for her safety.

Her skin tingled in the wake of his stare, and she swallowed. This side of Lord Castleton was rather difficult to resist.

Which was all the more reason she should resign. She and her sisters could not afford gowns, but they could afford a scandal even less. Any hint of impropriety could dash her sisters' chances of marrying well. Their very futures were at stake. "I understand the reasons for your decision, but I'm afraid we're debating a moot point."

"And why is that?"

Now that it was time to speak, Meg's throat tightened

and her mouth went dry. She licked her lips and forced herself to say the words. "The incident in the park this afternoon made me realize that I am not qualified to be a governess after all. I think you should find someone with more experience than I. Someone who understands children and—"

"What utter nonsense."

"I beg your pardon?"

"You were shaken by today's events—as anyone would be. But you reacted quickly. You saved Diana. No harm was done."

"But what if—"

"Don't torture yourself with *what if*s, Miss Lacey. It's tedious and, worse, useless." He pushed himself off the mantle, strolled to the sideboard behind his desk, and raised a decanter. "Brandy?"

Meg wrinkled her nose. "No, thank you."

"Very well, then—port."

"I don't care for a drink, my lord."

He proceeded to pour one for each of them. "Then you may simply hold yours and humor me."

He handed her a glass of port, sat in the chair opposite her, and leaned forward, propping his elbows on his knees. He swirled the brandy in his snifter, gazing into it thoughtfully.

Meg took the opportunity to study his chiseled cheekbones, straight nose, and large hands. Those strong hands had grasped her shoulders, those long fingers had brushed over her skin. And for a moment—as she had lain atop him, earlier—an awareness had sparked between them.

She felt an echo of it even now.

"To expanding your experience," he said, raising his snifter.

Dear Jesus. "What?" Meg fumbled her glass and the velvety red port sloshed close to the rim.

The earl reached out, quickly steadying her hand. "I was making a toast," he said, as though it were some exotic custom that required explaining.

"So I'd gathered," Meg said with a coolness that belied her burning cheeks.

His thumb grazed her inner wrist, lingering briefly on her wildly racing pulse before he released her, sat back, and raised his glass again. "To expanding your experience *as a governess*," he clarified.

A smile played about his mouth while he drank, and since she feared that any reply she made would only give him more ammunition to embarrass her, she raised her glass in a mock salute.

And drank.

A nice long draw, to numb her improbable and highly inconvenient attraction toward the earl. Sweet and potent, the port settled in her belly and warmed her insides.

At the sight of her drinking, he raised his brows and nodded his approval.

However, Meg was not about to bend to his will. "I thought that the desire to be a good governess, paired with hard work, would be enough," she said. "But I fear that it is not. The truth is that I am not qualified for this position."

Lord Castleton leaned back in his armchair, extended his legs, and crossed them at the ankles, his gleaming boots only inches from the skirt of her dress. As he seemed to consider what she'd said, he nonchalantly balanced the base of his snifter on his abdomen, loosely holding the rim between his thumb and forefinger. Meg had to concentrate in order to keep her eyes off of that intriguing spot just above the waistband of his trousers.

So she drank a little more port.

"I was twenty-three when I inherited my father's title. Do you think I was qualified to be an earl, Miss Lacey?"

"I don't know," she stammered. "But I'm sure it was difficult to lose your father at so young an age."

A shadow darkened his face briefly, then lifted. "It was, in some ways. I was trying to comfort my mother and attempting to run an estate at the same time. I had no idea what I was doing, but I learned. So will you."

"There is a difference in our situations."

"What might that be?" he challenged.

"You were born into this life." She waved a hand at the elegant surroundings. "You've always known you were destined to be an earl, and you were groomed for the title from an early age. But I was never meant to be a governess."

He shook his head, clearly dumbfounded. "A few days ago you stood in this very room and convinced me you would make a fine governess. Why the change of heart?"

She shrugged helplessly. "It's not fair to the twins." They were part of the reason, anyway.

"Don't do that," he snapped.

Meg pressed a hand to her chest. "Do what?"

"Lay the blame with the twins."

"I'm not blaming them," she said.

"Good, because this is about *you*. The job isn't as easy as you thought it would be, and now you want to quit."

No, she didn't *want* to. She needed this position far more than he knew, and had already spent her first week's salary ten times over in her head. But her attraction to the earl was unsettling, and living under the same roof with him could only invite trouble. "I just want what's best for Valerie and Diana."

"And you think that running away is what's best for them?" he asked, incredulous.

She closed her eyes. "No, but . . ."

"Then stay, damn it."

The words hung in the air between them, and she saw

it again. That raw, unfiltered glimpse into his soul. He took the glass from her hands and set it on a table next to his snifter. Then he reached for her hand and glided his thumb back and forth over her palm.

Perhaps it was the effect of the port, but that mere brush of his thumb sent ripples of pleasure through her limbs. Her nipples tightened beneath the stiff wool of her dress, and she squeezed her thighs together in a futile attempt to stop the pulsing between her legs.

"Stay," he breathed. "Please."

"Pardon me, my lord," Gibson intoned from the doorway, startling them both and shattering the intimate moment. "Your dinner is served."

Meg drew her hand back. "I really should go."

"Set another place, Gibson. Miss Lacey will be dining with me this evening."

Chapter SEVEN

"I'll see to it at once." Gibson bowed and glided out of Lord Castleton's study. If the butler thought it odd that the earl had invited the governess to dinner, he hid his surprise quite well.

Meg, on the other hand, did not. "What have you done?" she sputtered.

He shrugged, all innocence. "I invited you to dinner."

"I beg to differ, my lord. You did not extend an invitation. An invitation can be declined. What you did was . . . was . . . issue a *decree*."

He nodded approvingly. "You see, Miss Lacey, *this* is why you will make an exceptional governess. Those subtle nuances of language are lost on me."

"How convenient."

"In any event, Gibson is setting a place for you as we speak. And we still have a few matters left to discuss." He picked up their glasses and strolled to the sideboard where he proceeded to refill them.

Grasping at straws, Meg said, "I'm not dressed

properly." It was a gross understatement. Her utilitarian navy dress was meant for running errands in Town or performing light chores—not for sipping wine at an elegant candlelit table.

"Would you like to change?" the earl offered.

Meg's cheeks heated again. "I'm afraid I didn't bring any suitable gowns with me."

He returned to the armchair where she sat, handed her the glass of port, and rubbed the light stubble on his chin. She could almost see his mind replaying the scene in the dress shop earlier that afternoon. "It's taking a considerable amount of restraint not to say I told you so."

"Yes, you are ever the gentleman, my lord," she said through her teeth.

"Fortunately, only the two of us will be dining this evening, and I don't mind your dress."

She took a healthy swallow of port. "I think we both know that you do."

"Well then," he said quite seriously, "maybe I've become so accustomed to seeing it that it no longer affects me."

"Careful, Lord Castleton, or you shall turn my head."

He chucked, then offered his arm. "Allow me to escort you to the dining room.

Meg hesitated. Their bodies had touched in the park, but that hadn't been by choice. And she had an awareness of him now—so much so, that the simple act of taking his arm seemed fraught with peril.

Though it bordered on rude, she decided to refuse. "Thank you, but I don't require an escort." To demonstrate, she quickly hoisted herself out of the chair—and felt a sudden rush of dizziness. Her legs refused to obey orders from her head, and her knees buckled. Her glass crashed to the floor, and the dark port splattered everywhere.

She would have fallen onto the shards of glass if the earl hadn't wrapped his arm around her waist and steadied her against him. While the walls swirled around her and the furniture tilted, he held her tightly. Rock solid, he seemed to be the only thing in the room that wasn't swaying.

"Whoa," he said softly. He set down his glass and curled a finger beneath her chin, forcing her to look into his eyes. "Are you all right?" He didn't loosen his hold or give her space to test her legs. His hip was pressed snugly against her side, and his face was so close that she could see the individual spikes of his lashes and a small scar along his jaw.

"I stood too quickly, and . . . the port." But the port was not to blame for her inability to form a coherent sentence. That unfortunate development was entirely the earl's fault. "I am fine."

"Would you tell me if you were not?" The low timbre of his voice vibrated through her, and a teasing smile played about his full lips. At the small of her back, his large hand held her tightly. Almost . . . possessively.

"Perhaps not. But I will confess I am embarrassed about the mess." Her gaze flicked to the port-soaked rug. "I should get something to clean it up."

"Gibson will take care of it." The earl smoothly released her waist and grasped her upper arms lightly as if he were trying to balance her. "When did you last eat?"

"It's been . . . a few hours." Breakfast, actually.

He arched a brow. "You need food in your belly. I am going to escort you into the dining room. This can happen in one of two ways. Either you can take my arm, or I can carry you over my shoulder. It's your choice, Miss Lacey."

The glint in his eye said he wasn't jesting *and* that he'd relish the opportunity to prove it, so she made a quick decision. "Your arm will suffice."

He laughed again, a low, rich sound that made her pulse

thrum. "I thought you'd say that." But there was concern in his eyes as he tentatively released her and offered his arm once more. "Are you prone to fainting?"

"No. There was only the one time after I . . . well, after I received very bad news." She slipped her hand into the crook of his arm, and he flexed his muscles, pulling her close, demanding that she lean on him for support.

"I'm sorry about the bad news," he said sincerely.

"Thank you, but it was years ago." When she'd learned that her parents' carriage had careened off an icy bridge and they'd drowned in the river. All because she'd behaved like a spoiled chit. She could have asked for time to consider the engagement or simply been more gracious in her refusal . . . but, no. She'd embarrassed her parents so greatly, that they had no choice but to set out for the earl's house in treacherous weather in order to apologize for her rudeness. And they never came back.

"Tell me if you need to stop and rest."

"The journey to the dining room is not so far," she said, "and the dizziness has already subsided." But it had been replaced with a sort of headiness—one she very reluctantly identified as attraction. Blast it all.

He smelled faintly of brandy, soap, and ink, an oddly stirring combination. But his appeal this evening lay more in the undivided attention he paid her. Though not always polite, he was solicitous. She had to remind herself that he wanted something from her—namely, for her to stay on as his governess. And like most rakes, he could be very charming when it served his purposes.

"Here we are." He ushered her through the doorway and into the elegant pale-green room. Tasteful landscapes adorned the walls; classical urns occupied alcoves on either side of the fireplace. At the center of it all, a gold candelabrum holding a dozen flickering candles illuminated the long oval table.

That was elaborately set for two.

The place settings were on either end of the table, which could easily seat fourteen. Yards of pristine white linen separated mirror images of bone china, silver, and crystal.

Dear Lord, this was no place for her. Last night she'd taken a tray to her room. And she'd eaten breakfast that morning downstairs with the rest of the staff. *That* was where she belonged.

As though he sensed her urge to flee the formality of the place, Lord Castleton tightened his grip on her arm. He frowned at the immaculately set table and gestured to Gibson, who stood against the far wall, at the ready. "Move Miss Lacey's plate to my right," said the earl, "so we don't have to shout at each other throughout our meal."

"Of course, my lord." Gibson swiftly saw to the task, removed the silver covers from both plates, and poured claret in their glasses. Meg made a mental note not to drink it.

"Thank you, Gibson. That will be all. Miss Lacey and I will manage on our own."

"Very well. Ring if you need anything, my lord."

As the butler turned to leave, the earl said, "I bumped into a table in my study and knocked a glass onto the floor."

"I'll have someone take care of it immediately," Gibson said, smoothly pulling the doors closed as he left.

And Meg found herself alone with the earl once more.

As he pulled out her chair, she wondered if he normally ate alone. A handsome, wealthy gentleman must have plenty of dinner invitations, but none for tonight, apparently. It was one thing to take a meal alone in one's room, but to sit in a huge dining room by one's self seemed . . . sad.

"It's a simple menu tonight." He shot her an apologetic look as he sat. "Cook didn't know I'd have company."

"No one did," she said saucily.

"I normally eat dinner at my club, but once a week, I eat here, mostly to keep Mrs. Lundy happy. She insists that it's important for everyone to stay in practice because the day will come when I wish to host a proper dinner party. I do hope she's not holding her breath for that day."

Meg pitied the sweet housekeeper. She'd mentioned in passing that she longed to have a mistress of the house—someone to host balls and parties, but also to add a feminine touch here and there. "Mrs. Lundy is a treasure," she said. "Would it be so great a sacrifice to host a dinner party—for her sake?"

He'd been about to take a drink of wine, but froze at her impertinent question. "She works for *me*, Miss Lacey. As do *you*."

"For the time being," she reminded him.

He blinked slowly, as though summoning patience. "I have a proposal to make. What if, for the remainder of dinner, we agree not to discuss your position? We won't talk about the twins or their lessons or anything to do with governessing."

"Very well." Meg shrugged as if it mattered not to her, but she couldn't imagine how they would fill up a meal's worth of conversation.

The lamb cutlets, asparagus, and fish on her plate looked and smelled delicious, and she realized she was ravenous. She took a bite of lamb dipped in cucumber sauce and sighed as it melted in her mouth.

"Good?" he asked, clearly amused.

"Divine." And before she knew what she was doing, she washed down the delectable bite with the lovely claret.

"How are your sisters—Elizabeth and Juliette, is it not?"

Meg raised a brow. "I am surprised that you remember their names."

He made a show of placing his hand over his heart. "You wound me, Miss Lacey. We were practically neighbors growing up. I remember a lot of things."

"For instance?"

As the earl leaned forward, the candlelight accentuated his cheekbones and jaw. He spoke softly, creating an intimate space around them. "I remember riding through the fields, urging my horse over a hedge, and falling out of my saddle. I hit the ground so hard that my head rang for days." He drummed his long fingers on the table and smiled as if it were a treasured memory. "I remember nicking my father's brandy and drinking till I was ill—all over the rug beneath his desk."

Meg wrinkled her nose. "How positively charming. Have you no pleasant recollections? Something a bit more appropriate for dinner conversation, perchance?"

A roguish smile spread across his face, and a wicked gleam lit his eyes. "I have a pleasant memory or two. Unfortunately, the most pleasant ones happen to be the *least* appropriate." With that, he speared a hunk of meat with his fork, popped it into his mouth, and chuckled, as though inordinately pleased with himself.

He seemed to delight in pushing the boundaries of polite behavior—and making her feel uncomfortable. Well, turnabout was fair play.

Meg swallowed a tender morsel of asparagus, fortified herself with another sip of claret, and leaned back in her chair. "I suppose that one of the inappropriate memories you cherish is spying on me while I swam in the lake."

His devilish grin vanished, and his throat worked like

he was having difficulty swallowing his manly mouthful of meat. "I should explain," he managed to choke out.

"I quite agree. Please, take your time," she said sweetly. "I've waited eight years to hear your explanation; a few more minutes won't kill me."

Meg congratulated herself as she lifted her fork and savored a bite of fish. It tasted a bit like victory.

Chapter EIGHT

Will hammered a fist against his chest, dislodging the hunk of lamb in his throat, then chased it with a healthy swig of brandy.

Dear Jesus. Certain experiences from a man's past—particularly during the ages of 13 to 18 years—were best left undiscussed. The lake incident qualified as one of them.

He'd assumed Miss Lacey would want to avoid the topic as much as he did, if not more so. After all, *she* was the one who'd been caught swimming nude in the lake. Weren't vicar's daughters supposed to be modest and meek?

Apparently, no one had informed Miss Lacey. An errant curl dangled from her temple, all the way to the swell of her breasts, which were covered in their entirety by her abomination of a dress. A crime, that.

Her lips parted in expectation, and her eyes dared him to speak the truth. She would not be content with platitudes or niceties. She was willing to relive her profound humiliation—in order to see him squirm.

"Are you certain you wish to discuss this?" he asked.

She raised her chin. "I don't think we should let it fester any longer. Tell me, Lord Castleton. *Why* did you think it acceptable to spy on me?"

"It was August in Oxfordshire," he began.

"Yes." She rolled her eyes. "I was there."

"Do you want to hear my version of the story, or not?"

Heaving a sigh, she nodded.

"Patience, Miss Lacey. If you're always in a rush to get to the end, you miss all the fun."

She narrowed her eyes. "Your wisdom abounds."

"Thank you," he replied solemnly, as if her compliment had been sincere. "It was August," he repeated, "and everyone in the household was hot and irritable. I'd argued with my father that morning."

"About what?" she asked.

"He said I wasn't taking my studies seriously enough." He grinned at her. "That was true, incidentally. I didn't take *anything* seriously. But I suspected that my father's foul mood had less to do with my poor study habits than with . . . well, let's just say he had his own problems." Financial difficulties of his own making, to be specific—but Will saw no need to air that dirty laundry. "I didn't have to be a scholar to know it was in my best interests to leave the house. My cousin, Thomas, had just left for London, so I grabbed my fishing pole and headed for the lake alone.

"The air was heavy and still—the way it feels when an afternoon storm is brewing. But it hadn't rained in two weeks, and the lake was lower than usual. I walked to my usual fishing spot and cast my line, but nothing was biting. I couldn't return to the house, so I started walking along the shore."

She sniffed, skeptical. "And you just happened to end up near my family's house?"

"I think I'd been hoping to find you," he said. "I erroneously assumed you'd have your clothes on."

"While I was swimming?" she asked, incredulous.

Damn, he was enjoying himself. "No. I thought you might be out for a stroll . . . or fishing."

Her brow creased. "But we were barely acquainted. Why would you seek me out?"

"I didn't plan to; my feet simply took me there. And when I realized where I was . . . well, I hoped I'd see you."

"Why?"

"As I said, my cousin had returned to London. You were a serious, thoughtful girl. I thought you'd be a good listener."

"You wanted to *talk* with me?"

Will raked his fingers through his hair. What in hell had made him admit that? "Maybe. I wouldn't have walked to your front door and knocked, but I hoped I'd see you on the path."

She shot him a cynical look. "That doesn't explain why you were staring at me from behind a tree trunk."

"No, I suppose it doesn't." He stroked his chin, choosing his words with care. "When I heard splashing, I ran toward it, expecting to find you and your sisters fishing or wading. But when I reached the shore, it was you, alone— swimming in the middle of the lake like you'd been born with gills, dipping below the surface, then emerging, sleek as an otter."

She blinked and tilted her head, waiting for him to continue.

"At first, I just stared in admiration. You swam better than Thomas."

"But not you?" She rolled her eyes again.

Chuckling, he said. "That's hard to say, Miss Lacey. One day we shall have to put it to the test." He met her eyes and turned serious. "The point is that I stared because I found you mesmerizing. Not just your nakedness, but *you*. The way you glided across the water. The way the sunlight reflected off your skin. I'd never seen a creature so free . . . or so beautiful."

She swallowed as she stared back at him, her green eyes a storm of emotions.

"And the truth is," he continued evenly, "that I haven't seen anything as beautiful since."

Meg could barely breathe.

Everything the earl had said was improper. Good heavens, he'd referred to her *nakedness*. And at the dining table, no less.

His scandalous recounting had transported her back in time, to that day in the lake. Cool water had kissed her deliciously naked skin and swirled around her legs while the sunlight warmed her face. For a few blissful, stolen moments, she hadn't been a poor vicar's daughter, but a water fairy—magical, powerful, and free.

There was no denying it; his wicked words thrilled her. Like a feather slowly brushing over her bare skin, they teased and tantalized, awakening every inch of her body. She was all too aware of his gaze now, lingering on her mouth, neck, and breasts. Her heart beat faster; her nipples tightened, tingled, and strained against the confines of her stays. A sweet and seductive pulsing between her thighs made her squirm in her chair. It was all too difficult to fathom.

He had watched her and found her beautiful.

Even more unbelievable, his heavy-lidded gaze suggested that he still did.

But she could not allow herself to be taken in by his charms or overwhelmed by her own undeniable physical reaction. He was her employer—at least for now—and nothing more.

"That is quite a story," she managed.

"I told you it would be worth the wait." His wicked grin

told her he knew the effect his words had on her. He paused a beat, and his expression turned serious. "Do you believe me?"

God help her, she did. Oh, she knew rakes like him were quite capable of spouting pretty lies in order to bend women to their will, but she'd caught him off guard. In the centerpiece's flickering candlelight, she'd seen a glimpse of the boy he'd been. She was sure that he'd revealed more than he intended.

And that it was the truth.

"I believe you."

She could almost see the air rush out of his lungs.

"Then I am forgiven?" he asked hopefully.

"Are you apologizing, my lord?" She raised an eyebrow expectantly. Heady feelings aside, she could not make this too easy for him.

"That's a difficult question."

She snorted. "I don't think it's difficult at all."

"I would not apologize for being momentarily dumbstruck by the sheer beauty of a rainbow, nor for appreciating the awesome power of a storm."

Oh, he was good. Still.

She leveled her gaze at him. "Rainbows and storms aren't capable of feeling abject humiliation. They don't experience the helplessness that comes from having one's privacy violated. And most important of all, rainbows and storms can't . . ." She closed her eyes momentarily and breathed through her nose.

"Yes?" Lord Castleton leaned toward her.

". . . they can't be *naked*." Blast it all, now *she* was discussing nakedness at the dining table.

"Your point is well taken." He removed the napkin from his lap, placed it next to his plate, and pushed his chair back slightly. To make room for those long, muscular legs, she supposed. But then he reached across the corner of the table and took her hand, enveloping it in his own and sending a frisson of excitement through her limbs. She reminded herself to breathe.

"I do owe you an apology, Miss Lacey. I hope that you will forgive me for forgetting my manners and losing my head at the sight of you swimming in the lake. I'm sorry for the embarrassment and hurt I caused you. I'm sorry that I spoiled whatever friendship we might once have had." His thumb brushed lightly over the back of her hand, as he spoke, distracting her from his words.

But somewhere in the back of her mind, she knew they were the *right* words.

"I forgive you," she said.

He sighed with the sort of relief one reserved for passing a particularly difficult exam or for narrowly escaping a precarious fall. "Thank you, Meg."

Not Miss Lacey, or even Margaret, but *Meg*. Her mouth opened, but no sound emerged. Only a handful of people in the entire world called her Meg. They were the ones who knew about her fear of spiders and her weakness for chocolate—the ones she stayed up with, talking, crying, and laughing until the wee hours of the morning. Her inner circle.

"May I call you Meg?" He asked as though he already knew her answer would be yes. As though he were the Prince of Rakes, used to having his wishes granted in these sorts of matters.

"I don't think—"

"I'll still address you as Miss Lacey in front of the twins," he assured her, as if he'd deftly eliminated her only possible objection.

"I don't anticipate us spending a significant amount of time together when the girls are not present." Still very aware of the pressure of his hand on hers, she could not imagine why she didn't pull away. Clearly, any contact with him impaired her ability to think properly about what was, well, proper. Blast.

"Perhaps then," he said smoothly, "you can humor me. Permit me to call you Meg whenever we're alone, unlikely as those circumstances may be." He made a great show of looking around the spacious dining room populated by only the two of them, then shot her his signature smug grin. "In turn, you may call me Will. Whenever you like."

"Will," she repeated, more for her own ears than his. The name sounded innocuous enough, and they *had* been neighbors once.

What was the harm in allowing it? In eliminating surnames and titles they would simply be peeling away an unnecessary and often stiff layer of formality. It was akin to her dressing without a corset.

Far from prudent, but no one else would know. And after the earl had apologized, the least she could do was make a token gesture in return.

"Very well," she said evenly. "You may call me Meg when we are in private." Then, because she didn't want him to think she was in favor of throwing *all* the rules of propriety to the wind, she quickly added, "But now I must take my leave and prepare the girls' lessons for tomorrow. We have a busy day."

She pulled her hand away and stood, ignoring the way her fingers still tingled from his touch.

He frowned as he rose. "Will you be working in the library?"

"No," she said breezily. She did not want to risk having him join her there. She'd peeled away quite enough layers for one evening. "I believe I shall retire to my room."

"Very well. I'll escort you there."

Chapter NINE

Meg bristled. "I am quite capable of making the journey to my bedchamber without assistance."

"You almost swooned earlier," Will said.

"How gallant of you to remind me."

He shrugged. "And then you drank claret at dinner. Therefore, I will escort you to your room."

Feeling her blood heat, she crossed her arms. "I feel that I should have some say in this matter."

"I feel that I should be allowed to play the part of a gentleman. After all, you've already emasculated me once today."

Dear God. He was never going to let the incident go.

"Besides," he continued, "I won't have you tumbling down the stairs, creating yet another mess for Gibson to clean up." Ouch. He stepped closer, much closer than was proper, and offered his arm. "Indulge me this once . . . Meg."

Her name was a whisper on his lips. Soft. Seductive. Meanwhile, his eyes gleamed mischievously, daring her to say yes.

Though she knew she shouldn't, she slipped her hand in the crook of his arm and let him slowly lead her from the room and down the corridor.

They made their way up the staircase in companionable silence, but she was much too aware of his long legs brushing her skirts and his powerful thighs flexing as he took each step. Swallowing, she averted her gaze.

Thankfully, this sweet torture was almost over. When at last they reached the landing, she whirled toward him, intending to bid him goodnight. Mistaking her sudden movement for tipsiness, he gasped and steadied her, his large hands encircling her waist.

They stared at each other for several seconds, and Meg noticed he was breathing almost as hard as she was.

"You weren't about to fall just then, were you?"

"No. I am generally able to manage a staircase without catastrophe." Although she'd tried for a breezy tone, it sounded more breathy.

He frowned at his hands, still firmly settled just above her hips, as though they'd betrayed him. "Well then, this is embarrassing."

Embarrassing, yes, but also exhilarating.

"There has been no shortage of humiliation today," she agreed.

His brow wrinkled. "But today wasn't *all* bad, was it?"

"I suppose not—if you discount Diana's near trampling and me breaking your crystal glass and kneeing you in the—" She threw up her hands and leaned her forehead against his chest. "It's been a horrid day," she mumbled into his waistcoat.

He chuckled, but Meg didn't care. It felt so good to stop sparring with him, to let down her defenses for a moment and simply absorb his strength. She was tired of fighting him and perhaps, more specifically, the attraction she felt toward him.

As though he understood, he wrapped an arm around her and pulled her flush against him. "Everyone is safe," he reminded her. "Diana, you, and even me." He held her there at the top of the stairs and lightly caressed her back and neck till she was certain her knees had turned to jelly.

"Come," he said softly in her ear, "sit down next to me."

He helped her sit right there, on the top step, settled himself beside her, and slipped an arm around her shoulders. "It's not a bad view from up here."

Meg had to agree. Moonlight streamed through the transom above the door in the foyer, making the polished marble floors glisten below them like a river. The chandelier's teardrop crystals twinkled above them like stars. And the stairs, covered in a plush runner, rose up to meet them like a grassy hill in the countryside.

In was easy to imagine that they were miles away from London, and that only the two of them existed. "It's lovely."

"Do you want to know my opinion about today?" he asked.

"Please."

"As far as days go, I'd say today was a very good one."

She shot him an incredulous look. "I fear your standards are rather low."

"I don't think so. First, it must be noted that in spite of the near misses, all serious injuries were averted. Almost as remarkable, you and I reached a truce. But for me, the best part of today was dining with you and, well . . . right now." He reached for her hand and gave it a squeeze, which she felt somewhere in the vicinity of her chest.

She swallowed, then asked the question she simply had to know. "Why is now the best part?"

"I suppose I like having someone to share the view with."

Odd. He sounded almost lonely.

"And because," he continued, "while I do enjoy our

little battles of wits, I also like to see you smile. Your smile is . . ." He rubbed the stubble on his chin as he searched for the words. "Bright, fleeting, rare. Like a comet shooting through the midnight sky."

She blinked slowly, letting his words sink into her skin and thrum throughout her body. Dumbfounded, she stared at the chiseled perfection of his face. "That's . . . beautiful. But my smiles are not so rare."

"No? The ones directed at me are rare." Cupping her face in his palm, he lightly brushed his thumb across her cheek. "I suspect you'll make me wait seven years to see it again."

She smiled at that, because it was ridiculous and sweet and because she couldn't stop herself if she tried.

His gaze dropped to her mouth, and his expression turned serious. "Meg," he breathed. It was a question. A plea.

In response, she leaned forward.

And then his lips were on hers.

It was the height of foolishness to allow the kiss, even worse to invite it, but it seemed to be the predestined ending to their strange, emotional day. All of the fighting, the bargaining, and the revealing had led to this, the most unlikely of kisses.

And yet, here they were.

His mouth slanted across her lips, still parted in a soft smile. His hand cradled her cheek, pulling her closer and claiming her as his—at least for the moment. He growled and deepened the kiss, thrilling her with the knowledge that he wanted her. Desired her.

She wouldn't have believed it possible a few short hours ago, but there, on the earl's staircase in the evening's waning light, she could imagine that she was not a governess in a dowdy dress.

At that moment she was, as he'd said, a comet, bursting across the heavens in a shimmer of light.

A delicious shiver shot through her limbs as their faces bumped lightly, retreated, and came together again. He speared his fingers through her hair, cursing at the blockade presented by her tight bun. Changing course, he trailed his fingers lightly around her ear and down her neck, where the barrier of her modest neckline renewed his ire.

Unwilling to surrender, he teased the seam of her lips apart with his tongue, daring her to open to him. She did.

Never before had she been kissed like this—like it was meant to lead to something more.

Though her head was muddled with equal parts shock and bliss, she was certain of one thing: the earl could teach her all she needed to know about kissing. And other things as well, no doubt.

Yes, she was in excellent hands. And since the magical evening couldn't last forever, she might as well enjoy it while she could.

Tentatively, she curled a hand around his neck, lightly tugging the soft curls at his nape. When he groaned, she gave herself over to the kiss—and him.

The earth beneath her gave way, and she was floating, anchored only by his hand on her hip and his mouth on hers. She thought of nothing but the taste and feel of him, the pressure and heat of his body next to hers. Her breath came in short gasps and her skin heated. When the wall of his chest brushed against the front of her gown, her nipples tingled and hardened to tight, aching buds. As though he knew, he reached between them and caressed her breast, teasing its peak through the layers of lawn and wool, sending waves of pleasure through her body.

She cried out softly, but he swallowed the sound and murmured against her mouth. "I always knew."

Reluctantly, she broke off the kiss and pressed her forehead to his. "What did you know?"

His heavy-lidded eyes gleamed, reflecting her own desire. "That you were a magnificent, passionate creature."

In other circumstances, she might have been insulted, but since he clearly meant it as a compliment, she decided to accept it as such. "Thank you."

"I told you the day wasn't all bad. We managed to salvage the end."

He pressed a kiss to her palm and held her hand in his lap for a minute, giving her pulse a chance to return to normal. With each beat of her heart, she felt the spell between them slowly breaking, and the stark reality of their situation intruding once more.

She had *everything* to lose. Her virtue, her pride, her job. . . . her heart.

Suddenly self-conscious, she pulled her hand away and smoothed a tendril of hair behind her ear. She required time and space to think about what had just happened and to figure out what, if anything, it had meant. "This day did have some things to recommend it. However, I think that now I shall truly retire for the evening."

When she reached for the balustrade to pull herself up, he immediately stood and offered his hand, lifting her to her feet. With his hair disheveled and cravat askew he looked vaguely lost. Almost vulnerable. "Until tomorrow," he said, his words holding the hint of a question.

"Of course." However, she wasn't really sure of anything. Not while her lips were still swollen and her mind was still reeling from his kiss. "Tomorrow."

He walked beside her as she made her way to her bedchamber, crossing his arms as though he didn't quite trust his hands to be free. As she opened the door, he stepped aside but lingered.

Perhaps he wanted to say something, like *I shouldn't*

have kissed you. Or ask her a question, like *Could we pretend this interlude never happened?*

Or maybe he wanted to kiss her again.

Her skin tingled at the thought.

He leaned his long frame against the doorjamb, reached for the curl resting on her shoulder, and twirled it around his finger as though mesmerized. His gaze drifted to her mouth, and she knew. He *was* going to kiss her again.

But instead of coming closer, he dropped the curl and backed away solemnly. "Good night, Meg."

She closed the door to her room and rushed to the mirror above her washstand to check her reflection. She wanted to see if her face looked as flushed and her lips appeared as swollen as they felt. In short, she wanted to see if she had the look of a woman who'd been ravished.

But no. The change, it seemed, was primarily on the inside.

It was only after she'd washed, changed into her night rail, and slipped beneath the covers of her sumptuous bed that she realized the irony of the evening she'd spent with Will.

She'd gone to see him intending to turn in her resignation, but had ended up *kissing* him.

Even worse, she'd begun to think of him not as *the earl* or *Lord Castleton*, but as *Will.*

Clear signs she had begun the steady and inexorable descent into madness.

Chapter TEN

Despite the warm breeze wafting through an open window, the room reeked of stale sweat and blood. Will eyed his opponent, Alec, who lightly bounced from foot to foot, his boxing gloves raised in front of his torso. Their weekly match at Jackson's Saloon was a welcome diversion from the mental flogging Will had been giving himself since kissing Meg—his *governess* for God's sake—the night before last. It complicated everything, and complications were precisely what he did *not* need.

But Alec was no novice at the sport, and if Will wanted to preserve his month-long winning streak, not to mention his straight nose, he had to focus on the basics—footwork, jabs, and blocks. Damned difficult, since Alec had the *highly* annoying habit of initiating conversation while they sparred.

"I saw Marina at the opera last night," he gasped.

Will dodged a punch intended for his jaw. "That's nice." It had only been a week since Will had broken things off with his mistress but seemed more like a year.

"She asked about you." Alec swiped a forearm across

his brow. "Said she misses you. I'd wager she's willing to take you back."

Will deflected a blow with his left glove and landed a punch to Alec's abdomen with his right. "Lucky me."

Alec grunted and stumbled back a few steps before sticking out his chest and clapping his gloves together. "You could go back to your old arrangement. I thought you'd want to know."

"Don't care." A week ago, Will might have. But seven days without Marina had made him realize that he was better off without her—and there was no doubt that she was better off without him.

"Well, well, well," Alec drawled, "isn't that interesting?" He wore a grin that begged Will to knock his teeth out. "One of the most beautiful women in London invites you into her bed"—he feinted to his left, just out of Will's reach—"and you *don't care*?"

"None of your concern." Will wiped a trickle of sweat from his temple with his forearm and shot his friend a warning look.

"Would this sudden disinterest in your former mistress— by all accounts a skilled seductress—have anything to do with your new governess?"

A lightning quick burst of power surged through Will's arm as he swung and connected with Alec's cheek. He felt the satisfying smack of leather against skin, and—

Bam.

Alec hit the ground like a felled tree.

Shit. Will dropped to his knees beside his friend, who was out cold. "Somebody bring water," he yelled to the half dozen men who'd been watching, "and smelling salts." Then to Alec, "Can you hear me? Say something, you blazing idiot."

Alec groaned, pushed away the salts being waved under

his nose, and blinked. "Jesus, Will. You almost took off my head."

Relief flooded his veins as he helped Alec to his feet. "I should have. Next time, don't ask so many damned questions. We're in a boxing club, not a bloody ballroom."

Alec rubbed his face and winced. "Thanks for clarifying."

"You know, you might be a decent fighter if you could manage to keep your mouth shut."

Alec tugged off a glove, sipped from a ladle of water, and poured the rest over his head. "But then I'd never know what was going on in that mind of yours."

Will snorted. "Careful what you wish for."

They moved to the side of the room, where Alec slung a towel around his neck. "I struck a nerve when I mentioned Miss Lacey. Or is it Meg now?"

Will gave his shoulder a shove, backed him against the wall, and glared. "Tread lightly, Torrington. Tread very, very lightly."

Alec raised his hands in mock surrender. "Fine. But I happen to have some experience in this area—navigating a relationship with one's governess. You know where to find me if you want my advice."

Will blinked then laughed out loud. "The day I seek relationship advice from you, my friend, will be a cold, cold day in hell."

Alec started to laugh, too, but quickly stopped and cupped his cheek. "Damn, that hurts."

"I'll buy you dinner at the club later—*if* you vow not to speak of governesses."

"Fine," Alec said sullenly.

But as Will toweled off and dressed, he *was* thinking of Meg. Of how she'd responded when he'd kissed her and how he'd looked for her around every corner for the past two days. She seemed to spend all her time teaching the twins in the nursery or planning their lessons in her room.

He could hardly be cross about that—it's what he was paying her for, after all.

But he couldn't help wondering if she was avoiding him. If she regretted the whole evening. After all, she'd soundly rejected him once. Her infamous refusal of his proposal may have been eight years ago, but in his experience, people didn't change much, not at their center. And she'd obviously found him abhorrent then.

Regardless of whether her opinion of him had changed, the real problem was *him*. He'd crossed a line with the kiss. Granted, for that evening they'd shrugged off their roles as employer and governess. But as much as he'd enjoyed their interlude, he knew in his gut that they had no choice but to return to their assigned roles.

Meg had gone back to being Miss Lacey, dedicated teacher of unruly twins and steadfast wearer of ugly dresses. Will had gone back to being the Earl of Castleton, carefree bachelor of considerable means and consistent shunner of weighty responsibility.

He should be used to the playing the part. Hell, it wasn't even a part, it was simply *him*.

And if the role wasn't as satisfying as it once had been, if it left him feeling vaguely empty and lost, maybe it was a sign that, God help him, his mother was right.

Being an earl—at least a good one—meant doing his duty. He wouldn't repeat the mistakes his father had made—taking both his title and fortune for granted.

When his father died, Will had inherited more than an earldom; he'd inherited a mess of the first order. The entire estate was in a shambles, and the family's coffers were depleted. Every outstanding debt, ill-considered contract, and excessive expenditure had landed squarely in his lap.

Once he'd recovered from the shock, Will had rolled up his shirtsleeves. He'd dedicated the last five years of his life to restoring order where he could, making his land profitable, and generally cleaning up the remnants of his father's carelessness.

To be fair, he'd only worked twelve hours a day, which left plenty of hours to indulge in the sorts of activities bachelors normally enjoyed. Such as a highly pleasurable dalliance with one's fetching governess.

But when it came to being a truly fine earl, business acumen and hard work were only half of the equation. The other half was being honorable and, damn it all . . . doing one's duty.

It was time for him to stop keeping mistresses and seducing governesses and move on with his life.

It was time for him to find himself a proper countess.

"We have time for one more." Meg wrote $8-3=?$ on a small slate and showed it to Diana. "Try this."

She closed her eyes, moved her lips, and took a deep breath. "Six?"

"Close," said Valerie.

"Seven?" Diana guessed.

"Not quite." Meg patted Diana's knee. "But don't be discouraged."

"You almost had it," said Valerie.

Diana clenched her fists and let out an impressive growl. "It doesn't make *sense*. I started with eight and counted back three times. Eight, seven, six. The answer should be *six*."

"Ah, I think I understand the problem," said Meg. "You're starting with eight, when you should start with seven."

"No," said Diana, pointing her stubby finger to the

problem on the slate. "We're starting with eight. It says so right here."

Heavens, it *was* rather confusing. Meg looked around the neat but sparsely furnished nursery for small objects she could use to demonstrate. "Have you any marbles?"

Diana rolled her eyes. "We did, but Gibson took them away. He said that, in our hands, they were a hazard."

"He's probably right about that." Meg tapped her chin. "I know. Tomorrow we'll go for a walk and collect some small stones."

"Stones are going to help me with arithmetic?" Diana asked, clearly skeptical.

"Maybe they're good luck," Valerie offered.

Meg smiled at her charges. "Perhaps they will bring us good fortune, but mostly they're for demonstrating equations. You'll see."

"Why can't we go now?" asked Diana.

"She has the afternoon off." Valerie sighed.

"Off from what?"

Valerie sighed again. "From us."

Smiling, Meg erased the slate and returned it to the bookcase. "I'm going to spend a few hours with my sisters."

Diana pouted. "What are *we* going to do?"

Meg had wondered the same thing. She'd debated staying with the girls, but Mrs. Lundy had insisted she could manage them while Meg was gone. It was only a few hours, after all.

"You are going to have your lunch and take a nap."

"I detest naps," announced Diana.

"Then you may read instead," Meg said smoothly. "And Mrs. Lundy said that if you behave yourselves, you may go down to the kitchen and help Cook prepare a cake before dinner. Won't that be fun?"

"Grand," Diana intoned.

"I shall return this evening in plenty of time to tuck you into your beds."

"Do you miss your sisters?" Valerie asked soberly.

"Very much." It had only been six days, but Meg had never been apart from them for so long.

Valerie shuffled closer and wrapped her arms around Meg in a hip-high hug. "Enjoy the afternoon with your sisters," she mumbled into the skirt of Meg's gown, "but please, please be sure to come back."

"Oh, Val." Meg knelt, pulled her into a proper hug, and patted her golden curls. "I will. I promise."

But Diana sat on the edge of her bed with her arms crossed, brooding, and Meg could see the doubt in her eyes.

"In fact," Meg said to Valerie, "I would consider it a great favor if you could hold onto my locket for me while I'm gone—just until I return this evening." She took off the locket, dropped it into Valerie's palm, and curled her little fingers around it.

The girl's face split into a smile. "I'll take good care of it for you."

"What about me?" Diana marched over. "What shall I keep for you?"

"I don't suppose you could help Valerie with the locket?"

"No. I want to look after something on my own."

"Very well then." Meg had no other jewelry, but even if she had she would have thought twice before entrusting it to Diana. She pulled the lavender ribbon from her hair and gave it to Diana. "Why don't you hold onto this for me?"

"Yes, Miss Lacey," she said seriously.

"Wonderful. I feel much better now that that's settled. Mind Mrs. Lundy today, and I shall see you both this evening."

As she made her way to her bedchamber to change and gather a few things, she realized how desperately she needed a little time away. She didn't require a respite from teaching so much as from the earl. She'd done her best to avoid him over the past two days, but it was rather draining, trying to plan one's schedule with the sole purpose of minimizing the chances of random encounters.

Of course, if the earl had truly wanted to see her, he would have found a way.

But he hadn't.

In the two days since the kiss, Meg had done a considerable amount of thinking and had arrived at two conclusions. First, the impressive charm that the earl had employed that evening had no doubt been for the sole purpose of retaining her services as governess. He must have known she was on the verge of resigning and did not wish to be bothered with hiring another, so he'd shrewdly sought to distract her with pretty words and scorching kisses. And distract her, they had.

Second, these sorts of flirtations—replete with all manner of gazing, kissing, and caressing—had meant nothing to the earl. For her, their romantic interlude atop the staircase had been a glorious, magical, enlightening introduction to pleasure.

For him, it had merely been Friday evening.

Meg would not give him the satisfaction of knowing how much the kiss had affected her—how she'd lain awake at night remembering the sweet pressure of his lips on her neck and the thrilling feel of his hands on her body. Better to carry on as though it had been a perfectly ordinary Friday evening for her as well.

She peered into her satchel to ensure she had her first week's pay—more money than she'd ever held at one time. Mrs. Lundy had handed the note to her that morning and said it was well earned. If the dear housekeeper only knew.

Chapter ELEVEN

"Meg!" Beth and Julie catapulted themselves at her the moment she walked through the door. "How we've missed you!"

Meg managed to hug both of them at once, savoring the cozy, intimate atmosphere of home. "I've missed you too. How's Uncle Alistair?"

"He's well—the same as ever." Julie swept off Meg's bonnet and hung it on a peg in the front hall. "But we want to know about *you*. Your letters were vexingly brief, Meg. You must tell us about the twins. Are they ill behaved? Is Lord Castleton as overbearing an employer as I suspect he is?"

"You might at least allow her to catch her breath before you start bombarding her with questions," Beth scolded. Smiling at Meg she said, "You must be exhausted. Come sit in the parlor. Tea is ready."

"Wait. Take this." Meg reached into her satchel and gave Beth her first week's earnings. "It's certainly not enough to pay all our debts—it won't even make a dent—but please use it as you see fit. There's no need to mention it to Uncle Alistair; it would only embarrass him."

Beth stared at the note, her blue eyes wide with wonder. "I had no idea governesses earned so much."

"They don't." Meg blew out a breath. "The earl was desperate to hire me."

"Serves him right," said Julie in a sisterly display of loyalty. And for some unfathomable reason, Meg had to check the urge to defend Will.

"You've no idea how much this will help," Beth said. "I can give the staff a portion of their back pay *and* stock the pantry." Her eyes welled, and in that moment, Meg *knew* she was doing the right thing.

Working for the earl was dangerous—*especially* now that they'd kissed—but her family's well-being was worth the risk to her reputation. And to her heart.

"I'm glad I can make a small contribution. And tea sounds wonderful." She sniffed at the air. "Do I smell chocolate?"

"Yes!" Julie cried, as they entered the parlor. "To celebrate your first week as a governess. Look, Charlotte's here too."

"How lovely!" Meg exclaimed, giving her friend's hands an affectionate squeeze.

"I don't mean to intrude on your family visit, but I simply had to see you and hear how you've fared. You didn't write after that day in the park."

Meg gave a slight shake of her head. No need to recount the harrowing tale in front of Beth and Julie—they'd only ask scores of questions and worry needlessly. "There's not much to tell," Meg fibbed. "The week was a blur of planning, reading lessons, and sums. The twins are delightful."

Taking her cue, Charlotte nodded vigorously. "Darling girls."

Beth's gaze shifted between Meg and Charlotte, as though she suspected there was more to the story. "Is it difficult to tell them apart?"

"From a distance, it can be tricky, but Diana is left-handed and has a small dimple in her cheek; Valerie favors her right hand.

"If I had a twin," Julie announced, "she and I would have had great fun at the expense of our governess. You should be on your guard."

"Not everyone is blessed with your level of deviousness," said Beth. "Thank heaven."

As the four women squeezed themselves onto the threadbare settee, Meg reached for a cup, then paused. "You used the fine china *and* arranged fresh flowers on the table? Why all the fuss on my account?"

"We wanted today to be special," Beth said.

"Besides, you've been living in Castleton House," Julie pointed out. "You've no doubt become accustomed to elegant things. Home must seem awfully shabby by comparison."

"It is smaller and not as fancy, true. But it has much to recommend it. Especially the company." Meg covered the chip in the rim of her cup with her finger, sipped her tea, and sighed from sheer pleasure. "Now tell me, what has been happening here?"

"Here? Oh nothing of any interest," Beth said breezily, but she exchanged a look with Julie. "It's been dreadfully dull. I've started a new sewing project, and—"

"No." Meg set down her cup with a *clunk*. "Surely you don't intend to regale me with tales of your *sewing* projects. Please tell me something more significant than hemletting has transpired in the past week." The skin on the back of her neck prickled. "Why do I feel as though you're hiding something?"

Julie squirmed. "We should tell her, Beth."

Beth rolled her eyes at her younger sister. "I suppose that now we *must*." Exasperated, she turned to Meg. "It's Uncle Alistair. He has a preposterous notion."

Meg relaxed a bit and rolled her shoulders. Uncle Alistair's notions were hardly new. "What is it?"

"It's an absurd idea," Beth said, frowning. "But he's quite determined."

"Let me guess," said Meg. "He wants to buy an outrageously expensive telescope . . . or adopt some exotic animal—a hedgehog perhaps?"

"No . . ."

"He's decided to host a ball," Julie blurted.

"*What*? That's impossible."

Beth bit her lip. "Of course it is. Only, you know how he is when he resolves to do something."

"He wants to do it for *us*," said Julie. "He thinks that if we host the social event of the season, we shall soon be collecting suitors like buttons. That's the irony—instead of improving our reputation, we'd be laughingstocks. More than we already are," she added glumly.

Meg slipped an arm around her shoulders. "I can't imagine anyone would deign to come. At least there won't be more than a handful of witnesses to our humiliation."

"Are you sure about that?" Julie asked. "I rather think guests would line up outside our door to see the Wilting Wallflowers achieve the very pinnacle of disgrace."

"Do not fret. We will simply dissuade Uncle Alistair with a clear recitation of facts. We haven't the money, space, or staff to accommodate any gathering approximating a ball. I'll speak to him."

"I've already tried," Beth said. "He's adamant. Oh dear, here he comes."

"Can that be my darling Meg?" Uncle Alistair shuffled into the parlor, his tufts of white hair standing on end and his wizened face split into a grin. "Here she is, returned to us at long last."

"It's barely been a week," she said gently, "but it's wonderful to see you, Uncle." She embraced him, then pulled up his favorite armchair. "You're looking very well."

"As fit as a person can be at my age." He sank onto the pitifully thin chair cushion with a cheerful sigh. "And perfectly culpable of hosting a ball in honor of my three lovely nieces."

Meg cast him a wary smile. "Beth and Julie just informed me of your intentions. I must say, while it's wonderfully generous of you to offer, we wouldn't dream of putting you to the trouble or expense."

"But I want to do it!" Uncle Alistair said, clearly offended. "Of all people, I thought you'd understand."

"You've already done so much for us. More than we'll ever be able to repay."

"Stuff and nonsense," he scoffed. "We're family. You don't repay family. You simply love them and gracefully accept the gifts they offer."

Meg's eyes stung at the sweet sentiment, but she blinked away her tears. "What a lovely thing to say. You know we adore you and always will. But unfortunately, a ball takes a considerable amount of planning and effort. It also takes . . . well, it takes more money than we have."

He gripped the arms of his chair. "Then I'll sell some of my artifacts or, or . . . books!"

"Uncle!" cried Beth. "We couldn't allow you to do that."

"It's not just the lack of funds," Meg continued. "We don't have a ballroom or the servants to help us prepare." They didn't even have anything appropriate to *wear*, for heaven's sake.

"Why is it that young people look for all the reasons that an idea will fail instead of all the ways to ensure it succeeds?" In spite of the lines on his face, he looked like a toddler denied his favorite sweet, and it nearly broke Meg's heart.

She patted the back of his hand, willing him to understand. "We're just trying to be practical." *And keep you out of debtor's prison.*

He snorted. "Practicality is too often used as an excuse for complacence. You must have faith in me, my dears. What I lack in means and standing, I make up for in ingenuity and optimism. Our ball shall be the talk of the ton—a spectacle beyond repair."

Oh no. It *would* be a spectacle. And Meg had to stop it—or, at the very least, delay it.

"Your enthusiasm is inspiring, Uncle. However, I'm afraid that it will be several weeks at least before I'm able to attend a ball. You see, my governess duties require my full attention at the moment. Do you suppose we could postpone the festivities for a month or two?"

"A month?" He scratched the bald spot on top of his head.

"Or two?"

"Three weeks," he said firmly. "No longer. In fact, I'm off to make a list of eligible young gentlemen to invite." He hoisted himself from his armchair and headed toward the door like a man on a mission for the king.

Julie and Beth shot Meg a look of utter desperation—as though they were all in the back of a runaway wagon headed for a cliff. Meg had to do something, for her own sake as well as theirs.

"Will you allow me to help with the planning?" she blurted. Uncle Alistair turned to face her, his expression quizzical. "I've never hosted a ball," she continued, "and I've always wanted to."

He hesitated, then nodded. "Of course you may help me, my dear. Beth, Julie, and Charlotte are welcome to offer their suggestions as well. As long as you understand that I intend to entertain on a grand fail. You are by far the loveliest young ladies in London—nay, the Empire— and you deserve to be honored with the ball to end all balls."

For a few moments after he left the parlor, the women sat in stunned silence.

Julie dropped her head into her hands. "This is sure to be a disaster."

"Of monumental proportions," said Beth.

"At least we've stalled him for a bit. We'll try to reason with him over the coming weeks." But Meg suspected it was futile.

She felt as though she was now fighting battles on two fronts—one against a rakish earl in Mayfair and another against an eccentric uncle at home.

And she wasn't faring particularly well in either.

"What do you mean, Diana's gone?"

Mrs. Lundy fingered the tie on her lace collar. "She's not in the nursery or the kitchen or anywhere else I might expect to find her."

"Then I suggest you look in the places you don't expect to find her." Will strode past the housekeeper and out of his study. "Where is Miss Lacey?"

"She had the afternoon off." Mrs. Lundy followed in his wake.

Will consulted his pocket watch. "It's past seven. Shouldn't she have returned by now?"

"Why, I expect her shortly. After the week that young lady's had, she's entitled to enjoy a few peaceful hours with her family."

Will whirled on her. "It's not as though Miss Lacey has been laboring in the mines. Do not make me out to be some sort of beast."

Mrs. Lundy's face went white and she blinked rapidly,

clearly on the verge of tears. "Your lordship, I would never suggest such a thing."

Will paused in the foyer, drew a deep breath, and reined in his temper. "I know you wouldn't. Forgive me. Where is Harry? It's his duty to escort the twins whenever they leave the house."

"I believe he's cleaning and trimming the lamps, my lord. He didn't know Miss Diana was planning an outing."

"Summon him and Gibson to the drawing room. Then search the house again."

"Of course." Mrs. Lundy bobbed her capped head and hurried off.

Will paced the length of the foyer, his boot heels thudding ominously on the marble floor. Where in the devil would a six-year-old girl run off to? Perhaps she'd missed her mother—and home. But he didn't think so.

Maybe she'd missed Meg and had gone looking for her.

That he could believe. The damned truth was . . . he missed her, too.

Chapter TWELVE

Meg hurried up the brick path to Castleton House. Leaving her sisters and Charlotte had been more difficult than she'd thought. At home, she knew who she was. The eldest of the Lacey sisters. The practical, resourceful one who'd kept their little family together. The one who protected Uncle Alistair as much as possible and struggled to make ends meet. And of the three Wilting Wallflowers, she was . . . well, the most wilted.

But at least at home, she'd been surrounded by people who loved and understood her. At Castleton House, she wasn't at all sure who she was. Governess, yes. But who was she to the earl? Employee, friend . . . or something altogether different?

More important, who did she *wish* to be to him?

She paused on the front step, swung the gleaming brass knocker, and waited for Gibson to admit her. Except that when the door swung open a mere second later, it was not the portly butler who faced her on the other side of the threshold.

It was Will.

"Meg." His deep voice betrayed a strange mix of relief and desperation. Looking over his shoulder, he called out, "It's Miss Lacey."

"Thank the Lord above." Mrs. Lundy rushed toward Meg and pulled her inside.

Her stomach sank. "What's wrong?"

"It's Diana," said the earl. "We can't find her."

"Did you check under her bed? In the armoire? How about the kitchen? Or in the garden?"

"Yes to all of those." Mrs. Lundy's hand fluttered about her throat. "I've looked in every nook of every room in the house. She's nowhere to be found."

"I've got Harry searching the entire block," Will added. "Where else could she have gone?"

Meg shook her head helplessly. "I don't know. What did Valerie have to say?"

Will shrugged. "I haven't spoken with her."

"Why not?"

"I assumed Mrs. Lundy had already done so." He turned expectantly toward the housekeeper.

"Of course I asked if she knew where her sister was—forceful-like, so she knew I wasn't about to tolerate any nonsense. She claims that they laid down for a nap and that when she awoke, Diana was gone. More than that, I could not persuade her to say. She's a quiet wee one."

Oh dear. Mrs. Lundy may have meant well, but she'd probably scared Valerie half out of her wits. "She says little," Meg agreed, "but you can be sure it is the truth. I'll go speak with her."

"I'm coming too," the earl said.

Meg tossed her satchel on the side table and headed for the staircase. "Suit yourself—but do try not to frighten her."

"I shall endeavor to contain my ogre tendencies." He followed as she dashed up the stairs.

She shot him a too sweet smile. "Excellent, my lord."

Short of breath upon reaching the nursery, Meg opened the door to find Valerie sitting by a window that overlooked the street and the square beyond. Outside, dusk had begun to fall. Meg knelt beside her charge, eager to see the view from her perspective. Will remained behind, uncharacteristically quiet for now.

Valerie looked up at her, freckled face forlorn, and unfurled her fist to reveal the locket. "I kept it safe. Did you have a nice time with your family?"

"Indeed. But now I'm worried about Diana."

"I am too," the girl admitted.

Meg nodded past the window. "Do you think she's out there?"

"I don't know. Perhaps." Her thin voice quavered.

Slipping an arm around Valerie's shoulders, Meg said, "I'll find her. You may count on it."

"Will she be in trouble?"

"You needn't worry that she'll be punished harshly." Behind them, Will snorted; Meg ignored him and tried to reassure the girl. "We just want to bring her back here, where she's safe."

"I want that too."

Meg pulled up a chair beside Valerie. "What happened after I left today?"

She swallowed. "We took a nap. I did, at least."

"Did you and Diana talk before you fell asleep?"

She frowned as though trying to remember. "A little. She was still cross about not knowing her sums. I told her not to worry and to remember that you had a plan to help her."

"And what did she say to that?"

"She said she wished she didn't have to wait until tomorrow."

"Wait for *what*?" Will demanded, startling both Valerie and Meg. "What, precisely, does this plan of yours entail?"

"Nothing terribly sinister, my lord," Meg said dryly. "We'd simply discussed gathering a few pebbles to use as counting stones for tomorrow's lesson."

Will stepped closer, leaning over the pair of them as he gazed out the window. "Was Diana so eager that she might have tried to gather them on her own?"

"Maybe," Valerie said. "She's not very patient."

"Are her boots gone?" the earl asked.

Meg went to the armoire and checked. "Yes." She turned to Will. "Collecting pebbles wouldn't take more than a half hour. She's been gone for at least three." Heart pounding, she tried not to contemplate all the horrid things that could happen to a six-year old girl wandering the streets of London on her own.

Will's gaze flicked to Valerie before meeting Meg's. He didn't want to alarm the poor thing further. "I'm sure Diana just stopped to rest or lost her way a bit."

"We must go and help Harry search for her." Meg went to Valerie and squeezed her clammy little hands. "I'll ask Mrs. Lundy to send up dinner for you. You mustn't worry about Diana. The earl and I will find her. You'll see."

The twin's chin trembled, but she nodded bravely.

Will swept Meg outside of the nursery, closed the door behind them, and placed his large hands on her shoulders. "I think you should remain here."

"I'll do no such thing. Diana trusts me."

His brow creased as though he were mildly offended. "And not me?"

Meg shrugged. "She doesn't really know you, my lord." Although, the girl *did* seem to suffer from a case of hero-worship for the earl ever since the incident in the park.

"Fair enough. We'll go together—as long as you agree to remain in my sight."

Bristling, Meg tossed her head. "I've no intention of running away. At least not tonight."

"How comforting." He placed his hand at the small of her back and guided her through the hallway and back down the staircase.

They had just reached the foyer when they heard a yelp and several shouts from the back of the house. Will raced toward the commotion, and Meg followed closely on his heels.

"It's her!" he called over his shoulder. "It's Diana. She appears to be in one piece."

Meg pushed her way past the earl and the kitchen maid and footman who were fussing over the girl. "Diana." She pulled her into a hug, and tears she hadn't even known were threatening spilled down her cheeks. "Thank goodness you're safe."

The little girl cried too, her tears streaking the dirt smudges on her face. "I w-wanted to find some stones for our arithmetic l-lesson. B-but the square across the street didn't have enough, so I w-went a bit farther. And then I c-couldn't find my way back."

Meg swept Diana into her arms and rubbed her back. "Well you're home now. How did you manage it?"

"I asked a nice-looking lady to p-point me in the direction of Mayfair and then walked until I saw the earl's garden. It's the only one with a fountain."

"That was clever of you," Will said. "But I think you know you shouldn't have left the house. Especially on your own."

Diana's lower lip trembled. "Yes, sir."

"There will be time to discuss the consequences of your actions later. For now, you need a bath and dinner, in that order," Meg said.

"After dinner, may we have our lesson? I have plenty of stones—see?" Diana shoved a hand into the pocket of her pinafore and held out a palm full of dirt, pebbles, and Meg's lavender ribbon.

"Keep the ribbon. And you certainly have collected enough rocks for our purposes," Meg said, smiling.

"There will be no further lessons this evening," the earl pronounced in a booming voice, and Diana clung to Meg a bit tighter. "You will do just as Miss Lacey has instructed—a bath and dinner, followed by bed. Now run upstairs and see your sister. She's been worried sick about you."

"Yes, sir." Diana dumped the stones back into her pocket, wiggled her way out of Meg's arms, and took off for the nursery.

Will raised a brow at the kitchen maid and footman. "I presume you have duties to return to?"

"Of course, my lord," they muttered as they scurried off.

"Thank you for your assistance," Meg called out after them. She swiped at her eyes, suddenly self-conscious.

"Why are you crying?" The earl frowned as though thoroughly perplexed. "She seems well enough."

"It's just that I'm so . . . relieved. I don't expect you to understand."

His lips pressed into a thin line. "Regardless of what you may think, I care about the girls, too. I made a promise."

"A promise? What sort?"

He produced a crisp handkerchief from his jacket pocket and handed it to her. "It's a rather long story."

She dabbed the corners of her eyes. "If it relates to the twins, I'd like to hear it."

He considered that for a moment then gave a curt nod. "After the girls are settled and in bed, meet me in my study.

We'll have a much-deserved drink, and I'll tell you how the twins came to be here."

It warmed Meg to know that he would confide in her. "Thank you, my lord."

"Just Will, remember?"

Oh yes. She remembered. "Until this evening . . . Will."

A wicked grin lit his face, and her whole body thrummed in response.

Drat it all—it seemed she was suffering from a mild case of hero-worship herself.

Chapter THIRTEEN

The hour had grown so late that Will began to wonder if Meg would join him after all. Diana's disappearance had temporarily erased the awkwardness between them, for as long as she was missing, it had been impossible to dwell on stolen kisses and intimate encounters with Meg.

But now . . . it was nigh impossible to think of anything else.

He heard the patter of her slippers a moment before she rounded the corner, brightening the doorway of his study in spite of her damnable brown dress. "I wasn't sure if you'd still be here," she said without preamble. "I didn't want to leave the nursery until I was certain the twins were asleep."

"At least we can be relatively confident that they will remain out of trouble for the next eight hours."

"Yes." Her gaze flicked to the clock on the mantel, and he was almost sure she was contemplating how fast the time would pass and worrying about all that she wished to accomplish before then. She lingered by the door like Persephone debating the wisdom of crossing the river Styx.

But perhaps she didn't have to.

"Let us repair to the garden." He scooped up his decanter and a pair of glasses.

"Now?" she asked incredulous.

"Why not?"

She shrugged helplessly. "Well, for one thing, it's dark."

"There's some moonlight. I daresay our eyes will adjust. Come." He led the way down the hall toward the morning room, then handed the glasses to her while he unlocked the French doors that opened onto the garden patio. "Here we are."

He guided her to a stone bench beneath an ivy-covered arbor that offered shade in the daytime. Now, it afforded something more precious—a modicum of privacy.

She set the glasses beside her and perched on the edge of the bench with her hands folded in her lap, like she was there for an interview rather than a drink. To see her sitting there, her spine straight and expression impassive, one would never imagine that a few nights ago she'd been pliant and willing in his arms. Maybe she wished to pretend that evening had never happened. If he were wise, he'd follow her lead and revert to their old roles. She could play the part of prim and proper governess, and he'd be the overbearing and insufferable earl.

The problem was that he couldn't quite forget the taste of her lips or the feel of her body pressed against his. The rapid rise and fall of her chest suggested she hadn't entirely forgotten him either.

He splashed brandy into each glass, gave her one, and raised his. "Congratulations are in order. You've survived your first week."

She peered into her glass thoughtfully. "I suppose I have. More importantly, the twins have."

"Yes. Just barely," he teased.

She frowned adorably. "If something terrible had

happened to Diana tonight, I would never have been able to forgive myself."

"I know. I would have felt the same way." An unexpected but sobering truth.

"Are the girls related to you?"

"You could say that. Although I met them only a few days before you did. They were dropped on my doorstep by my late cousin's mistress."

"Why would she abandon her own children?"

Will shrugged. "Why indeed? Perhaps the more interesting question is, why did she hold onto them as long as she did?"

"I don't understand. What kind of mother wouldn't wish to have her children with her?"

He snorted. "The selfish kind. While my cousin, Thomas, was alive, it suited Lila's purposes to raise the girls herself. He visited them weekly and lavished them with gifts . . . even if he was never able to publicly acknowledge them as his daughters."

"Why ever not?"

"Lila forbid him to reveal to the twins that he was their father. She said he might only claim them as his own if he agreed to marry her."

Meg's nostrils flared in indignation. "How awful. She would deny the girls their father in order to procure a marriage offer?"

"Women have stooped to far worse to achieve their desired ends."

"As have men, my lord." Her eyes shot daggers at him over the rim of her brandy glass, and his blood heated in response. *This* was what he admired about her. *This* was what he'd missed.

"We are back to *my lord* then?"

She regarded him coolly, not deigning to answer. "So, Lila's plan didn't work. Thomas never proposed."

"He might have . . . if his life hadn't been cut short."

She placed a hand on his shoulder, awakening a host of feelings inside him. "I'm sorry."

"He was like a brother. Very much like me, but better. Thomas was wise and decent."

"Why didn't he marry Lila, then?" She went still and gazed at him intently—as though his answer were very important.

"His mother, my aunt, would not have approved. Lila is not the type of woman to grace genteel drawing rooms."

She pulled away and turned icy. "No? I suppose I am not that type of woman either."

Alarms sounded in his head. "Don't be ridiculous. You are a lady."

"And what does that *mean*, precisely? That I might kiss a man to whom I am not betrothed so long as I am not caught doing so?"

"You are twisting my words, Meg. Lila is an unscrupulous, conniving sort."

"Maybe she has had to be," she said quietly. "Besides, she must have some redeeming qualities. The girls seem to miss her."

"She's the only mother they've ever known. But she claimed she couldn't take care of them anymore. She said she'd have no choice but to deliver them to the foundling home unless I took them in."

She blinked, her long lashes guarding pretty hazel eyes. "And so you did."

"Yes."

"But surely you had other options. You could have sent the girls to live with a relative in the country or paid a kind family to raise them."

Will let out a long sigh. "Thomas wouldn't have wanted that. I promised him that I would be their guardian in the event that something happened to him."

"How did he . . . ?"

"A riding accident." Will's throat constricted. "A stupid, bloody riding accident."

Meg set down her glass and scooted closer to him on the bench. Her nearness was comforting and highly distracting at the same time. "It doesn't seem fair, does it?"

"No." He wondered if she was thinking of her parents and the horrific accident that had claimed their lives and ripped her family apart. "Little in life is fair."

"Your cousin Thomas was fortunate to have a friend like you. If you hadn't intervened, the twins might be eating gruel in an overcrowded orphanage." She shuddered at the thought.

"I can give them a roof over their heads. I can provide food and clothing. But they need more than that . . . and that's the part I can't give them."

"Can't . . . or won't?"

He took a large swallow of brandy. "Can't." All he knew of parenting was what he'd learned from his own father. The sting of a switch burning the back of his legs. The echo of vile insults ringing in his head. The indifference of a man too preoccupied with his own miserable life to spend a few moments with his only son.

"I think that perhaps you do yourself an injustice."

"No," he said firmly. He couldn't risk being a father—not in the real sense of the word. Of course, he'd need an heir one day, but he intended to parent from afar and leave the day-to-day responsibilities of child-rearing to someone more qualified than he—to someone who knew how decent and loving fathers were supposed to treat their children. "Trust me on this. I can't be anything to those girls but their benefactor. That's why I need you."

"I am only their governess. That's not the same thing as a mother."

"I know. But for now, maybe it's close enough." He

regarded her thoughtfully. "I confess, a small part of me was worried that you wouldn't return. That your sisters would convince you to give up your position and remain at home with them."

She looked away. "I wouldn't—couldn't—do that to the girls."

Ah. So, it had everything to do with the girls and naught to do with him. "You've been avoiding me these last few days."

Raising her chin, she met his gaze straight on. "I could say the same for you."

"That is true. I thought to make things easier for you. I assumed you'd prefer I stayed out of your way." He held his breath as he waited for her response. Because all she had to do was say the word, and he'd gladly pick up where they'd left off a few nights ago. Even now, as they sipped brandy in the evening air, he could barely resist the urge to plunder her mouth, unlace her ghastly gown, and tease the rosy tips of her breasts till she moaned for something more.

"It's doubtful that anything shall ever be easy as far as the two of us are concerned," she said, her voice oddly hollow.

He gave a bitter laugh. "Why must that be? Are we so different, you and I? Why does everything I stand for seem to repulse you so?"

"Repulse me?" Her eyes went wide. "Whatever gave you that idea?"

He shrugged. "Convents. Head-shaving. A general attitude of disdain."

At that, she blushed scarlet. "That was many years ago."

"And yet, it seems like yesterday." He smiled and swirled the brandy in his glass so that she'd never guess how deeply her words had cut him.

"Would you like to know why I said those things?"

Well, that all depended. Was the truth going to gut him? "If you feel the need to get your thoughts off your chest, I have no objection."

She cast a knowing smile his way and stood, her skirt rustling in the warm breeze. "Then I shall tell you. First off, it should be noted that I was a young woman of fifteen—an age that relishes drama as much as it eschews reason."

Will crossed his arms over his chest and nodded casually. So far, he liked this explanation—primarily because it kept his pride intact. "Duly noted."

"Second," she said, pressing her nose to a pink flower, "I had good cause to think you were a cad."

"Right—the incident at the lake."

"The *spying* incident at the lake," she corrected, "which gave me a most unfavorable impression of your character."

"A false impression that has since been rectified?" he asked, hopefully.

Rolling her eyes, she glided to another bush bursting with red blooms. "I concede that there may have been extenuating circumstances. However, you are not entirely absolved of guilt."

He could live with that. "Also duly noted."

"But neither of those reasons in and of themselves would have precipitated such an extreme reaction from me."

He went to her side, plucked a flower off the bush, and slid it behind her ear. The rich red petals accentuated the hue of her lips and the blush on her cheeks, almost blinding him to the unfortunate sludge color of her dress. Almost. "Then why did you reject me, Meg?"

Her lips parted, but she hesitated, as though afraid to form the words. At last, she said, "I don't expect someone like you to understand."

He felt his hackles rise. "What does that mean, *someone like me*?"

"It means you are a man. Someone with power and the ability to make your own decisions."

"And you resent me for that?"

"To a certain extent, yes."

"That hardly seems fair."

"Don't you see?" she pleaded. "I *craved* the independence you take for granted. I couldn't bear the thought of someone dictating who my husband would be or what my future would hold."

"You're a bluestocking," he mused.

She tossed her head. "Call me what you like. I chafed at the idea of taking a husband in order to please my parents. A successful marriage requires more than a handshake between prospective in-laws. It requires . . . love."

"It seems you're also a romantic."

She waved a hand, scoffing. "Hardly. I'm a practical sort, intent on keeping my family together and my uncle out of debtor's prison. My sisters deserve to own a new gown or two. That's why I'm here."

"So you wouldn't *really* rather shave your head than marry me."

She arched a wicked brow. "I didn't say that. But I will admit that the words I spoke that night—they were less about you than my frustration with the situation."

"I was frustrated too. And completely blindsided by our parents' announcement."

"Yes, but you were probably already plotting ways to extricate yourself from the betrothal."

Damn, but she had an uncanny ability to peel away his polished veneer and see the scoundrel who dwelled beneath. "Weren't you?" he countered.

"I fear I couldn't get past the shock. Besides, if the engagement had become public and was subsequently dissolved, no one would dream that it was by *my* choice.

Why would a mousy girl like me willingly break a betrothal to a rich gentleman who was heir to an earldom?"

"Don't forget handsome." He grinned at her.

"The point is," she said softly, "you had all the power. I had none. And I found that vexing in the extreme. I still do."

Contemplating her words, he reached for her hands and met her gaze. With her hair gleaming in the moonlight, her skin glowing with passion, and her eyes challenging him to deny the truth of her words, she appeared anything but helpless. "I think you underestimate your own power."

"I lack wealth, status, and beauty," she said matter-of-factly. "Pray tell, what power is it that I wield?"

Slowly, he lifted his hand to cup her cheek and brushed a thumb over her satin-soft skin. "You have power," he breathed. "You have power over *me*."

Chapter FOURTEEN

Meg's breath caught in her throat and her heart pounded in her chest. The earl's gaze dropped to her mouth like he wanted to kiss her but was waiting for her to grant him permission—with a sigh, a movement, or a sound.

It seemed the power *had* shifted to her, if only for a short time. She sought to prolong the heady feeling.

"How so, my lord? Are you not my employer and I your governess? How can I possibly exert power over you?"

"At this moment, madam, I am your servant," he murmured, his husky voice promising all manner of wicked delights.

"*My* servant?" She boldly placed her palm on his impossibly hard chest and heard his sharp intake of breath. "And what, precisely, are your duties?"

"To please you." As he leaned in, his lips a mere hair's breadth from hers, his eyes fairly burned with intensity. "Let me. Say the word."

Meg swallowed. She wanted to resent the earl, truly she did. But in spite of his carefully cultivated reputation as an incurable rake, he'd shown glimmers of decency and goodness. He'd honored a promise to his cousin and taken in two little girls with nowhere else to go.

Worse, he had the sort of dangerously handsome face and athletic physique that might well bring a woman to her knees.

The heat in his stare left no doubt he wanted her . . . and yet, he'd handed her the reins. All she had to do was say . . .

"Yes."

The word wasn't even out of her mouth before he hauled her against him. Their bodies bumped together, thrilling her senses and igniting her desire.

Everything else slipped away. Her earlier desperation to find Diana, her worry about Uncle Alistair's ball—even the shame she'd felt about kissing the earl. None of it mattered, or if it did, it was all eclipsed by the glorious sensations of his lips pressed to her neck and his hands cupping her bottom.

It was both liberating and exhilarating, living only in the moment. She was neither mired down by her past nor limited by her future. Surrounded by the vine-covered arbor and fragrant blooms, they were in their own small Garden of Eden.

In this paradise, there were no repercussions to sliding her hand beneath the earl's waistcoat and caressing the deliciously taut muscles under his shirt.

There was no one to frown upon her wantonness as she deliberately pressed her belly against the front of his trousers, reveling in the stark evidence of his desire.

Like Eve, she'd surely regret her brash behavior come dawn, but tonight she would surrender the need to control every maddening aspect of her life, from her family's pitiful financial state to her uncle's eccentric reputation.

Tonight she would willingly abandon the rules of polite society and simply feel . . . alive.

With a sigh, she speared her fingers through the hair at Will's nape and tilted his head toward her.

For *this* was what she needed. His hot, wet kisses trailing down her shoulder. His deft fingers waging war with her neckline. The slight stubble on his jaw abrading her skin in the most delightful way.

He was what she needed, and this once, she would not deny herself. Brazenly, she twisted in his arms, presenting her back to him. "Loosen my laces?"

He growled, making short work of them. But when she would have turned around to face him, he placed his warm hands on her now-bare shoulders and stilled her. "Wait."

He swept aside the tendrils of hair that tickled her back and tugged her gown lower, exposing her skin to a sultry night breeze. "Slip off your sleeves," he murmured in her ear. "I need to see more of you. I must touch you."

Her nipples tightened in response to his wicked words, and though she did as he asked, she held the front of her gown tightly against her breasts.

"Much better," he whispered approvingly. "But there is the small matter of your chemise." He reached around her, plucked the tie at her neckline, and pulled it free. "It must go as well."

He did not beg permission this time, but shoved the thin lawn garment down her arms so it was no longer a barrier between them.

And then he moaned. "Jesus, Meg." Though he was clearly exasperated, she rather thought he was pleased at the same time. And that pleased *her.*

He rested his chin on her shoulder and slipped his hands under the coarse wool of her dress, gliding his hands around her sides, up her belly, and beneath her swollen breasts. "So beautiful," he said. "So perfect."

The gown slipped through her fingers and bunched

wantonly at her waist. She leaned back against him, unsure if her own legs would support her and grateful for the
hard solid wall of his body behind her.

He cupped her breasts easily, taking their weight in his
hands as he kissed the sensitive spot behind her ear.

Oh God. This was more than a stolen kiss, far beyond
the realm of *allowing him a few liberties*. And that knowledge thrilled her all the more.

She whimpered as he caressed her with whisper-soft
strokes. Cried out when he lightly tweaked the tight
buds. She'd never imagined that he could induce such
bliss with a simple touch, but a delightful heat pulsed between her legs and echoed throughout her body. Every
nerve ending seemed connected and on fire—for him.

Somehow, he understood what she wanted before
she did.

"Come here," he said, guiding her to the bench. "Sit."

When she did, he knelt before her, letting his gaze rove
over her bare skin. She would have covered herself with
her hands, but he pinned them to the bench beneath his
own. "Don't hide yourself from me. Ever."

"I don't belong to you, and I am not yours to command."

"Perhaps not. It's one of the reasons you intrigue me so.
But one day soon, Meg, you *will* be mine." With that, he
bowed his head to her breast and drew the tip into his
mouth, his tongue tasting and teasing.

She sucked in her breath, dizzy from the sheer ecstasy
of it. "Do not stop," she begged.

As he left one breast to lavish attention on the other he
shot her a lazy, seductive smile. "I *am* yours to command,"
he said, throwing her words back at her. "Especially in
this."

Any retort she might have made died on her lips, and
her head fell back.

He slid his hand beneath the hem of her gown and stroked her leg, just behind the knee. "I want to make you feel even better. *Let* me."

"What, precisely, do you propose to do?" she asked breathlessly.

"I could tell you, if you like." He nibbled at her ear lobe. "Or I could show you. Trust me?"

He looked impossibly handsome and vulnerable at the same time. An irresistible combination.

"I trust you," she said.

A feral gleam lit his eyes as he lifted her dress, glided a hand up the inside of her leg, and gently spread her thighs. Her skin glowed pale in the moonlight, and the warm evening air kissed her . . . everywhere. When she would have squeezed her knees together, he leaned in to capture her mouth in a kiss.

With one hand he traced decadent spirals on her bare breast; with the other he found the sensitive folds at her entrance and stroked her, reacting to her every moan, responding to her every need. He circled the most sensitive spot until she was on the edge of something big, panting with desire and nearly incapable of coherent thought.

"I've dreamed of touching you like this, Meg. Of making you moan with pleasure and watching as you come undone."

"Why?" she gasped, leaning her head on his solid shoulder. "Why must you always push me to give up control?"

"Because you fight so hard to keep it." He slid a finger into her, and instinctively, she thrust against his hand. "And because I know that when you finally *do* relinquish control, it's going to be . . . exquisite."

"Help me," she begged. "I don't know what to do."

"It's very simple." He chuckled softly. "And you are closer than you think. But you might try thinking wicked thoughts."

"More wicked than being half undressed in your garden?" His finger moved inside her even as his thumb caressed her outside, setting up a hypnotic rhythm.

"More wicked than that," he confirmed.

"I am at a loss." Suddenly shy, she bit her lower lip. "But I've a feeling you could assist me."

"Wicked thoughts happen to be my area of expertise," he said smugly. "Just do as I say."

She was so tightly coiled, so ripe for release, that she didn't consider balking at his command. "Very well."

He plucked a petal from the bloom in her hair and held it before her face. "Imagine that this is ice cream."

"Ice cream," she repeated with some skepticism, even as she savored the pressure of his touch beneath her skirt.

"Mmm. Pineapple flavored. I'm dripping it here"—he swept the petal through the valley between her breasts—"and here"—he said, tracing a path to her navel. "Cold and sweet, it trickles down your sides, but I dutifully lick every drop off your skin." To demonstrate, he lapped an imaginary droplet from the swell of her breast.

"Ooh." The image of his dark head bent over her body and intent on pleasuring her filled her head. The pulsing in her core grew stronger, more insistent. "What else?"

"Close your eyes." She did. "Feel me touching you"—he stroked her entrance, teasing mercilessly—"here."

"Yes." Heaven help her, she was scarcely aware of anything else.

"Now imagine I'm caressing you here, not with my fingers . . . but with my mouth. Tasting and exploring to my heart's content. Driving you mad with every wicked stroke of my tongue."

Dear God. A thousand pinpricks of light gathered in her core and smoldered for an eternity. She whimpered, fearing they might never ignite, but then he grabbed a fistful of her hair, drew her head down, and breathed in her ear. "Come for me, Meg."

And she burst into flames. Fierce and beautiful, the fire roared through her, sparing not an inch of her body or soul. Her skin tingled, her heart pounded, and her toes curled. And all the while, Will stayed close, holding her and watching her with something akin to wonder.

Slowly, the world sharpened back into focus. A light breeze blew, the fountain gurgled, a toad croaked.

And Meg knew she'd never be the same again.

When at last the embers of her pleasure subsided, he pulled the skirt of her gown over her legs and sat beside her on the stone bench. "You're an excellent pupil," he murmured, brushing his lips against her temple.

Suddenly embarrassed, she'd swallowed and slipped her arms back into her sleeves. She'd surrendered to Will, and it was madness. Pure madness.

Clearly, the earl had not found the same sort of satisfaction she had, and yet, he did not urge her to venture any further down the lane of impropriety. Perhaps he was aware that she'd already strolled much further down that path than she'd intended.

"Allow me to help you with your laces."

Wordlessly, she turned and let him secure her dress while she attempted to repair the damage to her hair. A minute later, she could have almost passed for respectable.

But she knew very well that she was not—and what she must now do.

It was going to break her heart.

Chapter FIFTEEN

"After what just transpired," Meg said soberly, "I do not think it possible for me to remain in your employ."

Jesus. Will was still hard as a rock, drunk on the scent of her, and reeling from the raw power of her release. "Let's not be hasty." He nuzzled her neck, wishing he could take her to his bed and pleasure her a dozen different ways before morning. "There's no reason for you to leave. I will admit that this complicates things a bit—"

"It's more than a complication," she said. "It changes everything. A stolen kiss was one thing, but this . . . we cannot go back to the way it was before—at least, *I* cannot."

"Running away will accomplish nothing. You must give me time."

"Time for what?"

An excellent question—and one he wasn't quite prepared to answer. "To sort things out. To show you . . . that I care for you." God help him, he did.

She straightened her spine. "I harbor no illusions about the future."

"Maybe you should raise your expectations." The words had tumbled out of his mouth, unbidden—and yet, they rang true.

"So that I may ultimately be disappointed?"

Damn it, he was in no position to make promises. Meg was nothing like the type of woman he'd envisioned as his future countess. He needed someone born to the role—someone who could move about society with ease, visiting genteel drawing rooms during the day and hosting lavish dinner parties at night. Someone whose dowdy gowns wouldn't raise eyebrows in ballrooms or spark gossip amongst the town's elite. Someone who would give him an heir but not demand too much of his time or heart. That wasn't Meg.

But he sure as hell wasn't ready to let her go. Not after she'd just come apart in his arms.

Maybe he could slightly alter the vision of his future countess in his head. Perhaps Meg could change a little, too, and they could find some middle ground.

Of course, her stubborn streak was a mile wide, so the odds of reaching a compromise were not in his favor. He only knew he had to try.

He blew out a long breath. "Give me the chance to prove to you that my feelings are true."

She blinked at him, her heavy-lidded gaze innocently seductive. "Couldn't that be accomplished while I was at my uncle's?"

Undoubtedly. But the distance would also make it infinitely more difficult for him to crack her armor. "Selfishly, I want you here, under my roof. But you need not fear for your reputation. While we are in the company of others, I promise to be the model of propriety."

"That in itself is sure to raise suspicion," she teased.

"And though it will kill me to refrain from touching you all day," he murmured, "I will. I'll see you, and I'll remember the feel of your satin skin beneath my hands . . . the decadent taste of your lips . . . and the glorious sight of you coming undone."

He lifted her chin and gave her a tender kiss—both a promise and a plea. "The choice is yours, Meg. You may stay or you may go. But by God, I want you to stay."

She arched a brow, regarding him thoughtfully. "And you need a governess."

"There is that. But right now"—he slid his hand up her side and cupped her breast—"I swear I'm thinking only of you. Of us."

Her eyes fluttered shut and she sighed softly. "I'm quite certain that I've lost my mind."

"As have I."

"But I do need the money. I will stay. For now."

He ignored the stab he felt at her mention of money and brushed his thumb over her nipple, pleased to find it taut and straining against the fabric of her dress. "Good," he growled.

"You must understand, though. I cannot risk a scandal."

"I'll protect you," he vowed.

She shook her head as if he failed to understand the gravity of the situation. "I *cannot* bring shame upon my family or sully my sisters' reputations. I won't jeopardize their chance to make a good match. If it seems we are in danger of being discovered, I shall be forced to leave at once and sever our connection."

"I won't let that happen."

"Some things are out of our control, Will. Isn't that what you keep telling me?"

"I had no idea you were actually listening."

Smiling ruefully, she stood and shook out her skirt. "I must go. The girls and I have much to accomplish to-morrow."

He reached for her hand and pressed his lips to the back. "Perhaps you'll save time in your schedule for me?"

"That all depends," she said vaguely.

"On what?"

"On the success of naptime." She pulled away, and he reluctantly released her fingertips.

"I am a staunch supporter of naps," he said, watching her glide toward the house.

"As am I, my lord," she said over her shoulder. "As am I."

"Valerie has nine ribbons." Meg counted out nine pebbles and placed them in front of Diana. She and the girls had pushed the desks and chairs toward the walls of the nursery, opting to sit on the worn but comfortable rug in the center. "Then she gives four of them away."

Diana slid four of the pebbles to the side.

Meg nodded approvingly. "How many ribbons has Valerie now?"

"No one knows," Diana said cheekily, "because her dresser is such a mess."

"Not as bad as yours," Valerie retorted. "At least I don't collect weeds in my drawer."

"They're flowers!"

"They might have been *once*. Now they're just dead."

"Girls," Meg said smoothly, while making a mental note to help Diana tidy her drawer later, "let's finish our lesson, shall we?"

Diana considered the pebbles once more, her lips moving silently as she counted. Raising her head, she said, "The problem is nine minus four, and the answer is five."

"Well done!" Meg exclaimed.

"Bravo!" cried Valerie. "You've got it."

"Yes, I think I do," Diana said, preening. "Now it's Valerie's turn. I shall make up a problem for her. Let's see. *Diana has six turtles.*"

"Pardon me, ladies."

Meg looked up to find the earl standing in the doorway, leaning casually against the jamb and wearing a midnight blue jacket that might have been molded to fit his broad shoulders and trim waist. "Miss Lacey, might I have a word?"

"We're in the middle of a lesson, my lord." Heat rose up her neck and flooded her cheeks.

"I only require a moment of your time," he said firmly, inducing the same sinking feeling as a summons to the headmistress's office.

"Very well." She pushed herself off the floor as gracefully as possible, which was to say not very gracefully at all, and addressed the twins. "Take turns making problems for each other, and write the equations on your chalkboards so that I may see them when I return. I shan't be gone for more than a few minutes."

The girls nodded mutely, staring at the earl with saucer eyes.

Meg stepped into the hallway where Will waited, and shut the nursery door behind her. "What are you doing here?" she hissed.

"I missed you." He reached for the long, loose curl that hung over her shoulder and wound it around his finger. "So I thought I'd inquire about naptime. When is it?"

"Not for another two hours, at least."

"Damn." He scowled, and though his grave and obvious disappointment melted her a smidge, she was all too aware that the twins might have their ears pressed to the door.

"Perhaps this afternoon isn't the most opportune—"

"Just meet me in the library," he said, his gaze hot and hungry. "I promise to behave myself. Unless you'd rather I didn't . . ."

"I shall try to be there."

"That's all I ask." He released her tendril of hair, brushed his thumb over her lower lip, and stared at her mouth.

"I must go."

"Until later, then." He let his hand drop, but as she went to open the nursery door, he said, "How is Diana today?"

Puzzled by his question, she frowned. "She is well. Why?"

"I wondered if she had recovered from yesterday's adventure. It must have been frightening for her, to be lost and on her own—even if she didn't wander farther than Mayfair."

Meg's heart squeezed in her chest. "Do you want to know what I think?"

"Of course."

She placed a hand in the crook of his elbow and leaned toward his ear. "I think that you care more for the twins than you let on."

Scoffing, he shook his head. "They're terrors."

"If you say so." Unable to resist, she rose up on her toes and kissed his mouth, lingering longer than she should have dared.

He groaned, and she smiled as she returned to the nursery, already counting the minutes until naptime.

Will closeted himself in his study and surrounded himself with contracts and ledgers in an attempt to appear productive for the next two hours, even if he was not.

He wrote a few letters making discreet inquiries into Lord Wiltmore's finances. Meg's uncle was the closest thing she had to a father, and if she'd agreed to take the governess position, he must be in dire straits, indeed. Will had no doubt he could help the baron, but first he needed some idea of the extent of his debts and troubles.

Will was melting sealing wax onto the last of his

correspondence when Gibson cleared his throat from the doorway. "Begging your pardon, my lord. This just arrived for you." The butler held a letter between his thumb and index finger the way one might handle a dead rat.

The moment Will snatched the letter from Gibson, a wave of perfume assaulted his nose and stung his eyes. He recognized the expensive but cloying scent as Marina's. "Bloody hell."

"Precisely, my lord."

"That will be all, Gibson."

Will turned the letter over in his hands, debating whether to read or burn it. He'd broken things off with his ex-mistress, and no good could come of prolonging their attachment—even if he attempted to keep it strictly platonic. He had no wish to give Marina the wrong idea. Especially now that he was involved with Meg.

But, guilt niggled. He and Marina had been intimate for several months, and though their relationship had been more business than personal, he owed her the courtesy of reading her letter.

Cursing, he unfolded the note and breathed through his mouth as he read.

Dearest Will,
    I trust you have not changed your mind about us. I confess I am disappointed, however, I shall not beg you to come back to me. I'm sure it is no suprise to you that I've a multitude of options available. However, their is a matter of some import that I feel compelled to share with you, and I think we must discuss it in person. Please send word indicating where and when you'd like to meet.
                                                        —M.

Will read the note over again, shaking his head over Marina's spelling and searching for a clue about what the *matter of import* might be. For all her faults, Marina was not one to play games, so if she wanted to speak with him, the most likely reason was . . .

Shit. His mouth went dry and his head started to pound. He'd always taken precautions to avoid getting her with child, but French letters were hardly failsafe.

Maybe she was mistaken, or perhaps she wanted to speak to him about something else entirely . . . but his gut told him that whatever the news was, it wouldn't be good.

A cold sweat broke out on his forehead. If Marina was pregnant, it could ruin everything . . . but he had to know, and he had to do the right thing where the child was concerned.

He stuffed her letter in the top drawer of his desk and pulled out a sheet of paper to compose a reply. The sooner he spoke with her, the sooner he'd have his answers—and he wanted them now.

He'd barely begun the letter when Gibson returned, looking even more self-important than usual. Will kept writing. "I'm busy, damn it."

"I see that, my lord," the butler said dryly. "However I thought you might be interested to know that you've company in the drawing room."

Though Will had neither the time nor inclination to entertain, he couldn't help asking. "Who?"

"The Countess of Castleton."

"My mother?" Good God. She'd been at a house party for the last week and was probably eager to impart all the gossip that she'd amassed over the course of her stay.

"And she is not alone."

"It would be helpful to know the name of the person accompanying her," Will said through gritted teeth.

"Lady Rebecca Damant," Gibson intoned—as though Will should be impressed.

And he probably should have been.

The daughter of a marquess, Lady Rebecca was a classically beautiful and exceedingly rich debutante, widely acclaimed as the catch of the season. So much so that when she entered a ballroom, one could almost hear the collective groan of the other young women present.

Hell if he knew what such a paragon was doing in his drawing room.

Will glanced at the clock. He was supposed to meet Meg in the library in a quarter of an hour, which meant he would have to find a way to discourage his guests from lingering.

"Lady Castleton requested that you not keep them waiting," the butler said.

Will snorted. "Tell my mother that I wouldn't dream of it."

Chapter SIXTEEN

The twins were already yawning by the end of their arithmetic lesson, but Meg insisted they practice their penmanship, for good measure. When she turned down their covers and drew the curtains, they crawled into their beds, too tired to make their usual objection that naps were strictly for babies and old people. And within a few minutes, they drifted into the glorious, rosy-cheeked slumber of exhausted children.

As Meg slipped out of the nursery, her pulse leaped at the thought of stealing a few moments with Will. She stopped in her bedchamber, checked her reflection, and frowned. Her grayish gown did little to flatter her complexion, and though she'd never fretted about her appearance overmuch, she now found herself wishing to wear a dress that belonged to a color family other than, well, *drab*.

But there was nothing to be done for it . . . Unless. Hastily, she retrieved her portmanteau and rummaged through it till she found a length of green silk. Once when she'd worn the ribbon Julie had proclaimed that her eyes sparkled like emeralds, and if that wasn't quite true, a bit of color certainly couldn't hurt matters.

Meg wished Julie were here now. She'd artfully weave the ribbon through her tresses and tie a pretty bow at a jaunty angle. Meg's bow was limp, but it was adornment nonetheless. And thankfully, Will certainly hadn't seemed to mind her dreary wardrobe last evening.

She strolled toward the library, wondering if it were possible to recapture the magic they'd shared in the garden. When he'd visited the nursery earlier, she felt a glimmer of it in her belly—and she was all but certain he'd felt it too.

It was far too soon to say what they meant to each other, precisely, but last night he'd made her feel powerful and respected and . . . adored. And that was a very good start.

She pinched her cheeks as she glided into the library, slightly breathless and eager to see him.

But he was not there.

The cushions on the armchairs flanking the fireplace were perfectly plumped; the books on the side tables were neatly stacked. The room was orderly and quiet—the opposite of how it would have felt had he occupied it.

She'd arrived a few minutes later than she'd hoped, but surely he wouldn't have given up on her so soon. No, he'd probably gotten caught up in his work or been detained by a pressing estate matter. Mildly disappointed, she strolled the perimeter of the room, keeping an expectant eye on the door and debating whether to greet him with a flirtatious smile or a serene one, when the truth was she was incapable of either.

For the next half-hour she waited, trailing her fingertips over a spinning globe and perusing the pages of a volume of poetry. And still, he did not show.

She felt certain he had good cause, but how long, exactly, was one supposed to wait for the other party when meeting for an assignation?

If he were to walk through the door quite late only to find her still waiting for him, how would that look? She suspected he'd think her desperate, foolish, or smitten. And she feared all three assessments would be vexingly accurate.

But her time was valuable too. The earl no doubt thought his more valuable, but she had lessons to plan and letters to write and . . . well, other *things*.

No, she would not wait for him indefinitely. Clearly, the best course of action was to exit the library slowly, so that if he did happen to approach—as she hoped he would—she could say truthfully, *Oh, I was just leaving.*

A snail might have inched its way across the entire house in the time she took to make her way to the door. Drat it all. Had she not an ounce of pride?

Straightening her spine, she resolved to return to her bedchamber at once and make the most of the twin's remaining naptime. She'd do something more productive than wait about for the earl—like dusting the furniture or polishing her boots.

Or perhaps she'd follow the twins' lead and indulge in a nap.

With the book of poetry tucked under her arm, she whisked herself out of the room and down the corridor. As she rounded the corner and made her way to the staircase, she glanced toward the earl's study.

The door was ajar.

She'd been too preoccupied on her way to the library to notice it, but now she couldn't help but wonder if he'd been there the whole time. He *had* requested that she meet him in the library, hadn't he? Was it possible that he'd meant to say the study?

Almost of their own accord, her feet carried her toward the study. She peeked around the doorjamb, only to find the room as vacant as the library had been.

The difference was that the earl *had* been here. His desk was a shambles, with books and papers everywhere. His pen was propped in a pot of ink as though he'd been called away in the middle of his accounting or correspondence.

But something else about the room piqued her curiosity—a pungent, unfamiliar scent tickled her nose and enticed her to venture over the threshold. She sniffed at the air. Perfume.

As far as Meg knew, Will did not entertain women in his study. But she *had* found a rather incriminating handkerchief there during her interview. How well did she really know him?

Listening for sounds of anyone approaching, she leaned over the massive desk to peer at the paper next to the ink-pot and pen, which appeared to have been abandoned midsentence. Even upside-down, it was easy to read the earl's bold cursive.

Marina,
      It's imperative that I see you at once. Your discretion
is required.
      Meet me tonight at nine o-clock at the

Meg swallowed past the huge lump in her throat. Stomach churning, she considered possible explanations Will might have for arranging a clandestine meeting with another woman . . . and could think of none. She did not know anyone by the name of Marina, but it did not sound to her like the name of a feeble great aunt or dear old grandmamma. No, Marina was the name for a beautiful actress or a talented opera-singer or a . . . a mistress.

But Meg would not jump to conclusions. Will deserved

a chance to explain, and until then, she would give him the benefit of the doubt—even if the evidence before her did cast him in a bad light.

And make her question her sanity for becoming involved with him.

"Miss Lacey?"

Meg whirled around, her face burning. The twins looked up at her, their blond curls wild and blue eyes sleepy. "Valerie, Diana. What are you doing down here?" She gently herded them into the corridor.

Diana yawned. "We're hungry."

"Your ribbon is very pretty," Valerie said, shuffling her stockinged feet.

"Why, thank you."

"May we go ask Cook for a treat?" Diana pressed a hand to her belly as though she were about to perish from starvation.

Meg sank to her knees and hugged the girls. With them, she knew where she stood. And fortunately, they would keep her too busy to feel sorry for herself.

"I think we all deserve a trip to the kitchen, but first, we must go to the nursery and make you presentable."

Diana crossed her arms, obstinate. "I want to go *now*."

Meg stood slowly, directed her gaze at Diana, and attempted *the look*. Her face impassive and her voice frosty, she intoned, "We shall go the kitchen *after* we have brushed your hair and put on your shoes."

Diana stomped her foot. "But I'm hungry *now*," she screeched.

Blast it all, *the look* was nothing but quackery.

"I've no wish to make you suffer any longer than necessary," Meg said smoothly. "The sooner we make you presentable, the sooner you may have some refreshment."

Diana's nostrils flared, and her chest began to heave.

Her breathing grew heavier and heavier, as though she were building up to something big.

Valerie had the panicked look of a matador in the path of charging bull.

Meg blinked slowly, pretending to be unimpressed. However, she was rather worried about the scale of Diana's tantrum, which she perceived was both imminent and inevitable.

"I . . . don't. . . . *want* to brush my hair!" Diana yelled, loudly enough to rattle windows. She threw herself on the floor and kicked, her face rapidly turning red from her exertions.

Meg observed her thrashing as though only vaguely interested. "I regret to inform you," she said over the din, "that your hair is growing more tangled by the minute. At this rate, we'll be brushing out knots till breakfast tomorrow."

Valerie tugged on Meg's sleeve. "Sometimes Diana gets a little cranky when she's hungry."

"You don't say?"

Meg could empathize, as she'd been known to be a bit irritable herself when feeling peckish. But that was neither here nor there.

Because while Meg knew precious little of governessing, she knew this: one must never, ever, capitulate to a child who was in the midst of a tantrum.

And so, it raged on.

Before long, Mrs. Lundy rushed to the scene, frantic over the commotion.

"Diana is fine," Meg assured the housekeeper, even as the girl screamed and writhed on the floor like demons had possessed her. "This must run its course."

"Are you certain?" Mrs. Lundy pressed a hand to her chest and took a step backward.

"Yes, I—"

"Well, isn't this a charming display of manners." The earl strode toward them, his scowl suggesting he was far from amused. In his wake, a pair of women followed—one older and impeccably dressed, the other younger and impossibly beautiful.

Meg's stomach dropped. She wanted to grab the girls by the hands and flee up the stairs as quickly as possible . . . but it was not to be.

"Mother," he said politely while ignoring the chaos at his feet, "I'm sure you remember Miss Margaret Lacey. She is the twins' governess."

"I was not aware." The countess's cheeks hollowed.

"Lady Rebecca," Will continued, "allow me to introduce Miss Margaret Lacey. Miss Lacey, this is Lady Rebecca."

"A pleasure to meet you both." Meg curtsied, because even though both women had now learned that she was a deplorably inept governess, there was no reason they should think her completely devoid of manners.

Lady Rebecca pursed perfectly full lips as her gaze roved over Meg's unfashionable gown. "You look familiar, Miss Lacey. Have we met somewhere else—perhaps at your previous employer's?"

"No, I don't think so. This is my first real governess position." Blast. She couldn't imagine what had prompted her to confess such a thing.

The countess's thin white brows crept up her high forehead. "Your first, you say?"

"Miss Lacey came with excellent references," the earl lied.

Meanwhile, Diana's screeches gave way to sobs, drawing piteous looks from the women.

"I know," Lady Rebecca said, beaming. "You're one of Lord Wiltmore's . . . wards."

Meg's hackles rose instantly. "Lord Wiltmore is indeed my uncle and guardian. He was kind enough to take in me and my sisters after . . ." Her traitorous voice cracked, and she cleared her throat. "He's been very good to us."

Lady Rebecca eyed Meg's gown again as though it were evidence to the contrary. "I'm sure he means well. But it must be difficult for you and your sisters, living with a man who is so . . ."

Meg could feel a tantrum of her own brewing. She clenched her jaw and shot a warning look at Will. Lady Rebecca would do well to choose her next words very, very carefully.

". . . unconventional," Lady Rebecca continued, inordinately pleased with herself. "He can neither know nor understand the intricacies of helping young ladies make their entrance into society."

Meg took even breaths through her nose. In her own condescending way, Lady Rebecca was simply trying to express sympathy for Meg's plight. To magnanimously attribute her fashion faux pas and general awkwardness to her uncle's negligence.

When she thought she might respond without causing a greater scene than Diana had, she said, "Uncle Alistair may not be the most conventional of gentlemen, but he *is* the most generous and loving."

"The Viscount Wiltmore," the earl's mother murmured to herself. "I'm surprised they haven't carted him off to Bedlam by now."

Oh, *no*. Fists clenched, Meg turned to the twins and spoke through her teeth. "Go to the nursery. At once." The color drained from Diana's face as she scrambled to her feet. Valerie grabbed her hand, and the pair dashed up the staircase.

Meg smiled sweetly at the countess. For now that the twins were gone, she need not contain her rage.

Chapter SEVENTEEN

Meg's eyes blazed with ire.

Will had no doubt a firestorm was about to ignite. Tinder and sparks were everywhere, with nary a water bucket in sight.

"How *dare* you?" Meg accused the countess.

His mother sniffed. "I speak the truth."

"Have a care, Mother," Will warned.

She shrugged. "If Miss Lacey were honest with herself she'd admit it. Wiltmore's as buffle-headed as they come."

"He is one of the smartest people I know," Meg seethed. "He is exceedingly knowledgeable about a multitude of subjects—topics of far more import than the latest titillating gossip or . . . or the current season's fashions."

Lady Rebecca's gaze flicked to Meg's gown again, lingering on the high neckline, large sleeves, and low waist. "Lord Wiltmore appears to suffer from a knowledge gap spanning *several* seasons' fashions."

Meg gasped and narrowed her eyes; Rebecca tossed her perfectly coiffed head.

"Enough," snapped Will. Though he found Meg's gowns

beyond irksome and had himself expressed a strong dis-
like for them on occasion, he would not permit his
mother or Lady Rebecca to belittle Meg. Or her uncle. "I
was about to invite Miss Lacey to join us for tea, but given
our momentary lapse in civility, I think it best that we all
conclude our visit."

"Perhaps another time," his mother mused in a tone
suggesting she'd sooner be dragged through town by
horses.

Meg raised her chin. "I must go." She pressed her lips
together as she turned to ascend the staircase, and he could
see what it cost her to remain silent—well, relatively
silent—in the face of his mother's and Rebecca's barbs.

"I'll see you out," he said to them tersely.

His mother brushed her hands down the front of her
gown as though ridding herself of the nastiness she'd just
endured, then began walking toward the front hall at a glacial pace. "I'd not heard that you hired a governess, William. You might have consulted me."

Will flinched. He didn't have to explain his actions to
her, damn it, but old habits were hard to break. "Thomas's
twins arrived suddenly. There was no time to summon you
from the house party and parade a host of candidates before you."

"I hesitate to mention it," Rebecca said, "but Miss Lacey
seemed to have some difficulty controlling the girls. A
competent governess would never tolerate such churlish
behavior."

"Thank you for imparting that nugget of wisdom."

The debutante preened, deaf to his sarcasm.

"Let me assure you," Will continued. "Today's incident
was quite unusual."

"Was it?" His mother sucked in her cheeks, skeptical.

"Diana is simply overtired today because she suffered
an ordeal last night."

"And what sort was that?" Rebecca batted her eyes.

Damn, but he'd walked into that one. "Never mind. She is safe now, and that is all that matters."

"Your commitment to care for Thomas's by-blows is commendable," his mother said.

Will flinched again.

"But there are other aspects of this arrangement you must consider," she continued. "For example, it isn't proper for an unmarried miss—even one such as Miss Lacey— to live under your roof without some sort of chaperone."

"Are you volunteering to move back home, Mother?" Will looked straight into her icy blue eyes, praying she wouldn't challenge his bluff. Ever since Will's father had died, his mother had lived with her sister. She'd originally said it would only be for the mourning period, to help her adjust, but keeping separate residences seemed to suit her as much as it did Will.

His mother returned his gaze, unwavering, and after several beats of silence said, "I will move in, should I deem it necessary."

"Not that anyone would ever presume there was impropriety between you and Miss Lacey." Rebecca tittered as she navigated the stairs at his side. "After all, she's . . ."

Will's blood boiled, but his tone was deceptively calm. "She's what?"

"Well, she's hardly the sort of woman who would tempt a man. In fact, based on her choice of gown, I'd say she's doing everything in her power to discourage male attention. I can think of no other explanation for that unfortunate dress."

Will bit his tongue. Clearly, thinking was not Lady Rebecca's strong suit. Thank God they'd almost reached the front door and he'd soon be rid of her company. "Thank you for your visit. I regret that it was marred by Diana's outburst."

"Not at all, my lord," Lady Rebecca cooed. "I find children to be fascinating creatures." She made them sound like exotic animals in a royal menagerie. "Girls that age simply require a maternal influence. Someone to teach them proper etiquette and respect for their elders." She smiled as if to add, *Someone like me.*

Will suppressed a shudder.

"In any event," she continued, "I trust that our next meeting will be more conducive to . . . conversation." She held out her hand, and Will dutifully bowed over it.

"Rebecca," his mother said, "why don't you go ahead and settle yourself into the coach? I shall join you shortly."

"Of course, Lady Castleton." She covered her brunette ringlets with a gold silk bonnet that had probably cost more than Meg's weekly earnings and glided down the pavement to the coach.

Will turned to his mother, bracing himself.

"Lady Rebecca is precisely the sort of woman you should be courting," she said.

"She has plenty of suitors already."

"I've never known you to shy away from competition, William."

"I don't. When the prize is worthy."

"The *prize* could hardly be more worthy. She is descended from a long and respected family line. Her dowry would do much to pad our coffers—not that they need padding at the moment, but one can never accumulate too much wealth."

"You need not worry that you'll end up in the poorhouse, Mother."

"Do not be flippant. Your father, God rest his soul, has been gone for five years. I believed you when you said you needed time to adjust to your role and to make the estate prosperous again. Now it's time for you to do your duty—as you promised me you would."

Will stiffened at the mention of his father. "I have not forgotten my duty."

"Perhaps not, but you have precious little inclination to *act*. Fortunately, your wealth and good looks do much of the work for you. Indeed, Lady Rebecca has expressed to me that she might be amenable to a match. She is young, beautiful, and sophisticated—all that you could hope for in your future countess."

Unless one wanted loyalty, strength, and fire. Someone more like Meg.

But even Will could honestly not say what he wanted at that moment. All he knew was that he needed to meet with his ex-mistress before he made promises to anyone, particularly Meg.

"I will give the matter due consideration."

"Good. To assist you with your *consideration*, I shall host a dinner party three days hence and invite Rebecca. I expect you to be there."

"I'm afraid my schedule won't permit me to attend. I've much to do here."

"How terribly unfortunate." Tilting her head, she eyed him shrewdly. "I declare, it's a curious thing. It seems that hiring the governess has somehow resulted in *more* work for you. Perhaps I *should* take up residence here. To ease some of the burden."

He met her gaze and held it for several seconds. "That won't be necessary."

She smiled widely, revealing white, even teeth. "You'll attend then?"

Damn it all to hell. He'd inherited his negotiation skills from his mother. "Fine. But we'll have the dinner party *here*. Mrs. Lundy has been hinting that she'd like for me to entertain. She'll be delighted to host a social event."

"By all means, let's make the housekeeper happy," his mother said dryly.

He kissed the cheek she offered, and said, "Eight o'clock on Thursday evening."

"I shall inform Rebecca and her father, Viscount Redmere, of the plans." The countess stepped out into the balmy summer day, pleased as a cat. Looking over her shoulder, she added, "I'd advise you to make sure the children are in bed before the guests arrive. We do not wish to repeat today's dreadful scene."

"I shall chain them to their beds if necessary," he said, rolling his eyes.

She waved warmly, the picture of maternal grace and love. "Perfect."

"Do I look presentable?" Diana ran her hands down her braids and smoothed the front of her frock.

"Quite," said Meg. "Are you ready?"

"Yes," she answered bravely.

Valerie held her sister's hand in a show of support as Meg escorted them to the earl's study. "Maybe he won't be there," Valerie said, somewhat hopefully.

"We shall see." Meg wasn't certain, either. He hadn't come looking for her, but it wasn't yet time for his meeting with the mysterious Marina.

Meg burned with curiosity—about who the woman was and what she meant to Will. At the same time, she was desperately afraid of what those answers might be. And since she'd been snooping, she couldn't very well demand the information from the earl.

There was, however, someone else who might know, or who could find out. Charlotte. Earlier, Meg had scrawled a brief note to her and asked a footman to deliver it to Lord Torrington's townhouse a few blocks away. She felt better knowing she'd done something, even if it might take a few days for her friend to respond.

For now, Meg would focus on smoothing things over between Diana and the earl.

The study door was closed, and Diana faced it with the same caution that mortals used when approaching Mount Olympus. Meg sympathized more than the girl could know.

Diana released Valerie's hand and looked up at Meg, who nodded encouragingly, and knocked.

"Enter," the earl boomed with Zeus-like authority.

Her hand trembling, Diana pushed open the door. "Excuse me, sir."

Will's gaze—intense and indecipherable—met Meg's briefly, then landed on Diana. "Yes?"

She squeezed her eyes shut and sucked in a long breath before lifting her chin and looking the earl in the eye. "I've come to apologize for my behavior this afternoon."

"I see."

"I shouldn't have acted that way—especially while you had visitors."

"The timing was less than ideal." He rubbed his jaw thoughtfully.

"I can be a monster when I'm hungry, but that's no excuse. I'm sorry for embarrassing you."

"I accept your apology, Diana. However, I was not the only one you embarrassed. Miss Lacey deserves an apology as well."

Meg rested a hand on Diana's shoulder. "Thank you, my lord, but she has already made amends with me."

"Good." He rose from his chair, rounded the desk and sat on the edge, his long legs crossed casually in front of him. "I suppose that now it's my turn."

The twins stared at the earl, wide-eyed and wary.

"Miss Lacey," he began, "please forgive me for subjecting

you to my mother and Lady Rebecca. Their comments about you and your uncle were rude in the extreme. I made my displeasure with them known."

"Thank you, but I do not hold you accountable for their actions—only your own." She'd been unable to resist adding that last bit.

"Fair enough," he said slowly, like a man navigating a field of explosives. "I hope you'll give me the opportunity to explain, if I've done something to disappoint you."

Meg sighed. It wasn't so much what he'd done, but what he was presumably about to do—with the mysterious Marina. "Everyone deserves the chance to defend and explain their actions."

"I'm glad you feel that way," he said, but worry was written plainly across his face.

Valerie bounced to Meg's side and clasped her hand. "Miss Lacey said that once Diana had righted her wrongs we could go to the drawing room and have a lesson on the pianoforte."

"If you have no objection, my lord," Meg added.

"Not at all. I think it a fine idea, actually."

"Do you know how to play?" Diana asked him excitedly.

"A little."

"Oh, would you like to come with us?" Valerie blinked up at him, her blue eyes hopeful.

Will's gaze flicked to the clock on the mantel. "Much as I would like to, I'm afraid I have an appointment. Another time, perhaps."

Disappointment stabbed Meg in the chest. Some small, foolish part of her had hoped he'd cancel his plans to meet Marina and seek her out instead. To explain why he hadn't met her in the study earlier. To make up for the horrific things his mother and Lady Rebecca had said. But his decision to keep his appointment was nothing if not enlightening. Meg now knew exactly where she ranked with him.

The earl stood and stepped closer, looking at Meg over the heads of the twins. "I shall look forward to resuming our conversation tomorrow."

"As shall I," Meg said. "But for different reasons than I originally did."

His forehead creased in a mix of puzzlement and concern. "I do not follow your meaning."

"I would explain," she said breezily, "but I have no wish to detain you from your appointment. Come along, girls."

Chapter EIGHTEEN

Will strode into the Silver Fox, weaved through a maze of tables, and located Marina at a booth in the back, wearing black lace over her face. He should have predicted the veil, given his request for discretion and her flair for the dramatic.

"Marina," he said, taking a seat opposite her. "Thank you for coming."

"It's good to see you, Will." She lifted the veil over her head and let her gaze rove over him. "Even if the circumstances aren't what I would have wished."

"You're looking well." He hated that he was required to make polite conversation when all he wanted to know was whether or not she was with child. Now. But he knew better than to rush Marina. She would reveal all—when she was ready. So, he ignored the churning of his stomach, waved a barmaid over, and ordered a round of drinks.

"I've a new beau," she said with a shrug. "He lacks your skill, but he is young and eminently trainable."

Will raised his glass of ale and smiled. "Congratulations. I wish you both well."

"He is aware of our past, of course. It's hardly a secret. But he's a jealous sort and would not be pleased to see us together."

"He sounds like an insecure pup," Will teased.

She sipped her sherry thoughtfully. "Perhaps. But I will make it work to my advantage."

"I have no doubt you will." She had more acumen than most merchants. "I appreciate you meeting me in spite of your reservations. The matter you mentioned—it must be of some import." Will braced himself.

"It's hard to say," she mused. "But I will give you the facts and leave it to you to decide."

Relaxing a little, he nodded. "Go on."

"Two nights ago, while at Vauxhall Gardens, I was approached by a man wearing a mask. He was tall and light-haired." She thought for a moment. "And dressed like a gentleman."

"I trust you were not a victim of untoward behavior." The pleasure gardens were rife with it.

"No," Marina said. "But the man seemed to know who I was, and he inquired after you."

Will narrowed his eyes. "Really? How so?"

"He asked if it was true that you and I had parted ways. Normally, I would have refused to discuss such a personal matter, but the punch had loosened my tongue."

"How did you respond?"

She waved a hand. "I told him we were no longer seeing one another."

"Did he press you for any other information?"

"Yes, and this is the part I found most strange. He wanted to know if you had taken in a pair of twin girls. I'd told him I'd heard the rumor but didn't know if it was true." She raised a brow at him. "Is it?"

He nodded. "They're only six. And quite a handful."

Marina shuddered as though he'd confessed to taking

in not two small girls, but a pair of goats. "I would ask what in heaven possessed you to do such a thing, but I'm not certain I want to know."

"You don't know the man's identity?"

She shook her head regretfully. "No. When I asked for his name, he merely said he was *an interested party*."

"Did he say anything else?"

"He asked about the twins and your level of attachment to them . . ." Marina traced the rim of her glass with her fingertip. ". . . and their mother."

"The devil you say," Will murmured, more to himself than to Marina.

"I told him I did not know and that it was none of my concern. Or his."

"Thank you," he said sincerely. Marina really was a decent sort.

"It was the truth—even if he didn't care to hear it. He said that if I were to acquire information that was useful to him, he would pay handsomely for it."

The hairs on the back of Will's neck stood on end. "Jesus. How are you to contact him?"

"When I asked, he said that I should not worry about it. He would seek me out when the opportunity arose."

"I don't like the sound of that, Marina. Did he threaten you in any way?"

"No. As I said, he dressed and spoke like a gentleman, but he had a ruthlessness about him. Something in his tone and demeanor made me shiver."

"You should not go out alone for the time being. Tell your beau you require an escort everywhere you go."

"I will have a care for my safety," she said vaguely. "And if he should approach me again, I shall send word."

"Thank you. I'm sorry that you're involved in this at all. I don't know why anyone would be curious about my relationship to the girls. They're simply my—"

"No." Marina stopped him, holding up a hand. "I would prefer not to know. That way, if I'm interrogated, it will be impossible for me to reveal anything that I shouldn't—even if I *have* partaken of the punch."

"Anyone who dares to interrogate you shall deal with me," Will said. "But you need not worry about revealing too much. I have no secrets."

"No?" Ever the coquette, the hint of a smile played about her lips. "According to the rumors, there is also a governess—one of Wiltmore's Wallflowers. Perhaps she is not destined to be a wallflower for long?"

Damn, but this town loved gossip. "I've a feeling you'll know the answer before I do." He threw back the rest of his ale and clunked the glass on the table. "I must go. Allow me to see you safely home."

Marina smiled and gracefully draped the black lace over her face. "It warms me to know that chivalry is not entirely dead."

Meg sat on the edge of her bed, hands trembling as she unfolded Charlotte's letter. She hadn't expected a reply to-night—it was already quite late. But the footman who'd delivered Meg's note was friendly with one of Lord Tor-rington's kitchen maids, and they'd enjoyed a brief visit while he waited to see if Charlotte wished to respond.

And she had.

Dearest Meg,

I do not know anyone by the name of Marina but have made discreet inquiries. It seems that until quite recently, she was Lord Castleton's mistress. I'm sorry to relate such shocking news, but the urgency of your note suggested you'd want to know. My source informs me that they are no longer seeing one another. I do hope you find this information to be more helpful than distressing. Please write me again when you are able.

Fondly,
Charlotte

Mistress. Meg pressed a hand to her roiling belly. How could he arrange a meeting with his mistress just one day after the evening they'd spent in the garden where he'd . . . and she'd . . . Dear *God*, what had she done?

She'd been foolish to trust him so quickly. A master of manipulation, he'd seduced her with pretty words and wicked caresses. She'd willingly—nay, eagerly—surrendered to desire.

A mistake she would not make again.

After locking the door to her bedchamber, she hauled her hideous gown over her head and threw it on the floor. She wrestled with the laces of her wretched corset, wiggled out of it, and tossed it on top of her dress. In no mood to fold or hang her clothes, she simply went to her washstand, scrubbed and dried her face, and crawled beneath the covers of her bed, still seething with anger.

An hour later, after she'd thought of half a dozen methods of revenge, most involving highly creative forms of torture, a soft knock sounded at her door.

Heart pounding, she bolted upright. Assuring herself that the door was locked, she went perfectly still, listening for sounds from the hallway.

It had to be Will. The twins always slept soundly through the night, and no one else had cause to disturb her.

The knock sounded again, slightly louder. She pressed her lips firmly together.

"Meg?" he whispered through the door. "Can you hear me?"

She didn't make a sound.

Another knock. "Meg, are you awake? I need to speak with you."

She doubted very much that what he wanted to do was speak, for conversation could surely wait for the light of day.

After a moment, the door handle clicked, as though he were testing to see if it was locked. She clutched the sheets to her chest, her blood boiling.

When she heard the doorknob rattle, followed by his muttered curse, she smiled to herself.

What kind of a cad spent the evening with his mistress—or ex-mistress, if one cared to split hairs—and then had the audacity to seek out another lady in her bedchamber?

He did not deserve the courtesy of a reply. Let him wonder and wait, for her silence would sting more than an outright rejection. Besides, if she went to the door and told him to go away, her voice might crack. Or her resolve might waver.

And though she had very little, she did have her pride.

Before long, she heard him stride down the hall, away from her room.

So . . . he'd given up rather easily, which was certainly for the best. She ignored the slight disappointment in her chest and slipped back beneath the covers.

It had been a long day, and finally, it was over. Tomorrow, she would figure out how to deal with the earl. Once, she would have hurled a string of insults at him, walked out of Castleton House, and never looked back. But now her salary was keeping food in her sisters' bellies. And even if money weren't an issue, she'd become attached to the twins.

Diana had even confided in her this afternoon, and now . . . well, everything had changed.

Outside her window, moonlight silhouetted leafy

boughs shivering from a strong, sudden gust. She listened to the halting patter of rain beginning to hit the panes, wondering if Beth and Julie heard it as they lay in their beds, too. Her sisters had always gathered in Meg's bed during a storm, not because any of them were frightened, but because they wanted to savor the raw power of it together—every lightning flash, thunder boom, and wind burst. Though Meg was several blocks away from them now, it seemed to her that the sound of the driving rain brought them together in a way . . . and calmed her. Her eyelids grew heavy; sleep beckoned.

Crack.

Dear Jesus. Meg sprang out of her bed and ran to the window. It sounded as though a large branch had splintered off of a tree, and now there was another sound above the din—a voice shouting. Pulse racing, she pressed her forehead to the pane and searched the dark night. The tree outside her window still stood, its leaves twisting in the torrent.

A dream, perhaps. The kind that happens in the twilight just before sleep that can seem quite real. It must have been a dream.

Except then, she heard her name. "Meg!" Muffled but unmistakable, a man called out to her. And she was fairly certain he did so from the garden.

"Blast it all," she muttered, hauling up the window sash. Madness to do such a thing in the middle of a storm, but she'd detected an urgency in the voice. Rain pelted her face and drenched her chemise as she leaned out the window to peer at the garden below.

And then she saw the hands. Male hands, white-knuckled, gripping the sill outside her window.

Chapter NINETEEN

Meg nearly jumped out of her skin at the sight of a man dangling from her sill, but she managed to choke back the scream in her throat.

"Meg, it's me, Will." He sounded winded. "Back away from the window. I'm going to hoist myself up."

"Please tell me you're standing on a ladder," she begged.

"No." He grunted. "Stand back."

She gripped his wrists, slick with rain. "I can't. I'm afraid you'll fall."

"Stand. Back."

Her belly in knots, she stepped aside, watching him inch his hands to one end of the brick sill. "I'm going for help," she said.

"No. Time."

Blast it all, she had to do something. Frantic, she ran to her bed, yanked off the blanket, and grabbed the sheet beneath. She hastily knotted one end around her waist and prepared to throw the other out the window. "Hold on, I'm coming."

But just then, a large boot landed on the windowsill with a *thud*.

The rest of his large body soon followed, and he tumbled onto the floor of her room, soaking wet and gasping for air.

"What the devil do you think you're doing?" she cried. Tears burned her eyes and her throat constricted. "You almost . . . you could have . . . *Damn* you, William Ryder." Crumpling to the floor, she began to sob.

"Meg, I'm fine. Everything is fine." He scooped the blanket off the floor, draped it over her shoulders, and pulled her against his side. "I'm going to close the window. Just sit here for a moment and try to calm yourself."

Hackles rising, she blinked slowly. "Calm myself? Don't you *dare* tell me to calm myself," she warned, "unless you wish for me to push you back out that window."

"Very well," he chuckled, infuriating her even more. "If you prefer to remain enraged, that is entirely your prerogative."

In two strides, he reached the window, then lowered the sash. Without the wind and driving rain assaulting them, the room suddenly seemed smaller, cozier, more intimate—alarmingly so.

He lit the lamp beside her bed before returning to her side, on the floor. "The branch I was on broke," he said simply, as though that explained everything.

"Only an idiot would climb a tree in the middle of a storm." She was still crying, damn it all, and she had no idea why.

"I cannot disagree. Although, in my defense, the storm began *after* I was halfway up the trunk." He slicked his rain-soaked hair back from his face and looked down at his palms, which were scraped raw. "I'm sorry I frightened you."

"Why?" She cradled one of his open hands in hers. "Why would you do it?"

"You wouldn't answer the door."

"*No*," she said, throwing his hand back in his lap. "You may *not* blame your little brush with death on me. You had other options available to you. Such as waiting until morning—which, incidentally, is what a proper gentleman would have done."

"Morning," he repeated to himself. "And would you have agreed to speak to me then?"

She deflated a little. "Probably not."

"I was worried about you. I had to make sure you were all right." He brushed a wet strand of hair away from her face. "Are you?"

She shook her head. "I don't know. You could have broken your neck."

"I didn't. Besides, there were shrubs below me. Even if I fell, I would have escaped with a few scratches."

"Your confidence might well be impressive if it weren't so bloody foolish," she said sharply.

His laugh, low and rich, vibrated through her limbs. "That's one of the things I adore about you, Meg. You don't mince words. You don't believe in false flattery or blind agreement. On the contrary, you challenge me at every turn."

"*Someone* has to," she said sullenly.

"Yes. And if you want to know the truth of it"—he cupped her cheek in his palm—"I'm inordinately glad that person is you."

She couldn't help it—she warmed at the compliment. Most men thought her prickly personality was a liability— something to be hidden or apologized for. But Will liked her tendency to speak her mind. More than that, he seemed to genuinely like *her*.

He leaned in and touched his forehead to hers, looking very much like he wanted to kiss her. Her traitorous heart leaped and her lips parted.

He was but a breath away when she remembered and drew back. She had to ask, even though she knew the answer.

Especially since she knew the answer.

"Who is Marina?"

Good God. Will winced and pinched the bridge of his nose. "How do you know about Marina?"

"I hear things," she said vaguely. "But I know very little. That's why I'm asking you who she is."

No. He couldn't talk about his ex-mistress with Meg—especially not now, when she was already upset. He pushed himself to his feet and offered her his hand. "You've had a trying day. Let me bring a chair over and make you comfortable."

Refusing his assistance, she untangled herself from a web of blankets and sheets, and stood, facing him. Her hair was a glorious mass of dark, wet curls, and her damp chemise clung to her like a second skin.

"I don't require a *chair*," she said slowly. "I require the *truth*."

Damn. Will wished to God he was back on the windowsill, hanging by his fingertips. The truth was going to hurt Meg, and hurting her was the last thing he wanted to do. "Why would you ask about Marina? She has nothing to do with us."

"There is no *us*, Will. Especially if you cannot answer this simple question for me. *Who is Marina?*"

He could respond that she was a friend—nothing more—and it would be the truth. But Meg wanted the whole truth, and he had no choice but to respect that.

"Fine. I will tell you. But fair warning—you may not like the answer." He clasped her hand and guided her to the edge of the bed, where they both sat.

As he looked into her beautiful, wary eyes, his stomach clenched. He'd sooner have this uncomfortable conversation with his mother than with her, but there was no avoiding it now. No way to spare her the pain.

He drew in a deep breath, exhaled slowly, and let the words spill out. "Until recently, Marina and I were . . . lovers." She flinched at the word but did not look away. "She is a widow, and wealthy in her own right. Our arrangement was purely physical—that is, neither of us had any expectation of courtship or marriage." Until Marina changed her mind, prompting him to end things. In retrospect, she'd done him a favor.

"What happened?" The lamp's light flickered over her pale face.

"The relationship ran its course, as we both knew it eventually would. She's now seeing someone new."

Meg stared at him, long and hard, as though she doubted the veracity of his words. "When did you last see her?"

He hesitated a beat. She must already know. "Earlier tonight."

Her chin trembled and her eyes welled again. "I don't understand."

"I know it sounds bad. There was a matter we needed to discuss." He wanted to reassure her, and yet, he did not think it wise to mention the masked man who'd questioned Marina about the twins. The less Meg was involved, the better.

"I see," she said, but he could tell that she wished to know more.

"I promise you," he said, taking her hand, "that there is no romantic involvement between Marina and me. She has moved on, as have I."

"Will you see her again?"

"Possibly. But only if it's absolutely necessary. She's trying to help me with . . . something. I know it all sounds very vague, but I'm asking you to trust me."

"I want to. But I confess I can't begin to understand a relationship that is based on nothing but . . ."

"Pleasure?"

"Yes. And how it could end so . . . abruptly."

"You are right to question such things." God, he wished he had some brandy. "The truth is that such relationships are often shallow and ultimately unfulfilling." Only it had never bothered him before.

"That is rather . . . sad." She crossed her arms, stood, and paced beside the bed. "I suppose it was naïve of me to think that our tryst in the garden was anything more than a pleasurable encounter." Her cheeks flushed bright pink.

"No." He shook his head adamantly. "You are not naïve. It meant something to me, too."

She stood very still before him, silhouetted by the lamplight. "*What* did it mean to you?" She asked as though his answer had the power to change everything.

Though his jacket and trousers were still damp, a sheen of sweat broke out on his forehead. "I'm not skilled at putting these things into words."

"Try." It was both a demand and a plea.

"Very well." He took a moment to gather his thoughts, such as they were. "When I'm with you—it doesn't matter if we're kissing or arguing or just talking—I feel alive. Like I'm not just gliding through life, doing what little is expected of me, playing the self-indulgent rake. You make me feel like I'm . . . more." He speared his fingers through his hair. "Christ. That sounds ridiculous, doesn't it?"

She swallowed and slowly shook her head. "No."

"It's the same reason I sought you out as a teenager, that day at the lake, I think. You've always had a strength and confidence about you—a tendency to question things and to defy tradition. I like that."

"That tendency lands me in trouble on a regular basis," she admitted. "But I can't help it."

"I wouldn't want you to change." He grinned. "Well, *sometimes* I might wish you would follow simple requests—like backing away from the window—without an argument."

She arched a brow. "*Sometimes* I might wish that you would avoid dangling from my sill."

"You see," he said, pointing at her. "You take me to task when I deserve it—and I usually do. You won't permit me to skate by without examining myself or my actions."

"I am not certain that's a compliment," she said frowning, "but I shall take it as one anyway."

"It is indeed a compliment, Meg." He pulled her down beside him, wrapped an arm around her narrow shoulders, and rested his chin on her head. Her damp hair smelled like soap, citrus, and summer. "You demand more of me. Even better, you make me want to give more. Be more." He sighed. "Does any part of these ramblings make sense?"

"Not really," she murmured, snuggling against his chest. "Little has made sense since the day you interviewed me for the governess position. I detest you one minute and admire you the next. You mock me one minute and praise me the next. I know that we are not well-suited for one another. But I like being with you."

His heartbeat sped from trot to gallop. "You do?"

"Against my better judgment, yes."

He lifted her chin and gazed into her eyes, willing her to believe him. "Things between us are complicated, but I do know this—I want to make it work. Tell me you do, too."

"You know," she breathed, "I think I do." Tenderly, she

lifted his hand, uncurled his fingers, and kissed his abraded palm. Innocent enough, and yet, his trousers grew uncomfortably tight.

"Does it hurt?" she asked.

He grinned. "Feeling better by the minute."

"When I'm with you," she said, "I feel alive too." She placed his hand just above the loose neckline of her chemise, on the tantalizing curve of her breast, and held it there. Her heart pounded beneath his fingertips, echoing the rapid beat of his own. "It's very difficult to resist you."

"Meg," he said earnestly, "I know I shouldn't be here. I charged into your bedchamber uninvited, but I will go right now if you want me to. Just point me to the door."

"You don't care to exit the same way you entered?" she teased, twining her arms around his neck.

He slid his hand beneath her chemise and caressed her breasts. "No, vixen. I want to stay."

"In that case, I think we'd better remove your wet clothes."

Chapter TWENTY

This was madness. Pure, simple, impossibly sweet madness.

Meg shoved Will's jacket off his shoulders. Their arms tangled in a frenzy to remove it—along with his cravat, waistcoat, and shirt. Fabric ripped, buttons rolled across the floor, and garments were abandoned.

Leaving his torso completely bare.

He was a sight to behold, and, Lord help her, she couldn't tear her eyes away if she tried. All lean muscle and raw power, his chest and shoulders flexed as he bent over and tugged off his boots, one at a time. The sinewy strength of his arms made her mouth go dry, but it was his abdomen that mesmerized her. Her fingers itched to touch the fuzzy, flat planes above his waistband and test their hardness.

When he straightened, he wore only his trousers and a triumphant grin. With his dark hair hanging low over his brow and his damp skin glistening in the lamplight, he might have indeed been a marauding Viking or a dragon-slaying knight.

Either way, he was *hers*.

Perhaps not for forever . . . but for tonight.

"Any second thoughts?" His eyes searched hers.

"On the contrary. I fear my thoughts are very . . . wanton."

He released a breath, relieved. "I approve of wanton thoughts, as you well know." He sprawled his body diagonally across the bed and patted the mattress. "Come here."

She climbed up beside him, every nerve tingling with anticipation. "What now?" she asked, perhaps a bit too eagerly.

"Miss Laccy," he said, clucking his tongue. "Have you learned nothing?"

Heat flooded her face. "I think you know that I am still very much a novice."

His low chuckle made her body hum. "I'm referring to a lesson I gave you some time ago."

"*You* gave *me* a lesson?" she asked, incredulous.

"Indeed. I counseled patience, and told you that if you're always in a rush to get to the end, you'll miss all the fun."

Blast, he *had* said that. "That advice was given in an entirely different context," she pointed out.

"You had your context; I had mine. The most valuable lessons can be applied to many aspects of one's life."

"I see," she said, although it was nearly impossible to concentrate on his words when his mouthwateringly handsome, hard body was only inches from hers.

He found the loose string at her neckline and slowly tugged, inch by inch, his hot gaze roving over the swells of her heavy breasts. "It's best not to rush things."

The soft lawn of her chemise grazed the tight peaks, sending a sweet ache straight to her core. "If you say so." It was a relief to surrender control and let someone else take charge for a while. To give herself over to him, completely. She stretched out on the bed beside him. "I promise to be the very picture of patience."

A devilish gleam lit his eyes. "We shall see about that." He dragged her chemise off her shoulders and pushed it down to her waist, then pinned her wrists to the mattress, above her head. "Mine," he breathed. "You are mine."

He bent his head and took the tip of her breast in his mouth, sucking and teasing till she arched her back and moaned, aching from the sheer pleasure of it. He lavished the same attention on the other breast, then looked down at her with heavy-lidded brown eyes.

"I want to explore all of you, Meg. At my leisure. And even though we have all night, I already know that it won't be nearly enough time. I'll never have enough of you."

She melted, falling a little further under his spell. "Let's enjoy each other now," she whispered. "As much as we can."

He dedicated himself completely to pleasing her. With a growl, he wedged a leg between hers and caressed the tops of her thighs, working his way higher and teasing the folds at her entrance until she was dizzy with need. She strained toward him, seeking the glorious release he'd given her in the garden.

"Not so fast, vixen," he said, but he was nearly as breathless as she.

"I want to touch you too." She wriggled her wrists where he still clasped them gently above her head.

He arched a brow as though considering her request. "Maybe we can make a deal."

"A deal?"

"I shall release you, if . . . you remove your chemise."

She was about to point out that her chemise was barely on her but shrugged. "Deal." He let her wrists go, and she began to push the garment over her hips.

"Not like that," he said.

"I beg your pardon?"

"Stand over there, in front of the lamp, so I can see you properly."

Oh. She swallowed. He knew that she would not back down from a challenge. But perhaps she could torture him a little. "Very well."

She pulled her sleeves up onto her shoulders and pushed her hem below her knees, covering as much of herself as she could before she eased herself off the bed.

"I don't think you understand the game," he said, scowling.

"I think I do." She swayed her hips as she walked around the bed, letting her fingertips trail along the edge of the mattress. His hungry gaze tracked her every move.

When she reached the bedside table, she turned the lamp up brighter, fully aware that the thin lawn fabric she wore would be nearly transparent. "How's this?"

He sat up, and his jaw dropped. "Jesus, Meg."

"I shall assume that means you approve."

"God, yes."

"Good." Praying she didn't make an utter fool of herself, she faced him, slipped off her sleeves, and slowly lowered the chemise—over her breasts, belly, hips, and legs—till it puddled at her feet.

For the space of several breaths, he didn't move. His expression dark and unreadable, he devoured her with his eyes. "You are beyond beautiful."

Beyond beautiful. They were the heady sort of words a wallflower didn't dare hope to hear, but he'd said them—to her. Best of all, he looked at her in such a way that she couldn't possibly doubt the truth of them.

He held out a hand to her, and she crawled back onto the bed, kneeling before him.

"You more than fulfilled your end of the deal," he said approvingly.

"You should know," she said, gliding a palm over the hard planes of his chest, "that I intend to take full advantage."

"I would be disappointed if you did not."

She pressed her lips to his shoulder and nipped at his neck while her hands roved over his back, down his sides, and across his abdomen. Every inch of his body was coiled power, taut muscle, and male perfection. She pushed him onto his back and leaned over him, sighing as his light sprinkling of chest hair tickled her breasts.

"I want you, Meg," he said. "More than I've ever wanted anything."

"I want you, too." Dipping her head, she lapped at his flat nipple and smiled when he groaned in response.

"Christ." He rolled her over, pinning her beneath him. She savored the weight of his body on hers and the hard length of his arousal pressed against her hip.

"Who's impatient now?" she teased.

"Guilty." He stood, hauled off his trousers, and pulled her close. Cupping her cheek in his palm, he said, "Are you certain about this?"

"I am." God help her, she was. Women like her— genteel, poor, and plain—were rarely presented with these opportunities. When else would she have the chance to experience passion with a man who made her heart beat wildly every time he looked at her?

With a grateful moan, he pressed his lips to hers and kissed her till she was dazed. He seemed to know just how to please her, and with every touch he brought her closer and closer to the brink. She touched him too, curling her hand around the smooth length of him and stroking until he groaned.

At last, he nudged her legs apart and touched his forehead to hers. "Meg." He spoke her name like a prayer, sacred and true.

She speared her fingers through the damp curls at his nape and wrapped her legs around his hips. "Yes."

He entered her slowly, every muscle in his body quivering with restraint. She pulled him closer and urged him on, for there was no going back. She had already given herself to him.

In her admittedly naïve romantic fantasies, she'd imagined that coupling would be controlled and perfunctory, similar to a sweet, timeless dance. But their joining was *nothing* like that.

It was skin on skin, damp and hot. It was raw power and glorious abandon. It was wildly physical and, at the same time, heartbreakingly intimate.

Nothing existed outside of the two of them. The entire world had boiled down to this—the brief escape and exquisite pleasure they could bring each other. Her whole body and soul, it seemed, were wound up in him.

Every kiss drew her deeper under his spell; every touch drove her nearer to her release. His face was a study of intense concentration, as though pleasing her required his complete focus. But his eyes held a tenderness, too—a softness that shattered the shell around her heart.

"God, you feel good," he whispered, his breath ragged as he moved inside her. "I need you to come for me." He said it like he'd die if she didn't.

"Tell me . . . what to do."

Growling, he rolled over so his back was on the bed. She sat astride his hips, the hard length of him still buried inside her. He took her hand, kissed her palm, and placed it over her breast. "Touch yourself," he commanded, moving her hand in tantalizing circles, "while I touch you."

Good heavens. Heat crawled up her neck. "I don't know if I—"

"It will be pleasurable . . . for both of us." He guided

her, murmuring his encouragement, then let his hands fall away.

She felt terribly brazen and exposed, but she desperately wanted to please him—and herself. Swallowing her embarrassment, she did as he'd asked, lightly squeezing her breasts.

"A fine start," he said. "I think you can do better."

Gathering courage, she smiled. "Very well." She stared at his handsome face as she traced circles on her breasts with her fingertips, teasing the taut peaks until they tingled deliciously. Her wickedness was doubly rewarded when Will moaned in response. He gazed upon her as though she were Aphrodite, sent to earth to torture him.

"Damn it," he cursed, his thin thread of control snapping. He gripped her hip with one hand; with the other, he reached between them and caressed her, finding the most sensitive spot and the source of her pleasure.

It was too much. Her head fell back, the world went black. She was aware only of him, moving inside her, rocking beneath her, and touching her *there*.

"That's it," he breathed. "So. Damn. Good."

She whimpered as the pressure built, spiraling and beating out of control.

And then it took her. Release rolled over her like a storm, awesome and frightening in its intensity—but breathtakingly beautiful. She cried out, and Will was there, holding her as she crested, letting her savor every infinite, fleeting second.

When at last she emerged from the clouds, sated, she blinked at him. "Did you . . . that is . . ."

"Not yet." He flipped her onto her back and cradled her face in his hands. "But I will."

Slowly, he moved inside her, setting up a rhythm that ignited her desire once again. She grasped his arms, thrilling at the way his biceps flexed beneath her hands. With every thrust, he seemed to claim her as his, imprinting himself on her body and heart. She relished the friction of his skin against hers as their bodies collided, faster and harder, till they were both panting, reaching for something together . . .

The crescendo overtook her again, but this time, Will came too. She reveled in the pure power of it, crying out as he pumped one last time, groaned, and rolled off her, catching his seed in his hand.

They laid side by side for several minutes until their breathing had more or less returned to normal.

"How do you feel?" he asked.

"Amazing." Like she'd learned how to fly.

"I knew we would be this way." He kissed the side of her neck, the light stubble on his jaw abrading her skin delightfully.

"What way?" she asked, even as pleasant little tremors echoed through her body.

He stared at the ceiling for a moment as though searching for an answer. "Extraordinary. In every sense of the word."

The compliment warmed her. "I'll fetch you a towel."

On her way to the washstand she stepped over Will's boots, scooped a sheet off of the floor and wrapped it under her arms.

"Forgive me for saying so," he said, "but your bedchamber appears to have been ransacked."

She wrung out the towel over the basin and tossed it to him. "I fear it was. And for once, the twins are not to blame for the mess." Flopping on the bed beside him, she sighed happily. She had no idea how long the glow of their lovemaking would last, but she intended to enjoy it while it did.

With a chuckle, he washed up, returned the towel, and extracted the coverlet from the mountain of clothes on the floor. When he rejoined her, he snapped the bedspread in the air and let it billow down on them, forming their own little cocoon. She snuggled close to him, committing this moment to memory.

Years from now, she'd think back and recall what this night had felt like. He had made her feel beautiful and respected and special. Like he cared for her as more than a childhood friend, or a governess, or a lonely wallflower. In baring herself to him, she'd discovered both a power and vulnerability that she'd never known she possessed.

And no matter what happened tomorrow, that knowledge would change her forever.

Chapter TWENTY-ONE

Will would have given anything to know what Meg was thinking. When he'd climbed through her window a few hours ago, she'd been shaking with rage. And now . . . well, now she seemed content. Blissful, even.

She fit perfectly next to him, her lithe legs twining with his, her hand splayed over his chest. Everything about that night—at least *after* she'd interrogated him about his ex-mistress—had felt right and exhilarating and true. This was unchartered territory.

And it scared the hell out of him.

He wanted nothing so much as to hold her, sleep, and pleasure her once more before morning. But since there was no telling when he'd have the chance to speak with her privately again, and since he'd nearly broken his neck in order to do so, he needed to seize the moment.

"I never told you why I knocked on your door earlier tonight."

She raised her head and arched a brow at him. "When a gentleman knocks on a young woman's door in the middle of the night, it's rather easy to discern his mission. I trust you accomplished yours?"

"Vixen." He ravished her mouth with a kiss, already hungry for her again. "I confess your poor opinion of me is somewhat warranted. However, I really *did* want to speak with you tonight."

"Very well," she said, tracing lazy, swirling patterns on his chest with a fingertip. "You have my undivided attention."

"I wish to apologize for my mother's behavior this afternoon. And for Lady Rebecca's. They had no right to malign you or your uncle."

"No," she said soberly. "They did not."

"I do not know Lady Rebecca well, but I cannot think what possessed my mother to forget her manners."

"I am well aware of my reputation. Your mother and Lady Rebecca simply gave voice to the unkind barbs that others only dare to whisper behind my back. I must give them credit for that."

"They do not deserve any credit at all. But I would like to give them a chance to make amends for their deplorable conduct."

Her finger froze mid-spiral, and she looked up at him, wary. "What do you mean?"

Christ, this wasn't going to be easy. He sat up, and she did the same, leaning against the padded headboard. With the coverlet clutched to her chest and glorious curls tumbling around her shoulders, she was the portrait of sensuality. Damn it, he had to focus.

"I'm hosting a dinner party here, on Thursday evening. My mother and Lady Rebecca will be in attendance."

She stiffened. "The twins and I will be sure to stay out of their way this time."

"You misunderstand. I don't want you to stay out of

sight," he said. "I wish for you to attend the dinner party—as my guest."

"Will, I . . ." She gaped at him as though he'd lost his mind. "I think that would be a *terrible* idea. For many reasons."

"I disagree. Once they have the chance to better know you, they will revise their opinions and realize the error of their ways."

"And I thought *I* was naïve," she muttered.

"You don't believe in giving people second chances?" he asked.

"I don't believe in subjecting myself to unnecessary ridicule," she tossed back, but he was almost certain that her indifference was a mask for hurt.

"I would never permit them to mock you," he said earnestly. "Not under my roof."

"I know. You defended me earlier today." She shot him a wobbly, grateful smile. "But a dinner party is not going to convince your mother and Lady Rebecca to change their opinions of me . . . no matter how much you might wish it to."

He reached for her hand and laced his fingers through hers. "What if I asked you to attend the dinner party on Thursday . . . for me?"

A small, vertical line appeared between her brows, and she swallowed hard. "Why is it so important to you?"

Why, indeed? Because now, more than ever, he wanted a future with her. And if there was to be any chance of that, he needed to know she could mingle with his family and friends and host parties and be comfortable moving about in his world. "I care about you. My mother is the only close family I have left, and for all her faults, I care about her, too. I would like the two of you to get along—or at least be on civil terms."

She stared at him for the space of several heartbeats, then exhaled. "How many guests?"

He smiled. "No more than eight."

"Very well. I cannot believe I'm agreeing to this, but I shall attend, as a favor to you—on one condition."

"And what is that?" He planted a kiss on the inside of her wrist.

"You must invite my friend Charlotte, so that I'll have an ally there—and so that I won't be the only governess at the table."

"Done. I'll invite her and Torrington. You see? That was shockingly easy." And yet she still frowned as though troubled. "What else concerns you?"

"The risk we could be discovered. It's very important," she said slowly, "that no one knows about . . . us. I won't bring shame upon my sisters and uncle."

"Of course you won't."

"I'm quite serious. A mere whisper of scandal could spoil Beth's and Julie's chances to marry well."

"I understand." He pressed his lips to hers, pouring everything he couldn't say into the kiss. *I'm not going to hurt you. I want you for mine, always. Prove to me that this can work.*

When he pulled away, she looked up at him, her eyes dazed and lips swollen. "You are a very shrewd negotiator, Lord Castleton, to convince me to attend a dinner party."

"And you are a fine negotiator yourself, Miss Lacey."

When she leaned in for another kiss, her blanket fell away, and their bodies came together. His hands found her breasts, then cupped the sweet curves of her bottom. Damn if he wasn't hard and ready to bury himself in her again.

"Oh," she said, breaking off the kiss. "I almost forgot. I wanted to tell you something, too."

"Can it wait?" God, she smelled good. He lowered his head, intent on kissing a trail down her belly, all the way to—

"No." She raised his head by the chin. "It cannot."

Damn. "You sounded very much like a governess, just then," he said sullenly.

"I've been practicing." As if she realized she did not have his full attention, she pulled the blanket up to cover herself once more.

Reluctantly, he resigned himself to more conversation. But the sooner they finished, the sooner he could lay her back, spread her legs, and—

"It actually concerns the twins," she said, effectively dousing him with cold water.

"The twins? They seemed well enough this evening. Diana's apology was charming."

"She was very contrite about the tantrum. Afterward, I inquired whether there was any other reason for the outburst, beyond hunger."

"Was there?" He scratched his head. "Let me guess. She and Valerie had a quarrel."

"No." Meg sighed. "I wish it were that simple. Diana confessed that she misses her mother. Valerie does, too."

Will dragged his hands down his face. Of *course* six-year-old girls would miss their mother. "I should have known. In the space of a fortnight, their little lives have been turned upside down."

"Don't blame yourself. The girls are fortunate to have a guardian like you," she said. "But new dresses, trips to the park, and even ice cream can't heal the wounds of being abandoned by a parent."

"No." He knew the feeling. Not that his father had ever left him on a relative's doorstep, but there was more than one way to abandon a child.

"Two nights ago, when we couldn't find Diana, she wasn't only looking for rocks."

His heart sank. "She was trying to find her way home?"

Meg nodded. "When she left the house, she meant to

collect some pebbles, but once she began walking, she thought she would see if she could navigate her way back to her mother's."

Will's chest squeezed. "The poor mite. Lila, my cousin's mistress, lives at least five miles away—in Hackney. Diana never would have made it."

Meg bit her lip, hesitant. "I haven't mentioned anything to the girls, but I thought that perhaps . . . perhaps we could arrange for them to have a visit with their mother." Meg nestled her hand in the crook of his arm. "What do you think?"

"A mother who can't be bothered to care for her children and who threatens to leave them in an orphanage doesn't deserve to see them. I doubt Lila has a single maternal bone in her body."

Meg tilted her head, thoughtful. "That is possible, but it's more likely she simply isn't herself. She could still be grieving for Thomas."

At the mention of Thomas, Will felt the familiar hollow ache in his chest. He let it fill with anger. "It's been six months since he died. And I don't think Lila ever grieved for him. He left her a generous yearly allowance— more than enough to care for her and the girls—but she didn't think she should be required to spend any part of that sum on her daughters."

And that was not the whole of the story. On the day that Lila arrived on his doorstep with the girls, she'd demanded an exorbitant amount from him, saying that it was the least he could do for the girls, who were Thomas's own flesh and blood. Will had refused, for two reasons. First, he would wager his last shilling that she had no intention of using the money to care for the girls. Second, he assumed she was bluffing—that she would never actually leave behind her young twin daughters.

She had not been bluffing.

"That's awful."

"Agreed." As far as Will was concerned, she should be in prison. "Trust me—she doesn't deserve to see them."

"I'm sure you're correct," Meg said softly. "But maybe Valerie and Diana deserve to see *her*."

Will stroked his jaw as he considered this—and the anger drained out of him. Meg was right.

Still, the idea didn't sit well. "A visit could be quite distressing for the twins. If they were to spend an afternoon with their mother, they'd be reminded of all the things they're missing. They'd want to go home."

"I imagine they would. The question is, would Lila let them?"

He snorted. "She would, if it served her own selfish purposes."

But Will did not feel nearly as cavalier as he sounded. The girls *should* be with their mother, but what if she wasn't fit to raise them? In the space of a few short weeks, he'd come to care for the girls—more than he'd ever admit.

"I know you want to protect the girls," Meg said, smiling. "You might even like them a little bit."

"Heathens."

"Yes, well. They're adorable nonetheless. And they happen to like you, too. Diana was terrified that you'd never forgive her for her outburst."

Will winced. "I don't want the girls to ever be terrified of me." Like he'd been terrified of his father.

Meg squeezed his arm. "I only meant that your opinion matters greatly to her. You can be rather intimidating, but I think both she and Valerie know that your bark is worse than your bite."

Attempting a scowl, he said, "Do I intimidate *you*, vixen?"

"Not at all," she said, tossing her hair over her smooth, bare shoulder.

He grinned. "Damn."

"Will you write to Lila, then? And invite her to visit?"

Something in his gut told him that a visit was ill-advised. But Meg's hazel eyes looked so eager and hopeful that it was impossible to deny her.

"I will contact her and extend an invitation," he said. "But I don't think we should say anything to the girls about it just yet. If she declines, it could well devastate them."

"Thank you." She slipped her arms about his neck and nuzzled his cheek.

"You know, if Lila does deign to make an appearance, it will complicate everything. The girls could have some difficult decisions to make."

"That is true. But at least the decision will be theirs. They are strong."

"I confess I never really stopped to think how much they've been through in the past several months. They lost their father, were abandoned by their mother, and were uprooted from their home." He kissed the top of Meg's head. "I guess you can empathize with them better than anyone."

Meg nodded. "I was fortunate to have my sisters, and Diana and Valerie are lucky to have each other. They're going to be fine. We *all* are," she said with a yawn.

As long as Meg's sweetly curved body was pressed against his side, sleep was the furthest thing from his mind. But he supposed he could let her rest a little while before they enjoyed each other again.

He turned down the lamp and held her close, wishing he felt as optimistic as she. But he couldn't stop worrying about Lila, the twins, and the man who'd interrogated Marina . . . and about how they might all be connected.

Chapter TWENTY-TWO

Meg sat on a blanket in the shade of a tree, across from Charlotte. They'd decided to meet at Hyde Park once more so that the twins could play with Abigail. Harry—the footman Will had designated as their bodyguard—played on the lawn with the three girls, showing them how to roll a hoop to each other. When Harry tossed the hoop into the air, spun on his boot heel, and caught the hoop in one hand, the girls squealed with delight.

It was good to hear them laugh. And after the momentous night she'd spent with Will, Meg had simply had to escape the house. It wasn't that she regretted her actions, but more that she required time and space to determine what it had all meant. She rather thought she knew what the night had meant to *her*, but what, precisely, had it meant to Will?

And while Meg had no intention of discussing last night's events with her friend, they had many other topics to cover—not the least of which was the impending dinner party.

"I wondered if I might borrow one of your gowns."

Charlotte smiled at Meg's question, not bothering to hide her surprise. "Of course you may borrow a dress—any time you wish." She leaned forward, her blue eyes sparkling with curiosity. "May I ask what the occasion is?"

"Will, er, Lord Castleton is hosting a dinner party on Thursday. He intends to invite you and Lord Torrington as well."

Charlotte pressed a hand to her chest. "*Me*? How very odd."

Meg shrugged innocently. "The earl and Lord Torrington are good friends, as you know. Perhaps Lord Torrington suggested it."

"That is possible." Charlotte cast a sideways glance at her. "Were *you* surprised to receive an invitation?"

"I was," Meg said truthfully. "I suppose he needed me in order to even out the numbers," she added, less truthfully.

"Whatever the reason, I am delighted." Charlotte tapped a slender finger to her cheek and let her assessing gaze rove over Meg, from head to toe. "I'm thinking the green silk for you. It will look lovely with your eyes."

Meg shook her head vigorously. "No. That's too elegant. I don't require anything so fancy—just something a bit more suitable than . . ." She looked down at her plain brown dress and let it finish her sentence for her.

The sole reason she'd decided to borrow a gown at all was so that she wouldn't embarrass Will. Of course, no one at the dinner party would know they were involved, but appearances mattered to him. Besides, facing Lady Castleton and Lady Rebecca would be slightly easier if she wore a pretty dress—a sort of armor against their cruel barbs and critical stares.

"What about my blue muslin? It's more of a day gown, but very flattering. And we could switch out the blue sash with white satin to dress it up a bit."

Meg wanted to hug Charlotte but settled for squeezing her hand. "That sounds perfect. I don't know how to thank you."

"Don't be silly. Seeing you in it will be thanks enough. I'll ask a footman to deliver it to you tomorrow. Imagine—*us*, at a dinner party together. What great fun!"

Charlotte's enthusiasm could not quite overcome Meg's dread, but she did feel better knowing that her friend would be there. The epitome of grace and beauty, Charlotte handled social situations with the ease of a duchess. Even Lady Castleton would be hard-pressed to find a flaw in Charlotte's manners.

They watched the girls chase the hoop across the lawn, cheering when they caught it before it slowed and toppled. Meg sighed, feeling lighter than she had in days. Maybe even years.

Charlotte reached into her basket and offered Meg an apple.

"Thank you." She bit into it, laughing when juice trickled down her chin.

"May I ask you something?" Charlotte spoke softly, sounding alarms in Meg's head.

She choked down the bite of apple. "Of course."

"Why did you inquire about the earl's ex-mistress yesterday? Did she visit Castleton House? Or confront you somewhere else?"

"No. We've not met." Meg didn't like being circumspect with her friend, but it was hard to discuss Marina without revealing her feelings for Will—feelings that she herself was still trying to sort out. "I happened to overhear the name and was curious. Thank you for answering me so quickly."

"You know you can count on me, no matter what you need." As though Charlotte sensed that Meg wished to change the subject, she added, "Which reminds me . . . how are the plans for Uncle Alistair's ball progressing?"

Dear God. At the mere mention of the word ball, panic surged through Meg. "It's not a *ball* so much as . . . a *soiree*."

Charlotte arched a skeptical brow. "I see."

"In any event, I cannot think of that looming debacle right now. First, I must survive the dinner party." And the next few weeks of governessing. With a little luck, perhaps the twins would have their wish and be reunited with their mother . . . and then she could return home in time to rein in Uncle Alistair's plans.

Maybe once she'd dealt with all *those* problems she could figure out where she stood with Will and whether they had any sort of a future together.

"I feel obliged to point out," Charlotte said teasingly, "that most young ladies look forward to dinner parties. And in our case, we happen to know that at least two handsome men will be in attendance."

Meg rolled her eyes. "Catching the eye of a handsome man is far too lofty a goal for me. I am merely trying to survive the evening without embarrassing myself."

Charlotte tossed her pretty dark curls and grinned. "How positively boring."

"Oh, I doubt it will be that."

Will laid the newspaper on the dining-room table, too pre-occupied to care about either the latest maneuverings of Parliament or the latest episodes of scandal. He picked at his dinner, wondering how to best convince his stubborn governess that she wanted to be his countess.

He had been doing a hell of a lot of thinking since he sneaked out of Meg's room in the pre-dawn hours that morning. And what he thought was that he had to tread very, very carefully. No one in the household seemed to suspect that he'd spent the night with her, but it would only take one slip-up—an overheard whisper or an indiscreet glance—to jeopardize her reputation.

He would not take unnecessary risks where she was concerned, even if he *did* wish to take her to his bed and keep her there for a week.

Having her so close throughout the day but being unable to touch her was driving him mad. And while he meant to make her his, he knew better than to demand it or treat it as a foregone conclusion. That strategy had not served him well the first time he'd proposed to her.

No, Meg had to think it was *her* idea. Even if it was not.

Hell, he'd had to pull out every stop just to convince her to attend a dinner party. Persuading her to marry him was bound to be considerably more difficult.

The problem was that she had far too many distractions right now—ones he intended to eliminate. First, he needed to find a way to help her Uncle and sisters out of their dire financial straits without offending their pride—which the entire family apparently had in spades.

Second, he needed to settle the twins in the best possible situation for them—whether that was there with him or in Hackney with their mother. Either way, it was essential that they were well cared for. He'd made a vow to Thomas. But this was not solely about fulfilling the promise to his friend. It was about Valerie and Diana.

He'd just set aside his plate when he heard Meg and the twins chatting outside the dining room. Unable to resist the chance to see Meg, he met them near the staircase.

"Good evening, Miss Lacey." She spun around and the girls followed suit.

"My lord," she said, blushing prettily as she dipped a curtsey. The twins watched her and tried to mimic the motion; both nearly toppled over before Meg caught them by their hands. "We shall have to practice that," she murmured, as though adding it to a mental list.

He examined the twins' faces, grateful for Diana's distinguishing dimple, and greeted each of them by name. Meg raised her brows, clearly impressed.

"We were just going upstairs so the girls could prepare for their baths," she said a little breathlessly.

Will frowned. He didn't think most governesses oversaw bath time as well as lessons and shopping and trips to the park. Meg hardly had a moment to herself—which meant she hardly had a moment to spare for *him*.

"I won't keep you," he said. "However I had hoped to schedule a meeting with you. I have plans at my club this evening, but perhaps tomorrow afternoon?"

"Certainly, my lord." The soft look in her eyes made his heart beat faster.

Valerie tugged on her arm, pulling her close enough to speak in her ear. "Are you in trouble with Lord Castleton?" she asked in a stage whisper that could easily have been heard across a theater.

"I might be," Meg whispered back. "But I'm not worried." As she bustled the girls up the stairs, she smiled at Will over her shoulder. "Good night."

"Good night, ladies," he replied formally, causing a chorus of giggles.

He watched the gentle sway of Meg's hips until she was out of sight, trying to remember if *he'd* ever had a bath prepared by someone as lovely as her. But his own nanny had been three times Meg's size and sixty years old if she was a day.

And then the realization hit him. What the twins needed was a *nanny*. Someone to lighten Meg's load. Or, in the event that they returned home to live with their mother, someone to care for them there. He would pay the woman's salary, regardless, and have some peace of mind, knowing the girls were in good hands.

It was the perfect plan. And if he was able to find someone soon, she could watch over the girls on Thursday evening while Meg enjoyed herself at the dinner party.

Hiring a nanny shouldn't prove too difficult. He was tempted to solicit help from Meg when it came to interviewing and screening candidates, but the last thing she needed was another duty to add to her list. No, he'd take care of this on his own—and surprise her.

Meg propped her head on her hand and stifled a yawn, determined to finish tomorrow's history lesson on Mary Queen of Scots. She was close to done—just a murder, a third husband and a beheading to cover. She'd worried that the accounts might be too gory for the twins, but Charlotte had assured her that there was nothing like a little blood to hold children's attention. Meg wished it could hold hers, because on the other side of the room, her soft bed and its plump pillows beckoned like a siren.

"I thought I might find you still awake." Mrs. Lundy walked into Meg's bedchamber and handed her a parcel wrapped in brown paper. "This arrived for you just after dinner. I didn't have a chance to bring it up until now."

Charlotte's dress. Meg could hardly wait to try it on. "Thank you. You didn't have to do that."

The housekeeper's critical gaze swept over Meg's face, no doubt lingering on the dark smudges beneath her eyes. "You've made enough trips up and down the stairs today. I suggest you retire for the evening—and soon."

"Yes, ma'am," Meg replied with a smile.

But as soon as Mrs. Lundy said good night, Meg closed her door and tore open the package.

A cheery shade of blue peeked out from beneath the brown paper, instantly brightening the room. And though the muslin wasn't as fancy as silk or satin, it was finer than anything she owned, including the brown wool monstrosity she now wore.

She hauled off her old dress and held Charlotte's beneath her chin, letting the petal-soft fabric cascade down her legs and lap at her ankles.

The length seemed about right, but there was no way to know whether the gown would suit her until she tried it on. Why, then, was she suddenly reluctant to do so?

She swallowed. Abandoning her drab wardrobe was akin to shedding a shabby but comfortable skin. What if fine clothes made her look foolish or pretentious or absurd? In her old gowns, she expected to be mocked. But those dowdy dresses had one distinct advantage. If members of the ton did not embrace her, it was easy to lay the blame with her wardrobe. Charlotte's gown would provide no such excuse.

Shrugging off her anxiety, she slipped the sky-blue muslin over her head, secured the pristine white sash beneath her breasts, and spun to face the full-length looking glass.

Good heavens.

At first glance, she resembled the fashionable ladies she saw strolling in the park—the ones who regularly shunned her or, worse, acted as though she were invisible. So much so, that she resented herself for a moment.

But it was *her*. Her legs beneath yards of gauzy muslin. Her breasts framed by the low square neckline. Her arms revealed by the tiny puffs of sleeves. She twirled in front of the mirror, mesmerized by the way the fabric floated about her body.

It made her feel beautiful in spite of her dark circles and mussed hair and bare feet.

Chapter TWENTY-THREE

Will strolled toward the nursery, hoping that his visit coincided with the twins' naps. Finding the door slightly ajar, he peeked in, happy to see the twins tucked in their beds, if not asleep. Meg sat on the edge of Valerie's bed, gently stroking her hair.

"How long was she in prison?" the girl whispered.

"Eighteen years."

Valerie gasped. "That's almost as long as you've been alive."

"True," Meg whispered.

"And then they . . . ?"

Meg nodded soberly. "Yes."

"How did they do it?" Diana asked from her bed.

Meg hesitated a moment. "An axe."

"Oh," said both girls, properly awed.

Meg closed her eyes briefly and shook her head as though scolding herself. "I fear that was not the best bedtime story. But you needn't worry—England is a much more civilized place in the nineteenth century than it was

God bless Charlotte for lending her this gown and for guessing it would be perfect. Thanks to her thoughtful friend, Meg found herself almost looking forward to the dinner party—and in particular, Will's expression when he saw her in this gown.

That alone might make the evening worthwhile.

back then." She planted a kiss on Valerie's forehead, then glided to Diana's side and kissed her as well.

"If I had a cousin, I would never throw her in prison," Valerie said, yawning.

"I might," Diana confessed, "but I would visit her."

"I've no doubt you would. Rest your eyes, now," Meg said, "and we'll talk more about it this afternoon."

Will may not have known much about children, but he knew better than to dare venture into the nursery at this critical juncture. Instead, he watched from the corridor as Meg quietly drew the curtains, straightened her papers, and placed Valerie's doll in the crook of her arm. When at last she walked toward the door and him, Will waved, startling her.

She pressed a hand to her chest but smiled as she closed the door behind her. "I didn't know you were here."

"But you're glad I am?" he provided helpfully.

"I might be," she admitted.

"I consider this marked progress." He took her hand, turned it over, and kissed her palm. "I missed you last night."

Her cheeks turned a fetching shade of pink. "I confess I slept like a rock."

"I thought you might need your rest. That's why I went to my club. If I'd been here, I would have been unable to resist knocking on your door."

Arching a brow, she said, "My door? How positively ordinary."

"You prefer the window then?"

She shrugged, unimpressed. "That's been done. Perhaps next time you could try the chimney."

"It might be messy." He cupped her cheek and brushed a thumb across her lower lip. "But you'd be worth it. Shall I come tonight?" His heart pounded as he awaited her answer.

"I don't think that's wise." Her face clouded with regret, she glanced down the corridor. "We were very lucky not to be discovered last time."

Will tamped down his disappointment. "I agree we must be cautious. But you cannot blame me for trying."

"No." She squeezed his hand, instantly heating his blood. "Thank you for understanding."

"How are you?" He really wanted to ask if she thought about him half as much as he thought about her.

"I'm well. And the twins seem to be doing better, too. Diana's still a little quieter than usual."

"You say that as though it's a bad thing," he teased, but it concerned him as well. "I wrote to Lila this morning." It had taken him a damned hour to compose a letter that struck just the right tone, splitting the difference between barely civil and friendly. He'd made it clear that the twins were not pawns to be used for her personal gain and that he wouldn't allow her to hurt them again.

"Thank you." She beamed at him, making the whole letter-writing exercise worth it. "I'm nervous that she won't respond . . . and equally worried that she will."

"Whatever happens, we will make sure Diana and Valerie are well cared for. They're strong girls—not unlike you and your sisters." He pulled her into a light embrace, savoring the feel of her in his arms. "The dinner party is tomorrow night."

"I haven't forgotten."

"But you'd like to."

She shot him an impish grin. "I've resigned myself to going, and at least Charlotte will be there."

"You're fortunate I'm not easily offended, vixen." He nudged her toward the wall, pressed her back against it, and braced his arms on either side of her head. "I want you to think very carefully. Is there anyone beside Charlotte you look forward to seeing?"

"Well . . ."

While she pretended to consider the question, he kissed the side of her neck. God, she tasted good. Like vanilla and cream.

"Do you have an answer yet?" he murmured against her warm skin.

"Hmm . . ."

He wedged his leg between hers and leaned into her hips, loving the way her breathing quickened in response.

"Will." She speared her fingers through his hair and pulled him down for a kiss that made his head spin.

Jesus. He was trying to listen for anyone who might be coming down the corridor, but the truth was, as long as Meg was kissing him, a parade could march right by and he'd be none the wiser. Desperate to quench the desire that engulfed them, he swept his hands down her sides, over her hips, and beneath her bottom, rocking against her until she moaned.

"You are mine," he breathed. "Now. Always."

She pulled back and blinked up at him. "What does that mean?"

"We will discuss it. Soon. For now, all you need to do is trust me. And endeavor to enjoy yourself at the dinner party tomorrow night." He brushed a loose curl away off her cheek and tucked it behind her ear.

"I will try," she said doubtfully.

"I think you'll be pleasantly surprised." It was all he could do not to give the surprise away.

He'd wanted to do something special for her in advance of the dinner party. Something that would let her know how much she meant to him and boost her confidence. His first thought had been to purchase her a new gown. But they'd sparred about her wardrobe on several occasions before. He'd invariably lost. Besides, he didn't give a damn what she wore as long as it eventually ended up on the floor of his bedchamber.

No, Meg didn't want a new dress from him; what she wanted was a *gesture*.

And Will had thought of one. Everything was arranged, and he couldn't wait to see her reaction tomorrow night.

In the meantime, he had scheduled interviews with two potential nannies for later that afternoon. Both women came with excellent references, and he hoped one would have the right temperament for Diana and Valerie. If she could start tomorrow, all the better.

Meg narrowed her eyes. "Why do you look as though you're plotting something?"

"Because I am." He nibbled on her lower lip.

"Dare I ask what?"

"Simple. How to get you into my bed."

Meg had devised a strategy to keep the twins in the nursery and out of trouble during the dinner party that evening. The first step was to exhaust the girls through a series of lessons, outings, and games. The second step was to allow them to forego nap time. With a bit of good fortune, they would voluntarily dive into their beds an hour before their bedtime and sleep soundly through the night.

Alas, the plan went awry.

With barely an hour to go before the dinner-party guests were scheduled to arrive, the twins displayed no signs of fatigue. None. In spite of the day's grueling schedule, the girls bounced around the nursery, full of energy and brimming with questions. And the only one exhausted was Meg.

"Will there be any dukes at the dinner party?" Diana asked.

Heaven forfend. "I don't think so."

Diana's shoulders slumped. "Drat. I should have liked to meet a duke."

Meg wiped a sleeve across her forehead as she turned down the girls' beds in a most-likely futile effort to make them appear inviting. "As I've already explained—several times—you shall not meet any of the guests this evening because you'll be *sleeping*."

Valerie spun around on her heels in an apparent attempt to make herself dizzy. "What if I'm not able to fall asleep?"

"I feel certain that you shall fall asleep quickly," Meg replied, placing all her hopes on the power of suggestion. She narrowed her eyes at Diana, who leaned back in her chair as though trying to balance it on the back two legs. "Please don't do that—I don't want you to fall."

"Will there be dancing?" Diana's chair rocked forward, thumping on the floor. "And who would you most like to dance with?"

Meg shook her head as she began moving about the nursery, picking up dolls, ribbons, and assorted toys. "No music or dancing. It's only a simple dinner party—not a ball." Something she'd do well to remind herself. Her nervousness was entirely out of proportion to the event.

Valerie stopped spinning and began staggering like she'd drunk three pints of ale. Heading directly toward Diana, who once again balanced precariously on the hind legs of her chair.

Meg's fingers tingled with fear. "Careful, Val!"

But it was too late. Valerie's arm brushed Diana's shoulder, and the chair toppled over, taking both girls with it. Diana let out a blood-curdling scream and Valerie began to wail. Meg dropped her armful of toys and rushed to the girls.

Diana was sprawled on the floor, gasping dramatically. "Where does it hurt?" Meg asked.

"*E-e-everywhere!*"

Meg scanned the carpet for blood, relieved to find none. "Did you hit your head?"

"M-m-my back."

Valerie rocked on her bottom, sobbing. "I'm sorry. I didn't mean to."

"Of course you didn't, darling."

Diana sat up and pointed a finger at her sister. "She knocked me over!"

The accusation provoked a fresh round of tears from Valerie; however, Meg was relieved to see Diana sitting. For she was fairly certain that a child with a broken neck wouldn't have been able to sit. But then, what did she know?

She ran a hand up and down Diana's back, hoping to soothe her. At the same time, she hugged Valerie, whose sobs had turned to body-racking hiccups.

"Shh," murmured Meg, huddling the girls together. "We all had a bit of a fright, but you're both fine. I think."

The sound of a throat clearing startled their trio, causing all three of them to look toward the nursery door.

It was the earl, of course, already dressed for dinner in a midnight blue jacket and cerulean waistcoat. He scanned the room, his gaze lingering on the scattered toys, the toppled chair, and the twins' tear-stained faces. "I see today's lessons are going well."

He was, no doubt, teasing; however, at that particular moment, Meg failed to find a smidgen of humor in the quip. In fact, she longed to throttle him with his pristine cravat.

"It's going swimmingly," she snapped. "We've just concluded a physics lesson in which we demonstrated the unintended effects of gravity on an object. Or a person."

Diana crossed her arms. "I *detest* gravity!"

"I'm afraid it's here to stay," Will said, oh so helpfully.

Meg rose to her feet and heaved a sigh as she faced him. "We apologize for the commotion and did not mean to alarm the household. Now, if you'll excuse us, I have much to do and less than an hour in which to accomplish it."

He shoved his hands in his pockets and rocked on his heels smugly. "That's why I'm here, actually."

She raised a brow and shot a pointed look at his vexingly lint-free trousers and polished boots. "You're here to *help*?"

"Er, not directly. But I have brought reinforcements. Allow me to introduce Mrs. Hopwood." He waved an arm at the doorway, and a petite, older woman wearing a cap over her bright red hair toddled into the room, beaming as though she found the combination of unruly children and wrecked nurseries utterly charming.

Will smiled, inordinately pleased with himself. "Mrs. Hopwood is the twins' new nanny."

Chapter TWENTY-FOUR

Meg blinked. She must have misunderstood. "Nanny?"

"I hired her this afternoon, and she was kind enough to agree to start right away," Will declared, like it was cause for great celebration. "I thought you'd be better able to enjoy yourself downstairs this evening if you weren't worried about the girls."

No, instead she'd be worried about the strange woman who was upstairs in the nursery with the twins.

Valerie screwed up her face. "What do we need a nanny for? We have Miss Lacey." Meg's thoughts, precisely, but she located her manners and extended her hand to the woman. "Welcome. It's a pleasure to meet you, Mrs. Hopwood. This is Diana." She patted the girl's mop of hair. "And this is Valerie," she said, repeating the gesture.

"The pleasure is mine, dearies."

"Miss Lacey is your *governess*," Will told the twins. "She is here to assist you in your studies, not see to your every need."

"We like how she sees to our needs," Diana pouted.

"I am sure you do," Will said sternly, "but she isn't your

personal maid. Neither is Mrs. Hopwood, for that matter."
He pointed to the scattered toys. "Tidy the room now. You
may become acquainted with Mrs. Hopwood when you are
done."

The girls jumped to the task with an urgency that made
Meg resent Will a little. Beginner's luck.

"Please forgive all the chaos," Meg said to the nanny.
"We were not expecting visitors to the nursery." The
woman's sympathetic look said they both knew advance
notice would not have made a whit of difference.

"No worries at all." Mrs. Hopwood waved a plump
hand. "Children should not be required to comport themselves like miniature adults. I believe in allowing them to
play and explore—within reason of course."

Meg nodded. She had never paused to consider her personal philosophy regarding the best way to raise children,
but if she had, she might have arrived at the same conclusion. She had to admit Mrs. Hopwood was a likable sort.
Even the smattering of freckles across her nose lent her a
merry look.

But that didn't excuse Will from springing the news on
her like this. He should have consulted her on something
so important—especially since it involved the twins.

"Mrs. Hopwood comes highly recommended. In her
previous position, she cared for six siblings under the age
of twelve."

"Six?" Meg tried to imagine being responsible for half
a dozen children and began to feel faint just thinking
about it.

As though she'd read Meg's mind, Mrs. Hopwood
leaned in and whispered conspiratorially, "The trick is
training the older children to look after the wee ones. Most
of the time I was left with nothing to do but my needlework." She laughed and planted her hands on her round
hips. "Lord Castleton tells me you're attending the dinner

party this evening. You should go and make yourself ready. Do not worry—I have the girls in hand."

"I don't know . . ."

"Yes, Miss Lacey, go." Will placed a hand on the small of her back and guided her toward the door. "In honor of Mrs. Hopwood's first day here, I've asked Cook to send up a treat for her and the girls."

"That's . . . nice." But Meg couldn't help feeling like she was being pushed aside. She hadn't even said goodnight to Valerie and Diana.

They didn't seem overly concerned, however. At the earl's mention of a treat they'd begun cleaning even faster. No, they didn't give her a second thought.

Meg hesitated at the doorway. "I suppose I'll see the twins in the morning, then."

"Yes, of course," Mrs. Hopwood said. "But you mustn't wake early. I'll see to their breakfast, and then perhaps we'll take a brisk walk before they begin their lessons."

It seemed Meg's duties had suddenly reduced by half. Any normal governess would have been ecstatic. But she thrived on being busy. It kept her from having to think about Uncle Alistair's mounting debt, her sisters' precarious plight, and her own bleak future.

Will gave her a knee-melting smile and a pointed look. "I look forward to seeing you downstairs shortly, Miss Lacey. We're gathering in the drawing room for drinks at eight."

Good heavens. She had less than a half hour to dress and mentally prepare herself to face Lady Castleton. Meg nodded and hurried to her bedchamber, glad she'd had the foresight to lay out Charlotte's dress that morning.

She stripped off her dress, washed her face, and brushed her hair till it was a mass of shining curls. If Julie were there, she'd know just how to tame them into a proper hair-style, but Meg would have to settle for a top knot with some loose tendrils, adorned with a white silk ribbon that matched the sash on Charlotte's gown. It took a few attempts to wrap the ribbon and secure it, but Meg had to admit she was pleased with the overall result.

A light dusting of face powder concealed the smudges beneath her eyes, and a bit of blush added a healthy glow to her cheeks. At first glance, no one would guess that she was a harried, sleep-deprived governess.

She glanced at the clock. Ten minutes to dress—more than enough time. She slipped the blue gown over her head, taking extra care not to muss her hair. The muslin skimmed over her skin like a kiss, soft and whisper light, instantly lifting her spirits. She did not feel like a princess, precisely, but rather like a sprite. Magical, spirited, and free.

For once, she approached the mirror with anticipation, eager to see the entire effect. As she laced the gown and tied the sash, she tried to see herself through Lady Rebecca's critical eyes. The dress's soft blue color was feminine without being garish. The low neckline was eye-catching without being vulgar. The lines of the gown were elegant without being ostentatious. Even the uncharitable debutante would be unable to find fault with Meg's appearance this evening.

Better yet, she knew Will would love everything about this gown. The way it clung to her curves and swished about her legs when she walked. The sleeves that constantly threatened to fall off her shoulders and the lace trim that seductively framed the swells of her breasts. She couldn't wait for him to see her in it . . . and perhaps, much later tonight, he could take it off her.

She checked the clock again and took a deep, fortifying breath. Almost time.

No matter what happened that evening, she knew she'd succeeded on at least one count. *No one* could accuse her of being a wallflower.

She stepped into her prettiest pair of slippers, grabbed a shawl, and summoned her courage before heading to the drawing room. Once in the corridor, however, she paused, listening to the sounds coming from the nursery—giggles and humming. The girls were not in bed, obviously, but all seemed to be well. Smiling to herself, she turned to go.

And the nursery door swung open.

Valerie rushed out. "Miss Lacey!" she squealed. "I wanted to say goodn—*Oh*, you look *beautiful*."

Meg's heart squeezed. "Thank you, Val. Are you feeling better?"

"Oh yes. Is that a new gown? You look like . . . like a queen."

"Miss Lacey?" called Diana from inside the nursery. "I want to see!" She burst through the doorway, pushed past Valerie, and tripped on the carpet runner. The teacup in her hands went sailing.

Straight toward Meg.

The cup hit her squarely in the chest. Thick, gooey brown liquid splattered everywhere and dripped down her dress. Chocolate.

No. No, no, no. "Diana!" she cried. "How could you? You've ruined . . ." She breathed through her nose, holding back tears. ". . . everything!"

Dear God. She spun on her heels, strode to her room, and slammed the door behind her. This could not be happening. Not tonight, when she was about to attend the most important dinner party of her life.

Perhaps there was a way to clean the gown. She rushed to the washstand, grabbed a wet cloth, and frantically rubbed at the sticky dark blob.

And only succeeding in smearing it all over her bodice.

She swallowed, willing herself not to cry. All was not lost. She'd take off the dress and soak it properly to remove the chocolate. The fabric was thin and shouldn't take long to dry. Some women dampened their gowns on purpose, didn't they? She would miss drinks before dinner, but it couldn't be helped.

A knock sounded at the door. "Miss Lacey? It's Mrs. Hopwood. I'd like to help. Is there anything I can do?"

Meg bit back the harsh words in her throat. *You might start by not permitting the girls to prance around the house while carrying cups of sticky chocolate.* "No, thank you. I just require some time to repair the damage." She wrestled the dress off her body, but a sleeve caught on her hair, turning her neat top knot into a messy bird's nest.

"The girls are very sorry," the nanny called from the hallway. "So am I."

"Yes, Miss Lacey," piped Diana, on the other side of the door. "I'm sorry I spilled my chocolate on your pretty dress."

Meg plunged the bodice of her gown into her washbasin and counted to three in her mind before she spoke. "I know it was an accident."

"Then you forgive me?"

She dabbed at the spot, and when that proved useless, she scrubbed. Harder than she should have handled the delicate muslin. The water in the basin turned brown, but the stain barely faded. And that was when she *knew*.

Charlotte's dress was ruined, quite beyond repair.

Heart pounding madly, Meg rushed to her armoire, yanked open the doors, and perused the half dozen unfashionable gowns she owned. Russet brown, greyish lilac, faded navy, and other, even less identifiable, shades. Blast, blast, *blast*. What had she hoped to find? It wasn't as though she had a fairy godmother to conjure the gown of her dreams. She slammed the doors, crumpled to the floor, and erupted into tears.

"Miss Lacey?" Diana called again, banging her fist on the door. "Please, please, *please* say you forgive me."

Meg's self-control snapped like a twig. "*Leave. Me. Alone.*"

Diana wailed in response, and Mrs. Hopwood tried to calm the girl as she ushered her away. Meg felt a twinge of guilt, but honestly, was a half hour to herself too much to ask?

She could plead a headache. It would be the easiest way to avoid humiliation. Possibly the only way.

But she couldn't do that to Will. For reasons she didn't fully understand, this night was important to him.

At that very moment, he was probably glancing at the clock, expecting her in the drawing room. And, like it or not, she was going to have to make her grand entrance wearing a dress that would make most kitchen maids turn up their noses.

Chapter TWENTY-FIVE

A quarter of an hour later, Meg was as ready as she could possibly be—which was to say not very ready at all.

She'd decided that her navy dress was the least of all evils, and had coaxed her hair into her usual, simple style. She still felt as though she were on the brink of tears, but most of the red splotches on her face had faded to light pink.

Her belly twisted in knots, she headed for the drawing room. She didn't know what she'd say to Charlotte or how she'd ever repay her for the gown she'd ruined.

But she knew precisely how to deal with Lady Castleton, Lady Rebecca, and the rest of the guests, whoever they might be. She had exactly one weapon in her arsenal, and it was pride. She'd hold her head high—and refuse to let them see her fear or pain.

In her considerable years as a wallflower, this tactic had served her well. She'd perfected the art of acting as though she didn't give a fig what people thought of her. So much so that she'd almost convinced herself she didn't care. *Almost.*

She paused outside the drawing room doors and took a deep breath. The muted, civil tones of adult conversation made her long for the lively, uninhibited ruckus of the nursery. But for the next three hours, she could manage to play the part of a proper young lady—for Will's sake.

She went in and immediately spotted his dark head and broad shoulders among the smattering of guests who'd formed a loose circle around the room's main seating area.

The warm smile he gave her as she approached melted some of her anxiety. "Miss Lacey, I'm delighted you're here." He took her hand and led her into the circle. "Allow me to introduce you to my friend, Torrington." More loudly, he said, "Lord Torrington, this is Miss Margaret Lacey—a friend of Charlotte's and my new governess."

"A pleasure, Miss Lacey." Shorter and stockier than Will, Lord Torrington had an athlete's physique and a poet's eyes. She could easily see why her friend was smitten.

"Charlotte has told me much about you, my lord. I'm delighted to make your acquaintance." She offered him her hand, which he bowed over gallantly, as though he didn't notice her lack of gloves. Her one and only pair had fallen victim to the chocolate.

"I've heard much about you and the twins as well," he said, kindly. "My daughter, Abigail, is fond of them."

"Meg!" Charlotte hurried toward her, leaned in for a hug, and whispered in her ear. "Did you receive the gown?"

She swallowed the lump in her throat. "Yes. I'll explain later."

"You look lovely, as always," her friend assured her.

God bless Charlotte. "Well, you look even lovelier than usual." Her friend's violet satin gown shimmered in the candlelight—a perfect complement to her dark tresses.

As Will talked with Lord Torrington, Meg began the inevitable greetings around the circle, bracing herself for a chillier reception from the other guests. Will's mother, the countess, acknowledged her with a tight smile. Dressed in gold silk and dripping with jewels, she looked as though she might have been attending a ball. Or a meeting with the queen. "Miss Lacey," she sang. "I see you've managed to escape the nursery this evening."

Meg curtsied. "They do let me out from time to time. While I adore the girls, I must confess it's nice to have the chance to converse with adults."

"Without having to shout above the screams of a child in the midst of a tantrum," Lady Rebecca chimed in as she glided over. A vision in white with a light blue shawl and satin sash, she would have been the very picture of innocence, if her gown's neckline had left something— anything at all, really—to the imagination. Meg had to resist the urge to tug it up for her.

"Diana is usually very sweet and charming. I wish you could have met her under different circumstances. You would have seen that she and her sister are delightful girls."

"I'm gratified to hear that, as I've no doubt I shall see them again," Lady Rebecca purred.

Meg knitted her brows. "Oh?"

Lady Castleton's eyes twinkled mischievously. "I suspect Lady Rebecca will be spending a good deal of time here in the upcoming weeks and months."

The younger woman fanned herself with impressive vigor and cast a conspiratorial glance at Will's mother. "I do hope so. Papa would be so pleased, as would I."

Meg's blood boiled, and she bit the inside of her cheek to prevent herself from saying something she'd regret. She couldn't fault Rebecca for setting her cap at Will, but to hear her declare it—in front of his mother no less—while her breasts spilled out of her dress . . . It was too much.

The debutante couldn't know the nature of Meg and Will's relationship—Meg barely knew it herself. But she *did* know that the mere suggestion of a match between

Rebecca and Will made Meg want to do one of two things, both of which were entirely unacceptable.

First, she dearly would have liked to take Rebecca's glass of claret and pour it directly into her cleavage. Barring that, she wanted to drag Will to the center of the room by his cravat and kiss him soundly in front of the entire party—so that there could be no doubt he was *hers*.

But was he?

When they were alone, it certainly seemed so. It was difficult to doubt his feelings for her when his mouth was pressed against her lips and his hands were caressing her body. But here, among his family and friends, it was harder to know where she stood.

Anyone who walked into the room would easily spot her as the outsider. And it was due to more than just her horrid dress.

"Papa," Lady Rebecca said to a tall man with dark brows and an angular face, "allow me to present Lord Castleton's governess, Miss Margaret Lacey. Miss Lacey, my father, the Marquess of Redmere."

"Miss Lacey," the marquess said in a gravelly voice, "it's a pleasure." His discerning gaze roved over her, but once he'd determined that she was no threat to his daughter's marriage ambitions, his shoulders relaxed, and his smile turned easy. "How long have you been in Castleton's employ?"

"Just a fortnight or so. But we have known each other since we were children." Meg couldn't imagine what had possessed her to reveal that bit of history; she supposed she didn't want to be so summarily dismissed as a potential competitor for Will's affections.

"You don't say," the marquess drawled, his interest clearly piqued. He was on the verge of continuing the conversation when the butler cleared his throat and announced that dinner was served.

"Wait," Will said, glancing at the clock on the mantel. "We're expecting one more guest, Gibson. Let's give him another quarter of an hour. If he hasn't arrived by then, we'll proceed to the dining room."

The butler scowled, making no secret what he thought of rescheduling dinner to accommodate a tardy guest. "Very good, my lord," he said with a curt bow.

At least Meg hadn't been the very last person to arrive. She turned her attention back to the marquess, who gestured to the sideboard. "May I pour you a drink, Miss Lacey?"

"That would be lovely." While he applied himself to the task, she took a moment to congratulate herself on managing the introductions quite well. Perhaps the night would not be as wretched as she'd feared.

Lord Redmere handed her a glass of wine and frowned at the drawing-room doorway. She followed his gaze and saw the last, mysterious guest.

Oh no.

"Greetings, all. Please forgive my tardiness. I was unexpectedly dismayed."

"Uncle Alistair?"

"Meg, my dear!" Wisps of white hair wafted above his ears as he toddled over happily and pulled her into a warm hug. "So good of Castleton to invite me to dinner, wasn't it? Capital fellow."

"Yes." She forced a smile for Uncle Alistair's sake. But truly, what could Will have been thinking? Was he trying to make her more of a laughingstock than she already was?

"Julie and Beth send their love. They made me change my jacket three times. How do I look?"

"Very dashing." She kissed his cheek, and he blushed.

"Welcome, Lord Wiltmore." Will shook his hand. "Thank you for joining us. I'd hoped to surprise Miss Lacey . . . and I think we succeeded."

"You certainly did," she said through her teeth.

Will clasped a hand on Uncle Alistair's rounded shoulder. "I regret having to rush you into the dining room when you've only just arrived, but if we aren't seated soon, I'm afraid Gibson's head may explode."

"Gibson?" Uncle Alistair asked, more than a little alarmed.

"Lord Castleton's butler," Meg explained. "He's only jesting."

"Oh, of course."

The incredulous murmurs of the other guests and their pitying stares filled Meg with rage she only barely managed to suppress. Perhaps Uncle Alistair interpreted things a bit literally and occasionally confused his words. He was still one of the most intelligent, generous men she knew, and these shallow people had *no* right to judge him.

Will offered his mother his arm, and the rest of the group began to pair off as well. Lord Redmere escorted his daughter. As it happened, they were the next highest rank, which meant Lady Rebecca—and her impressive décolletage—would be sitting beside Will. The very thought set Meg's teeth on edge.

Lord Torrington offered his arm to Meg. "Would you do me the honor?" She glanced worriedly at Uncle Alistair, but Charlotte was already asking him about his latest project, putting him at ease.

"Thank you." They filed into the dining room and took their seats. Will's mother was on his right. Seated next to her were Lord Torrington and Charlotte. On Will's left were Lady Rebecca, Lord Redmere, and Uncle Alistair. Meg sat at the end of the table, opposite Will, where she would have an excellent view of him as he conversed with the well-endowed debutante.

She took a long draw of her claret and prepared for a trying evening.

"I'd like to make a toast," Will announced, raising his glass. "Forgive me for beginning on a somber note, but as most of you know, when I lost my cousin, Thomas, my life was turned upside down. Lately I've realized, however, all that I have to be grateful for and all that I have to look forward to . . ."

As his voice trailed off, Meg looked down at her plate, afraid to meet his eyes. He was alluding to a future with *her*, she was sure of it. Or maybe she just hoped it.

The wistful, self-satisfied expression on Rebecca's face said she hoped for the same.

Lord Torrington coughed into his hand and arched a sardonic brow. "Do you have some news to share, Castleton? Some big announcement perhaps?"

Rebecca and her father edged forward on their seats. Will's mother stared at him, slack-jawed. Meg held her breath.

Will hesitated. "Not yet."

"Good." Lord Torrington wiped a hand across his brow, feigning relief. "You hosting a dinner party is odd enough. If you were to blindside me with something else, I might well fall off my chair."

"Lord knows we would not want that," Will said dryly, then raised his glass again. "To the future."

Chapter TWENTY-SIX

"Hear, hear," Will's guests murmured, even though they were clearly puzzled by his toast. He didn't give a damn what anyone thought—except Meg. He'd wanted to reassure her, to let her know that he was changing because of her—and trying desperately to meet her in the middle.

He gazed down the long table, wishing she weren't so far away.

She was supposed to be enjoying herself, secure in the knowledge that the twins were in Mrs. Hopwood's capable hands. She was supposed to be delighted by her Uncle's arrival, touched by Will's thoughtful gesture.

But her red-rimmed eyes and anxious expression told him that something was wrong—and that he was most likely to blame.

Even with Charlotte on one side of her and her uncle on the other, she appeared ill at ease. As though she'd rather be anywhere but in his dining room.

"That was a lovely toast," Lady Rebecca cooed. Her breasts were precariously close to spilling out of her dress, but the effect was more ridiculous than seductive. It was a wonder she could converse, much less eat, with her corset tied tightly enough to squeeze up everything north of her navel.

"It's kind of you to say so. It wasn't my most eloquent speech."

"I think I understood it, though. Sometimes the loss of a loved one makes us realize what's truly important in life. It puts everything in perspective. Suddenly, decisions we've been struggling with become clearer."

Will blinked and set down his fork. "Well said."

"I felt much the same way when my mother died two years ago."

"That must have been very difficult for you."

Lady Rebecca nodded thoughtfully. "In the months afterward, though, I realized that we mustn't settle for less than we deserve. And that if we want something badly, it's up to us to pursue it."

Will hazarded a glance at Lady Rebecca's father, on her left. He pretended to be wholly preoccupied with the fish on his plate, but Will suspected he hung on every word of the conversation.

"I agree with the sentiment," Will said slowly. "But sometimes, what we *think* we want is not what's truly best for us."

"True, Lord Castleton. That's something we'd *all* do well to remember."

Good God. Will took a large gulp of wine and turned his attention to the other side of the table. While Alec droned on about the adorable—to him—antics of his daughter, Abigail, Will's mother cast furtive glances at Meg, as if she feared Meg would run off with the silver candlesticks. And as Meg listened to Torrington and Charlotte's tale of how they'd searched for Abigail's white cat in a snowstorm, she grew increasingly pale. She'd barely touched the food on her plate.

He wanted to ask her if she was all right, but he would have had to shout across the table, which was not only the height of bad form, but would have also drawn all eyes to her. And, somehow, he knew Meg wouldn't be pleased.

He couldn't do anything right, damn it.

"Please excuse me for a moment." Meg abruptly pushed back her chair and stood.

Charlotte gasped. "Meg, are you well?"

"Yes, forgive me. I don't want to interrupt your meal."

Will's mother rolled her eyes. "You already have."

Meg regretfully placed her napkin on her chair. "I must see to something but will return shortly." She shot Will a brief but pointed look that begged him not to intervene.

"Certainly," he said, standing quickly, even as he heard his mother clucking her tongue in disgust.

Charlotte appeared as worried as he felt; the rest of the group merely looked bewildered and a bit pitying as Meg rushed from the room, almost colliding with Gibson on her way out.

Why in God's name did she have to make everything so *difficult*? He wasn't asking her to change who she was, but was it too much to ask that she show up to a damned dinner party at the appointed time and remain in her seat throughout the meal? The whole point of this bloody affair was to show his family and friends that she was more than a wallflower.

And to maybe convince her too.

But Will didn't think he'd changed anyone's mind tonight.

Meg's conscience had propelled her from her chair. She couldn't sit and make polite conversation while guilt twisted her belly in knots. Every story that Charlotte told about her charge, Abigail, reminded Meg of Diana and the awful way she'd treated her before she'd come down for the dinner party. She'd been so wrapped up in her own problems that she'd snapped at a six-year old—even when she'd tried to apologize.

Meg had seen the disappointment in Will's eyes as she'd fled the room, and she would eventually have to apologize to him as well. But first, Diana.

She reached the nursery and put her ear to the closed door, for once hoping that the girls were still awake. When she heard Mrs. Hopwood humming softly inside, she released the breath she'd been holding and entered quietly.

The nanny sat in a rocking chair situated between the girls' beds, the lamp beside her burning low. She knitted as she hummed and rocked, and Meg fought a stab of envy. The nursery rarely seemed so peaceful when she was in charge.

Upon seeing her, Mrs. Hopwood froze, concern written plainly upon her face. "My dear," she whispered. "Whatever's the matter? You look very pale. Come sit and let me fetch a cool cloth for your head. It's just the thing when you're overtired."

Meg shook her head, too full of emotion to speak. Mrs. Hopwood's solicitous and caring nature reminded her so much of her mother. Like the nanny, Mama had had a knack for dispensing just the right amount of sympathy while somehow making her believe that everything would work out fine. Meg felt a sudden, raw longing to hug her mother and hear her voice again.

One sleepy head popped up in her bed. "Miss Lacey?"

"Yes, Valerie, it's me. I'm sorry to wake you."

Diana bolted upright, too. "We weren't asleep. Mrs. Hopwood was singing to us."

Meg kissed Valerie's forehead, then sat on the edge of Diana's bed. "I'm glad you're still awake. I wanted to speak with you."

"With me?" Diana's asked, her voice thin and small.

"Yes. I owe you an apology. Earlier, when the chocolate spilled, I shouldn't have raised my voice. I shouldn't have been upset with you."

Diana hung her head. "I don't blame you. I would have been angry with me too. Trouble follows wherever I go. That's what Mama says."

Meg pulled the girl against her side and rubbed her thin shoulder. "No, the chocolate was an accident, and those kinds of things can happen to anyone."

"True," Valerie chimed in thoughtfully. "But they happen to Diana a lot more."

For a moment, nobody spoke. And then Diana giggled. Which caused Valerie to fall into a fit of laughter, and soon, Mrs. Hopwood and Meg were giggling as hard as the girls.

Wiping tears from her eyes, Meg blew out a long breath. "You asked me for forgiveness, but I should be asking *you*. Will you forgive me, please?"

Diana's bottom lip trembled, and she threw her arms around Meg's neck. Valerie hopped off her bed, jumped into Diana's, and latched onto the hug.

"You see?" Mrs. Hopwood said soothingly. "All's as it should be."

Meg sat with them for a while, feeling more at peace than she had all day. When Diana's head grew heavy on Meg's shoulder, she patted her back. "Are you falling asleep?"

She answered with a yawn.

"I'm sleepy too," Valerie admitted. "Would it be all right if I stayed in Diana's bed tonight?"

Meg looked over the girls' heads at the nanny. "That's up to Mrs. Hopwood."

"Oh, I think it would be fine just this once," she said, winking at Meg. "Now *you* should return downstairs."

Meg extracted herself from the twins' embrace, settled

them, and pulled the covers up to their chins. "I suppose I should," she said, not bothering to hide her reluctance.

"Do you feel better?"

"Two stone lighter."

"Then you've done the right thing. Do not be overly concerned with what the guests think. Stay true to yourself."

"Thank you." Meg smiled over her shoulder as she slipped out of the nursery and closed the door behind her. Earlier she'd bemoaned the fact that she had no fairy godmother . . . but perhaps, in a way, she now did.

When she returned to the dining room, she was greeted with varied expressions —concern, relief, disgust, and pity. Taking Mrs. Hopwood's advice, she shrugged off the negativity. "I apologize for leaving in the middle of dinner. I needed to speak to the girls."

Will frowned. "I trust they're well?"

"Yes," she assured him.

"Making the entire episode rather unnecessary," Lady Castleton murmured.

Will ignored his mother and smiled at Meg. "I'm glad you're back in time for the dessert course."

"It's my favorite course." She patted Uncle Alistair's hand and smiled at him. "My uncle's, too."

"That it is," he said jovially. "But a fine gathering such as this is about far more than culinary delights. I am honored, Lord Castleton, that you would think to include me among your redeemed guests."

"I believe you mean to say *esteemed*," Lady Castleton corrected.

"Pardon?" Uncle Alistair's bushy white brows formed a *V*.

Meg glared at Will's mother, then spoke slowly, through her teeth. "I think everyone understood his meaning."

Uncle Alistair scratched his head. "Didn't I say *esteemed*?"

"I believe you did," Charlotte replied, ever loyal.

"In any case," he said, "I'd like to take this opportunity to make an announcement, Castleton. With your provision."

Oh no.

Lady Castleton and Lord Redmere snickered, but Will gave Uncle Alistair an encouraging nod. "Of course. You have the floor."

He blinked as though puzzled, but took a bracing breath and—

Meg had to stop him. "Uncle, I'm sure Lord Castleton's guests would be interested in your latest observations of the moon's movements."

"I'm sure I would *not*," muttered Lord Redmere.

"No, no. I won't be distracted from my purpose, dear Meg." He pushed back his chair, stood, and cleared his throat.

Meg wanted to slink under the table.

Her uncle waved his arms expansively. "I would like all of you to be the first to know, that in honor of my three young and extremely lovely nieces, I intend to host a grand ball."

"How delightful!" Lady Rebecca cried, her breasts jiggling in proportion to her considerable excitement. "A ball!"

Dear God. "It's more of a *soiree*, actually," Meg added quickly.

"And what is the date of this momentous event?" Lady Castleton asked.

"Two weeks from tonight," he said firmly.

A fortnight? It was not nearly enough time. Even a year would have been insufficient. "We'll send out proper invitations with the pertinent details," Meg hurried to add. "We still need to discuss some of the arrangements with my sisters."

"No, no," Uncle Alistair protested. "It's all settled. The ball shall go on, and I humbly request the honor of your pretense."

"I'd love to attend," Charlotte said graciously. "I look forward to it."

"As do I," said Lord Torrington, who could be forgiven for his lack of enthusiasm.

"You may be sure I'll be there." Will said, and the rest of the guests took their cue from him, murmuring their agreement.

"Very good!" Uncle Alistair proclaimed. "I have long wanted to give my nieces a proper introduction into society, and now at last, I shall. There shall be much music, dancing, and reverie."

Meg sighed as Gibson set a dessert dish in front of her. Even orange and lemon ice cream couldn't salvage the disastrous evening.

Chapter TWENTY-SEVEN

Will couldn't wait for the evening to end.

After dinner, he and the other men drank the obligatory glass of port before going through to join the ladies in the drawing room. But shortly after that, Torrington and Charlotte bid their farewells, as did Meg's uncle.

Meg excused herself immediately after, scurrying out of the room as if she were fleeing the Underworld.

Which, Will supposed, made him Hades.

The only poor souls who remained with him were his mother, Lord Redmere, and the scantily clad Lady Rebecca.

As Will poured himself a brandy, his mother glided over and hissed in his ear. "Take her for a turn about the room."

He took a gulp of his drink, then shook his head. "I don't wish to encourage her."

"No one could accuse you of that. You're lucky she hasn't run away screaming after this farce of a dinner party." She narrowed her eyes. "Now, go play the part of a gentleman. Unless you'd like me to make good on my threat of taking up residence here again . . ."

Damn it. "I'm going."

While his mother conversed—and no doubt plotted— with Lord Redmere, Will approached Lady Rebecca, who perched on the settee, delicately sipping her tea. He didn't bother with flattery, preferring to keep the entire encounter as short as possible. "Would you care to walk about the room?"

"I'd be delighted!" She stood, bouncing predictably.

He offered her his arm, and she clung too tightly as they ambled around the perimeter of the drawing room. "Tonight was the first dinner party I've hosted in ages," he admitted. "It didn't go as smoothly as I'd planned."

"It wasn't terrible," Rebecca said, which was about as diplomatic as one could be under the circumstances. "I confess I barely noticed the other guests." Her demure smile and pink cheeks seemed completely incongruent with her revealing neckline.

He attempted to steer the conversation in another direction. "My mother tells me you have a bevy of suitors."

"I do." He respected that she didn't deny it. "And Papa is eager for me to marry one of them."

"But you are not equally enthused?" They paused at the far end of the drawing room and gazed at the moonlit garden. The secluded spot would forever remind him of the night he'd gone there with Meg—when she'd surrendered to desire.

"I wish to have some say in whom I marry, but the group of gentlemen my father deems suitable and the group I find acceptable barely intersect. In fact, there is exactly one man who meets both my father's criteria and mine."

Good God. "When making such a monumental decision, it's best to explore all options—to the extent possible, that is. You may trust your father to know what is best for you."

"And does your mother know what's best for *you*?" she challenged. "Because *she* certainly seems to think I'm a catch."

Will began walking again, guiding Rebecca toward her father as fast as good manners would allow. "I'm sure she does. But I make my own decisions, Lady Rebecca, and my affections are otherwise engaged."

She frowned slightly, as though putting together all the pieces of a puzzle. "I see. And does the lucky lady return your affections?"

"That's a very good question," he said. He was certain that Meg cared for him, but would it be enough? "I wish I knew the answer."

Will said good-bye to the last of his guests, drank a well-deserved glass of brandy in his study, and trudged upstairs to his bedchamber. He'd just shrugged off his jacket and waistcoat when he heard a light knock at the door.

Meg. God, he hoped it was she.

He cracked open the door and spied her in the corridor. Her hair hung in loose waves around her shoulders, begging to be touched. Her faded blue dressing gown revealed the sweet curves of her breasts and hips. "Good evening, Miss Lacey."

She glanced nervously over her shoulder. "May I come in?"

"I don't know if that's wise. It's awfully late and you have lessons to teach in the morning."

"Will, please."

As if he could deny her. He grinned and opened the door wide. "Be my guest."

She rushed passed him, plainly relieved to have avoided detection. But now that she was in his bedchamber, she seemed curious. Barefoot, she padded around the large room, lingering over the small portrait of him and Thomas on his dresser. Eventually, she walked toward the pair of chairs in front of the fireplace. "How was the rest of your evening?"

He crossed his arms. "You should have stayed and seen for yourself."

She winced at the unsubtle barb. "I deserved that. I'm sorry about tonight."

He wanted to understand her, damn it. The dinner party had been an attempt to invite her into his world, his *life*. And it seemed she was rejecting him yet again—albeit in a different way. "Tell me this. Why is something as simple as attending a dinner party so difficult for you?"

Swallowing, she sank into a chair and tucked her feet beneath her. "I don't know. I truly thought tonight would be different. That I might fit in. But then a chocolate splotch ruined Charlotte's dress, and Uncle Alistair bungled three sentences in five minutes, and I was consumed with guilt over the way I'd treated Diana."

Rubbing his head, Will lowered himself into the chair opposite her. He didn't pretend to comprehend all she'd said, but he could read between the lines. "You've had a trying day."

"Extremely."

"And I contributed to your difficulties by inviting your uncle."

"I'm ashamed to admit it, but it would have been easier if he hadn't come." She dropped her head into her hands. "I can't believe I'm saying such a thing about the man who took in me and my sisters. I must be the most horrible, ungrateful person in all the British Empire."

"I can think of a few people worse than you," he said.

"I'd hoped to dissuade Uncle Alistair from hosting the ball, but now that he's publicly announced it, my sisters and I will have no choice but to go through with it." She paused for a moment. "Can I tell you something? Something I've never dared to say aloud—even to my sisters?"

"Go on."

"Sometimes I worry . . . that he's as mad as people say."

The stark fear in her eyes made him choose his next words carefully. "Madness takes a variety of forms and afflicts us all, to some degree. Some may be more skilled at hiding it than others, but none of us is immune. It seems to me that your uncle is a fine gentleman with a generous heart. That's hardly evidence of insanity."

"I suppose that's true. Oh Will, I would defend him with my dying breath. But no matter how well-intentioned he is, there's no denying his tendency to make things . . . complicated."

He propped his elbows on his knees and leaned forward. "I know how much you care about him, and I thought inviting him tonight would make you happy. I'm sorry if I was wrong."

Meg shook her head slowly and sniffled. "You weren't wrong. Seeing him *did* make me happy. But the way some of the other guests treated him . . ."

"Made you angry?"

"And sad."

He reached out, grasped one of her feet, and set it on his lap.

"What are you doing?" she asked, as though appalled.

"Making you feel better."

He kneaded the arch of her foot, and she sighed contentedly. "Oh."

After a minute, some of the tension drained out of her. He tugged lightly on her toes. "How do you like Mrs. Hopwood?"

"She seems very nice—perhaps too nice."

Will arched a brow. "Too nice?"

"I'm afraid the girls will soon prefer her to me." She smiled, but he could see the worry was real.

He reached for her other foot and massaged the heel. "I don't think you have any cause for concern."

"No? Well, you didn't see how harsh I was with Diana earlier."

"I'm certain the little hoyden deserved it."

"Not this time," she said, her expression grim.

"Listen to me." He squeezed her calves firmly, willing her to look into his eyes. "You needn't berate yourself just because you lost your temper with Diana. And you shouldn't feel guilty about your uncle or the ruined dress either. Some things are simply out of our control."

"Doesn't that frighten you?"

He considered the question. "Occasionally. But the way I see it, I could waste a lot of time feeling guilty about things that have happened in the past and even more time worrying about things that might happen in the future. I prefer to spend my time in the present—finding happiness where I can."

Meg let her head roll back against the chair. "I wish I could be like that."

Jesus, she was beautiful. Though her dressing gown was modest, her breasts strained against the thin lawn. Her lips parted as though she, too, had wicked thoughts.

"I think I may be able to help you."

Chapter TWENTY-EIGHT

Will's soulful brown eyes held the promise of passion—and perhaps something else too novel to define.

He tugged lightly on her outstretched feet, set them on the floor, and knelt in front of her. "Untie your dressing gown."

There were a dozen reasons why she should not do as he asked, but she ignored all of them and loosened the sash at her waist. He was right. Guilt and worry had not served her well. Tonight, she needed to be with him, seizing happiness while she could.

Possessively, he peeled open the sides of her dressing gown and growled when he discovered she wore nothing underneath. "Jesus, Meg." He raked a hand through his hair like she'd be the death of him.

He looked at her with undisguised hunger, letting his gaze linger on her bare breasts and the juncture of her thighs. He didn't touch her, but her body tingled like he did.

"You have no idea how much I'm going to enjoy this," he said.

Oh, but she had an inkling. She leaned forward, intending to wrap her arms around his neck, but he clasped her wrists and placed her hands firmly on the arms of the chair. "Keep them here."

She arched a brow at him, but smiled. "Very well."

Nodding approvingly, he pressed her shoulders into the velvet cushions behind her. "Now make yourself comfortable."

Obediently, she shifted on the soft seat, resisting the impulse to cover herself with her dressing gown. The sides of the robe gaped open, exposing everything but her arms and leaving her deliciously vulnerable. Though the room was warm, the peaks of her breasts tightened to hard buds. And as she drank in the sight of Will, her belly flipped in anticipation.

Gone was his formal dinner attire. He still wore trousers, but only a thin lawn shirt covered his torso. The beginnings of a beard darkened his chin, lending him a dangerous air. The dark slash of his brows across his face made him look more pirate than earl.

And though much of the evening had gone very wrong, she had the distinct impression that it was about to take a sharp turn for the better.

His expression intense, he sat back on his heels and gently nudged her knees apart. Heaven help her, he was practically eye level with her . . .

Good Lord. She hadn't forgotten the wicked words he'd whispered to her that night in the garden. Sometimes, while lying in her bed at night, she'd tried to imagine, but the idea was beyond shocking. "Will, I—"

He bent his head and kissed the inside of her thigh. With a tenderness that nearly broke her heart, he looked up at her. "Give me this."

Exhaling slowly, she nodded. She wanted to please him, and she knew he wanted to please her. She may not have fit in at his dinner party, but here, in the privacy of his bed-chamber, they were perfectly attuned.

He seduced her thoroughly, caressing her legs, hips, and bottom as he kissed and licked a path up the inside of her thigh. He murmured naughty words against her flesh, setting her on fire.

Soon, she was gripping the armrests, squirming in her chair, eager to feel the warm pressure of his mouth. He spread her legs farther apart, eased one over his shoulder, and moaned as he bent his head once more. She rocked toward him, just short of begging.

"Meg," he said, as breathless as she. "You're mine."

"Y-yes." She arched her back, desperate for release.

"Say it," he demanded. "Say you're mine."

Her head spinning with desire, she speared her fingers through his hair. "Yes. I'm yours." *Always.*

The first touch of his mouth almost sent her over the edge. He found the rhythm she liked best and did not stop. The sight of him kneeling before her, his dark head between her thighs was somehow both highly erotic and deeply touching. Release barreled toward her, fast and furious, almost frightening in its power.

And then she was gone—a thousand miles above the earth, where only the stars existed. She called out his name as her body convulsed in wave after wave of pleasure until, at last, she drifted to the ground, a feather floating in the wind.

She collapsed on the chair, utterly spent and totally sated. Will scooped her into his arms, carried her to his bed, and laid her gently across the mattress. "This is where you belong," he whispered. "With me."

He covered her with a sheet and kissed her forehead just as her eyelids fluttered shut and she lost the battle to sleep. Jesus, after the day she'd had, she needed to rest. And as long as she was in his bed, he'd never complain.

Hell if he knew where he stood with her, but slowly, he was breaking down her walls. Tonight she'd told him secrets and revealed her feelings—more than ever before. And she'd opened to him physically, too, making at least a dozen of his fantasies come to life.

He longed to claim her publicly, just as he had tonight in private, but he knew better than to pressure her to accept him. As long as he was making steady progress, he intended to stay the course. And if it was still difficult to envision his feisty governess as his future countess, well, he trusted Meg to work with him. To find a way for them to be together.

He hauled off his shirt, kicked off his trousers, and climbed into bed next to her, still painfully aroused—but inexplicably happy.

Meg slept straight through the night, so soundly that if Will hadn't seen the subtle rise and fall of her chest, he might have worried.

He kept a close eye on the clock, and minutes before the servants would begin their chores, he reluctantly caressed her shoulder. "Meg."

She rolled over to face him. In spite of her mussed hair and puffy eyes, he'd never seen a more beautiful sight.

"Oh no." She bolted upright, clutching the sheet to her chest. "What time is it?"

"Not quite morning. But we need to return you to your bedchamber."

Fueled by panic, she had already leapt from the bed and was scooping up her dressing gown.

It killed him that she had to go. "I wish we didn't have to worry about what other people thought."

"I'm afraid we do," she said, grumpily thrusting an arm through the sleeve of her robe. "While I'm sure the ton would be all too happy to ignore *your* libertine behavior, they would gleefully crucify me. And my sisters would suffer for my mistake."

He flinched, all too aware that *he* was her mistake. "I won't allow anyone to speak ill of you."

She scoffed as she cinched the sash at her waist. "Then you should plan on fighting duels by the dozens. I do hope you're a good marksman."

"I am an *excellent* shot." Cautiously, he opened his bedroom door and checked the corridor. All clear. "Come. I'll walk you to your room."

She shook her head. "I'll go alone. It will be easier to devise an explanation in the event I'm caught in the hall wearing my robe."

"You won't be caught," he said soberly, "if you leave right now." He kissed her quickly but soundly and guided her into the corridor. "I shall see you later today."

"Good-bye," she mouthed, the hint of a smile softening the worry in her eyes. Her hips swayed seductively as she glided down the hall, making him seriously question his own judgment in letting her leave his bed, damn it.

But while he'd lain awake all night, he'd thought of at least one thing he could do this morning that would help him pass the time until he saw Meg again. It involved a trip to the attic where his father's old things had been stowed, locked away, and mostly forgotten.

Somewhere in that collection of rusty-hinged trunks, a single priceless item was hidden. And Will intended to find it.

Mrs. Lundy fumbled with the large key ring at her waist, clearly distressed. "It's been an age since anyone's been up here. Shall I have one of the footmen dust off the trunks and take them down to your study?"

"No need," said Will. "I'll go through them here."

The housekeeper frowned as she slipped a black iron

key into the attic door lock. "If I'd known you needed something in this room, I would have sent a maid up to dust, at least."

"I'm certain you and the staff have more pressing matters to attend to. A little dust won't kill me."

Ignoring that bit of blasphemy, Mrs. Lundy swung the door open and sighed in dismay.

The closet-sized room had steeply sloped ceilings and a small round window near the roof peak. Tiny specks floated in the shaft of light that shone above half a dozen stacked chests and boxes.

"Thank you, Mrs. Lundy. That will be all."

She coughed and waved the dust away from her face. "If you're sure. Please let me know if you require anything, anything at all." She hurried off as though the sight of the dirty, cluttered room was simply too much to bear.

In deference to the low ceilings, Will ducked as he entered and dragged one of the sturdier trunks closer to sit on. He shrugged off his jacket, rolled up his shirtsleeves, and stared at the stack of boxes before him.

His father's entire life had been distilled into this sad pile and relegated to a distant corner of the house. After he'd died, servants had packed up his things; neither Will nor his mother had seen to the task themselves because they didn't need keepsakes or mementoes. Didn't want them. They'd just as soon forget the man and the things he'd done.

Will unlatched a large trunk, gripped the lid, and hesitated. Despite the room's stifling heat, a chill stole over him. His father couldn't hurt him from his grave, but rummaging through his personal belongings was sure to conjure memories better left buried. Drunken rants about his lazy, stupid son. The stinging smack of his palm across the face. The disgusted looks he shot across a silent dining table.

Will shook off his apprehension. He was not his father, and certainly not doomed to repeat his mistakes. Of course, he hadn't the slightest clue how a good husband or father should behave, and that scared the hell out of him. He wanted to do the right thing . . . the problem was knowing what the right thing was.

The old earl had been a miserable bastard. But five years had passed since his death, and Will was no longer a fly trapped in his diabolical web. True, he might have sustained a few scars during his youth, but lately he'd felt a glimmer of something unexpected and completely foreign: hope.

Will threw back the lid of the trunk and began examining the contents, determined to find something good in the sorry remnants of his father's existence—for Meg's sake and his own.

Two hours later, sweat dripped from his forehead and dampened his shirt. He leafed through a stack of letters in the second to last trunk, most of them from hard-working estate tenants or poorer relatives begging assistance from his father. Will would bet they'd all gone unanswered.

The next layer in the trunk consisted of his father's old, treasured articles of clothing. He spotted a small, faded blue jacket that his father had worn in a childhood portrait and a powdered wig, the likes of which he hadn't seen in decades.

And then, beneath an assortment of hats, shoes, and boots, Will found it: a large, water-stained satin pouch.

His heart pounding, he loosened the drawstring and spilled the contents onto the dusty floorboards. A collection of snuffboxes tumbled out, but there, in the middle of them, was a small, antique hinged box, inlaid with pearl.

His hands trembled as he opened it.

Nested in folds of velvet, his grandmother's diamond ring sparkled in the light. The diamond was not huge, but it was a fine stone, and any pawnshop would have paid his father a fair price for it.

But the old earl had held on to it. Even when he'd been willing to sell everything in the house that wasn't nailed down, he couldn't bring himself to part with Grandmamma's wedding ring. She had been the best part of their family, showing Will love and kindness when her own son had been unable to.

Meg was like her in many ways. Loyal, generous, and stubborn. Unwilling to bend her principles for anyone, but willing to sacrifice anything for those she cared about.

Will wanted her to wear his grandmother's ring, the ton be damned. All he had to do was convince Meg that, this time, she'd be better off with him than in a convent. But he knew better than to take her agreement for granted.

Now that he'd found what he was looking for, he was eager to leave the stuffy room and maybe pay a visit to the nursery to see Meg and the twins.

Invigorated by his success, he tucked the ring box into his pocket and tossed the snuffboxes and clothes back into the trunk. He threw the stacks of letters on top, but as he did, one of the strings binding them broke, and the letters spilled everywhere. He was tempted to leave them on the floor, but poor Mrs. Lundy had been distraught over the state of the room even before he'd created this additional mess. Cursing to himself, he scooped up handfuls of paper and threw them into the trunk.

And then one particular scrap of paper caught his eye.

Dated nine years ago, it appeared to be a note promising payment of a gambling debt. There was nothing odd about that; his father had written scores of them, and often collected them when—and if—he paid off his debts. But this one was different from the rest. The payee was Mr. Gregory Lacey—Meg's father. And the amount owed was a staggering ten thousand pounds.

Will's fingers went numb. For Gods' sake, how could his father have played so deeply with the local vicar—and lost?

He examined the IOU more closely. Beneath his father's cursive, however, a few lines of unfamiliar handwriting were scrawled:

In lieu of payment of the aforementioned sum, the debtor, Lord Castleton, may arrange for the marriage of his son and heir to my daughter, Miss Margaret Lacey. Upon consummation of the marriage, the debt shall be considered paid.

G.L.

Jesus. *This* was why his father had tried to force him to marry Meg all those years ago. And when her parents had died in that horrible coach accident, his father had not thought it necessary to honor his debt, much less mention it. He'd been content to stand by and watch as Meg and her sisters lost their childhood home. He'd remained silent as they were shipped off to live with their uncle, who could barely support himself.

The discovery of the IOU answered many of Will's long-held questions, but it raised a few, too. Had his mother been aware of the debt? Had the coach accident that killed Meg's parents *really* been an accident? He dragged his hands down his face, unsure he wanted to know the answers.

He'd spent years trying to fix his father's mistakes, but how in hell could he ever begin to repay his father's debt to Meg and her sisters?

Will carefully folded the IOU and tucked it into his pocket next to the ring box. His mother was forever nagging him to visit more often.

Her wish was about to come true.

Chapter TWENTY-NINE

An afternoon jaunt to the park had somehow become an elaborate production, partly due to the size of their party—five, including Meg, the twins, Mrs. Hopwood, and Harry—and partly due to the extravagant picnic that the nanny had suggested they ask Cook to pack. She reasoned that it would be easier for Meg to tell Charlotte about her ruined dress if everyone enjoyed a scone or two. It certainly couldn't hurt.

Meg spread out two large quilts. "Miss Winters and Abigail will be here soon," she told the twins. "Shall we read a book until they come?"

Valerie heaved a sigh. "If we must. But I'd rather play catch with Mr. Harry."

"It's fine with me, Miss Lacey." The footman threw a ball high into the air and easily caught it behind his back, causing the girls to cheer wildly.

"How can I possibly compete with that?" Meg playfully shooed the girls away. "Go, have fun."

"Hooray!" They ran after Harry and the ball like hoydens.

Meg sank onto the blanket, mentally rehearsing what she'd say to Charlotte, while Mrs. Hopwood sat on a nearby bench, plying her needle.

"There they are now," Meg murmured, spying her friend and her young charge strolling down the path.

"Remember," Mrs. Hopwood said sagely, "a dress is only a possession, an object. No matter how beautiful it is—"

"*Was*," Meg corrected.

"—it can't destroy a true friendship."

Several yards away, Charlotte waved cheerfully and pointed Abigail in the direction of Harry and the girls before joining Meg and Mrs. Hopwood.

Meg introduced the nanny, and Charlotte raised her eyebrows. "I didn't realize Lord Castleton was even interviewing for a nanny—how wonderful!"

"He's a decisive sort of gentleman," Mrs. Hopwood mused. "Once he makes his mind up, he acts, which is how it should be, if you ask me." She stood slowly, stretched, and set her needlework in her sewing basket. "I believe I'll stroll for a bit and leave you young ladies to talk. You must have much to discuss after last night's dinner party. I shan't be gone long." Giving Meg an encouraging wink, she toddled off.

"I was so happy to receive your invitation." Charlotte rubbed her hands together eagerly as she plopped herself onto the blanket. "I'm desperate to hear what you thought of the evening."

Meg swallowed hard. "Charlotte, there's something I must tell you. The beautiful gown that you lent to me . . . Blast, there's no easy way to say it. I . . . I ruined it. I'm so sorry. I'll find a way to replace it or reimburse you, I pro—"

"Meg, it's really not—"

"It may take me a while—"

"*Please* do not fret. It's only a dress." Charlotte clasped her hand and gave it a firm squeeze.

"A one-of-a-kind dress. You entrusted it to me, and now it's destroyed." Meg swiped at the tears that threatened.

"Destroyed?" Charlotte repeated, incredulous. "What in heaven's name happened to it?

"There's a stain on the bodice the size of a dinner plate," she choked out. "Chocolate."

"Well, if a gown must be ruined, I can think of no better way than chocolate." She shook her head solemnly, then giggled. "We should all be so lucky."

Meg let out a long breath and smiled, feeling inordinately better. "Honestly, I can't imagine what I did to deserve a wonderful friend like you."

"Like *me*? I'm a horrid person. If you need proof, I was just going to indulge in a nasty bit of gossip about last night."

Bracing herself, Meg asked, "You were?"

"I must confess that I did not care for Lady Rebecca *or* her father a whit. And though it's uncharitable of me to say, it's the truth."

"Oh, Charlotte. If you must know, I adore your uncharitable side."

"Good, for I feel the need to expound on the utter ridiculousness of Lady Rebecca's gown. Honestly, have you ever seen anything so ghastly?"

After returning from the park, Mrs. Hopwood and Meg tucked the girls into their beds for a nap. The nanny settled into her rocking chair, declared she planned to rest her eyes, and suggested that Meg do the same.

A nap sounded heavenly. Meg kissed the girls and headed toward her bedchamber but was intercepted in the corridor by Mrs. Lundy.

"Ah, there you are," the housekeeper said. "The earl wishes to see you in his study. He asked me to give you the message as soon as you'd returned."

Meg's heart did a cartwheel, but she endeavored to look only mildly interested. "Oh? How odd. I shall go at once."

She found him in his study, not sitting behind his desk as she'd expected, but standing near the window, looking much more serious than he had last night. Alarms sounded in her head. She glanced over her shoulder to make sure no one was about. "Will, is everything all right? Mrs. Lundy said you wanted to see me."

He waved her toward a seat and closed the door halfway, giving them some semblance of privacy without flouting convention entirely. He leaned on the corner of his desk, his expression softening. "I always want to see you. I can't stop thinking about last night."

Her face heated. "Nor can I."

"There's much we need to discuss—in another time and place, when we are truly alone."

Meg nodded. She and Will seemed destined to have two distinct relationships—their intimate one in secret, and their distant one in public. It wasn't ideal, but she would rather have those few stolen moments with him than none at all.

"There's another reason we need to talk. This came today." He pulled a folded paper from his jacket pocket and tapped it against his palm. "It's a letter from Lila. She's agreed to come visit the girls . . . tomorrow."

"That's good news." And yet her belly twisted at the mention of the twin's mother. "The girls will be so pleased."

"Do you think so?"

"I do. They miss her, and they should spend time with her. You're doing the right thing by bringing them together."

Will's forehead creased, and if the door hadn't been half open, Meg would have slipped her arms around his waist, pressed her head to his chest, and told him not to worry.

"We haven't a clue how the girls will react to seeing her, or what she'll say to them. Hell, we don't even know if she'll show at the appointed time. I'd hate to tell Diana and Valerie, only to have their hopes dashed in the event she doesn't come."

Meg pressed a finger to her bottom lip as she considered this. "Let's not mention it to them. Mrs. Hopwood and I will make sure the girls are prepared for company. Once Lila arrives, I'll give them the news and they'll be happily surprised."

He nodded his agreement. "I'd like you or Mrs. Hopwood to chaperone the visit—or at least remain within earshot. I know she's their mother, but I don't trust her."

His concern for the girls' welfare warmed Meg's heart. He was not the same callous man who'd interviewed her in this very room just a few weeks ago.

"I'll keep watch," she assured him.

"Good." His gaze flicked to the doorway before returning to her. "I'm afraid I won't see you tonight."

"Oh?" She tried not to let her disappointment show.

"I need to pay a visit to my mother and attend to some other business."

How vexingly vague. "I understand."

"Do you?" he asked, his voice husky. He bent his head close to her neck and his lips brushed the skin just above her collar. "There's *nowhere* I'd rather be than with you. I'd suggest you sleep as much as you can tonight because tomorrow night you'll be very, very busy."

A delicious shiver stole over her. With a few naughty words and the lightest of touches, he'd made her believe she was special.

Had he charmed his ex-mistress the same way? And

what of the countless women who'd no doubt come before her?

One thing was for certain. As much as Meg cared for him, she couldn't go on this way. Every night she spent under his roof tempted fate.

They could be discovered.

She could become pregnant.

Or, she could lose her heart to the one man she had no right to love. To do so would amount to the ultimate betrayal of her parents' memory.

He searched her face like he suspected the direction of her thoughts. "Trust me, Meg." It was both a demand and a plea.

She gave him a weak smile. "I do." It was true. The person she didn't trust was herself.

Chapter THIRTY

"This is ancient history." Will's mother waved a bejeweled hand at the IOU he held. "I see no reason to revisit it."

He glared at her as she sipped tea in her sister's elegant but cluttered drawing room. A man couldn't walk two feet in his aunt's house without bumping into some priceless but useless damned trinket.

"It's important to me," he ground out. "I want the truth. Did you know that an arranged marriage to Miss Lacey was meant to be repayment of a gambling debt?"

"Wasn't her father a vicar?" She knew very well that he had been. "It seems wholly improper for a man of the cloth to indulge in cards."

"Do not attempt to change the subject. Were you aware that my father owed him ten thousand pounds?"

She choked on a sip of tea and pressed a hand to her chest. "Ten thousand?"

"Yes."

"I knew your father owed the vicar a substantial amount . . . but I didn't realize . . ."

Will sat forward, leaning his elbows on his knees. "And

what did he think of Mr. Lacey's proposal that I marry his daughter, Margaret, in order to have the debt forgiven?"

The countess sighed dramatically. "I'm sure he thought to appease the vicar while he devised a way to extract you from the engagement. As it turned out, that wasn't necessary."

Good God. He raked a hand through his hair and stalked across the room, unable to sit politely while she defended his father. "Do you hear yourself, Mother? You speak of the Laceys' accident as though it were some fortunate twist of fate. It's sickening."

"I did not say it was *fortunate*, but it did prevent you from having to marry a stubborn chit too proud for her own good."

"Don't," he warned.

Her pale eyes narrowed. "Don't what? Malign your governess? From what I've witnessed, she's wholly incompetent. I cannot know what you were thinking to hire her."

"Maybe you should ask yourself why she accepted the position."

"I'm not certain I care," she sniffed.

"You should. If your husband—my father—had honored his debt, Miss Lacey and her sisters might not have been forced to leave their home. They certainly wouldn't have found themselves in the precarious position they're in today—poor relations to a elderly uncle who is also in dire financial straits."

She shrugged, raising his ire even further. "Your father was not a saint. Neither are you, incidentally, and it's rather rich to pretend that you are."

"I'm no saint, it's true. But I honor my debts, and I have tried to honor his."

Her powdered face paled. "You cannot mean to pay her the ten thousand pounds."

He snorted. "There is another option."

"William, no." Her fingers fluttered at her throat. "I know I've pressured you to marry, but there's really no need to rush. You are still a young man. You should not be required to pay for your father's mistakes. Not in this way."

"I would not marry Miss Lacey out of a sense of obligation, but rather by choice."

"Do you hear *yourself*, William?" she asked, throwing his words back at him. "You are acting like an infatuated schoolboy. Margaret Lacey is not fit to be the next Countess of Castleton. We both know it. She could not even manage to behave appropriately at a small dinner party. Asking her to step into the role is hardly fair. It's like asking a stray mutt to act as your prize hunting dog."

"I don't like your analogy, Mother," he said, his voice low and lethal. "Have a care."

"Forgive me," she said, her chin trembling. "I only want what's best for you, and I fear that your feelings and actions are being swayed by guilt."

He shook his head. "No, I've always admired Miss Lacey."

"If you care for her," she said cautiously, "there is an option besides marriage. You could make her your mistress and marry someone respectable—someone like Lady Rebecca. If your father were alive today, it's what he would advise."

"If I hadn't already made up my mind, that fact alone would have been enough to dissuade me from that path."

He sat down again, directly across from his mother, and pinned her to the settee with his stare. "I'm going to ask you one more question. I'll only ask it once, and I expect you to answer truthfully."

She raised her chin. "Are you sure you want to know the truth, William?"

No, damn it. He wasn't at all sure. "The carriage accident that took the Laceys' lives—did Father or his agents have anything to do with it?"

His mother recoiled as though he'd slapped her. "What are you implying?"

"I'm asking whether he did anything that led to the accident. Maybe someone loosened the bolts on a wheel or persuaded the driver to take the turn too fast?"

"The bridge was icy," she ground out. "Surely you don't blame your father for the *weather*."

Hell, he didn't know what to think anymore. "Factors besides the weather might have contributed to the danger."

She leaned back onto the settee, too upset to be concerned with good posture, let alone pretense. "Whatever sins your father may have committed, I do not believe him guilty of murder."

Will sighed, relieved to know that his mother, at least, had not been complicit. He would have known if she were lying. "I'm glad to hear it."

"If you are looking for someone to blame for the Laceys' accident, you need look no further than their daughter, your dear Margaret. *She's* the one who cruelly rejected you and forced her parents to brave the treacherous conditions so that they might apologize to us on her behalf. She has no one to blame for her sad situation—no one but herself."

Will stood, clenched his fists, and counted to ten in his head. "You will *not* disparage Miss Lacey in my presence. You will treat her cordially. And if you do not, I will cease to acknowledge you as my mother. I will not acknowledge you at all."

With that, he stormed out of the drawing room, leaving

his aunt's collections of vases, sculptures, and ornaments shivering violently in his wake.

Meg had been on pins and needles all morning, and even Mrs. Hopwood seemed a bit nervous, nearly jumping out of her rocking chair when Valerie toppled a tower of blocks. But Diana and Valerie didn't blink when Meg suggested they wear their pretty new dresses and neatly braid their hair.

And Meg worried about more than Lila's visit with the girls. She had to make a decision about her relationship with Will, soon. She hadn't seen him since the day before, and the longer they were apart, the more she doubted his feelings for her—and her own good judgment. Thankfully, tomorrow was her afternoon off. Spending an evening with Beth and Julie would restore her confidence and give her much-needed perspective.

The twins were practicing their penmanship when Mrs. Lundy popped into the nursery. "Miss Lacey," she said breathlessly, "might I have a word?"

Meg hurried to the corridor and closed the door behind her. "Is she here?"

The housekeeper nodded. "She's waiting for the girls in the drawing room. I told her they might be a few minutes, in case you need time to prepare them."

"Thank you. Does the earl know she's here?"

"Yes, he's speaking with her now, although I do not think he means to stay for her visit. He said something about going out."

"I see. Thank you, Mrs. Lundy."

Meg paused before she returned to the nursery. For the twins' sake, it was important that she handle this calmly. She went to the window seat and called them over. They both threw down their pens and raced for the same spot beside her.

"I was here first," Diana said.

"But that's my seat," Valerie protested.

"Just because you sat here once or twice doesn't make it yours for all eternity."

Goodness. Meg scooted to the middle of the bench and patted the cushions on either side of her. "Both of you, sit."

They flopped themselves down, each of them steaming over the injustice.

"I have some happy news for you," she began, and the girls immediately perked up.

"We're going back to the park?" Valerie bounced on her bottom.

"No."

"To Gunter's?" Diana said, hands clasped beneath her chin.

"No, this is a different sort of surprise." Meg put her arms around them and took a fortifying breath. "Your mother's come to visit you."

"Mama's here?" Diana's face paled.

"Yes, she's waiting for us in the drawing room."

Valerie frowned. "Why?"

"Why has she come to visit?" Meg clarified. "Well, I'm sure she misses you both."

"So it's only to be a visit? We're not going home with her?" Diana asked the question in such a way that Meg couldn't be sure what she was hoping for.

"For now, why don't we assume that you're just having a nice visit? Then we shall see what happens."

"What will we say to her?" Diana asked.

Meg swallowed and looked helplessly at Mrs. Hopwood.

The nanny set her needlework in her lap. "You could tell her about your picnic in the park, and I'm sure she'd love to hear about your new friend, Abigail."

"I could show her my new dress," Valerie said soberly.

"A grand idea," said the nanny.

Diana brightened. "And I could demonstrate how I do my sums."

"She'll be quite impressed," Meg said.

"Will you come, too?" Valerie asked.

"I will," Meg assured her. "I shall be there the entire time. Are you both ready?"

"Yes!" they said, clearly warming to the idea.

Meg painted on a cheerful face. "Then let us go."

Chapter THIRTY-ONE

"My darlings!"

The twins ran into Lila's outstretched arms, embracing her with a raucous mix of laughter, tears, and kisses.

Meg's belly twisted inexplicably. This is what she'd wanted for Diana and Valerie—to be reunited with their mother. Why then, did their sheer joy at seeing her cause a pang in her chest?

"I know it's only been a few weeks, but I would swear you've each grown an inch." Lila's hair was a shade darker gold than her daughters', but just as lovely. "Let me see you. You look so beautiful in your new dresses!"

Will stood on the far side of the drawing room, wearing a brooding expression that made Meg wonder if he felt the same ambivalence she did. While Lila and the twins chatted merrily, she went to him.

"You don't seem pleased," she said.

"Two weeks ago, she abandoned them. Now she's acting like an adoring, devoted mother. I'm not convinced."

"It *is* difficult to understand," Meg said. "But maybe there were extenuating circumstances we're unaware of.

She may have been ill or suffered some crisis that made her temporarily unable to care for the girls."

Will snorted. "You wouldn't have left the girls with a virtual stranger."

"No, but I can't stand in judgment. I have little experience with children and no idea what it's like to be a mother."

"Perhaps not," he said. "And yet, I already know you'll be a wonderful mother. There's no comparison between you and Lila."

Meg blinked at his off-hand remark, not because he assumed that she'd be a good mother, but because he assumed she'd be a mother at all. Which necessarily implied that she'd marry and not end up a spinster dependent on the generosity of a distant relative. So much had changed recently, and she hadn't had time to re-envision her future. But perhaps it *was* possible . . . just not with Will.

She and Will watched as Lila reached into her reticule and withdrew peppermint sticks, which she handed to the girls. "A treat for you."

"Thank you!" Valerie climbed onto her mother's lap and snuggled against her chest.

Diana stared wide-eyed at her candy. "But . . . but it's not even our birthday."

"No, darling," Lila said, laughing. "It's only because I've missed you so."

Cheering, Diana spun in circles, happier than Meg had ever seen her.

Will turned to the window, cursing under his breath.

"What's wrong?"

He hesitated for the space of several breaths. "She wants to take them home."

Meg's heart sank. "For good?"

"Yes. She claims she's been giving the matter a lot of thought and that she's realized she can't live without them. She wants the girls back."

Her throat constricted. "When?"

"Today."

Meg pressed a hand to her belly. "*Today?* But it's so sudden. The girls—"

He discreetly squeezed her hand. "I told her I wanted a chance to discuss it with Diana and Valerie this evening, but that if they wished to go with her, I would allow it. Unless I send word otherwise, she plans to come back for them tomorrow."

Tomorrow. She swayed, but Will steadied her with a hand at the small of her back. "Come, sit."

"No, I'm fine," she insisted.

Frowning, he said, "I asked Lila to let me be the one to tell the girls. Will you help me?"

"Of course." Her head was still spinning, adjusting to the news. No more math problems or history lessons or bedtime stories. No more spontaneous, messy hugs.

"I must go out for a while, but I'd like you and the girls to join me for dinner tonight. We'll tell them then. Hopefully, we'll be able to see from their response whether this is the best course for them. If we have any misgivings, we can delay their departure."

Departure. The word sounded so dismal, so final to her ears. "Yes, that's a fine idea. Diana and Valerie will be excited to dine with you."

"And you," he reminded her.

"Yes."

"Watch Lila closely. I don't want her saying or doing anything to upset the twins."

Meg nodded.

"I'll see you at dinner," he said softly, "and again after the girls are asleep? There's much we have to discuss."

"I'll see you at dinner," she repeated. "And we'll see about after that." She wanted nothing more than to spend the night with him, but she had to begin drawing some lines. On the other hand, if the twins left tomorrow, he would no longer need a governess.

This could well be her last night in Castleton House.

He scowled at her vague response, then leaned close to her ear. "I promise to make it worth your while, vixen," he whispered, leaving her wobbly-kneed as he strode out of the drawing room.

Will's first stop was a modiste's shop teeming with women who pored over fabrics and design books. They parted like the Red Sea as he strode to the counter and addressed the startled shop owner. "I require a nightgown."

"But of course," she said in a predictable French accent. "What sort would you like? Linen or silk? Modest or revealing?"

All questions should be so easy. "Silk. Revealing."

The woman shot him a knowing smile, adjusted her spectacles, and picked up a pen. "I'd be happy to place an order for you."

"I'll need it by this evening," he said.

She fumbled the pen and set it on the counter. "*Mon dieu*. Let me see what I can find for you," she murmured, disappearing into a back room. The five minutes until her return seemed an eternity.

"Here we are," she said, laying a swath of pale blue, shimmering fabric before him. "Satin trimmed in exquisite French lace. It will fit a woman of medium stature. I can assure you she will love it." She leaned forward and lowered her voice. "As will you."

"Send it to Miss Margaret Lacey at this address, please," he said, producing his card.

"Shall I include a note with the nightgown?" the shopkeeper asked.

He shook his head. "She'll know who it's from."

A half hour later, Will's coach rolled to a stop in front

of Marina's flat. Before he'd even reached the door to her building, she emerged, once again wearing a black lace veil. She rushed past him and climbed into his coach, clearly hoping to avoid detection.

He hoped her precautions were in deference to her new beau and not because she feared the strange man who'd pressed her for information about the twins earlier, but the latest note she'd sent Will requesting a meeting had revealed little—only that she had a bit of information to share.

He instructed his driver to circle through the park and around town, then joined his ex-mistress in the coach, settling himself on the bench opposite her.

"Has there been a new development?" he asked.

Slowly and deliberately, she lifted her veil and placed it over her head. "It's nice to see you, too, Will."

Damn it. "Forgive me. You're looking well, Marina. I'm sorry you've somehow become involved in this but grateful that you're keeping me informed. Did the strange gentleman approach you again?"

"My, my." She clucked her tongue. "That was still not the most congenial of greetings. However, what you lack in charm you've always made up for in other ways." She let her sultry gaze slide down his torso.

He had zero interest in flirtation. "You and your new beau are getting on well, I presume?"

"I'd say so." She smiled like a cat. "He thinks he's died and gone to heaven. I must say, having a young man who's so very appreciative of my efforts is good for my confidence."

It was probably good for her purse as well. Chuckling, he said, "I'm happy for you, Marina."

"Now then," she said, her tone turning businesslike, "I thought you should know that the gentleman from Vauxhall Gardens questioned me in my box at the opera last night."

Jesus, that was bold. "What did he look like?"

"I'm afraid I didn't see," she said, clearly vexed. "But I've no doubt it was him. He had the same gravelly voice. It was just after intermission. Philip had left the box in search of drinks. The lights went down for the start of the second act and the stranger slipped into our box. I sensed him behind me before he spoke. He pressed a cool blade to the side of my neck and ordered me not to turn around."

A knife? Will clenched his fists. "Bastard."

"Precisely," she said coolly. "I told him that my escort would be returning soon. He seemed unconcerned."

"He'd probably arranged for him to be detained in the lobby."

"No doubt." Marina sniffed. "He asked whether I'd learned anything else, and I said I had no idea what he was referring to. Then he pressed the blade a bit harder and asked what I knew about the twins . . . and your relationship with Margaret Lacey."

Holy hell. "He asked about Meg?"

Marina arched a brow. "I said that as far as I knew, she was the twins' governess—nothing more."

"How did he respond to that?"

"He said if I believed that, then I was as blind as the rest of the ton. Only, he said it a bit more colorfully."

What kind of miscreant threatened and insulted a woman? "When I discover who this coward is, he will pay for his deeds, I promise you. Did he give you any clue as to his identity?"

She shook her head and stared out the coach window, watching the trees slide by. "I asked if he had an address where I could contact him, should I learn anything more, but he snickered and said that wouldn't be necessary. A second later, he was gone."

Will scrubbed his chin in frustration. He had to be missing something. "What did Philip say when he returned?"

"Nothing. I asked what kept him so long, and he said a nice gent offered him a cigar." She gave an elegant shrug. "I didn't tell him about the incident, but pleaded a headache and asked him to take me home."

"I think you should tell the authorities, Marina. I'm concerned for your safety."

She gave a husky laugh. "Please, Will. It's not the first time I've been held at knifepoint, and it probably won't be the last. I'm accustomed to living on the edges of society. I know how to take care of myself. Involving the authorities would only invite more trouble."

He raked a hand through his hair. "Fine, leave them out of it if you wish. But know this: I will find out who the scoundrel is . . . and I will exact revenge. He won't bother you, the twins, or Meg, ever again."

Chapter THIRTY-TWO

The twins sat on either side of Will, with only their shoulders and heads visible above the massive dining room table. Before they'd come down to dinner, Meg had reminded them of proper table manners. Now, they stared at their soup bowls, virtually paralyzed, as though they feared one false move would result in their permanent banishment from the dining room.

Oblivious, Will dove into his soup with gusto. Meg cleared her throat and made a great show of picking up her spoon and sipping her broth, hoping the girls would follow suit. Nodding bravely, Valerie lifted her spoon and dared to take a dainty sip. Meg smiled approvingly.

Diana shrugged and attempted it as well, only there was nothing dainty about the sound she made—*slurp*.

Meg cringed and Valerie gasped.

From his post near the buffet, Gibson closed his eyes, horrified.

Will raised a dark brow and glared at Diana. "Is that the best you can do?"

"Sir?" Her spoon slipped from her trembling fingers and plunked into the bowl.

"Listen to this," Will said. He raised his spoon to his lips and slurped twice as loud. "*That* is how it is done."

Diana bounced in her chair. "May I try again?"

"Please," Will replied. "And do try to make it respectable this time."

Her blue eyes twinkling, she pursed her lips like a fish and slurped impressively.

"Not bad, Diana," he said.

"Not bad? I was *magnificent*."

"You'll improve with practice," he teased.

"Oh, my turn?" asked Valerie.

Will nodded. "If you think you can manage it."

She did, setting off a noisy slurping battle that drove poor Gibson from the room, his nostrils flared in disapproval.

The girls relaxed for the rest of the meal, responding politely to Will's inquiries about their studies and activities, but he avoided any mention of Lila's visit. They had been teary when they said their good-byes to their mother that afternoon but had seemed fine since—perhaps just a bit more subdued than usual. It was hard to know what they were feeling, but Meg guessed that seeing their mother made them miss home.

Even living like royalty in the earl's luxurious townhouse couldn't replace the comforts of home—something she knew better than anyone.

Diana caught a glimpse of herself in a silver tureen and preened. "Do you like our new dresses, sir?"

Will shot Meg a grin before replying. "I do. You and your sister look very grown-up."

"We do?" Valerie sat up, her spine straight as a rod. "How old do I look?"

He rubbed his chin, as though the question merited great thought. "Nine, at least."

Both girls clapped gleefully at first, then Diana's face fell. "Miss Lacey had a beautiful dress, too."

Will's fork froze in mid-air. "Did she?"

Valerie nodded. "She looked like a princess in it, and she was going to wear it to the dinner party, but—"

"But I ruined it," Diana admitted.

"It was an accident," Meg added quickly. "These things happen."

"It was a tragedy," Diana said solemnly.

"Miss Lacey tried to fix it, but there was nothing that could be done." Valerie shook her head. "When I see it hanging in Miss Lacey's room, all brown and twisted, it makes me so sad."

Will nodded in empathy. "I can understand why."

As Meg watched him conversing easily with the girls, a wave of longing rushed over her. Something in his manner with them touched her deeply. He was attentive without being condescending; genuine without being overly sentimental. And he was truly enjoying them—almost as much as they enjoyed him.

Dear heavens. He would make a wonderful father.

"Do you want to know what I think?" he asked, eyes gleaming.

The girls' heads bobbed in the affirmative. Meg fanned herself with her napkin.

He leaned back in his chair and steepled his fingers under his chin. "A special dress like that should not hang about making people sad. It deserves a send-off—a proper good-bye."

Meg blinked. "What do you mean?"

"We need to arrange a funeral."

An hour later, the four of them were assembled in the nursery. The twins wore veils that were actually lace handkerchiefs that Meg had pinned to their blond curls. Charlotte's poor gown was folded into a pitiful splotchy brown bundle and tied up with a pretty white bow that had once been the sash. It rested atop a velvet pillow that Will placed on a desk in the center of the room, and they all joined hands to form a circle around it.

"Dearly beloved," Will said, "we are gathered here to celebrate a special gown."

Awkward silence ensued.

He looked helplessly at Meg. "Ah, would anyone like to say a few words . . . in memoriam?"

She was tempted to let him flounder on his own but took pity. "I will." She cleared her throat and addressed the bundle on the pillow. "You were a friend to Miss Charlotte, and I am certain you would have been a friend to me if you hadn't . . ."—good heavens, she felt foolish—". . . fallen victim to a cup of chocolate. We thank you for your service, which sadly, came to an unfortunate and untimely end."

"Amen," Will said. "Any other words?"

"I'd like to say something," Diana ventured.

Everyone bowed their heads.

"You were a blue dress. So very, very . . . blue. And pretty."

"Amen."

"Anyone else?" asked Will. They all looked pointedly at Valerie who shook her head and rolled her eyes as though she thought the lot of them mad.

"Some music would be nice," Diana said.

"An excellent suggestion." Will turned to Meg. "Miss Lacey, would you be so good as to hum a requiem for us?"

Good Lord. "I'm afraid I don't know one," she said through her teeth.

"No matter. You may hum any song as long as you hum it slowly."

"Perhaps *you* should hum a song slowly, my lord."

"Unfortunately, none of the tunes I know are suitable for young, impressionable ears. Really, Miss Lacey, any song will do."

Meg opened her mouth to toss a retort at him, but Diana looked up at her with pleading eyes.

"Very well," Meg huffed. And because she could think of nothing else, she hummed *God Save the Queen*. Everyone joined in on the second verse.

"A stirring rendition," Will said soberly. Blast him. "Now, at last, it's time we laid this gown to rest."

"We're going to bury it?" Diana asked excitedly.

"Not quite. I thought we would follow the Viking tradition," Will said.

Valerie's eyes went wide. "What's that?"

"Surely, in the course of your studies Miss Lacey has taught you about the Norse customs?"

"No, my lord," Meg said dryly, "we've focused solely on English history thus far, and I fear we were unable to cover eight centuries in the two weeks since I've arrived. Perhaps *you* would like to tutor the girls in a bit of Norse history?"

He nodded as though conceding the point. "We haven't the time to delve into the finer points of funeral pyres, ship burials, and Valhalla. Suffice it to say we're going to burn the dress. Follow me."

With great deference, he lifted the pillow, balancing it on his outstretched arms as the girls and Meg formed a small procession behind him. He led them down the stairs, into the drawing room, and in front of the dormant fireplace. Reverently, he placed the bundled dress on the grate, added some firewood and kindling, and reached for the tinderbox on the mantel. "Ready?" he asked.

The girls nodded and watched as Will knelt and lit the fire. They stared raptly as the tinder ignited, followed by the kindling and the dress and the logs.

For several minutes, no one spoke. The twins sank onto the carpet, mesmerized by the flames that licked the gown, slowly turning it to ash and smoke.

At last, when the dress was no longer recognizable, Diana sighed. "I'm not sure why, but I feel better now."

Meg did too. Sometimes letting go of things felt good. But most of the time it was very, very, difficult. Letting go of her parents and her home had nearly broken her. Even now, eight years later, a simple sound or smell could resurrect the grief and bring it back in full force.

And now she was going to have to let go again. Of the twins and Will. And while it couldn't possibly be as bad as losing her parents, she suspected she'd feel the loss keenly.

As though he'd read her mind, Will sat on the floor between Diana and Valerie. Meg pulled up an ottoman and perched on the edge. "I'm glad you feel better," he said to Diana. "You and your sister have shown a great deal of courage over the past few weeks. We may have gotten off to a difficult start—"

"What does that mean?" Diana asked.

"He yelled a lot in the beginning," Valerie offered helpfully.

"—but Miss Lacey and I have been impressed by your hard work and your loyalty to each other. That is, when you're not fighting."

"Why are you telling us this?" Valerie asked, ever perceptive.

"An excellent question. I spoke to your mother when she visited today, and she would like you both to go back home with her, tomorrow."

The girls gaped at one another, unbelieving.

"I told her the choice is yours. Would you like that?"

"Home," Valerie repeated. "Yes."

Diana bit her lip then burst into tears.

"Oh dear." Meg flew to her side and rubbed her back. "What's wrong?"

She shook her head and sputtered, "Nothing's wrong. Mama really *does* want us."

"Of course she does, darling," Meg said. "You mustn't doubt that."

"It sounds as though you've made your decision," Will said. "But I want you to remember that you *do* have a choice. You are welcome here—and you always will be."

For several heartbeats, no one spoke.

"We're really going home tomorrow?" Valerie breathed.

Will squeezed her shoulder and smiled. "Your mother will be here at noon."

Above the twins' heads, he and Meg exchanged an un-expectedly poignant look. So this was truly good-bye. Their motley little crew would soon disband.

And as they sat on the floor of the elegant drawing room, watching the charred remnants of her dress sizzle in the grate, Meg reminded herself that this was the outcome she'd wished for—that they'd all wished for. It was time for them to move on.

Chapter THIRTY-THREE

Will swore he'd wait till after midnight to visit Meg's room, but it was only half past eleven when he knocked lightly on her door. She answered quickly, admitting him into her dimly lit bedchamber wearing the silky blue nightgown he'd purchased earlier that day. The lace bodice and thin satin clung to her curves, leaving little to the imagination and setting his blood on fire.

"I see you received my gift." He leaned against her door and drank in the sight of her luminous skin and lithe limbs. "Do you like it?"

She smirked as she leaned her hips into his and walked her fingers up his torso, starting at his waistband and lingering at the open neck of his shirt. "You say it is a gift for me," she teased, "but I think, perhaps, it is more for you."

"It's the most selfish gift I've ever given," he confirmed. "I regret nothing." He resolved to return to the shop tomorrow and order a dozen more, one in every color of the damned rainbow.

"I do like it," she admitted. "Er, what there is of it."

Despite her playfulness, there was a sadness in her eyes he couldn't ignore. And as much as he wanted to drag her to the bed and rip that pretty nightgown off of her, he knew they had to talk. "Come." He laced his fingers through hers and pulled her toward the chair in the small sitting area. She sat, tucking bare feet beneath her, and he perched on a footstool opposite her.

"You seem melancholy. Do you have reservations about letting the girls return home?" Strangely, part of him hoped she'd say yes, so he'd have an excuse to delay their departure.

"Nothing specific. It seems so sudden, though. I'm going to miss them."

He grunted.

"And I think you will, too."

"Yes," he said dryly, "I'm sure I'll be at loose ends without all the bickering, tantrums, and chaos." But he knew he wasn't fooling Meg.

She rolled her eyes. "And I suppose *you* were the perfect child. A true angel."

Grinning wickedly, he said, "I think you know better than that." He leaned forward. "I spoke to Mrs. Hopwood earlier. She's agreed to go with the girls and help care for them at Lila's."

"That's good," she said. He could see the relief plain on her face. "They're fond of her already, and I like her too. Perhaps it will make their transition easier."

"Yes." And it would give him peace of mind, as well. He would continue to pay Mrs. Hopwood's salary and had no qualms about asking her for regular updates on Valerie and Diana's well-being.

"I'll help the girls pack their things in the morning." She pressed a palm to her forehead, frowning. "I wish I'd ordered cloaks for them. I'd thought it could wait till the weather turned cooler."

"Make a list of anything you think they might need, and we'll see that the items are delivered to Lila's."

She nodded and tears welled in her eyes. "Thank you. Saying good-bye to the twins tomorrow is going to be . . . difficult. I wonder if I'll ever see them again."

"Of course you will," he said, even though he had doubts himself. "*We* will."

"I don't know. This may be a painful time in their lives that they'd just as soon forget. And if that's what they wish, perhaps we should let them."

"I made a promise to my friend—their father. I'm responsible for them and will be for as long as I live." But the truth was that they'd become more than a responsibility. More than a burden. They'd become . . . family.

"You have that connection to them, but I . . . I don't."

"Yes, you do." *Through me*, he wanted to say. *We're in this together.* But he had to go about it in the correct way, and that meant being honest with her. About everything—his father's debt, the possibility that he'd played a part in her parents' deaths, and his mother's complicity in the entire affair.

Most of all, he needed to be honest with Meg about his feelings. He loved her. And not because he liked sparring with her or kissing her or watching her melt in his arms—although he was *very* fond of all those things.

The truth was that he loved her for who she was at her core—loyal, compassionate, funny, and kind.

And she deserved to know.

He reached for her hand, brought her fingers to his lips, and met her gaze. "Meg, there are a few things I need to tell you."

The day had been fraught with emotion, and if this was Meg's last night under Will's roof, she didn't want to spend it *talking*. They needed to transcend words and conversation with intimacy and pleasure.

After all, some day, several months from now, assuming she was able to keep Uncle Alistair and her sisters out of the poor house, she and Will might well have a chance meeting in the park or at a soiree or on the street. And there would be time for talking *then*. They'd smile politely at one another, and he'd inquire about her family, and she'd ask after the twins, and they'd each respond in a pleasant, if vague manner. It would seem almost impossible that she'd once pressed her bare skin against his, or that he'd whispered impossibly naughty things in her ear, or that he'd made her cry out in ecstasy.

Her decision made, she pushed herself out of the chair, walked behind the footstool where he sat and slipped her arms around him, pressing her chest to his back.

"Meg—"

"Please," she breathed, gliding her hands over his shoulders and reveling at the hard contours of muscle and flesh. "Whatever you want to discuss can wait. Right now, I . . . I need you."

The muscles in his back tensed, and she knew he was battling desire, fighting attraction . . . and losing. She slid her palms down his arms and brushed her lips over the warm skin above his collar. "I've missed you," she murmured.

His hands gripped the edge of the stool. "Jesus, Meg. I've missed you too. I dream about you every night and a dozen times throughout the day."

She came around to kneel in front of him. "And now you're here." She slid her hands over the tops of his thighs and caressed the hard length of him. "With me."

The curse he muttered thrilled her. "You are making it damn near impossible to resist you."

"That was my plan," she admitted as she unbuttoned his trousers.

When she touched him, his eyes glazed with desire, but she was far from an expert in these matters. "Show me," she said. "I want to please you."

Swallowing, he guided her hand.

"Like this?" She savored the feel of him, hard, large, and warm.

"God, yes," he choked out.

Emboldened, she bent her head and licked the bead of liquid off the tip.

"Meg." He cupped her cheeks in his hands. "You're driving me mad—in the best possible way."

"Good." She loved seeing him like this, drunk with desire and burning for her. She tasted him again, tentatively at first, mimicking the motion she'd used with her hand. He moaned each time she took him deeper, gasping from pure restraint.

"Enough," he said at last, pulling back and closing his eyes as though he needed a moment to regain control. Meg sat on her heels, pleased with her efforts.

"You've bewitched me." He gazed at her hungrily. "And now you must pay."

Laughing, she scrambled away from him but managed only two strides before he scooped her into his arms, stalked to the bed, and tossed her unceremoniously onto the mattress.

"The governess in me feels obliged to tell you that jumping and rough play on the bed is inadvisable, as it often results in damage to something or someone."

He chuckled as he hauled off his shirt, and the sight of his rippled torso left her mouth dry. "You are one part vixen," he said, "one part governess. I adore both sides of you, however, right now, I believe I'd like to see more of the vixen." He crawled over her, pinned her wrists above her head, and kissed her until she could barely form a thought, let alone a sentence.

"Need you." Her body arched toward him, aching from desire.

But he took his time, suckling her through a layer of silk lace and stroking her slick entrance until she was dizzy with wanting.

"You and I, Meg," he whispered seductively, "we are perfectly matched. No one else makes me feel like you do. And I know just what you like, too." His wicked fingers demonstrated his meaning, caressing the spot that brought her the most pleasure and bringing her closer and closer to pure bliss.

She heard herself begging as her fingers dug into his shoulders. "Please, Will. I need you. Oh God . . . oh . . ."

With a growl, he thrust inside, filling her perfectly. He speared his hands through her hair and rocked his hips in a rhythm that drove her mad. Doubts and uncertainties may have lurked in the back of her mind, but they were no match for the solid weight of him lying atop her and the delicious feel of his hair tickling her neck. Her body responded to him as it always did, and she hurtled toward the abyss, crying out as they came together in an exquisite, soul-shattering release.

They drifted off after that, their legs tangled and his arm draped across her waist. Never before had she felt so safe, so content, so . . . loved.

But when she woke a couple hours later, a chill skittered down her spine. She reached behind her and patted the cold mattress. "Will?"

"It's all right." He stood by the window, gazing down into the garden wearing only his trousers. "I'm here."

She sat up, rubbing her eyes. "Why are you out of bed?"

He gave a hollow laugh. "If I stayed there beside you, I would have taken you again."

Her pulse quickened and she stretched a hand toward him. "Come back."

Regret plain on his face, he shook his head. "We do need to talk, Meg."

She shuddered again, but not because of the cold. She'd known this time would come—the time when they'd have to face hard truths, and she could delay it no longer. "Yes, of course." She tucked the blanket beneath her arms, turned up the lamp on the table next to her, and steeled herself for whatever he would say.

As though he didn't trust himself to stand too close to her, he leaned against the post at the foot of the bed, arms crossed over his chest. "Yesterday, I learned something about your past—*our* pasts, really. I think it's important that you know."

Chapter THIRTY-FOUR

"My past?" Meg swallowed. When the past was filled with grief, guilt, and loss, one expended a great deal of energy attempting to *avoid* thinking about it.

Will nodded. "I've discovered a secret, and while it can't change the events that happened, it may shed some light on them."

Her heart pounded in her chest. What if she was happy to remain in the dark? She suspected the secret had to do with her parents, and new information about them was likely to reopen the wound from their deaths. "Are you certain it's necessary?" she asked. "Some secrets are best left untold."

"Maybe, but I thought you'd want to know the truth—especially since it has some bearing on your current situation."

"You're speaking in riddles." She blew out a breath, exasperated, but Will was right. Deep down, she *needed* to know the truth. "Very well. Tell me."

"I was going through some of my father's things and

found a promissory note. It seems he owed a large gambling debt—to your father."

Meg frowned. "To Papa? Are you sure? I never knew him to play cards."

"I don't know what they bet on, exactly, only that the stakes were high. My father owed yours—ten thousand pounds."

Her chin dropped. "That's impossible. My father had a very modest income."

Will sat on the edge of the bed, his tousled hair gleaming in the moonlight. "Then he must have been a very shrewd gambler."

But that did not fit with her memories of Papa, who had spent most afternoons visiting the sick and most evenings reading the Bible. It was possible he'd had some hidden vices, but ten thousand pounds was not the sort of bet one made on a casual game of loo.

"I inherited my father's estate and, with it, his debts," Will said soberly. "I owe you and your sisters ten thousand pounds."

Dear God. It was an amount too great to fathom. Had they known about it, it could have changed the course of their lives. "Forgive me, but I find it all rather difficult to believe. It's a fascinating story, to be sure, but with both our fathers gone, it's likely we'll never know the truth."

"I have the IOU, Meg. I spoke to my mother about it, too. She confirmed it's true."

She felt a little stab of betrayal. "You spoke to your mother about this, but not me?"

"I'm telling you now," he said softly, "and there's more. Our fathers agreed to an alternate form of payment."

"I don't understand." Suddenly cold, she began to shake. "What sort of payment?"

"Your father agreed to forgive the debt if—"

"No." Hands trembling, she covered her ears. But it was

too late. She knew what Will was going to say—and it broke her heart.

In an instant he was at her side, trying to comfort her, but she ducked out of his embrace. "Please, don't," she begged.

"I'm sorry. I didn't realize this news would upset you so."

She blinked, aghast. "You didn't realize it would hurt me to know that my father thought he had to pay *ten thousand pounds* to the boy next door in order to marry me off?"

"To be clear," Will said, "he wasn't offering to pay *me*, merely to forgive my father's debt."

"It is the same thing," she spat. "It seems everyone involved in the deal had a rather low opinion of me."

"Meg," he said softly, "I don't think that's true at all. Your father simply wanted the best possible future for you."

"And my best possible future was marriage to *you*?" With a snort, she leaped out of bed, snatched her robe off of the chair, and stuffed her arms into it.

He shrugged his impossibly broad shoulders in a most vexing manner. "You could do worse."

"Your arrogance, my lord, is truly amazing."

"We're back to *my lord*?" Shaking his head, he gave a hollow laugh. "Why do you insist on blaming *me* for a deal struck by our fathers?"

"Because *you're* the one who brought it to my attention and . . . and because you're blind to the offensiveness of it." She tied her wrapper tightly around her and paced the side of the room farthest from him.

"I was just as much a pawn in this charade as you were," he said.

"Men are never pawns in the same way that women are. You were the heir to an earldom. Even if you had been forced to marry me—a fate I saved you from, by the way—you would have been free to pursue your own life, your own pleasures. I'm sure you would have had a mistress or two."

He speared his hands through his hair, frustration plain on his face. "Now you're condemning me for hypothetical mistresses?"

Very well, perhaps she'd gone too far. "I'm only trying to explain why our situations were so very different. *My* future was almost decided by the turn of a card, without any consideration for my wishes or feelings. I would have been trapped in a loveless sham of a marriage for the rest of my life."

The hurt look that crossed his face made her instantly regret her words. "Do you truly think our marriage would have been loveless?" he asked.

She threw up her hands. "We were young and foolish, Will. Neither of us knew anything about love."

"And now?" His brown eyes had never looked more vulnerable. But she had everything to lose—including her heart.

Wrapping her arms around her waist, she said, "It is a moot point."

"What if it isn't?" He approached carefully, like a hunter tracking a deer.

"I don't take your meaning." In no mood for games, she stepped back, needing some distance between them.

"In the last couple of weeks, I've come to care for you deeply," he began.

Oh no. She knew what he was going to say and wanted nothing more than to freeze the words on his lips. "I care for you, too," she said, "but we both knew this relationship would eventually have to end."

"I don't think it does, Meg." He reached for her hands and clasped them tenderly between his own. "I understand that you want to determine your own future and make your own choices . . . so I'm giving you a choice now."

Swallowing, she closed her eyes. It wasn't supposed to happen like this. It probably wasn't supposed to happen at all. "You don't have to—"

"I'm not doing anything because I *have* to, damn it." He looked down at their hands before meeting her gaze again. "Allow me to finish. I *want* to marry you, and not out of obligation. I'd planned to ask you even before I learned of the debt."

He *wanted* to marry her? Or had he merely convinced himself that he did out of a misplaced sense of honor? Either way, it was a *proposal*—not the most romantic sort perhaps, but her chest squeezed nonetheless. After all, wallflowers could hardly expect bouquets and poetry.

And they most certainly could not expect declarations of love.

Which was just as well, since she could not possibly accept his proposal.

"Will, I—"

"Please, wait. I said that you have a choice. If you do not wish to marry me"—his voice grew rough—"I will, of course, honor my father's debt. I want you to know that, no matter your decision, you, your sisters, and your uncle will be provided for." Slowly, he raised her hands to his lips and kissed them. "I want you to be my wife, but your future will not be determined by what *I* want. And it won't be determined by what your parents wanted or by your dire financial straits. Your future will be determined solely by *you*."

The room tilted and her fingers went numb. Yes, she'd wanted to control her own destiny, but neither of his options felt like true choices.

It wasn't that she didn't want him for a husband. Lord save her, she did, with all her heart. But to marry Will after her initial rejection of him—which had directly led to her parents' deaths—seemed like the ultimate betrayal. How could she live with herself, knowing that if she'd simply obeyed Papa and Mama's wishes eight years ago, she'd be happily married to Will and her parents would be alive and well today?

And while the ten thousand pounds would solve many problems for her family, it felt an awful lot like blood money—a windfall that would never have come her way but for her parents' deaths.

She had to wonder, too, whether Will would have insisted on paying the debt if she and he hadn't . . . if they hadn't made love. The very idea that the money might be compensation for their intimate relationship . . . well, it made her stomach roil.

Pulling away, she pressed a palm to her forehead.

His brows knitted. "Are you all right?"

No. "Yes, it's all just a bit overwhelming."

"I . . . I thought you'd be happy," he said. "I'd hoped we would be celebrating our engagement."

"I'm not suited for this life." She flung a hand at the elegant bedchamber.

"A life with me? Of course you are."

"Your mother would never approve of me. Nor would half the ton."

He shrugged. "Then we shall have to change their minds."

Dear God, her belly was in knots. "I'm sorry that I can't give you an answer right now. I'm afraid I need some time to think."

His face fell. "I understand. You may take as much time as you need. But don't push me away." He jabbed a thumb over his shoulder. "An hour ago we laid together in that bed, as close as two people can be. Nothing's changed since then."

Oh, but it had. She'd just learned that her own father had wagered her like she was a breeding mare. Then Will's proposal had jarred her out of the fantasy world she'd been living in, forcing her to take stock of what they'd done and to somehow reconcile it with her past. "The twins are going home tomorrow, and so am I."

"I wish you wouldn't, Meg. Stay a few days at least—so we can sort this all out." His heavy-lidded eyes pleaded with her, and he sidled closer. "You belong here, with me."

"I'm not certain where I belong," she said hoarsely. "I promise to consider all you've said, but I think I'd like to be alone for a while now."

He pressed his lips into a thin line. While he silently pulled on his boots and wrestled with his shirt, she tried to keep her knees from wobbling.

"I'll leave you now," he said, "but think about this. You and I are good together—and not just in bed. If you gave us a chance, we could be *great* together."

Her cheeks burned. She could not deny that they were well-matched in passion.

He stalked to the door and gripped the knob, frustration written plain on his face. "I don't know why you're upset, but I do know that if you trusted me, we could face anything together. I swear to you, Meg, if you say yes, I'll make you happy—or die trying." As he quietly left her room, his words echoed in her head.

She believed that he wanted to make her happy.

She even believed that with him, she could be.

But she'd once rejected him and sent her parents on a chase that led to their sudden, pointless, and tragic deaths. Maybe a girl who'd do something like that didn't *deserve* to be happy.

Chapter THIRTY-FIVE

"Pardon the interruption, my lord. Miss Lacey wondered if you might have a trunk to spare for the twins' belongings. They came with nothing but the frocks they wore and a small satchel of clothes to share between the two of them. Now they have a closetful of dresses—thanks to you." Mrs. Lundy smiled approvingly.

"Of course, there are plenty of trunks in the attic. Give Miss Lacey and the girls whatever they require."

"Thank you." The housekeeper bobbed her head, started to scurry off, then hesitated in the doorway of his study. "Funny how those two managed to worm their ways into my heart. I'm going to miss the little mites."

Will knew just what she meant but snorted anyway. "Yes, all the peace and quiet will be unbearable."

Chuckling, she hurried toward the stairway once more.

Will checked the time. Almost noon, and he hadn't seen Meg all morning. She was avoiding him, and that was a very bad sign.

Gibson shuffled into the room, proffering a small stack of envelopes. "The mail, my lord."

"I see that, Gibson. Place it there." He inclined his head to the corner of his desk. "Like you do every other damned day."

"Very good, my lord." A tortoise could have traveled to his desk faster than the butler.

"Is there a problem, Gibson?"

The butler pursed his lips. "I was just thinking about how Miss Diana and Miss Valerie liked to help me sort the mail each morning."

"You put them to work, did you? Brilliant, and also shameless. I approve."

Jowls waggling, the butler nodded vigorously. "Industriousness is its own reward. And the girls insisted on reciting your address to me each day. I tested each of them separately."

"How fascinating." Will rolled his eyes, but his sarcasm was lost on Gibson.

"They were rather proud of the accomplishment. Miss Lacey insisted that they commit the address to memory after the evening that Miss Diana disappeared." The butler rubbed his chin. "Perhaps I'll write them a letter now and then, just to let them practice. I'd hate for them to regress."

"It would be a tragedy." Will glanced at the ledger on his desk so Gibson wouldn't see him smiling. "I think you should write to them at least every fortnight or so."

The butler tilted his head thoughtfully. "I was considering writing a weekly missive," he mused.

"Even better."

"If you insist, my lord."

"Thank you. That will be all, Gibson."

Will couldn't deny that he'd miss the girls too. But he'd

been quite content with his life before they'd arrived. He'd adjust to life without them again. It wasn't as though a person could completely change in a few weeks . . . or could he?

Rather than contemplate the question, Will sifted through the letters that Gibson had delivered. One envelope in particular caught his eye, and he opened it.

It was an invitation to Lord Wiltmore's ball.

Will immediately penned a response indicating he'd be delighted and honored to attend. He knew Meg was dreading the ball, but if he leaned on his friends and acquaintances, they would all attend, ensuring the ball's success and sparing her further embarrassment.

The ink had barely dried on his reply before Lila arrived and everyone congregated in the drawing room to say good-bye. Diana and Valerie beamed at the attention, and bounded around the room excitedly, towing Lila in their wake.

All the staff wanted to wish the girls well; some gave them candies and small gifts. Mrs. Hopwood directed a footman to load two trunks and two bags in the hackney cab out front. Meg hung back, letting the girls slowly transition from her care into their mother's. She'd put on a brave face, but her pink-rimmed eyes betrayed her.

Eventually, the servants returned to work and Lila clasped the twins' hands. "Well, my darlings, are you ready to go home?"

"Yes!" they cried.

"Then we shall. Say good-bye to Miss Lacey and Lord Castleton."

A look of alarm crossed Diana and Valerie's faces—as though they'd just now realized that going home necessarily involved *leaving* the earl's house. They ran to Meg and threw their arms around her. "You'll come visit us, won't you?"

Over the girls' heads, Meg glanced at Lila, who gave her a blank stare. "I shall try. I will most assuredly write to you. Be good for your mama and for Mrs. Hopwood. Be kind to each other, because sisters are the friends you shall have your whole life."

"We'll miss you, Miss Lacey," Valerie said.

Diana nodded vigorously. "You were the best governess we ever had."

Her eyes brimming, Meg smiled and kissed each girl on the cheek. As though she didn't trust herself to speak, she waved them in Will's direction.

"Ladies," he said formally, "I wonder if we might have a brief word in private?"

They stared at him, bewildered.

"Let's have a chat in the hall," he said.

They nearly tripped over themselves trying to be first through the doorway, and once they were in the corridor, Will crouched so he was approximately at a six-year-old height. "I have a couple of important matters to discuss with you," he began.

Two pairs of strikingly blue eyes went wide. "Yes, sir," Diana replied.

"First, I need your help selecting a thank-you gift for Miss Lacey. I thought we could give her something from the three of us."

Valerie clasped her plump hands beneath her chin. "Ooh, a gift would make her happy. What shall we give her?"

"I was thinking a dress, to replace the one that . . ."

"We stained with chocolate and burned to ash?" Diana provided.

"Precisely." Will smiled. "But you must tell me what you think Miss Lacey would like."

"A fairy princess dress," announced Valerie.

"Done." Will turned to Diana.

"What color?"

"Dark pink—like the square of fabric we saw the first day we went dress shopping. I could tell that Miss Lacey admired it."

"Perfect," Will announced. "I cannot tell you how helpful that information is." The girls lifted their chins proudly.

"What was the second thing?" asked Valerie.

"I have a secret to tell you—an important one."

Diana shivered in anticipation. "Oh, I do love secrets."

Will placed his hands on their shoulders, drew them closer, and lowered his voice.

"One day when you are older, I will tell you more, but for now, I want you to know that your father was a dear friend of mine."

"You know who our father was?"

"I do. And he loved you . . . very much."

"I thought that . . ." Valerie blushed. "I thought that perhaps *you* were our father."

"I am not," Will said carefully. "But I can tell you this. Any man would be lucky to have you two for his daughters."

They hugged him—surprisingly hard for such tiny girls—and he hugged them back, oddly reluctant to let go.

When they returned to the drawing room, Lila tapped her toe impatiently. "I'm afraid we must be off now," she said. "I want to have the girls settled before naptime."

"We have to take naps at home, too?" Diana moaned.

As the twins, Lila, and Mrs. Hopwood bustled out the front door, Will spotted a trunk in the foyer. "Wait, there's one more trunk to be loaded. I'll see to it." He leaned over and prepared to heft it onto his shoulder.

"That's not the girls'," Meg said. "It's mine. I wondered if Harry could deliver me home."

"Damn it, Meg," he murmured. "If anyone's going to take you home, it will be me. Let's see the twins off first."

They stood on the doorstep as Diana and Valerie clambered into the cab, chatting endlessly. Their blue eyes shining and little noses pressed to the windows, they waved enthusiastically.

Will waved back until the hackney disappeared from view. For Meg's sake and his pride's, he remained stoic.

He told himself that the hole left in his heart by two tiny hoydens couldn't possibly take very long to heal.

And he hoped to hell he was right.

Chapter THIRTY-SIX

"It's not too late to turn around." Will sat across from Meg on the plush squabs of his elegant coach as it rumbled through the streets of London. The shattered look in his eyes nearly broke her heart. "Let's go home and discuss your concerns over dinner."

"No," she said softly. "When we are alone together, we have a tendency to engage in activities other than talking."

"That's not a bad thing, you know."

She took a deep breath. "I can't be with you anymore, Will. A relationship shouldn't be based on secret wagers, verbal sparring, and . . ."

He raised a dark brow. "Amazing sex?"

"Exactly," she choked out.

"That's not fair, and you know it."

She did know it. But she couldn't very well tell him about her guilt or the fear that if she married him, she'd wake up every day knowing that she was living the life her parents had wanted for her—only, due to her stubborn pride, they weren't there to witness it. Her selfishness had made her sisters orphans. How was she supposed to tell them that she'd capriciously changed her mind about the decision that had led to their parents' deaths?

"Perhaps in time . . ." But she already knew she and Will had no hope of a future; she merely pretended otherwise in order to make a graceful exit from the coach—and from his life.

As the coach rolled to a stop in front of Uncle Alistair's house, she scooped her bag off the floor. "Thank you for seeing me home."

He shook his head, bewildered. "That is all you have to say to me? I asked you to *marry* me, Meg. We shared everything. And you act as though I'm a stranger who escorted you home from the park."

Dear God, she had to go. Quickly, before she lost her resolve and the last threads of her composure. "I shall write to you in a week or so."

"A week?" he asked, incredulous.

She nodded, not trusting herself to speak.

He reached into his pocket, produced a wad of bank notes, and thrust them at her. "Here. It's your last week's salary and three month's pay."

Meg had never seen so much money at one time, but his offer turned her stomach. Hands firmly clasped in her lap, she kept her voice low and even. "I don't want it."

"Why not?" he said harshly. "You've earned it."

The words stung. "Will. Please, don't."

"Take it. It's what I'd do for any of my employees whose service was cut short due to circumstances beyond their control."

She eyed the roll of bank notes warily. Lord only knew when she'd be able to find another position, and the money could keep them afloat for another year. She should take it.

But it made her think about her father's wager, and each time she did, she felt ill. How well had she really known him?

"I don't want your money." She scooted across the seat toward the cab door.

Will cursed and stuffed the notes into his pocket. "I'll carry your trunk in."

"That's not necessary," she said quickly. "I'll ask the driver."

She reached for the door handle, and he covered her hand with his. "One more thing before you go," he said.

She swallowed, one part suspicious and one part hopeful. Maybe he wanted to kiss her—a final kiss, to say good-bye. It wouldn't change anything, and it might well haunt her forever, but she wanted it all the same. Desperately. She leaned forward, parted her lips, and—

"I'm leaving town for a couple of days," he said. "But if you should need to contact me, for any reason, Gibson knows how to reach me."

Feeling as though she'd been slapped, she nodded numbly. "Good-bye, Will."

He didn't reply, and she didn't look back.

Meg marveled at her ability to alight from the coach, talk to the driver, and navigate the walkway to the door. She even managed a smile as he deposited her trunk in the foyer, swept off his cap, and bowed.

It was only after he left and she closed the door behind him that she crumpled to the floor right there in the foyer and cried—for the twins, Will, her sisters, and herself. She hadn't wept so hard or so long since the day she buried her parents, but once the tears started coming, she was powerless to stop them.

She was heartbroken, penniless, and unemployed.

But at least she was home.

It had been a few months since Will had visited Castleton Park, the estate where he'd spent much of his childhood, within walking distance of the Lacey family's residence.

He'd thought it would be good for him to leave London and the townhouse where he still expected to see Meg and the twins each time he rounded a corner, but damned if he didn't see Meg everywhere he looked in the country, too.

As he left the manor house, traveling on horseback by green fields spotted with wildflowers, he recalled the scent of her hair. The moss at the base of the trees that lined the road was the same shade as her eyes. And the lake itself brought back memories of the day he'd watched her swimming, undulating through the clear water like a mermaid.

It was foolish to think he could forget her, even for a couple of days.

And it was probably even more foolish to think he could find the answers he sought—answers to questions that were at least eight years old.

But he started in the most logical place he could think of—the Red Griffin.

The inn's taproom was crowded with villagers who greeted him with slaps on the back and gap-toothed grins. He made small talk with a few, asking after their families and their farms and thinking how different these conversations were from the ones in London's ballrooms.

Here, there were no minefields to avoid, no hidden agendas, no one pretending to be anything but what they were. Just hardworking, simple people who required a couple of glasses of ale after a day in the fields.

Will made his way to the bar. "Evening, Jack."

The innkeeper, a spry, redheaded man in rolled shirt-sleeves, nodded and slid a pint toward him. "Good to see you, my lord. Any news from the manor house?"

"Cook's daughter had a baby boy. Everyone seems to be well. Hobbes runs a tight ship." His steward and the staff kept the estate functioning perfectly, even in Will's absence. He paid Hobbes handsomely for his service but made a mental note to give him a raise.

The innkeeper rubbed a towel over the bar's dented wood top. A bar that old surely had heard a lot of stories and seen a lot of fights. "Staying long this time?" Jack asked.

"No." Not if he could help it. He needed to discover the extent of his father's involvement in the Laceys' deaths and return to Meg, soon. Somehow, he had to convince her to marry him, and his gut told him that with each day that passed, his odds worsened. Will lowered his voice. "I'm trying to uncover some of the details of a coach accident that happened years ago."

Jack nodded. "The vicar and his wife." At Will's raised brow, he added, "It's the only real tragedy we've had here in the last decade. Who are you looking for?"

"I thought I'd start with the one witness to the accident, the Laceys' driver. I don't even know his name."

The innkeeper pulled a pint and placed it on the barmaid's tray. "That'd be Dan Ostrey. Sad what's become of him. He hasn't been the same since the accident."

"Was he injured?"

"Not seriously. But he rarely leaves his cottage these days. His wife relies on the charity of neighbors for all the necessities."

"I'll talk to him." Will threw back the rest of his ale and slid his glass forward for a refill. "Wrap me up a couple of shepherd's pies and a loaf of bread, would you? I'll take them with me."

"The invitations have all gone out." Beth delivered the news to Meg with the same gravity as one relates the death of a beloved pet. "There's nothing we can do but ready the house for the ball."

Meg pressed her fingertips to her temples. "This is

awful. We have only a week to prepare. Maybe no one will be able to attend?" she asked hopefully.

Julie waved a handful of responses. "All but Lady Tutley have accepted. She's taking the waters in Bath. We haven't yet heard from a few others, but it's going to be a crush."

Wincing, Meg asked, "How many are coming?"

"Including us and Uncle Alistair?" Beth asked.

"Yes." She may as well know the worst-case scenario. "By my estimate . . . sixty."

All three sisters sat, staring at the crowded parlor, wondering how on earth they were going to manage to accommodate sixty people.

"We shall have to tidy Uncle Alistair's study and push the furniture against the walls," Julie said.

"If we move the table, the dining room could be used for dancing," Beth said uncertainly. Both Meg and Beth squinted their eyes, trying to picture it.

"Where would the musicians go?" Meg asked—as if they could afford musicians.

"If it's a nice evening," Julie ventured, "we could put them just outside the French doors, in the garden."

Meg and Beth exchanged a look. It wasn't a bad idea, except their *garden* was little more than a weed pit.

"We have a lot of work to do," Meg said. "Let's make a list of all the tasks we must complete and split them up."

"I'll spruce up the garden," Beth said. "I've been meaning to, anyway. And I shall ask Patrick if he and a few of his friends would be willing to provide the music." Patrick was a baker who was fond of playing the cello. He'd probably never performed for an audience before, but neither beggars nor the Lacey sisters could be choosers.

"I'll attempt to make the study presentable," Julie offered.

Beth and Meg gasped as if she'd announced she'd just

volunteered to charge into battle. Tidying the study was the most daunting task of all because it required maneuvering around their uncle, who did not take kindly to interlopers—even his beloved nieces—in his hallowed room.

Julie shrugged slender shoulders. "If I do a little each day, while Uncle Alistair naps, perhaps he won't notice." But they all knew he would, and he wasn't going to be happy about it.

Meg volunteered to prepare the parlor and foyer and speak to their overworked housekeeper about the menu. It was all a bit overwhelming, but at least they had a plan. And if there was one thing that Meg and her sisters enjoyed, it was a challenge.

Maybe she'd be so busy with ball preparations that she'd be able to put Will out of her mind. Unless . . . surely he wouldn't . . . "May I see the guest list?"

Julie leaned across the settee and handed it to her. There, nine lines from the top, was his name—*William Ryder, Earl of Castleton.*

"Blast," she muttered.

"What's the matter?" Beth asked.

"I'd hoped Lord Castleton wouldn't come." She should have known he wouldn't respect her request for time to consider his proposal. Perhaps because he knew she wasn't truly considering it. How would she be able to bear seeing him?

"Oh, I almost forgot," Julie said. "You received a package this morning. I fear it was buried under all the ball responses." She shuffled through a stack of papers on the desk, produced a large envelope, and handed it to Meg. The front read: *To Miss Margaret Lacey.*

She'd recognize that bold, scrawling handwriting anywhere. Will's.

Inside she found the wad of bank notes he'd offered her the day before, wrapped neatly in a crisply folded letter.

Dear Meg,

This money is rightfully yours. You've earned it, and I suspect you need it. I'm sorry if I've offended you—that was never my intention.

My offer from the other evening still stands. It will be good tomorrow, next week, and next year. In case you were wondering, it stands for all eternity, so take as much time you need.

You still have a choice, Meg, and I pray to God you choose me.

—Will

Meg pressed a hand to her chest, as if that could slow the beating of her runaway heart.

Beth gasped. "That looks like . . ."

"Money," Julie finished for her.

"It's my last week's pay . . . and three month's severance." In truth, it was so much more. The money was security, but the letter was even more precious, because it gave her time and autonomy—and hope. Hope that in spite of all she'd said and done, Will wasn't giving up on her.

"You look very pale, Meg," Beth fretted. "Do I need to fetch the smelling salts?"

"No. But we do need to add one more item to our list of preparations."

"Ready!" Julie piped up, her pen poised.

"You must purchase ball gowns."

Julie and Beth sat in stunned silence.

At last, Julie said, "But that's so . . . impractical."

Beth nodded. "And frivolous."

"And completely necessary," Meg retorted. "We cannot

possibly host a ball while wearing rags. If we're going to make suitable matches for you, we need to create an illusion of wealth and well-being, and that begins with appearances."

Beth raised a skeptical brow. "So you will buy a gown for yourself as well?"

Julie clasped her hands together. "If anyone deserves it, Meg, you do."

"I will buy a gown," she said, but failed to mention that it wouldn't truly be a ball gown. Her sisters would provide enough beauty and sparkle for the family. She would purchase something pretty but practical—something she could wear on her next interview. Which she'd already decided would be another governess position.

"I can't believe we're really hosting a ball," Beth breathed.

"I can't believe it's only seven days away." Julie, who was probably contemplating the cluttered state of Uncle Alistair's study, bit her lip.

"All the more reason we should go dress shopping today," Meg announced. "Fetch your bonnets and gloves, ladies. We're off to Bond Street."

Chapter THIRTY-SEVEN

Will ducked through the doorway of the cottage where Dan Ostrey and his wife lived. Inside, it appeared even smaller than it did from the outside, and the air tasted stale and warm. Will handed the shepherd's pies to Mrs. Ostrey, who smiled gratefully.

Her husband sat in a rocking chair in front of the dormant fireplace. His sunken cheeks and hunched body probably made him look a decade older than he was. He barely glanced up as his wife announced he had a visitor.

"It's the earl, Dan. Lord Castleton. He'd like to speak with you."

"I have eyes in my head, Hazel."

She threw up her hands and gave Will a look that said *you try dealing with him for a while* before donning her apron and returning to the pot of potatoes she was peeling.

"There's a matter I'd like to ask you about," Will began.

Ostrey scowled. "I don't need a job."

At the kitchen table behind them, Hazel snorted. "Yes, you do."

"That's not why I've come." Will clarified. He looked out the small, smudged windowpane, envious of the branches swaying in the breeze. "It's a fine day. Would you like to go for a walk, Mr. Ostrey?"

Hazel guffawed at this, as though it had been an age since her husband had stepped foot outside the cottage.

"You know, Lord Castleton"—Ostrey gave his wife a spiteful look—"I believe I would."

He stood slowly, his knees unsteady, and Will handed him the cane propped beside the fireplace. Ostrey hobbled along with Will behind him, and when at last they emerged from the cottage, the older man staggered into the sunlight like a newborn colt finding its legs.

They'd only walked to the narrow, tree-lined road when Ostrey asked, "You'll be wanting to know about the accident, won't you?"

"How did you know?"

"It's the only significant event in my life," he said bitterly. "A horrible, tragic event, and I relive it every day."

"So, you were driving the coach that afternoon?"

"Aye. The weather 'twas not fit for driving, but the Laceys insisted on visiting Castleton Park. They said it was imperative that they meet with your father immediately. So I pulled the coach around and they climbed inside."

Ostrey was already huffing from the short walk, so Will led him to tree stump situated in the shade. "Come, sit."

The old driver sank gratefully onto the stump and continued. "When we started out, I thought we might reach our destination after all. The horses were able to maneuver in spite of the snow and ice. But then, as we were crossing the bridge, the coach wheels turned into ice skates and the whole cab slid sideways. It crashed into the low, stone wall on the edge of the bridge, and balanced there. I was thrown from the driver's seat and landed hard on the frozen ground.

"I heard the vicar and his wife screaming from inside the cab." His voice cracked as he recounted the tale. "I scrambled to my feet—I was much faster then—but just as I reached them, the cab shifted and toppled into the icy river, dragging the pair of horses with it.

"I jumped in and nearly drowned trying to rescue the Laceys. The door was jammed shut and the cab filled . . . By the time I pulled them to the shore, it was too late—their faces were already blue." The agony in his voice was palpable.

"I'm sorry," Will said. "It sounds as though you did everything you could. No one blames you for what happened to them."

"Not true, my lord. I held the reins that day, and I blame myself."

"Mr. Ostrey, this may seem an odd question, but is it possible that someone had access to the coach or horses prior to the accident? Could someone have tampered with the equipment, causing it to fail?"

"No, sir. I had been concerned about the weather, so before I climbed into the driver's seat that day, I inspected everything twice—the axles, braces, reaches, wheels, and fifth wheel. All were sound. I checked the horses' harnesses, too—every strap, band, and buckle."

Will considered this. "The extra precautions you took that day, were they all due to the weather?"

Ostrey inhaled deeply before he answered. "You'll think me strange for admitting it, but I had a feeling in my bones—a feeling that something dreadful was about to happen. I don't know how, but I knew. And still, there was nothing I could do to stop it. I'd never had a sense of foreboding so strong before then, and I haven't since."

In spite of the heat, a shiver stole down Will's spine. "What about the bridge itself? Was there anything suspicious in the road, any sort of slippery substance?"

"Besides the ice?" Ostrey shook his head sadly. "No, that was treacherous enough."

Will felt as though a weight had been lifted off his chest. He had no reason to doubt the truth of the man's claims, which meant his father, in this case at least, was not a murderer. But neither was Ostrey.

Pacing slowly in front of the tree stump where the old driver sat, Will said, "I remember that day, too. You were right—the weather wasn't fit for driving, but you didn't have a choice. If you hadn't driven the Laceys, they would have found someone else to do it. You must accept that the accident was just that—a horrible, tragic accident. You bear no responsibility for their deaths; if anything, you should be commended for your valiant attempt to save them."

Ostrey dragged a bony hand down the side of his face. "Guilt is an insidious thing, Lord Castleton. A man can know a thing as fact in his head"—he tapped his temple—"but guilt can convince him otherwise where it matters"—he patted his chest—"in his heart. It hobbles a person and weighs him down. Do you think I want to waste the rest of my life like this, a prisoner in my home and a burden to my wife?"

"Come work at Castleton Park. I could use someone knowledgeable and safety-minded in the stables." A lie, but an extra body in the stables certainly couldn't hurt.

"I don't know," Ostrey wavered. "I've grown weak."

"Work an hour or two every day to start. As you regain your strength, you can extend your hours. What do you say?"

The old man regarded him thoughtfully. "I'll give it a

try, for Hazel's sake. She's been so desperate to get me out of the cottage it's a wonder she hasn't set it on fire."

Will smiled, offering his hand. "Very good, Mr. Ostrey. I'll inform my steward that you'll start tomorrow." They shook on it, and Will took his leave.

But as he mounted his horse and rode back to Castleton Park, he kept thinking about what the man had said—about guilt holding a person back.

Meg was in the grips of guilt. Guilt over the death of her parents, the orphaning of her sisters, and now, her relationship with him. Somehow, he had to pry her free.

Even if she decided she *didn't* want to marry him, he couldn't let her go on flogging herself and pushing people away. He had to convince her that she deserved to be happy.

With someone.

Even if that someone wasn't him.

Meg had attacked the parlor with the dust cloth for most of the morning, and while the room was starting to look marginally better, it seemed that every speck of dust she'd removed from shelves, tables, and other surfaces had settled onto *her*. She heaved open a window and shook out the cloth, then did the same with her apron.

She was about to begin organizing the contents of several cabinets when a knock sounded at the front door.

Her heart leaped in her chest. Charlotte was working, and they rarely had other visitors. It could be a delivery, but it was far too soon for the dresses and other items they'd ordered yesterday to arrive.

Will had said he was going away for a while, but was it possible he'd returned already?

Despite her attempts to keep busy, she couldn't stop thinking about him. And even though they'd only been apart a few days . . . God, how she missed him. The way he could make her breath hitch with one wicked grin; the way he pretended as though he wasn't wrapped around Diana and Valerie's little fingers; the heart-stopping way he looked at her when he thought she wasn't watching.

Swallowing, she walked to the door and opened it.

There on her front step, was Mrs. Hopwood, looking disheveled and frazzled. "Mrs. Hopwood," she said, trying to hide her disappointment. "Why, what a pleasant surprise! Please, come in, and do forgive the—"

"It's awful!" the nanny interrupted, anguish plain on her face. "Lord Castleton isn't in town, and I didn't know where else to turn."

A frisson of fear skittered across the back of Meg's neck. "Where are the twins? Please, tell me they're all right."

"I don't know," she cried. Seeing the normally unflappable Mrs. Hopwood at her wit's end frightened Meg more than anything. "I tucked them into bed last night and went to sleep on a cot in the very same room, but when I awoke, they were gone. Their mother's gone, too."

"You did the right thing in coming here." Meg coaxed the nanny into the house and guided her to the settee in the parlor. "Perhaps Lila and the girls are merely visiting the park or doing a bit of shopping?" she asked hopefully.

Mrs. Hopwood shook her head. "They took most of their things with them. Everything except for this." She pulled Valerie's well-worn and much-loved doll from her satchel.

"How odd. Valerie would never leave Molly behind."

"I found it at the foot of my bed. It's as though she left it there for me . . . a clue."

Meg suppressed a shiver. "Did Lila mention anything about taking a trip? Had she been behaving suspiciously?"

"No, but when I slept till noon this morning, I knew something wasn't right. I'm usually up with the birds, but

I could barely move my legs when I first awoke. I'm wondering if someone slipped something into my tea before bed last night."

"You were *drugged*?" Good heavens, it did seem as though something sinister was afoot.

Meg leaned forward and patted the nanny's hand. "How do you feel now? Would you like something to eat or drink?"

"Thank you, dear, but no." Mrs. Hopwood's eyes brimmed with tears. "I just want to find the girls and make sure they're well."

"As do I." Meg stood and began to pace. "You stopped at Castleton House before you came here?"

Mrs. Hopwood nodded. "I could tell that Mr. Gibson was as concerned about the twins as I. He said that he didn't expect the earl to return for another day or two but that we had the staff at our disposal and that if there was anything we needed, all we had to do was ask."

Meg desperately wished Will were there. But he wasn't . . . and if Diana and Valerie were in jeopardy, there wasn't a second to waste.

"I think we must begin by returning to Lila's flat and looking for any evidence that might indicate where they've gone."

"It's so sad, isn't it?" Mrs. Hopwood said. "The safest place in the world for children *should* be with their mother. And yet, my intuition tells me that woman can't be trusted. I'm terribly frightened for the girls."

"I am too." Meg closed her eyes and said a brief prayer. *She* was the one who'd urged Will to let the girls visit with their mother and ultimately return home.

If harm came to Diana and Valerie due to her recklessness, she'd never, ever, forgive herself.

Chapter THIRTY-EIGHT

Will had barely crossed the threshold of Castleton House when Mrs. Lundy and Gibson descended on him like a pair of homing pigeons.

"It's the twins, my lord," Gibson said, taking his hat and bags. "I would have sent word, but I suspected you were already on your way home.

"What the devil are you talking about?"

Mrs. Lundy wrung her hands. "Mrs. Hopwood's upstairs, beside herself. The girls' mother drugged the nanny, took the twins, and left Town."

Will shook his head, certain he'd misunderstood. "Why would Lila drug Mrs. Hopwood?"

"Because she was up to no good," Gibson declared. "And she didn't wish to be stopped."

"Do we know where Lila and the girls have gone?"

The housekeeper shook her head. "No, but Miss Lacey is looking for them."

Dear Jesus. "Miss Lacey?" How the hell had she gotten involved in this mess?

"Yes, my lord. Mrs. Hopwood sought her help." The

butler stood tall. "Miss Lacey left this morning, and I insisted that Harry go with her. I thought you'd want the young lady to be escorted."

"Damned right, Gibson. Where are they headed?"

"To a village named Brinhaven in Essex," Mrs. Lundy piped up. "Apparently, the twins' mother has a sister who lives there. Mrs. Hopwood may know more specifics."

"I'm going to talk to her now." Will stalked toward the stairs and called to Gibson over his shoulder. "Have my horse saddled immediately. I leave for Brinhaven within the quarter hour."

"I wish we could return to London tonight," Meg said, her belly tied in knots.

Harry gave her a sympathetic smile as he helped her alight from the coach. "The horses require rest, and so do you. We'll leave at first light—I promise."

Meg had found Lila's sister in a tidy cottage on the outskirts of the village, but during their brief conversation, she hadn't been able to glean any information about the whereabouts of Lila or the twins. On the contrary, she had more questions than ever.

And they were hours away from London.

Harry guided her to the front door of a quaint, bustling inn located in the center of the village. "I'll secure a room for you and have some dinner sent up."

"Thank you, but I'm not hungry."

"You must eat," the footman said. "Lord Castleton would want you to."

"I rarely do what Lord Castleton wants," Meg snapped, instantly regretting it. "Oh, forgive me, Harry. I know you're only trying to look after me. I'm just so worried about the girls."

"It's all right, Miss Lacey. I'm worried about the mites, too. Wait here, please." He approached a counter, spoke to the innkeeper, and returned with a key. "Come. I'll see you safely to your room."

Before long, she was ensconced in a clean, comfortable room with a dinner tray . . . quite alone. Harry and the driver were having dinner in the taproom downstairs and would be sharing a room down the hall that night in case she should need anything.

But what she really needed was a clue. Some hint of where she could find Valerie and Diana. Or better yet, some way of knowing they were safe.

She lit the lamp by the bed and managed to eat a few spoonsful of stew and nibble at the bread before pushing the tray away.

Not tired in the least, she sprawled on the mattress, glad that she'd thought to pack a small satchel with a nightgown and a book. She'd brought Valerie's doll, too, and she pulled it out, squeezing it to her chest as though it could somehow bring her closer to finding the twins.

As she lay on the bed listening to the raucous shouts and laughter drifting up from the taproom below, she tried to convince herself that it was all a huge misunderstanding. That the girls were merely enjoying a spontaneous outing in the country with their mother. Perhaps they had already returned home and were tucked safely in their beds.

A knock at her door startled her, and she leaped up. Harry must be checking on her, or perhaps a servant had come to retrieve her dinner tray. She opened the door and there, filling the doorframe with his broad shoulders, was Will.

Her heartbeat hammered at the sight of him. How was it that in the space of a few days she'd forgotten how big, brooding, and breathtakingly handsome he was?

"Why, in God's name," he snapped, "would you open the door to a random stranger?"

"I am already regretting it," she answered, even as hope blossomed in her chest.

He swiftly closed the door behind him and hauled her against him. Her cheek pressed against the solid wall of his chest, and she almost wept with relief.

She was not alone anymore.

He speared his fingers through her hair and kissed the top of her head. "Don't worry, Meg. I will find them. I won't rest until I do."

"I don't understand why Lila would do it." She looked up at him. "Why would she drug sweet Mrs. Hopwood and whisk the girls away in the middle of the night?"

"Come, sit." He pulled her toward the room's one chair and raised an eyebrow at the doll she still held in one hand. "You brought Molly."

She smiled to herself, a little amused and deeply touched that he remembered the doll's name. "I hope to give it to Valerie. If we find her, that is."

"Don't say *if*. We will find her." He sat on the edge of the bed, opposite her, elbows propped on his knees. "Did you speak with Lila's sister?"

Meg nodded. "She said she doesn't know where Lila and the girls might have gone, and I believed her. She seemed truly concerned about Diana and Valerie and said she would have offered to raise the twins herself if she wasn't so feeble."

"Did she mention whether Lila has any other family? Other friends she might turn to?"

"She said she suspected Lila was staying with a mysterious new gentleman friend that she mentioned a couple of times in her letters. But her sister knows nothing about him."

"Damn."

Meg could tell from the concerned look on Will's face that he was thinking the same thing she was—that if Lila was indeed meeting with a romantic interest, he probably wouldn't appreciate having the twins about.

"If she wanted to run off with a lover, why didn't she just leave Diana and Valerie with us?" Will muttered. "She is the sort of woman who always acts in her own self-interests . . . so what did she have to gain by taking back the girls?"

Meg had asked herself that question, too. "Maybe she wished to appear a devoted, loving mother?"

He scowled. "I must admit, she fooled me."

"Where do we go from here?"

"Back to London. We need to discover who she's involved with."

Meg groaned in frustration. "May we leave now? I hate to waste another minute when the twins could be in danger."

"No. The journey will be faster and safer if we wait until morning. You need to rest and eat something." His eyes flicked to the dinner tray she'd barely touched. "That bad?"

"I've no appetite, but help yourself."

He frowned. "Would you like some wine? It might help you sleep."

"No, I don't think so." She hugged the doll to her belly.

"It's a shame that Molly can't talk." Will smiled ruefully. "She probably knows everything."

A chill ran down Meg's spine. "Do you think they're frightened?"

"Maybe. But they're brave girls, and they have each other. That's something we can be grateful for."

"Yes." Meg clung to the thought.

"Tomorrow, when we return to London, I'll question Lila's neighbors and try to learn who she's involved with. Once I have a name, I can track him down."

"I want to help, too."

"Of course, and you shall." He captured her hands and pressed his lips to the backs of them. "Tonight, however, there's nothing to be done. If you'd like, we can join Harry in the taproom for a while. Or, if you'd prefer to be alone, I can leave you here—with the door locked—and retrieve you first thing in the morning."

She swallowed. "Or?"

"Meg," he said softly, "I would do anything for you. I would leave. I would stay. I would sit by your bed and watch over you as you sleep or make love to you all night long. I would do anything to give you a measure of peace. Just tell me what you need."

"I don't want to be alone." She stood, set the doll on the chair, and circled her arms around his neck.

"It just so happens that I don't want you to be alone either." He chuckled, soothing her frayed nerves.

She pressed her forehead to his, breathing in his familiar, masculine scent. She didn't want him to go, but she couldn't fall into bed with him just because she was distraught. Their situation hadn't changed since she moved out of Castleton House. God willing, they'd find the twins . . . but then they'd go their separate ways.

"Perhaps we could just lie beside each other?" She felt her face grow hot. "Unless that would be too difficult . . ."

"It will be damned difficult," he murmured, "but I will take as much of you as you're willing to give. Now, and always."

"Thank you. I think that I might be able to fall asleep now that you're here."

"Would you like me to leave while you change?"

Her face got even hotter, but after all they'd been through and all they'd shared, it seemed silly to insist on privacy. "No, but perhaps you could face the wall?"

He did as she asked and thoughtfully turned down the lamp as well. She'd never hauled on her nightgown so fast, and she tossed her dress over the back of the chair before scrambling beneath the covers of the narrow bed. "Done," she said a bit breathlessly.

"You can trust me, you know." Amused, he sat on the chair and ate a few bites of her stew, shrugged off his jacket, and removed his boots. They chatted as he washed up and slid under the covers beside her, still dressed in his shirt and trousers.

"If you'd be more comfortable without your shirt . . ."

"I'd be more comfortable if *you* were naked," he teased, propping himself up on an elbow.

"I'm not certain I want you to be *that* comfortable," she said dryly, "but I would not mind if you chose to remove your shirt." His bare chest would be a pleasant distraction from her troubles. Tempting, too—but she would resist the pull.

Shrugging, he pulled his shirt over his head and threw it on top of her dress. "Try to sleep," he said, turning the lamp all the way down. "I'll be right here if you should need anything. Anything at all," he added suggestively.

Emboldened by the darkness, she snuggled close to him and slipped an arm around his waist. He caressed her arm lightly, lulling her into a content, trancelike state.

"Everything will work out," he whispered into her hair. "You'll see."

How she longed to believe him. "If any harm should come to the twins, I'll never forgive myself."

For several heartbeats, he was silent. Then he said, "Forgive yourself for what—wanting the girls to be happy? Wanting what's best for them?"

She appreciated what he was trying to do but wasn't about to let herself off the hook. "I should have been more cautious about reuniting them with Lila."

"You couldn't have known what she intended to do."

"I should have questioned her more, waited longer before entrusting them to her care."

"I don't mean to split hairs, but *I'm* the one who decided to let the twins return to their mother. Setting that fact aside for a moment, would you condemn one of your sisters for acting as you did?"

"They would never intentionally put a child in danger."

"Of course they wouldn't. Neither would you. And you didn't answer my question."

She thought for a moment, trying to find the crack in his logic. "I wouldn't condemn Julie or Beth, but this situation is different. *I* should have known better."

"And why is it that you are held to a different standard? Are you more intelligent, more powerful, more responsible than they?

She swallowed, glad that it was too dark for Will to see the tears gathering in her eyes. "No."

"Then why do you make yourself personally responsible for the safety and well-being of everyone around you?"

"Maybe because the alternative is just too awful to contemplate."

He wrapped his strong arms around her and kissed her temple. "And what is that?"

"That I can't protect the people I love," she said hoarsely. "That they could be snatched away from me at any time. That our happiness—our very existence—is subject to the whims of Fate."

"I'm afraid that has always been true, Meg. It's the reason we need to love freely and fiercely while we can." He stroked her hair, making her scalp tingle pleasantly. "Sure, we make our own choices, but Fate . . . well, she is squarely in charge."

"I admit, I find that terrifying."

"Sometimes. But it's also liberating. Once you accept

that many things in life are beyond your control, you might let go of the guilt . . . and realize you deserve to be happy."

She nuzzled his neck, letting the truth of his words sink in. "You're not talking about just the twins anymore, are you?"

"No."

He might have a point. But the guilt she'd been carrying around since her parent's death was a heavy, palpable thing, and it had been with her so long that it seemed a part of her. She couldn't shrug it off just because Will told her she deserved happiness.

"I will think about what you said."

"Good."

"In the meantime, promise you won't give up on me?"

He chuckled. "Never even crossed my mind."

Chapter THIRTY-NINE

Will traveled back to London in the coach with Meg. Normally, he'd have preferred to ride horseback and feel the wind on his face, but her company made the close quarters of the cab more than tolerable.

Proving what a damned lovesick fool he was.

As they approached London, he reached between them and squeezed her hand. "Would you like me to take you home?"

"No!" she said. "You promised I could go to Lila's and help look for clues to the identity of her lover."

He raised a hand in mock defense. "I only thought you might like to change or let your sisters know you're safe."

She shot him an apologetic smile. "I don't need anything, and my sisters won't worry. I'll send word to them this afternoon."

"Very well. I told the driver I want to stop at Castleton House briefly, to see if we've received any messages related to the twins."

He was thinking about Marina, and wondering if the mysterious man had approached her again. Will suspected he had something to do with this. He considered telling Meg about him, but decided against it. She was worried enough as it was.

"A good idea." Meg's forehead creased as she looked out the window.

"You're not going to find them roaming the streets, you know," he said.

She frowned at him. "I hope not . . . but it cannot hurt to look."

Half an hour later, they finally arrived at Will's house. The coach had barely rolled to a stop when Gibson sprinted down the steps, moving faster than Will had ever seen.

Throwing open the cab door, he leaped to the ground. "What's the hell's gotten into you, Gibson?"

"It's the twins, my lord," he said, gasping for air.

Jesus. Dread turned his veins to ice. "What have you learned?"

"They're here," said the butler. "And they're fine."

"What? Thank God!" Meg scooped up Molly and jumped out of the coach into Will's arms. He lowered her to the ground, grabbed her hand, and together they sprinted toward the front door.

"They're in the nursery," Mrs. Lundy cried as his boots slid across the foyer's tiles, "with Mrs. Hopwood!"

They dashed down the corridor and up the staircase. Will was tempted to take the steps two at a time but wouldn't dream of leaving Meg behind—as if she'd let him. "Are you all right?" he asked her over his shoulder.

"I just need to see them with my own eyes," she said in a trembling voice. "Then I'll believe it's true."

"Miss Lacey? Lord Castleton?"

Will recognized the slightly raspy voice. "We're here, Diana!"

Both girls tore out of the nursery and met them on the landing. The moment Will's knees hit the floor, he was smothered in sloppy hugs. He scooped the girls up, one in each arm and presented them to Meg, who embraced all three of them.

"We were so worried about you two," she said through her tears.

"Why are you crying?" Valerie asked.

"Because she's so happy to see you," Will said. "We both are."

Mrs. Hopwood emerged from the nursery as well, smiling at the reunion. Will had scores of questions for her and the girls but didn't think it wise to launch into an interrogation. Not right away, at least.

"Here's Molly." Meg handed the doll to Valerie. "I thought you might have missed her."

"I did." The girl squeezed her eyes shut as she clutched the doll to her chest. "But I missed you more."

"Oh, Valerie." Meg turned into a watering pot, and Will laughed.

"We missed you, too, Lord Castleton," Diana assured him, melting his heart a little.

Before he knew what he was saying, he blurted, "Maybe you should call me something else—like Uncle Will."

"Really?" Diana squealed.

Valerie hugged him tighter. "You're not angry with us?" she asked.

"No, darling," Meg said firmly. "Why would we be?"

"We ran away from the orphanage." Diana's voice held a hint of defiance, reminding him of a certain someone else he knew. He and Meg exchanged a look.

"How did you come to be at an orphanage?" he asked, almost afraid to know the answer.

"Mama took us there," Valerie said softly. "She said she'd come back for us after a while . . ."

"But I didn't believe her," Diana said. "After two nights in that awful place, we couldn't stand it any longer. So we managed to sneak out of the dining hall and onto the street just before breakfast. We ran around the corner and hailed a hackney cab."

"You hailed a cab all by yourselves?" Meg asked, incredulous.

"I told the driver that we were going to see the Earl of Castleton, and then I gave him the address," Diana said proudly. "I know it by heart."

"Well done," Will said. "How did you pay the fare?"

She blushed a little. "I told him you'd pay and that you'd tip handsomely."

Will laughed at that. "I certainly would have. I assume Gibson saw to it?"

"Yes, Mr. Gibson paid the driver with his own money and said he was happy to do it," Diana said, beaming.

"You did the right thing," Meg said to them both. "You're not hurt, are you?"

"No." Valerie shook her head. "But we had to leave all our beautiful new dresses and things behind. We were afraid if we tried to take them with us, someone would know we were running away."

"Do not worry," Will said. "I'll retrieve them for you. And if anything is lost, we'll simply replace it. As long as the two of you are safe, nothing else matters."

"That's what I told them, too," Mrs. Hopwood said.

"You'll be living with me from now on," Will told them, just to be sure there was no confusion. "And I'm very glad about that."

He knew it would take them some time to come to grips with what their mother had done, but he hoped they were young enough that the memories would fade over time . . . and be replaced with happier ones.

As if echoing his thoughts, Valerie piped up, "Will Miss Lacey be staying with us, too?"

Meg swallowed. "I . . . I won't live here, as I did before,

but I promise to visit often. And you may visit me anytime you like."

The twins' faces fell. Will's stomach sank as well, but he pasted on a smile for the girls' sake. "I'll take you to visit Miss Lacey as often as you wish. But right now," he said, "I think we should celebrate the fact that we are all back together."

"How?" the girls cried.

"By making a trip to the kitchen and seeing if we can convince Cook to spoil us."

"Hooray!"

"Why don't I take them down," Meg offered smoothly, "while you chat with Mrs. Hopwood? You can join us shortly."

Carefully, he set the twins on the ground, oddly reluctant to let them go. "Yes, run along with Miss Lacey," he said.

Once they were out of earshot, he turned to Mrs. Hopwood. "Were you able to learn anything from the girls?"

The older woman frowned. "When their mother left them at the orphanage, she gave no hint as to where she was going. She simply said she was sorry to leave them, but that she'd received an offer she couldn't refuse."

Interesting. "Where was the orphanage?" He presumed there was more than one in London and felt somewhat ashamed that he didn't know for certain.

"Mr. Gibson said the hackney driver came from Whitechapel. There's a foundling home for girls there." She shuddered. "Terrible places, orphanages."

"I promise you that Diana and Valerie will never see the inside of one again."

"Thank heaven." The nanny pressed a hand to her chest.

"I'm sorry you were involved in this and very grateful that you and the girls are unharmed. I do hope you'll stay on with us, in my employ."

"Of course I will. Trying to keep up with the wee ones is what keeps me young." She looked like she wanted to say more, but pressed her lips firmly together.

"What is it, Mrs. Hopwood? Please, I'd like you to feel free to speak your mind."

"It's none of my business," she began, "but I do hope you'll be able to convince Miss Lacey to stay. Not because I need someone to share the responsibilities with, but because I think Diana and Valerie need her. And I suspect she needs them as well."

"Never fear," Will said with significantly more confidence than he felt. "I'm working on it."

"Oh, Julie, it's lovely!" Meg and Beth circled their sister in the dress shop's changing room, admiring her new gown from every angle. Wispy and white with petal sleeves and a shimmering, silver sash, the gown flattered Julie's statuesque figure.

"You look like the goddess Athena," Beth announced dreamily.

"Be careful," Julie teased. "Mortals have been turned into spiders for lesser offences."

Meg sighed a breath of relief. Julie's ball gown had required a few extra alterations, but every farthing they'd spent and every trip they'd made to the modiste had been worth it. She looked exquisite—and happier than Meg had seen her in ages. She'd be the belle of tomorrow night's . . . er, soiree.

The seamstress carefully lifted the gown over Julie's head. "I'll take this into the back and wrap it for you, miss," she said, before whisking yards of frothy white silk out of the dressing room.

"We'd better hurry home," Beth said. "I want to finish up a few chores in the garden."

"I hope Uncle Alistair's still napping when we return."

Julie presented her back so Meg could lace up her old navy dress. It seemed especially drab and heavy in comparison to the ethereal white one. "I need to straighten one last bookshelf in his study."

The sisters gathered their reticules and shawls, chatting merrily as they walked out of the changing area and through the front of the shop. Meg picked up the wrapped parcel at the counter, and the shopkeeper smiled broadly. "Thank you, Miss Lacey. I hope your ball is a smashing success."

Meg cringed. "Actually, it's more of a soir—"

"Miss Lacey?" A stunning woman with dark hair and almond-shaped eyes glided toward Meg. "Miss Margaret Lacey?"

"Yes." Meg searched her mind for where she might have met the woman and found nary a clue. "Forgive me. Have we met?"

"We haven't. However, I know of you. Please, forgive *me* for being so forward. I'm an old friend of Lord Castleton's." Meg shook the hand she offered. "My name is Marina."

A wave of nausea hit her. Meg had no claim on Will but couldn't deny the fierce jealousy that bubbled up inside at the sight of his ex-mistress.

Frown lines marred Marina's face, smooth and flawless in every other respect. Lowering her voice, she said, "I had heard that Lord Castleton was searching for his young wards, the twins. Do you happen to know if he has found them?"

Guilt sliced through Meg. She'd let jealousy consume her, while Marina was clearly concerned about Diana and Valerie's welfare. "Yes," she assured her. "They're safe at Castleton House."

"I'm delighted to hear it," Marina said, her relief palpable. "Especially after all the odd things that have been happening. Perhaps Will, er, Lord Castleton mentioned the strange gentleman to you? The one who's been asking questions about the twins?"

"He did," Meg lied. So *that* was why Will had met with Marina. She tilted her head, thoughtful. She'd assumed that the twins' ordeal had simply been a result of Lila's neglectful parenting. But was it possible that someone else was involved too? And for perhaps more sinister reasons? "Do you think that the strange incidents are related to the twins' disappearance?"

"I don't know for certain," Marina admitted. She glanced around the dress shop suspiciously. "But my intuition has never failed me before. Something evil is afoot. You and your sisters should have a care when you're out and about—just in case."

"Thank you," Meg said earnestly. "We will. Allow me to introduce my sisters, Elizabeth and Juliette."

"Please, call me Beth."

"And I'm Julie."

"It's a pleasure to meet all of you," Marina said with a sincere smile. "And I do apologize for interrupting your outing. I haven't any sisters, but if I did, I'd spend at least one day each week just as you are, shopping for gowns, hats, and shoes."

"Oh, this is a rarity for us," Beth said, laughing.

"The shopping part," Julie clarified. "We're always together. It happens to be our motto."

Meg saw the longing in Marina's dark eyes. It appeared that she suffered a twinge of jealousy, too.

"If you're free tomorrow evening, we're hosting a little soiree at my uncle's house," Meg blurted. Clearly, she'd lost her wits. "We'd love it if you'd come."

"A soiree? How wonderful!"

Beth rolled her eyes. "It's actually more of a *ball*."

Chapter FORTY

Everything was ready.

And while Uncle Alistair's humble townhouse would never resemble the grand ballrooms of the tôn, it had a charm all its own. Meg preferred the warmth of stuffed bookshelves to high ceilings and the ambiance of flickering candles to glittering chandeliers.

She, Beth, and Julie had pushed most of the furniture to the sides of the rooms, leaving the centers free for guests to mingle . . . or even dance. They'd placed freshly cut flowers on windowsills and mantels, making the whole house colorful and fragrant.

Though it had rained most of the morning, the clouds parted, leaving Beth's newly revitalized garden damp but refreshingly cool.

Meg smoothed the muted gold bombazine of her new dress, glad she'd opted to purchase something more practical than a ball gown. Her dress didn't float when she walked, like Julie's. It didn't shimmer in the candlelight, like Beth's. But even if it could best be described as *serviceable*, it was new and flattering and far nicer than any other dress she owned.

In less than an hour, when the first guests arrived, she'd greet them with her head held high. She scurried out of her bedchamber and, in a deliciously unladylike display, shouted down the stairs. "Julie? Beth? Do either of you require help with your hair?"

"No, we've finished," Beth called back from the vicinity of the parlor.

"But a package just arrived for you," Julie added.

"Coming!" Meg wanted to take one last walk through the rooms and check with the staff to make sure the refreshments were ready.

As she glided down the stairs, the sight of her sisters looking so beautiful and elegant made her breath catch. Her brief stint as a governess in Will's employ may have led to heartbreak and pain, but it had also led to this—a new start for her sisters. She would be forever grateful for that.

"Oh Meg," cried Beth. "You look lovely!"

"Radiant." Julie handed her a tidy parcel wrapped in brown paper. A small note was tucked beneath the string. "A messenger delivered it."

"I can't imagine what it could be." Meg went to the settee, which they'd centered under the picture window for the evening's festivities, and opened the note. She recognized the handwriting at once.

Dear Miss Lacey,
     We hope you like your new gown. We chose the color. We think you will look like a fairy princess. Uncle Will agrees with us. Take our advice and stay far away from chocolate. Please visit us soon.
                                    Most sincerely yours,
                                    Diana and Valerie

"Who's it from?" Julie craned her neck to see the note.

"The twins. It's a new gown." Meg swiped at her eyes, determined not to cry. "I think I'll open it tomorrow, when things are calmer."

"Tomorrow? Are you *mad*?" Julie placed her hands on her hips. "If you don't open it now, I will."

"Very well." While her sisters hovered over her, Meg tore off the paper and opened the box's lid. Nestled inside was the most lovely, sparkling, sigh-inducing dress she'd ever seen.

"That's no ordinary gown," Beth whispered reverently.

Meg pulled it from the box and gasped as several feet of deep rose silk cascaded to the floor like a waterfall. The gown's tiny, puffed sleeves were meant to be worn off the shoulder, and its low, square neckline was meant to frame her décolletage. The shimmering light pink satin sash matched the delicate lace that graced the hemline.

It was the sort of dress Meg had never even dared to dream about.

In a tone that brooked no argument, Julie said, "Go upstairs and change."

Meg swallowed. There would be no hiding in this gown. "I've already dressed and done my hair with a ribbon to match. Perhaps I should save—"

"*Now*." Julie gave a death stare, and Meg desperately looked for an ally in Beth.

"I concur with our younger sister. You *will* wear the rose silk gown tonight—even if Julie and I have to wrestle you into it."

Will shouldered his way through the crush of guests in Lord Wiltmore's townhouse, looking for Meg. He greeted his mother, Lady Rebecca, and Miss Winters who were chatting in the parlor and sipping champagne. It was Miss

Winters who suggested that he might find Meg in the dining room-turned-dance floor.

The moment he spotted her in the crowded room, shining like a rose-colored diamond, he regretted buying the gown. Now every man at the bloody ball recognized her for the beauty she was. He should have purchased her a shawl to go with it—something to cover all that luminous, smooth skin. Hellfire and damnation.

He stalked toward her, intent on breaking up the circle of young bucks vying for her attention but was halted by someone pulling on his arm. Irritated, he turned.

Dear God. What on earth was his ex-mistress doing at Meg's ball? "Marina?"

"Will," she said in an urgent whisper, "may I speak with you privately?"

"It's really not a good time." He glanced over at Meg, who was valiantly resisting an invitation to dance. Sooner or later, however, she was bound to cave to the relentless pressure, and if she were going to dance with anyone, it would damned well be *him*.

Marina heaved a sigh. "I've no wish to interrupt your evening, but this pertains to the strange encounters I've had. I think I know the identity of the mysterious gentleman . . . and he's *here*."

"What?" She had his full attention now. "Follow me. The garden will afford us some privacy."

Will angled past the musicians, and Marina followed him out onto a small stone patio bordered by well-manicured bushes and a vine-laced trellis.

He dragged a hand through his hair. "What in God's name are you doing here?"

Marina rolled her eyes. "Miss Lacey invited me, if you must know. I feared it might be awkward—"

"I'll say," he interrupted.

"—but she and her sisters couldn't have been more

gracious. And I'm glad I came, because I'm almost certain that the man who approached me at Vauxhall Gardens and threatened me at the opera is here."

Will's hands curled into fists. "Who?"

"Miss Lacey introduced him as Lord Redmere."

Will shook his head, disbelieving. "The marquess is the last person I'd suspect. What makes you think he's the one who's been harassing you?"

"I can't say exactly," Marina said. "But he has a very distinct voice. When he addressed me tonight, I felt a shiver in my bones. I'd wager my best pearl necklace—it's him."

Will would have liked to have a bit more evidence to go on than a familiar voice and Marina's intuition, but it was a start. "I'll see what I can find out."

Already his mind was scrambling, trying to make sense of the theory. What motive could Redmere possibly have for stalking Marina? The stranger had asked about the twins, their mother, and Meg. Nothing added up.

"Thank you again for the information," he told Marina. "I doubt Redmere would be so bold as to corner you at the ball tonight, but to be safe, I'd suggest you try to avoid him."

She shrugged. "I will stay out of his way . . . but I look forward to seeing what transpires." With that she turned to make her way inside, and Will followed.

As he entered the dining room, he spotted Meg, still fending off admirers. Fickle bastards. He searched the other clusters of guests peppered around the perimeter of the room, looking for Redmere.

"If I didn't know better," a feminine voice at his side said smoothly, "I'd think you were avoiding me."

He glanced down at Lady Rebecca, trying to mask his exasperation. "Not at all. In fact, I was just looking for your father. I'd like a word with him."

She arched a brow, and he could tell from her sudden intake of breath that she'd jumped to the wrong conclusion.

"Papa was conversing with Lord Wiltmore when last I saw him. Shall I fetch him for you?"

"No. I'll find him." Bowing hastily, he took a step toward the parlor. "Excuse me."

Will barely made it to the doorway before Redmere approached, his gaze calculating. "Evening, Castleton. I saw you talking with Rebecca. I must say, the two of you make a striking pair."

Redmere had tried to make it sound like a casual observation, but Will knew the man had an agenda . . . and a piece of the puzzle suddenly fell into place. "I was just looking for you, Redmere. What do you say we step outside for a moment?"

"If you wish. A nice night for a bit of fresh air." He patted the front pocket of his pristine evening jacket and smiled conspiratorially. "I've smuggled in a couple of cheroots if you'd like to indulge."

"Not a bad idea," Will lied. He walked through the dining room once more, catching Meg's eye this time, and casting a regretful look her way. She frowned slightly, and he vowed to himself that he'd spend the rest of the evening making up for his inattentiveness.

As soon as he dealt with Redmere.

The trio of musicians didn't miss a note as Will and Redmere angled past them, spilled out into the garden, and moved away from the noise.

The older man reached into his pocket, pulled out a cheroot, and offered it to Will.

"No, thank you."

Redmere pursed his lips as though vaguely insulted. Will didn't give a damn.

"Something on your mind, Castleton?" He held the cheroot under his nose and inhaled deeply.

"I understand you've been making inquiries into my personal affairs."

"I don't know what the hell you're talking about," Redmere said coolly, "but I can tell you this—I don't care for your tone."

Will squared his shoulders. "Then you should cease harassing and questioning innocent parties regarding my business."

"There's nothing *innocent* about your ex-mistress. What makes you think I have any interest in your *affairs*?"

"I suspect," Will said conversationally, "that you're trying to facilitate a match between your daughter and me."

Redmere shook his head, incredulous. "You're a cocky son of a bitch, Castleton. For the life of me, I don't know what Rebecca sees in you. But for some goddamned reason she's rather smitten. And you'll be lucky to have her."

"I'm certain *someone* will be lucky to have her, but it won't be me."

"You might want to rethink your position." Redmere paced the patio slowly. Threateningly.

"And why is that?"

"You seem to like that governess of yours. The oldest of Wiltmore's Wallflowers."

A chill skittered down Will's spine. "Careful, Redmere. Your fascination with my personal business grows tiresome."

"Take her as your mistress if you must . . . but *don't* make her your countess."

"I don't recall asking your advice." Will seethed but fought to keep his temper in check. He still needed more information.

"We both know that my daughter is far more suited to the role of countess than the Lacey chit. You'll soon become bored with the wallflower, toss her aside, and turn into a loving, devoted husband . . . to Rebecca."

Will swallowed, struggling to contain the rage pounding in his chest. "*That's* why you convinced Lila to take the twins? So I'd have no need for a governess?"

Redmere shrugged. "I didn't *convince* Lila so much as *bribe* her."

Jesus. Will took a step toward him, backing the marquess up against the trellis. "Were you aware she deposited them in an orphanage at the first opportunity?"

Redmere snorted. "Honestly, what Lila chose to do with the hellions was no concern of mine. All I cared about was removing them from your household before you took Rebecca as your wife. A young bride shouldn't be expected to rear your by-blows. If you had any brains at all, you'd be thanking me for getting the rascals out of your hair."

"They are not pests to be exterminated, you bastard. They're *children*. And for the record, all your sick, twisted plans were for nothing. The twins are safe at home, with me. Furthermore, I'm going to marry Miss Lacey."

"No, you're not." Redmere sneered.

"What did you say?" Will took a menacing step toward the marquess, bumping chests with him and hankering for a fight.

"You won't marry her, because if you do, I'll tell her you've been consorting with your mistress, right under her nose." Redmere gave a sinister laugh. "I saw you out here with her earlier, and I'd wager I'm not the only one." He paused to let the implied threat sink in. "I have to hand it to you, Castleton, you've got more stones than most men, consorting with one mistress while attending the ball of another."

The thin thread of Will's control snapped. He grabbed Redmere by the lapels of his jacket, lifted him off his feet, and shoved him against the trellis, shaking the entire structure.

"What's going on out here?"

Will looked over his shoulder to see Meg rushing toward them.

"Go inside," he ordered.

True to form, she ignored him. Jabbing him in the arm, she said, "Lord Redmere is a guest in my home. I must ask you to release him."

"I'm afraid I can't. We have unfinished business." He slammed the marquess into the trellis again, splintering the wood at his back. "Isn't that right, Redmere?"

"I feel obliged to inform you, Miss Lacey," the man sputtered, "that Lord Castleton has been meeting with his mistress while here, at your ball."

"Don't listen to him, Meg. He's trying to blackmail me into marrying his daughter."

Meg shot the marquess, who was already quite red in the face, a withering governess stare. "Really, Lord Redmere, your behavior is less than gentlemanly." Turning her critical eye on Will, she added, "However, I cannot condone any sort of violence toward a guest at a gathering in my home. Once more, I must request that you release him."

"For God's sake, Meg, he's responsible for what happened to the twins."

"*What*?"

"He bribed Lila to get rid of them."

Her eyes narrowed, and her chest rose and fell as she grappled with the knowledge. "In that case," she said deliberately, "you have my permission to give Lord Redmere *exactly* what he deserves."

Before the words were out of her mouth, Will landed a punch squarely in the marquess's gut. His back broke through the trellis and Will swept Meg out of the way just before the structure collapsed on Redmere, burying him in a pile of lattice and greenery.

At the loud crack of wood, the musicians ceased their playing and craned their necks toward the terrace. The lively strains of a reel were replaced with the pitiful groans of the marquess.

A few curious souls rushed outside, gasping at the utter chaos. Within seconds, it seemed every guest at the ball had squeezed onto the patio to witness the spectacle.

Meg stared at the mess, her face pale with shock. Will could kick himself for ruining her ball . . . but damn, it had felt good to punch Redmere. And she *had* given him her blessing.

He shrugged to himself and patted the bump in his breast pocket. He might as well give the ton something else to gape at.

Chapter FORTY-ONE

Heat flooded Meg's face as London's elite craned their necks, eager to see the unfolding scandal. Her sisters pushed their way to the front of the crowd, their expressions crestfallen. Beth's beautiful garden was in a shambles. Lord Redmere's legs and boots protruded from the pile in a manner that might have made Meg laugh if it hadn't occurred at the first ball she and her sisters had ever hosted. Or ever would.

She still reeled from the news that he'd orchestrated the twins' abandonment at the orphanage and had to summon every ounce of self-control she possessed to prevent herself from kicking him in the side as he lay writhing on the ground.

Lady Rebecca emerged from between two rather large matrons, her face contorting with dread as she realized the flailing legs belonged to none other than her father. *"Papa?"*

It seemed all eyes were on Meg, waiting for her to explain or provide some commentary on the decidedly odd turn the evening's festivities had taken. She opened her mouth, unsure of what she might say, when Will placed a steadying hand on her back and whispered in her ear, "Allow me."

To the crowd he said, "Lord Redmere had an unfortunate encounter with the garden trellis"—several ladies gasped sympathetically—"but I am happy to report he is none the worse for the wear." He found his friend in the throng and addressed him. "Torrington, perhaps you'd be so good as to extract Redmere from the debris and escort him and Lady Rebecca home."

Lord Torrington unceremoniously grabbed Redmere by one leg, dragged him out of the pile by his ankle, and hauled him to his feet as the guests looked on, aghast. The marquess appeared dazed but not gravely injured.

"You see," Will said jovially, "I told you he was fine."

"Oh, Papa!" Rebecca ran to him and threw her arms around his middle, causing him to grimace.

"The ribs may be a bit sore," Will explained as Lord Torrington ushered the marquess and his daughter through the garden's back gate.

Meg breathed a sigh of relief as they left without further incident, but the damage had already been done. Just once, she wished that *something* in her life would go as planned.

"Now then," Will said to the stunned crowd, "since you're all gathered here, you might as well stay and hear this."

Meg blinked. Hear *what*, precisely?

Will looked into her eyes and took her hands in his. Just as he was about to speak, Uncle Alistair fumbled his way through the guests and stumbled onto the patio, his white hair waving triumphantly.

"At last, congratulations are in order! It is with heartfelt joy and immense delight that I have given this upstanding gentleman my blessing to marry Margaret, my beloved niece. Never was a couple more deserted of happiness. May they live long and improper!"

His nonsensical words echoed through the garden, which then fell silent.

Meg closed her eyes. By all accounts, she should be truly and utterly humiliated. Yet, she felt no shame. Only love.

It surrounded her. Love for her uncle, her sisters, and Charlotte. Love for the twins and Mrs. Hopwood. And, above all, love for Will.

She felt her parents' presence too, in the twinkling stars above and warm evening breeze tickling the curls at her nape. Their greatest wish had been to make Meg and her sisters happy. Who knew? Perhaps they'd been the ones to bring her and Will together again.

When she opened her eyes, he was smiling, still holding her hands. Beth, Julie, and Charlotte stood to one side of her, nearly bouncing with anticipation. Marina gazed at them, a wistful look in her eyes. Even Will's mother, Lady Castleton appeared rather misty and uncharacteristically sentimental.

Will cleared his throat. "Thank you for your kind wishes, Lord Wiltmore. However, I haven't asked her yet."

Uncle Alistair blinked and waved his cane impatiently. "Then get on with it, man!"

Meg cast an apologetic smile at Will, but he seemed unflustered—and focused on no one but her.

"I confess this evening has not gone even remotely as I planned," he began. "But that's the way life is—full of surprises, some wonderful and some tragic. We cannot change the past any more than we can predict what trials we'll face in the future. But we *can* choose who's by our side . . . and Meg, I want to be by yours, now and always."

Her chest nearly bursting, she swallowed, then nodded.

"Miss Margaret Lacey," he said soberly, "you have my

heart and my soul. And if you agree to marry me, you'll make me the happiest man in the world." He gazed at her, his brown eyes aglow with love. "Please. Say you will."

It took her a moment to respond, not because she had to consider her answer, but because her throat was thick with emotion. "I love you, and yes. Of course I will!"

The crowd erupted in a chorus of cheers as he lifted and spun her around.

"I almost forgot." He set her on her feet, reached into his pocket, and presented her with a lovely antique ring. "It belonged to my grandmother," he said, slipping it onto her finger. "She would have adored you."

"You know," Lady Castleton said softly, as she dabbed the corners of her eyes with a handkerchief, "I believe she would have. And even I can see how happy you make my son. You'll be a fine countess, Miss Lacey."

The next several minutes were a blur of tears, embraces, and felicitations, but at last, the musicians picked up their instruments and began to play. The guests slowly retreated into the house for refreshments, dancing, and gossip, leaving Will and Meg alone on the terrace.

"Thank you for my lovely gown," she said, turning so that the pink silk sparkled in the moonlight. "It's perfect."

He shrugged. "Valerie and Diana helped me select it. They had very specific requirements."

"I'm sure they did." Her heart melted a little more. "You're going to be a wonderful father, you know."

"I'm going to try," he said soberly. "I used to think that the twins would be better off if I kept my distance."

"And now?"

"I realize they need me as much as I need them."

She arched a brow. "That's very sweet."

"I'm not sweet," he said with a scowl.

"No?"

"I'm demanding."

She arched a brow. "How so?"

"Like this." He pulled her much closer than was proper and twirled her around the patio in time with the music. "I've been waiting all night for a dance. But now that we're dancing, all I can think of is stripping this gown off of you and kissing every inch of your skin."

Wantonly, she pressed her hips against his, feeling the long, hard length of him. "Is that all?"

He growled, making her shiver deliciously. "Careful, vixen, or I'll take you to that bench, lift your pretty skirt, and ravish you until you're crying out in pleasure."

She glanced at the bench, picturing it. Wanting it. "I miss you," she admitted.

"Come visit the twins tomorrow. During their nap, you and I can steal a few minutes alone."

"I suppose I can wait till then," she said with a sigh.

He gave her a long, lingering kiss that made her toes curl. "Trust me, I'll make it worth the wait."

"Miss Lacey!"

Valerie and Diana dashed across the nursery and sandwiched her in a fierce hug.

"Did you like your gown?" Diana asked.

"I adored it. Thank you."

"I'll bet you looked pretty," Valerie said.

"Indeed she did." Will guided them all to the window seat and settled the twins between him and Meg. "Miss Lacey and I have something to tell you."

"Oh no." Valerie's face crinkled with worry.

"Don't fret," Will said, chuckling, "I have a feeling you'll like this news."

"Just tell us," Diana said bravely. "Whatever it is, we will face it."

Meg's heart melted. The poor dears had been through so much. "Your Uncle Will has asked me to marry him"—the girls' eyes grew impossibly wide—"and I've said yes."

"Hooray!" they cried, jumping on the window seat in a spontaneous and heartfelt celebration that made Meg love them even more.

"My two favorite people in the world." Valerie flopped onto Will's lap with a sigh. "And they're going to marry!"

"That means Miss Lacey will live here," Diana said cautiously, "with us?"

"Of course, with you!" Meg assured her.

"We're a family," Will said. "We belong together."

"Truly?" Valerie asked, desperate to believe.

Will nodded. "I think the four of us will make an excellent team."

Meg had never seen the twins look so happy.

A few hours later, while Mrs. Hopwood coaxed the girls into their beds for a nap, Meg and Will tiptoed downstairs and snuck into his study. He locked the door behind them, drew the curtains, and sank into his chair, propping his crossed heels on the corner of the desk.

Meg's body thrummed with anticipation.

Steepling his fingers under his chin, he let his gaze rove over her body. "So, Miss Lacey, what makes you think you're qualified for this position?"

She arched a brow and perched on an arm of the chair opposite him. "Why, is this an interview, my lord?"

He shot her a slow, wicked grin that turned her insides to jelly. "It is."

She blinked innocently. "I suppose I'm confused because you're not hung over."

"You're perceptive—a fine quality. But I must confess that I'm dismayed by your lack of experience."

"I have gained some experience of late," she purred,

"but will readily admit I'm still a novice." She reached for the laces at the side of her gown, untied them, and eased the sleeves off her shoulders. "Perhaps I can make up for it in other ways."

His eyes dark with desire, he stood and stalked to her side of the desk, leaning a hip against it. "I'm afraid you'll have to be more specific, Miss Lacey. How else am I to determine if you're qualified?"

"Well, there's this." She pushed her bodice down to her waist, wriggled the gown over her hips, and let it puddle to the floor. Dressed in only her chemise and corset, she arched her back seductively.

"It seems you *do* have some skills." He swallowed, clearly struggling to stay in character. "But before I can make a decision I'll need to see more."

"Why do I suspect you'll be a very demanding employer?" She loosened the tie at the top of her chemise and tugged at the neckline, exposing taut, rosy peaks to his scorching stare.

"Damn, you're beautiful." He pushed himself off the desk, moved behind her, and cupped her swollen breasts in his hands. "I'll never have enough of you, Meg."

Her breath hitched as he hiked up the hem of her chemise. "Does this mean I have the position, Lord Castleton?"

He kissed the back of her neck, making her knees go weak. "How soon can you start?"

"I'm ready . . . now," she breathed.

"Very well, Miss Lacey, we'll need to begin by clearing off my desk . . ."

Read on for an excerpt from Anna Bennett's next novel
in the *Wayward Wallflowers* series

I DARED THE DUKE

Coming soon from St. Martin's Paperbacks

"Well then, Miss Lacey"—Lord help him, he must be mad—"I believe we have a bargain."

She thrust her hand forward, but Alex shook his head. This called for something more momentous than a handshake. "We shall seal the deal with a toast."

He strode to the sideboard, grabbed the decanter of brandy, refilled his glass, and topped off hers. They sat on a settee in front of the fireplace, the blue silk of her gown almost touching his knee.

After thinking for a moment, he raised his glass. "To ostrich feathers, which are far more utilitarian than most people realize."

Grinning, she raised her glass as well. "To leprechauns. Who are far more real than most people realize."

He clinked his snifter against hers and met her sultry gaze as the brandy slid down his throat. Damn, but those blue eyes of hers bewitched him.

She certainly wasn't *acting* like a wallflower. And in that moment, as a saucy smile played about her full lips, he knew that he'd rue the day he'd foolishly referred to her and her sisters as the Wilting Wallflowers. His stupid, careless, jocular quip had become the cruel label that she and her sisters hadn't been able to shake for three seasons—and it would no doubt come back to haunt him. Maybe it already had.

Miss Lacey set her glass on the table in front of them and smoothed the skirt of her gown, as though signaling she meant to return to business. Pity, that.

"There are a couple of terms we should clarify," she announced.

Holy hell. "Such as?"

"For one, our little deal must remain a secret. I would not want your grandmother to know I had to coerce you to spend time with her. That would rather defeat the purpose."

Why must she always make him feel two inches tall? "Agreed."

"Some subtlety on your part shall be required. A bit of finesse."

He shot her a wicked look. "I've no shortage of finesse. Perhaps you've already heard."

Her cheeks pinkened, and she brushed an imaginary speck of lint off her shoulder. "What I mean to say is that you cannot be too obvious or rush your grandmother to make a decision with respect to her three wishes."

He draped an arm over the back of the settee, his fingertips tantalizingly close to a curl that dangled from her nape. "I do understand, Miss Lacey. However, time is of the essence. I feel confident that we shall be able to accommodate each other's needs."

The blush on her cheeks deepened and spread down her neck over the delectable swells of her breasts, triggering a highly inconvenient wave of desire.

Dragging his gaze away from her neckline, he arched

a brow. "Have you any other last minute rules you wish to impose?"

"Yes, as a matter of fact. It's not a rule so much as a request." She bit her lip as she glanced up at him, her expression uncharacteristically hesitant and—unless he was mistaken—vulnerable. The shrewd negotiator in him should have smelled blood, and yet, it was all he could do not to blurt, *I'll give you anything you want. Anything. Everything.*

Attempting a droll tone, he merely said, "Go on."

"I don't know if you've noticed, but your grandmother becomes distressed when we argue. I think that—for her sake—we should refrain from bickering when in her presence and strive to treat one another kindly."

It was hardly an unreasonable request, and yet, he couldn't resist teasing her. Rubbing his jaw thoughtfully, he let his gaze linger on her plump lower lip. "How kindly, exactly, shall I treat you?"

She narrowed her eyes suspiciously, then shrugged. "Somewhat more kindly than you'd treat a mangy stray dog, and somewhat less kindly than you'd treat your . . ."

"My *what*, Miss Lacey?"

"Your mistress."

Good God. He leaned forward, wanting to read every nuance of her expression, every emotion written on her face. Her eyes held a flash of defiance and a spark of pride, neither of which was particularly surprising. But beneath her bravado lay a blush of something raw and wholly unexpected—longing.

Then again, maybe he'd simply had too much brandy.

"You made two assumptions just now," he said smoothly, "both of which I feel obliged to correct."

She batted her thick lashes mockingly. "By all means, please enlighten me."

"First, you implied that I wouldn't treat a stray dog with kindness. The truth is, I'd be more inclined to treat a mongrel well than I would most men of my acquaintance."

"That is good news for dogs throughout London and rather unfortunate news for your friends."

"Indeed," he conceded. "I must also correct your second assumption—that I have a mistress. I do not."

"Forgive me, your grace," she said dryly. "I did not mean to impugn your character."

Alex relaxed against the plush cushions of the settee and flashed his most charming smile. "No offense was taken, Miss Lacey. I just thought you should know."

Beth could not imagine how the conversation had devolved to talk of mistresses, but perhaps the brandy toast was partially to blame for that—and for the headiness she felt from sitting so close to the duke.

"I'm delighted that we've cleared up the matter of your non-existent mistress," she said primly. "And I do hope that in the future we shall be able to keep civil tongues in our heads—at least while in the duchess's presence."

"Oh, I don't know," the duke drawled. "Surely we can do better than mere civility. I thought we were striving for kindness."

"True, but I've since realized the folly of it."

He leaned forward and propped his elbows on his knees. "No, I think we're quite capable."

Beth wasn't so sure. The duke seemed to bring out the worst in her. But perhaps if they aimed for kindness, they'd manage to achieve civility. "Very well then. Our goal shall be kindness."

"Excellent. Let us practice."

"You want to *practice* being kind?" she asked, incredulous.

"It may come naturally to you, but I suspect it will require rather more effort on my part." He steepled his fingers beneath his chin, then mused, "How to start? Perhaps I could begin by paying you a compliment."

Her cheeks heated. "That's not necessary. Besides, you should save your kindness for when we're in the company of your grandmother. No sense in using it up now."

"But kindness is not a limited commodity, is it, Miss Lacey?"

"It isn't for most people," she muttered uncharitably.

He shot her a mildly scolding look. "Tsk, tsk. I think you could use some practice too."

She bristled and set down her glass. "Believe it or not, I'm practicing right *now*. I find myself refraining from all manner of retorts and instead, bidding you a good night."

When she would have risen from the settee, he grasped her hand, making it suddenly hard to breathe. She could easily pull away. It's what she should do. But she didn't.

"Wait," he protested. "If you leave now, you won't hear my compliment."

She savored the warmth of his hand and the fluttering in her chest. "Nor will I hear further insults."

"I wouldn't insult you." He frowned, as though truly offended.

"An empty compliment would feel worse than an insult." She was amazed by her ability to keep her voice cool, even as her skin heated from his touch.

He slid closer and looked earnestly into her eyes. "I will *always* be truthful with you—to the extent that I can."

"Fine." She couldn't endure much more of this closeness, enthralling as it was. "Pay me a compliment, if you wish."

His gaze traveled over her face and lingered on her

mouth before dropping to her breasts and hips. As she braced herself for something wholly inappropriate and wildly titillating, she could already feel the heat climbing up her neck.

"There are a great many things I could compliment you on, Miss Lacey, but the thing I admire most about you . . ."

She closed her eyes, not certain she could bear it if he should mention a body part south of her chin.

". . . is your devotion to my grandmother. Your loyalty to her is commendable."

She opened her eyes to see if the duke mocked her, but he seemed quite sincere. The breath she'd been holding rushed out of her. "Thank you. She is a rather amazing woman."

"So are you."

Beth swallowed. They'd both had too much to drink. She shouldn't have allowed him to hold her hand. Blast, she shouldn't even have come to his study. He needed her services—such as they were—and as a certifiable rake, he was not above using pretty words to achieve his aim. Something she'd do well to remember.

"Tomorrow I will start to determine what the duchess might choose as her first wish," she said. "But for now, I think it is well past time I retired for the evening."

Almost regretfully, he released her hand and stood. "I appreciate your assistance, and I have the feeling we shall make an excellent team."

Beth remained skeptical. If she was on anyone's team, it was the duchess's. But her knees were too weak for her to spar with him further. "Good night, your grace," she said, rising and making a beeline for the door of his study.

"Good night, Miss Lacey. And please do me one favor, if you would."

Drat. She'd almost made her escape. She halted and

looked over her shoulder at his dangerously handsome face. "What might that be?"

"Make sure you lock the windows and door of your bedchamber tonight—just as a precaution, of course."

A chill ran the length of Beth's spine. Good heavens. A precaution against what? Was he concerned about were-wolves? Was *he* a werewolf? "Don't worry," she choked out. "I will."

Indeed, if she could manage it, she might just block the door with her dresser for good measure.